THE HEARTBREAKER

USA TODAY BESTSELLING AUTHOR

SARA CATE

For the hot professors

Dear Reader

You know the drill by now. This family is going through some heavy shit, and Lucas's story is no exception.
There are some potentially triggering scenes in this story, including: on-the-page child abuse, homophobia, sexual assault and rape (off page).
This is a pregnancy romance, to include every wonderful and awful part of pregnancy and childbirth like awkward ultrasound probing and throwing up in the least convenient place possible.
As always in my books, the kink and elements of BDSM are entirely fictional and meant to be read as fantasy, not reality. Should anything in my novels serve as inspiration to you, you and your partner(s) are responsible for your own research and safety—especially, if you're pregnant.
I hope you enjoy Lucas and Sadie's wild ride into parenthood.
If you love a little rebellion and a whole lot of brattiness, this might be the book for you.
Enjoy!

Love always,
Sara

PROLOGUE

Lucas
13 years old

My mother sets a cake in the center of the table as I stare at my brother over the thirteen individual flames.

"One, two, three, go," Adam announces.

Caleb starts to laugh, but quickly presses his lips together as he gazes wide-eyed at me across the table.

Mom starts singing first, her sweet soprano voice louder than my brothers' or dad's. Isaac and Adam are standing on either side of the table, trying to make one of us blink as Caleb and I battle each other in a staring contest. The same staring contest we have every year on our birthday.

I won last year, and neither of us has won two years in a row yet, so I'm trying my best to beat him again.

"Boys, knock it off," my father booms from the head of the table in the middle of the song.

When Isaac waves his hand in front of Caleb's face to get him to blink, Dad swats him in the back of the head, and I flinch, blinking immediately.

"I won!" Caleb proclaims, throwing his hands in the air.

I can't take my eyes off Isaac as he clearly fights the urge to cry.

"Blow out your candles!" Mom says excitedly.

Still tense from watching my dad hit my brother, I forget to make a wish as I lean forward and blow out the candles with Caleb. Mom kisses the top of my head before she cuts the cake and hands me a piece.

"Happy birthday, my sweet boys," she says.

Then, she hugs Isaac to her side and I see a single tear fall down his cheek, so I push my cake away and glare at the man at the head of the table.

I think my mom notices because she immediately tries to distract us and lighten the mood—ever the mediator.

"What did you boys wish for?" she asks excitedly as she takes a bite of cake from her own plate.

"I bet Luke wished to finally get a girlfriend," Caleb jests with a laugh.

I scowl at him. "I don't even want a girlfriend," I reply. "I bet you wished for an extra brain cell since you probably lost the last one playing football."

He flips me off where our mother can't see it and I laugh to myself. Even my dad cracks a smile at seeing my brother and I poke fun at each other.

But when the room goes quiet for a second, little Isaac asks, "Do you want a boyfriend?"

The sound of a fork clinking against a small dessert plate is the only sound in the room as we all stare wide-eyed at Isaac.

"What did you just say?" our dad asks with a cruel, biting tone.

Isaac starts to shrink into himself. The tension creeps in as I wait for him to say something, trying to understand why he would ask that.

"Be—because Luke said he doesn't want a girl...friend."

Isaac's only six years old. He doesn't understand why a

teenage boy doesn't want a girlfriend, and his innocent mind only assumes that means I want the opposite.

"It's okay, buddy," I say, staring at him with warmth in my expression. "That's not what I meant, but it's not wrong to ask that. Some boys do want boyfriends." I know full well this response will not go over well at our family table with our dad at the head.

A loud booming sound fills the dining room as my father's fist lands against the table, rattling the dishes.

"Lucas, so help me God," he shouts. "If you don't stop it, right now."

I feel his angry gaze on my face so I turn to glare right back at him. "Stop what?"

"That's enough now," my mother chirps next to my little brother. "Isaac was just confused."

But no one is paying her any mind. The focus is on my father and me right now and a very different stare-down than I just shared with my twin.

"You know damn well what," he grits through his teeth. "We don't talk about such deadly sins at the table and you know it."

"How could love be a sin?" I argue.

"Lucas, stop," Adam mutters in frustration.

Caleb is watching our dad across the table as if he's ready to pounce, waiting for me to tag him in like this is a wrestling match. I'm the brains, and he's the brawn.

"That's all Isaac is asking about," I say. "He doesn't know any better. What's so wrong with asking if I want a boyfriend?"

"Because it's a sin," he grunts.

"And I asked how two people loving each other could be a sin." I'm poking the bear, and I know it.

"Lucas, that's enough," my mom snaps. It grates on my nerves that she asks *me* to stop but not him.

My dad's face is red and I imagine smoke billowing from his ears. At this point, I'm too energized by his frustration to stop. I want to see just how mad I can make him.

"How can it be a sin?" he argues. "Because the Bible tells us so, and no son of mine is going to speak against the word of God. Now don't you dare go and put those disgusting ideas in your innocent brother's head, you understand me? I don't care that it's your birthday. One more word out of you, Lucas Goode, and I'll remove you from this table myself."

I swallow down the bile rising in my throat. The dining room falls silent as I turn my clenched jaw expression down to the uneaten cake in front of me. Slowly and quietly, everyone starts eating again, but the room is bathed in so much tension that I can't move.

Overwhelming hatred for everything swarms inside my head. Hatred for my father and his hypocritical lies. Hatred for my older brother who feeds into everything he says. Hatred for my mother who never stands up against my father but just tells us pretty lies to keep us happy.

That familiar desire to run away floods through me. Every time we get into one of these fights, I resist the urge to run. And these fights have been happening more and more lately. But where would I go? I am stuck in this prison for five more years.

Once I'm old enough, I'll get a scholarship somewhere and I'll never look back.

I lift my gaze from the plate and stare at my little brother across the table. His bottom lip is quivering as he resists the urge to cry.

Who's going to stand up for him when I'm gone? If I don't do it now then Isaac will never learn that we *can* and we *should* stand up against our dad. He's not God. He's not a king. He's just a man. And I'm not afraid of him.

"What kind of God would condemn someone for who they love?" I mutter under my breath.

"What did you just say?" my dad barks.

"I won't worship a God who condemns people for who they love."

I barely get the words out when all hell breaks loose.

I see Caleb burst out of his chair as a heavy hand clamps down on the back of my neck. My chair tumbles backward as my mother screams, and I'm hauled out of the dining room.

"Truett, stop!" she shouts, but my father puts up a hand and huffs in her face.

"Mel, sit your ass down! These boys need to learn some discipline."

All I can see is the floor as my father holds me with a punishing grip on my neck. I'm wincing in pain, but the fear is worse. The fear of what awaits me when he gets me alone.

I already know Dad will win. He always wins.

Caleb tries to pry Dad's hand off my neck, but then he's shoved violently away. He crashes against the wall, knocking a family photo from the nail as it comes crashing to the floor and shatters at his feet.

Isaac wails in fear as my dad continues his tirade, forcing me away from the rest of the family. I stumble on the steps, falling onto my face before he picks me up again and continues the march toward his office.

I'm not strong like Caleb or brave like Adam. I'm no match for my giant of a father. All I have to fight with are my words and those can't protect me now. So, whatever happens next is going to hurt. I know that much.

Once we reach the office, he tosses me inside and slams the door, closing us in together.

I expect a lecture first, but he doesn't waste time with words. At least none more eloquent than, "Ungrateful little brat."

Suddenly, I'm hit so hard against the side of my face, it knocks me off my feet. It's the blow of a lost temper. And it's followed by more. Fury-filled and rampant, as if beating me is something he needs to get out of his system.

"You will listen to me, boy," he barks through gritted teeth.

"I don't have to listen to you!" I shout defiantly through tears and rage. My face is on fire, red and throbbing.

"Oh, you don't think so?" he snaps back. "As long as you live in this house, you live under my rules, and I will not tolerate your rebellious bullshit!"

"I'll never be a bigot like you!" I shout. I've never yelled at my parents. I hardly even yell at my brothers. But I'm thirteen now. A teenager. Nearly a man. And I'm drunk on it.

I want to scream my way out of this family. I want to punch and yell and fight until I've dismantled the entire house. Until there is nothing left of the Goodes.

He picks up the Bible from his desk and waves it at me. "You *will* learn some respect!" he shouts.

Then, I feel the blunt end of the book crashing against the side of my head. It's a dull thunderous feeling that rattles my brain and makes my eyes feel like they're going to fly from the sockets.

It shuts me up fast.

I'm holding the side of my head, looking for blood, and still in shock. It hurts so bad I can't think straight. Can he do that? Is he allowed to hit me so hard? Spankings and smacks I'm used to, but beaten with an object... This is new. It never even registered to me that parents could do something so awful to their own kids.

My vision pulses and throbs and my hearing is deafened by a ringing noise. Am I dying?

Would he kill me?

He's angry enough. And he hates me enough.

But surely my mother would stop him. Or Caleb.

But no one comes. I'm sitting on the floor of his office alone without any strength left to fight.

He won. He always wins.

"You think you're so smart," he says. He sounds breathless and almost remorseful. "You think the rules don't apply to you. But trust me, son," he says with a bite of anger. I slowly trail my eyes upward toward where he stands over me. "I *will* break you."

My teeth are pressed together so tightly I'm afraid they'll shatter.

"I hate you," I whisper.

"I know you do," he replies. "And you can hate me all you want, but you'll serve the Lord eventually, Lucas. To save your very soul, I'll be sure of it."

He slams the book on his desk and storms out of the room. I'm still holding my head when I glance up to the door. Caleb is on the other side, glaring at him with rage in his eyes.

"Leave him in there," my father bellows. "He'll sleep on the floor tonight."

I hear my mother argue, but my dad shuts her down immediately. As the door slams, shutting me inside alone, I slump against the floor and cry into the expensive rug.

It's the first night I've spent away from Caleb, and it's all my fault. Why couldn't I just be quiet? What good did it do to argue with him? It scared my baby brother and upset my mom. Not to mention, I probably have a concussion now.

From now on, I'll never speak up. In fact, I may never speak to him again.

Then, when I'm old enough, I'm gone. For good.

FIRST TRIMESTER

ONE

Sadie

"**H**e's coming!"

The security screens display the Land Rover parked out front. I let out a scream as I scurry out of the office and dash toward the entrance of the club.

Sage meets me at the black curtain separating the lobby from the main area.

"Breathe," she says, putting her hands up. "He's just a guy, remember?"

Just a guy.

Just a guy with two million followers on Instagram and twice as many on FanVids.

Just a guy I've been negotiating with—and maybe sorta flirting with—for the past three months.

Just a guy who could put our club on the map.

With a deep breath, I force my shoulders to descend from my ears and my eye to stop twitching. When we hear the car door slam outside, Sage and I pull back the curtain together.

The first man to walk in is stout and balding.

For a moment, I panic, thinking that maybe I've been catfished—along with a few million people.

But then, Jax Kingston walks in behind him. All six and a half feet of Adonis-level hotness.

"Mr. Kingston," I beam as I close the distance, putting out a hand toward him.

Like the suave and sexy motherfucker that he is, he pauses near the door and licks his bottom lip. His tongue is red and just the peek of it sends a jolt of warmth to my core.

"You must be Sadie," he says in a cool, raspy tone. "Sexy Sadie."

Laughing at his own joke, he grins, and deep dimples pierce his perfectly chiseled cheeks.

Naturally, I giggle way too much and for far too long. *He said my name.*

Sage, ever the valiant heroine, steps in and saves the day. "Jax, we're so glad you could make it to Sinners and Saints. I hope you understand that we cannot allow filming in the main public areas of the club, but should you feel inspired, you are welcome to film in any one of our private rooms. And if there is anything we can offer you while you're here, please let us know."

He crosses his arms and smiles down at Sage as if she's a small poodle who just learned how to walk on her hind legs.

"Look at you two. I gotta say...a sex club owned by two women is so fucking cool."

Out of the corner of my eye, I see Sage's tight-lipped smile. My headstrong boss has worked her ass off to make this club what it is, and she doesn't take kindly to men patronizing her in any way, shape, or form.

Not that that's what Jax is doing. He's just being playful. She doesn't understand his content.

Jax is young and progressive. He's a true ally and wants all the same things she does—female empowerment and the destigmatization of sexual culture. He talks about it all the time on his Instagram.

"All right then," he says with a wink. "Let's check this place out." He waves at the stout man who stays in the lobby as if that's his job.

As we enter the club, I try to keep myself at Jax's side. I want him to feel free to explore. It's important for the club that he gets a good first impression. If he films content here and shares it on his socials, it could mean so much for us.

Our dreams of opening another location could be easily within reach with just a nudge of national attention.

"Wow," he says, standing in the middle of the room. "This place is sick."

There's a lively crowd on the dance floor tonight. People are glancing this way, some of them clearly recognizing Jax.

"We have a full bar," I say, pointing to the left. "And over twenty private rooms with various themes and supplies."

Jax smiles down at me, and I feel my cheeks start to flame. "Supplies, huh? Are you going to give me a tour of those too?"

I laugh, looking away as I slap him playfully on the arm. When I look up and see Sage staring wide-eyed at me, I realize I might be acting *too* flirty.

"Sage," one of our escorts calls from the hallway. "There's a call for you."

She waves at Dean before turning toward me and Jax. "I hope you'll excuse me. Sadie is our floor manager and is more than qualified to give you a tour. But I'll be around if you need anything."

Jax slings an arm over my shoulders. "I'm sure we'll be just fine."

Sage gives me a pointed glare, and I know what she's thinking. That he's being too flirty, too touchy, too unprofessional. But she's just being protective.

Little does she know I'd let Jax Kingston do just about

anything he wants to me in here—full stop. And even if I didn't want it, we have extensive security that would step in the moment I needed it—but I won't.

"Yep," I say to her subtly, trying to speak with my eyes. "I've got it from here."

With a deep sigh, she turns and ambles toward the office.

"All right, sexy Sadie," he says, ruffling my hair. "Show me this sex club of yours."

I lead Jax through the main areas of the club first, but his attention span is weak at best. Most of the time, I notice his gaze slighting from his surroundings to *me*. I don't want to get ahead of myself, but I feel on fire tonight. And I'm feeling very optimistic about where this evening is going.

What if he films having sex with *me* for his page?

Whoa, Sadie. Slow down. He just walked in the door five minutes ago.

Not to mention, most of the girls on his page are rail thin with perky breasts and platinum hair—not five-foot-eight stacked gingers.

Ouch, that sounded self-deprecating, even in my head. So what if I rock a size sixteen and double *Ds*? He'd be fucking lucky to have me on his page.

Much better.

Still, I find myself pressing my tits up and sucking my stomach in as he talks. He's leaning his shoulder against the wall with a vodka Red Bull in his hand, telling me all about how his page got started and how he was *shocked* when it started to take off.

He's so humble and down to earth.

"Well, I have to admit," I say, tilting my head as I stare up at him. "I've been a fan for a long time."

The corner of his mouth lifts in a sexy smirk. "Is that so?" Reaching out, he tugs gently on one of my strawberry curls. "And what exactly is your favorite, of my content?"

I pinch my bottom lip between my teeth to keep from grinning. "You want to know?"

"Always."

"Your solo content," I reply, feeling a blush rise to my cheeks. Without even looking in the mirror, I know my neck and cheeks are tomato red.

I just admitted to this man I'm crushing on that I watch him masturbate, and I like it. The way he angles the camera to show his face as he strokes himself. The moans. The *whimpers*. I'm getting hot just thinking about it.

"So," he says with a sly wink. "Do you ever use the rooms for yourself?"

It feels as if we've given up on the tour altogether. I should probably feel bad for stealing his focus from the club, but I am too busy eating up all the attention he's giving me.

I give a flirtatious shrug. "Sometimes."

"Do you have a favorite?" He leans in closer.

"I have a couple." I feel like I'm sparkling under his heated gaze. His cologne smells amazing, and he's even more handsome in person than he is online.

"Will you show me?" he asks, letting his gaze dart down to my breasts and back up to my face.

Without another word, I take his hand and pull him down the hallway. This section was once a VIP area, but Sage did away with that when she took ownership of the club. I was here before the change—when her loser ex-boyfriend was in charge, and this whole wing was nothing but skeevy rich perverts who thought they ran the place.

Now, it's classy and safe and open to everyone.

When we pass the door to the back office, I pray Sage doesn't come out and see me tugging one of our potential influencers into a room alone. I could argue that this is just part of the tour, and if I show Jax just how stunning this place is, he is bound to return and share it with his followers.

We enter the old VIP bar area, which is decorated in luxe green and warm pink. It has a disco ball in the center and flowers adorned across the ceiling.

"Wow," Jax mutters to himself. "I've never seen a sex club like this."

"We cater to a diverse demographic," I reply confidently.

"I like it," he says with a smile.

A sense of pride swarms inside me. And then my brain does that thing it always does. It begins to imagine the possibilities. What if Jax really takes a liking to this club and to *me*? What if we start dating and we strike up a partnership between his brand and ours? We would be unstoppable. This club could be the best in the whole country. Or the whole world.

I continue dragging him toward the room on the left. After unlocking it with my manager's key, I glance around to be sure no one watches as I pull him inside.

I'm being reckless—or at least that's what the little voice in my head is reminding me. I'm moving too fast. Not thinking clearly. Eating up his attention and letting my desires take control without a second thought for the consequences.

But how can I stop? Especially now as he tugs me toward him, my body pressed against his tall, muscular frame.

"This isn't how this meeting was supposed to go," I mumble softly as he tips my chin up.

"Really? Because I think it's going very well," he replies with a smirk.

After he takes my lips in a soft but hungry kiss, everything starts moving too fast. Like a gust of wind that turns into a tornado, we kiss and kiss until we're lying on the soft peach-colored bed, and he's hiking my dress while tugging open the buckle on his jeans.

It's nothing like the scenes he films for his channel. Those are usually drawn out with loads of foreplay.

In fact, it's moving so fast that it feels as if I'm getting left behind.

"You're safe, right?" he mutters against my neck.

"Ugh..." I groan, not wanting to answer that question. We don't say *safe* around here. It implies that someone else is *unsafe*. "I'm tested regularly and always negative," I say with a wince.

Sex without a condom isn't a good idea, regardless of test results. I have no reason to trust Jax. I know that. Hell, I preach this sort of thing almost daily.

But there is no rationale. There is only the yearning and the passion and the way *I wanted this*.

So who am I to stop it now?

The next thing I know, his cock is thrusting between my legs. It's rushed and a little painful, but I shut my eyes and try to put myself in a place mentally where I can find pleasure. It just happened so fast.

He's grunting in my ear as he fucks me, and I'm silently reminding myself—this is Jax fucking Kingston. He's a sex god. Any person would be lucky to be fucked by him, and every woman in his videos is practically out of her mind with pleasure, so what is wrong with me?

I tilt my hips, tweak my nipples, kiss his neck. Anything to try and catch a brief, fleeting moment of ecstasy before it's over.

But all too soon, his grunts grow louder and more strained, and then he's shuddering, and I know it's done.

He slumps against me, and I stare at the cherubs painted on the ceiling, trying to convince myself of how great this was.

"Wow," I whisper with a sigh.

"Shit, I'm sorry," he groans into my neck. "I don't know what came over me. You're just so fucking sexy."

Forcing a giggle, I shake my head. "It was...great."

Without a response, he rises up and climbs off me, tucking his dick back in his jeans. "This club is something else," he says to himself.

I'm still lying on my back with my tight blue dress bunched above my hips. His cum is leaking out of me, and I keep waiting for him to at least bring a towel or something.

It's not like he's trying to be rude. He's just a little...dense. And I'm sure he's under a lot of stress with his newfound fame and all. It's okay.

Squeezing my thighs together, I ease up and reach for the tissues on the side table. While he looks down at his phone, I subtly wipe up the mess and toss the balled-up paper in the trash.

"So..." I say, fixing my dress. "Did you want to film some content for your page? This would be a great room to do it in."

I wouldn't turn down round two, especially if it means I might be able to get off, too.

Without looking up from his phone, he replies, "Nah, babe. I gotta be at a shoot in an hour. Wish I could, though."

Disappointment stains my insides like toxic fumes.

Finally, he glances up at me with a forced smile. "Mind if I come back, though? I really like this place, and I'd love to see you again."

My spine straightens, and my brows perk up. That was sweet of him.

"Yeah, of course! Come anytime. And you can film by yourself...or with me."

I paste a bashful grin on my face and he feeds right into it, pocketing his phone and pulling me against him again.

"You are just sweet as pie." I expect a kiss, but instead, he bops me on the nose. "I would *love* to film a solo scene in here, and since you love them so much, maybe you can get a live show."

"I'd like that very much," I say before biting my lip.

He glances down at his watch. "Fuck, I gotta go. I really hate to just bail like this."

"It's okay!" I say with a shake of my head. "You're busy, but that really was fun, and I hope we can do it again."

Grabbing my shoulders, he stares down at me with a twinkle in his eye and dimples in his cheeks. *Fuck, he's so hot.*

"Sugar, I would fucking *love* to do that again with you."

Quickly, he presses his lips to my forehead before turning

toward the door. With one last sweet wave, he disappears and leaves me standing alone in the middle of the room.

I'm left with a swirl of excitement and regret in my gut. I just had sex with Jax Kingston, and he was so overcome with lust *for me* that he just couldn't help himself.

I should be ecstatic about that.

So why on earth do I feel so crummy?

Two

Lucas

My phone is clutched tightly in my hand as my heart nearly pounds its way out of my chest.

"Are you serious?" I ask, stopping in my tracks and waiting for the voice on the other end to reply.

My old friend and colleague from my job in New York laughs through the line. "I know better than to tease you about this, Luke."

"I'm a finalist? Holy shit, Alan."

He laughs again. "You're on their short list. They were very impressed with your Marlowe article, and they'd love to schedule a virtual interview to discuss your ideas for the Stratford Project some more."

I could scream. My jaw is practically on the floor. This can't be happening.

I've been applying for the Stratford Project since grad school. To live in London, collaborate with some of this generation's greatest minds, and do nothing but study the classics for months on end...would be a dream come true.

It would catapult my career. No more teaching introductory English courses at a small state university. If I get into this program, I'd be at Oxford. *The* Oxford. I could be teaching *real* literature courses. No more idiotic essays on *Hamlet* or *Animal Farm* written by communication majors struggling to pass ENG101.

"Don't start celebrating yet," my friend replies. "It's a rigorous vetting process."

I stop in the quad and adjust my satchel on my shoulder. "Of course. I understand, but, Alan, this is the furthest I've gotten—an actual interview."

"Congratulations, Dr. Goode. Someone from the program will be in touch soon."

"Thanks, Alan."

When the phone line goes dead, I stare straight ahead at the bright-purple bougainvillea growing along the green pathways between buildings. This was the boost of confidence I needed. The past few years have been tough.

Finding work in New York was harder than I expected—even with a doctorate. It's what drove me back to Texas. Accepting this job at Austin State was humbling, but on the bright side, it meant I could be closer to Caleb again. And I could watch my niece grow up.

That's about the only silver lining I could find to living in Texas again.

Working at this mind-numbing job, watching my expensive education waste away, and seeing all of my potential and dreams of something greater vanish like dust in the wind.

Getting a place in the Stratford Project would change all of that.

With this renewed sense of purpose and possibility, I continue my walk across campus to the Humanities Building. It's the first day of the semester—the first day of my sixth year teaching here. And hopefully, my *last* first day at Austin State.

When I reach the room, the lecture hall is raucous and full of fresh-faced students. For many of them, they've just sprung out of high school and this is their first foray into university studies. I'll be lucky if half of them can even piece together an entire essay or read an entire book, let alone Shakespeare.

By now, this process is old hat. I get their attention, introduce myself, explain the coursework and reading list, and pass out the syllabus. Before I can even pick up a weathered copy of *Paradise Lost*, I've *lost* half of them to their phones.

"This will be our first reading assignment of the semester—"

Leaning against the desk at the front of the room, I'm interrupted by the door crashing open. All eyes dart to the entrance as a tall redhead busts through, staring wide-eyed at me and the John Milton novel in my hand.

"Shit! Sorry," she stammers as she tiptoes into the room.

It's not that she's late or causing a scene that has me tripping over my words. It's that...I know her. I've met Sadie before. She manages the sex club my brother's girlfriend owns. I see her from time to time at gatherings or their monthly book club.

For a moment, Sadie and I pause like two deer stuck in the middle of the road.

"Sorry I'm late," she mutters while backing up toward the steps leading up to the empty seats of the lecture hall. Her eyes are still trained on me.

When I notice the students fidgeting in their seats, I blink my gaze away from Sadie. "That's all right. Just...uh, have a seat, Miss..."

"Green," she blurts out, stumbling up the stairs.

"Miss Green."

As she takes her seat, I struggle to recover my train of thought. *What was I just talking about?*

I glance down at the book in my hand. Oh yeah.

"Our first reading assignment," I manage, "will be *Paradise Lost*. If you have not purchased your copy yet, you need to do so by the end of the week."

Out of the corner of my eye, I track her movement as she pulls a pen from her back pocket and scribbles something on the palm of her hand. As her eyes dance back up to where I'm standing at the front of the lecture hall, I notice she bites her bottom lip, and her brows lift expectantly.

I clear my throat. "We will have our first essay assignment due at the end of September about *Paradise Lost*, but you will choose your topic. You should be thinking about this as you read."

She nods, then scribbles on her hand again.

If I keep going, she's going to have the entire syllabus scrawled across her forearm.

"Miss Green, do you need a piece of paper?" I ask, furrowing my brow.

Her spine straightens as she releases her bottom lip from between her teeth. "Nope."

The rest of the class types their notes on a computer or their phones, but as I continue discussing the readings and assignments, Sadie proceeds to use her body as her own personal notepad.

With a sigh, I freeze midsentence and turn toward the male student in the front row. He's writing in a notebook and when I stare down at him, he glances up at me with confusion and a hint of fear in his eyes. Without another word, I take his notebook from his desk and flip to a blank page. Quickly I tear a piece out as the entire class watches in tense silence.

With the blank paper in hand, I march over to where Sadie is sitting in the third row. Her eyes are wide as I place it on her desk.

She glances down at it before shooting her terror-filled gaze up to my face.

"From now on, Miss Green, please come to my class prepared."

I watch her throat as she swallows. "Okay," she mumbles softly.

"And on time," I add.

Her eyes narrow, and her mouth closes in a tight, straight line.

She doesn't respond, and in the back of my mind I consider that I should probably feel bad for how I'm treating her mostly because *I know her*. But I don't.

She should know better than to show up in a college class without the bare minimum. I don't know how she gets by normally, but in my class, I have expectations.

Turning her attention to the paper on the desk, it feels like she's obstinately ignoring me as I turn back to the front of the room and continue my lecture on the class readings and assignments.

Toward the end of the period, the entire class starts to appear restless, packing up their things and checking their phones while I'm still talking. I glance up at Sadie, who is finally writing on the paper I gave her.

About five minutes before the end of the class, I announce to everyone that they can leave. They practically stampede out of the lecture hall, but Sadie hovers at her seat until the rest of them are gone. I've never spoken to her privately before, but after that little incident in class, I'm dreading this interaction.

I should apologize.

Shouldn't I?

With a huff, she stands from her seat, snatching the paper in her hand.

"Look, I'm sorry for being late, but just because we know each other in real life doesn't mean you can be such a jerk to me," she says. My back is to her as I close my laptop and slide it into my bag.

"I assure you, Miss Green, I was not treating you differently because we know each other," I reply without turning around.

"Oh, so you're just an asshole all the time then?"

My head spins toward her. "Excuse me—"

With a smirk, she interrupts me. "I assure you I would have said that to you even if we didn't know each other."

My eyes seem to be stuck, my jaw hanging open. Suddenly, I

can't tear my gaze away, and I realize I'm focusing too long on her hair, her freckles, her lips, her eyes. Which is weird for me. Normally, I avoid eye contact or staring at anyone for more than a split second, but Sadie has this gravity about her. I can't look away.

Finally closing my mouth and crossing my arms as I turn toward her, I let out a sigh. "I think we got off on the wrong foot, Miss Green."

"Please call me Sadie," she replies with an eye roll.

Ignoring her request, I continue. "If you're going to be in this class, *Miss Green*, then I think we need to set some expectations."

"Fine," she says, placing her hands on her hips. "I expect you to not humiliate me in front of the whole class."

"And I expect you to come to my class on time and prepared," I argue. "Is that clear?"

With a scoff, she flinches as if I've insulted her. After a moment, she shakes her head and rolls her eyes again. "Yes, Luke. Crystal clear."

"Dr. Goode," I snap.

Again, she scoffs. With her eyes trained on my face, she balls up the piece of paper in her hands and tosses it at me. I catch it as it lands against my chest.

"Whatever you say, *Dr. Goode*." I don't miss the way those words are seeping with cynicism.

Without another word, she marches out of the room, letting the door slam loudly behind her. A little struck by the entire encounter, I stand in shock for a moment before glancing down at the wad of paper in my hand.

Opening it up, I'm taken aback by the notes scrawled across the page. In her neat and meticulous handwriting, she has nearly every single word I spoke today written down. She even has a list of potential essay topics noted on the side—*good* essay topics too.

How would she even have these ideas? Has she read *Paradise Lost* before?

I flatten the page out as much as I can and slide it into my satchel before slinging the bag onto my shoulder. Revisiting every moment of that encounter, I make my way across campus toward my car.

I was already dreading the start of this semester, and now I'm suddenly feeling ten times worse.

THREE

Sadie

"He said that?" Sage asks as she dries glasses behind the bar.

"Yes!" I reply as I fold pamphlets for tomorrow night's demonstration. "He was a total asshat."

"Luke? Really?" Her dark brows are pinched together as if she's trying to imagine the entire scenario I just spelled out for her.

"Yes, Luke."

"But he's always so quiet and nice. I can't even imagine him being so rude."

I shrug. "Well, apparently, Luke and Dr. Goode are two different people."

"Huh," she says nonchalantly as she appears to contemplate it some more. "Are you going to drop his class?"

"I can't," I reply. "I've been putting off the English credits I need for my business degree, and that's the only class that will fit into my schedule. If I drop it, I'll have to graduate a year later than planned."

"Bummer," she says with her mouth twisted in disappointment.

"Yeah, major bummer."

This entire week has been shit. First, there was that totally awkward encounter with Jax on Saturday night. He hasn't texted me back since, and I'm trying not to take it personally, but before that lifeless quickie in the Ethereal Room, he and I would chat almost daily. Sure, it was mostly about the club and his visit, but now he won't reply to me at all.

Then, Monday morning rolled around, and Luke—sorry, *Dr. Goode*—had to go and remind me that all men do, in fact, suck.

I don't know why I even try. It feels like everywhere I look for love or attention is one letdown after another. Not that I was looking at Luke for any chance of romance—hard pass—but I'm just so tired of being hopelessly disappointed over and over again by men.

For once, I just want a man to surprise me. Blow me away.

My standards could *not* be lower.

I mean...look at Sage and Adam. She should have hated him for the way he was before they got together. He was pompous, ignorant, and self-righteous. But then he had to go and fall in love with her, and now they're married with a baby on the way, and he treats her like the queen she is. He'd kiss the floor for her.

I'm not asking for anyone to kiss the floor. But, I don't know, just be nice to me. If a man said one nice thing about me, I'd probably marry him on the spot. That's how low the bar is at the moment.

Is it me?

No. Surely not. I have so much to offer, even if I do tend to show up late for everything and never seem to have my shit together. And I still live at home with my family.

Okay, other than that, I manage a sex club, and I'm damn good at it. I get stellar grades at school. I have a luscious ass that I'm pretty proud of, and I have gotten a lot of compliments on my blow job skills.

All things considered, I should have men knocking down my door. But I refuse to settle, and every day it feels more and more like that's what is going to be expected of me.

"So..." Sage says, letting her voice trail.

I tense, afraid of where that tone is going.

"Are we going to talk about Saturday night?" she asks.

Fuck.

I drop my head, unable to look her in the eye. "Shit, Sage. I'm sorry. I know I crossed a line with him, but I just had a lapse in judgment and he was so hot and—"

"Sadie, relax," she says, touching my arm. "You're not in trouble. I figured you had something going on with him. I just want to check in and make sure you're okay."

I stand upright and stare at her with softness in my eyes. "Really? You're not mad?"

With a scoff, she tilts her head. "No. Of course not. I trust you to do what's best for the club. What you do with your body on your own time isn't my business. But as your friend...is everything okay?"

My brows fold inward. "Of course," I reply too eagerly.

"How was it?" she asks with a lift in the corner of her mouth. Leaning back, she winces as she rubs the top of her belly as if she's trying to separate her stomach from her rib cage. God, pregnancy looks miserable and amazing at the same time.

My mouth opens to reply, but the words don't come out. Finally, I manage to stammer out a response. "I mean...he's Jax Kingston. What do you think?"

I can tell by Sage's expression that she doesn't entirely buy my response. "Will you see him again?"

"I hope so. I really do want him to come back to the club to film his content here."

"I don't care about that," Sage replies. "But if he hurts you, I'll kill him."

"Whoa!" I say with a laugh. "You're cute when you're murderous."

With a flirty smirk, she poses with her hands under her chin, making her look both angelic and a little unhinged. I'm laughing out loud when I feel my phone buzz in my back pocket.

Pulling it out, I see my brother Jonah's name on the screen.

> Guess who made the soccer team again.

"Shut up," I mutter to myself as I read his message. Quickly, I type out my response.

> Congratulations!!!

> Not that I'm surprised. You're a natural.

The typing bubbles pop up immediately, followed by his response.

> Thanks. SMILE EMOJI. I LOVE YOU IN SIGN LANGUAGE EMOJI.

> THREE I LOVE YOU EMOJIS.

> I'm off tomorrow night. We have to celebrate.

> That's what Mom said, too.

> You pick the place, and I'll be there.

I'm grinning proudly at my phone before sliding it back into my pocket. Jonah really is a natural. He's been playing soccer since he was three years old, but every year, he acts like suddenly they're going to stop picking him for the team.

My little brother is unstoppable. He excels at everything he attempts. My parents couldn't be prouder of him and everything he accomplishes. And it has nothing to do with how much harder Jonah has to work at everything or how much he's overcome. He's perfect in every way.

Meanwhile, I'm twenty-five. I live at home. I'm single, and it feels like everything I attempt, I fail at. Sure, I manage a sex club, but I can't tell *them* that. They think I work the night shift at a nightclub. And even that they don't approve of, but they don't bother fighting with me about it anymore.

I just want to do something that will make them proud. Graduate college. Find a nice partner. Buy my own house.

Instead, I fell into bed with a guy I just met who won't text me back now. I pissed off my English professor. And I continue living in my little brother's shadow.

"So when do you have Luke's class again?" Sage asks, drawing my attention away from my self-destructive thoughts.

"Tomorrow," I reply. "Every Monday, Wednesday, and Friday. Lucky me." My tone is dripping with sarcasm—a language my friend and I speak fluently.

"Yikes," she says with a wince. "Well, if it were me—and this is *not* meant to be advice—I would give him hell. Show him you're not just some meek woman he can boss around and treat like garbage."

Smiling to myself, I fold another pamphlet and let those words sink in. I don't say this out loud, but I can't help but think... Maybe I *do* want someone to boss me around. I mean... not in a degrading or dehumanizing way. But sometimes, I wish someone would tell me exactly what to do.

"He doesn't treat me like garbage," I mumble quietly.

"Okay, then, what would you call it?" she asks.

Thinking for a moment, I realize the answer stings even worse than him treating me like garbage.

"He treated me like he expected better from me."

FOUR

Lucas

Walking up the steps to my house, another day of draining and unfulfilling work so heavy on my body that it feels like it's dragging me down, I tell myself this is the *last* year. Even if I don't make the program at Oxford, I won't be here. I can't do this anymore. I've never been more miserable.

After unlocking the front door, I slip inside and drop my bag on the bench at the entrance. My mind is so preoccupied that I almost don't notice that something feels off. Instead, I mindlessly pull off my shoes, sliding them neatly into their place. My keys go into the dish on the table.

I'm two steps into the house when I freeze. Turning back, I stare at the weathered brown boots discarded by the door.

"You're out of milk."

My heart nearly flies out of my chest as I spin to stare at the man in my kitchen, leaning against the island with a bowl of cereal in his hand. He lifts a spoon to his mouth and crunches on the dry flakes with a smirk on his face.

"Jesus, Isaac. You scared the shit out of me!" I bark, clutching my chest. My heart is hammering against my rib cage as I wait for my blood pressure to return to normal.

"Sorry." My brother laughs. "I would have called, but this was more fun."

I roll my eyes as I walk farther into my house. "I don't drink milk. And that cereal has been in my pantry since you bought it six—no, seven—months ago."

"It's still good," he mumbles around the food in his mouth.

"What the hell are you doing here?" I ask, going to the fridge for a sparkling water. "I thought you were going to stay in Nashville with that teacher."

He shrugs. His now brown hair is wet, so he must have already showered. I'm willing to bet his bedroom is already in disarray, too. It usually takes him less than an hour to make a mess of it when he comes home.

"Things didn't work out with him. Or the bartender," he replies, setting the cereal down.

"There was a bartender?" I ask, leaning my back against the refrigerator.

He picks up a handful of his cereal and tosses it at me. "Don't slut-shame me."

When I hear the sugary flakes landing on the floor, I give him a terse glare. "You're cleaning that up."

He tries to act rebellious, staring at me as if he's not going to do what I just said. Finally, with a huff, he goes into the laundry room and comes back out a moment later with the broom.

At the sink, I rinse his dirty dishes and lather up the sponge with soap.

"That's your problem, Isaac," I say over the sound. "You need to grow up. Stop acting like such a kid all the time."

He groans with frustration. "And that's *your* problem, Luke. You grew up too fast. You're no fun, and you take everything too seriously. No one is ever going to want to settle down with you. You're *impossible* to live with."

"And yet, you keep coming back," I say over my shoulder.

"Besides," I add. "I had to grow up fast because *someone* had to take care of your immature ass."

"Oh please," he argues. "You were already an uptight bore by the time I left home. So don't blame your lameness on me."

"You should be thankful I'm such an uptight bore. Who else would have taken you in when you decided to run away at seventeen?" I bark in return. "And for your information, I have *no* interest in settling down with anyone anyway, so I'm perfectly content being impossible to live with."

"God, how do you walk around all day with that stick so far up your ass?" he shouts as he dumps the dustpan full of cereal into the trash.

"Alone. That's how I do it," I shout back.

He huffs as he walks toward the laundry room to put the broom back where it belongs. When he doesn't argue back, I smile to myself. Not because I won this argument or because I'm right and he's wrong, but because it is kind of nice having Isaac back. I missed these little arguments.

Of course, in true brotherly fashion, the fights aren't real. We're not really mad at each other. Not mad like Adam was when he found out Caleb took a meeting with our bastard of a father. Not mad like I'm sure both of them would be at me if they found out I've been caring for our "estranged" brother since the day he disappeared ten years ago.

"You hungry?" he asks nonchalantly as he returns to the kitchen. "I'm thinking about ordering Thai."

"Thai sounds good," I reply as I set the cereal bowl on the drying rack before using a paper towel to dry the stainless steel sink.

While we're waiting for the food delivery, I retreat into my bedroom and change into a pair of joggers and a T-shirt. A run to clear my mind is exactly what I need. I only get about two and a half miles on the treadmill before the front door buzzes and the scent of spicy tofu and noodles wafts into my room.

Isaac is sitting on the couch, scrolling on his phone and eating with a pair of chopsticks when I finally come out. I glare at him because he knows how I feel about food in the living room, but he slurps a noodle instead of apologizing or offering to move. When I take a seat at the table, though, he eventually joins me.

We eat in silence for a bit, each of us staring at our devices. Finally, I look up and ask, "How long are you staying this time?"

Normally, he'll respond with something funny or casual. But this time, I notice he tenses.

"Just a few days," he mumbles without looking up.

"Going back to Nashville?" I ask.

He clears his throat. "No."

I don't pick up another bite of food as I stare at him, waiting for him to elaborate.

"I didn't renew my lease at my apartment there," he says as he finally meets my gaze.

"Is everything okay?"

Once Isaac became more focused on his career, I moved back to Austin for work. He was uncomfortable with living here again, so he kept a place in Nashville to escape to. For the past few years, I've been helping Isaac afford it while he worked to get his music career off the ground. He used to come home every month, but with time, his returns became less and less frequent.

Since he built his following online and went on tour, he's had enough money to cover the apartment himself. But if he hasn't renewed his lease, that must mean...

"I signed with a label."

The words fly out of his mouth so fast it takes me a moment to register what he's saying.

"Wait...what?"

"They're not based in Nashville, though. They're based in Austin."

I shake my head in confusion. "Whoa. Slow down. You signed a deal with a record label?"

"Yeah."

I drop my chopsticks and nearly bolt out of my seat. "Isaac!" I shout.

"Don't make a big deal out of it, okay?"

"Don't make a big deal?" I echo in astonishment. He's been trying to secure a publishing deal since he was seventeen. We must have sent out a thousand demo tapes that first year he came to live with me in New York.

"And they're here in Austin?" I add with a grin. "This is amazing!"

"Is it?" he asks with a wince.

"What are you talking about? It's perfect. You can stay here and save up for your own place—"

"Actually...I'm moving out."

It's like his words slice through mine. Or right through *me*.

"You don't...have to..." I stammer as my mood begins to settle from elation to anxiety. "I can take care of you. I'll sign on for another year at Austin State."

Any plans to leave Austin seem like a pipe dream now. If Isaac is staying, he needs me, and I'll stay.

"They're putting me up in my own apartment."

"Why do you look so upset about that?"

He shrugs. "Because I think you like having me around. If I'm gone, what are you going to do?"

When I laugh, I admit it feels forced. "I'll have you know, I could be moving to England next year, so, uh...this is...perfect."

Pressing his lips together, he's giving me a look like maybe he's not buying it. And yeah, maybe I am tamping down the rising feeling of discomfort at the idea that Isaac won't need me anymore. He won't show up out of the blue in need of laundry or money or guidance. He won't have a safe place to land when he gets tired of the world.

He is twenty-seven now. Did I really think he'd have a room here forever?

"Of course I like having you around," I add under my breath. The more I speak, the harder it is to hold back my emotions.

Squeezing my molars together, I struggle to keep myself in check. "But I'm proud of you."

Looking up at me, his mouth lifts in a crooked smile. "Awww..." he teases. "You *love* me."

Rolling my eyes, I stand from the table. "Grow up."

"You can say it, Lucas. You love me, and you'll miss having me around."

As I set my food container on the kitchen island, I glance over at my little brother. He's grinning up at me like a fool, and I simply shake my head. Sometimes I feel bad that I got so much time with Isaac that my other brothers didn't get.

I've never asked Isaac if he's been in contact with our brothers. He talks to Mom, and that's all I need to know. Part of me suspects Adam or Caleb have reached out or found him, but that's not up to me.

Growing up, Caleb and Adam were stuck in their own ignorance to be any good for Isaac. They never meant our little brother any harm, but I was the only one standing up to the miserable bigot that is our father. Caleb was too busy looking out for me and Adam was following in the old man's footsteps.

And yet, getting to watch Isaac grow up has felt like a privilege I don't deserve.

At least he had someone. At least Isaac got to keep one brother. Even if it is the lame, boring, uptight, no-fun brother.

Even if it is all about to come to an end.

But if the one person I've focused on caring for doesn't need me anymore, what the hell am I going to do now?

FIVE

Sadie

There's an incessant buzzing in the distance, and it's distracting me from this peaceful, dreamless slumber. When I roll over on my bed to shut my phone up, something light and papery lands on my face.

Opening my eyes, I pick up the weathered copy of *Paradise Lost*.

"What the fuck?" I croak.

Then, everything hits me at once. My eyes pop open as I scramble for my phone. It's on the floor next to my bed, hidden under a pile of clothes. When I uncover it, the blaring alarm grows louder, and I curse to myself when I see the time.

I'm late.

"Fuck, fuck, fuck!" I shout as I scurry out of bed and rush toward the pile of clothes on my dresser. The moment my feet hit the floor, the room starts to sway and my head becomes a balloon, weightless and woozy. Nausea blooms in my stomach.

With a hiss, I freeze and grab my head, waiting for the blood, bile, and oxygen to return to where it belongs inside my body.

If I didn't know any better, I'd think I was up until four in the morning doing tequila shots instead of reading a dusty old literature book.

Oh no. Don't think about tequila.

My stomach clenches, and I swallow down the excess saliva in my mouth.

Get it together, Sadie.

After an eternity spent convincing my stomach not to revolt against me, I grab a pair of leggings and a T-shirt from the pile and quickly get dressed. By the time I make it out the door with only my book, a pen, and a notebook I had to buy to keep Dr. Goode off my ass, I know I'm going to be late.

Really late.

And I'd skip it altogether, but if I miss class, then I have to talk to him to get the lecture I missed, and I'd rather eat my own socks than have another private conversation with that pompous dickhole.

It's been four weeks since the start of the semester, and I've managed to go mostly unnoticed this long. Four down. So many to go.

Although who am I kidding? If Luke sticks around to teach English 102, it's more than likely I'll be stuck with him again next semester. No need to stress about that now. At the moment, the only thing I need to do is get through this semester.

By the time I park my car and start my sprint across campus, my stomach does another somersault, but I choose to ignore it. My forehead breaks out in a cold, damp sweat.

My limbs turn heavy like mud.

I have myself convinced that all I need to do is get my ass in my seat and I'll be fine. I'm just a little out of shape.

But the moment I fly through the Humanities Building and the cold air-conditioning hits my skin, it's all over. I pull open the door to my English class and turn absolutely useless in the fight against my own stomach.

Just before I dive toward the *very small* trash can near the door, I lock eyes with Dr. Goode. His brows are practically in his hairline, and his mouth is hanging open in shock at my sweaty, pale appearance.

And then I'm hurling loudly into the metal can, the eyes of roughly seventy-five people boring into my clammy form as I drop to my knees and expel last night's dinner and any shred of my dignity.

"Miss Green," Lucas says as he stands over me. "Are you all right?"

With my face still buried in the metal vomit can, I lift my arm to give him a thumbs-up.

He lets out a sigh of exasperation. And I'd sooner wear this can as a hat before I'd turn to look into those disappointed eyes.

"Class is dismissed early," he announces loudly. "Use this extra time to work on your essays. They're still due next week and my email is available for rough draft analyses if you think you need it."

I fold my arms over the trash and rest my cheeks on them, squeezing my eyes shut as the entire class stampedes past me. I feel like one of those village idiots they put in the stockades so people can throw tomatoes at them as they go by.

Hear ye, hear ye. Feast your eyes on the world's biggest hot mess and royal fuckup.

I really should have stayed in bed.

When the room grows quiet, I clench my eyes tighter, squeezing out a few tears. Then, something soft touches my cheek. I lift my head and stare at the tissue Dr. Goode is handing me.

In his other hand is a bottle of water.

"I'm sorry," I mumble as I reach for the tissue and quickly wipe my mouth. He doesn't reply as I take the water and uncap the lid before guzzling down half the contents.

"Are you sick?" he asks.

I shake my head as I take another gulp.

"Hungover?"

Again, I shake my head. "And before you ask, I'm not pregnant either. You'd have to have sex for that to happen."

He lets out another sigh, but rather than disappointment, this one sounds like discomfort. Glancing up at him, I notice the way his brows are folded in, and his eyes won't land on my face. It makes me smile a little to realize how easy it is to make Luke uncomfortable.

Noted.

"Do you need medical attention?" he asks.

"No," I reply with a groan. "What I need is to skip cardio in the Texas heat."

"Well, if you would manage your time better, you wouldn't have to run."

With a scoff, I rise from the floor. "Save it. I just barfed in a can in front of a room full of my peers. I don't need a lecture from you."

The doors to the classroom open and one of the janitors stands in the doorway, looking at us expectantly.

"It's right here. In the trash," Dr. Goode says, pointing to the scene of the crime.

"You called them?" I shriek, covering my face with my hands as the poor man picks up the can I just desecrated. I can't even look at him, this poor elderly man who now has to deal with my mess. "I'm so sorry!" I cry through my hands.

"It's okay," the man replies, although it's so not okay.

When the door shuts, I turn toward my professor. "I could have cleaned it up."

"How?" he asks, turning his back toward me to pack up his things.

"I don't know. I would have figured it out. I don't like other people cleaning up my messes."

"Then, don't make messes," he replies calmly.

Ugh, I *hate* him so much. I want to slap that stupid, high-and-mighty tone right out of his mouth.

"You're so perfect, aren't you?" I ask in frustration.

"No one's perfect, Miss Green. But some of us just make smarter choices."

"Fuck you, Lucas," I snap. My fists are clenched at my sides. This day is already unsalvageable, so what's the point in even trying? I'm sure there are consequences for cussing out your professor, but it certainly couldn't be any worse than what I've already experienced today.

He spins and stares at me, looking appalled. I expect him to threaten me with some arbitrary punishment or lecture me some more, but after a moment, something like resignation washes over his face.

"Go home, Miss Green," he mumbles before turning away again.

My jaw drops. "That's it?"

"What more do you want from me? I already dismissed my class for you."

"I don't know," I argue. "I just figured you'd tell me what a screwup I am. Or give me some talk about how you're so much more mature and smarter than me. Fight with me or something!"

"You are not my responsibility, Miss Green. And if you are so sure that I'm more mature and smarter, then why do you need me to tell you? It seems to me that you want someone to tell you how to make your own life better, but that's your job."

"I'm sure you would *love* to tell me exactly what I'm doing wrong just so you could hold it over my head."

"What exactly would I gain from that?" he snaps in return.

"Oh, you would *so* get off on that, and we both know it," I reply with a sarcastic laugh.

He takes a step toward me. "You're crossing a line, Sadie. Watch yourself."

My features go stone cold at the sound of him saying my name. "Why?" I continue. "Because I said something true?"

Another step closer. "Because you said something inappropriate."

"So it is true?" I ask, a smirk returning to my face.

"Miss Green..." he says in a warning.

"What's wrong, Dr. Goode? You don't like me pointing out that you're a—"

Saliva floods my mouth as my abdomen clenches. It cuts the words straight from my mouth. I feel myself pale as Luke's eyes widen.

"There's another trash in the corner," he says flatly.

I spin away from him and barely make it in time, heaving what's left in my gut into the second innocent victim of a metal can today.

Just like last time, a soft tissue touches my face. But this time, instead of handing it to me, he wipes my lips and chin.

"Don't call the janitor again," I mutter with my eyes closed.

"Already did."

"I hate you," I reply.

"Come on. I'll drive you home," he replies.

"I brought my car. And I refuse to accept help from you."

"Why?" he asks as he uncaps my bottle of water and lifts it to my lips. "Because you know I'll get off on it?" he adds.

My eyes pop open to find him fighting a smile. The corner of his mouth lifts but only briefly. In the blink of an eye, he's scowling again.

After the janitor returns for the second time and I die of embarrassment again, Dr. Goode slings his bag over his shoulder and guides me out the door.

"I must have eaten something bad," I say as I reach my car. "You really don't have to drive me home. I'll be fine."

"Are you sure?" he asks.

With a sigh, I nod. "I'm sure. I don't live far."

"Okay," he says, relenting. "I'll see you Wednesday, then."

He turns and walks away toward his own car. He's in a blue plaid button-down shirt, rolled at the sleeves, and a pair of tight, black slacks. Suddenly, I can't stop thinking about our conversation in the classroom. I doubt that even if Luke had some controlling Dom kink, he would ever express it. He's too uptight and too much of a prude.

Although, if I'm honest, picturing him in that role is sort of hot.

"I'm sorry again," I call across the parking lot.

Without turning toward me, he holds up a hand as if to say, "It's okay."

My stomach settles down enough for me to drive home. When I get there, I'm relieved to find the house is empty. My parents are at work, and my brother is at school. Which means I can fall right back into my own bed without having to answer to anyone.

The blankets on my bed are cool and inviting, and even after my now empty stomach starts to growl, I ignore it. I refuse to reward it after the way it's behaved today.

It's so weird that I would just throw up out of nowhere. It's not like I'm sick. There are no other symptoms. And if it were food poisoning, I'm sure there would be other signs.

Maybe it's just a fluke.

Because what I said to Dr. Goode was true. Unless it's an immaculate conception, there's no chance I could be pregnant. The last time I had sex was...

I'm staring at the ceiling of my bedroom as a memory flashes through my mind.

No.

The last time I had sex was with Jax Kingston that night at the club, but that barely counts. It was nothing. Just a quickie. Just a...

I bolt upright as the panic starts to set in. I replay every moment of those short but intense five minutes. He put on a condom...didn't he?

No matter how many times I try to remember the moment he paused to wrap up his dick, it's not there. But the memory of his cum leaking down my leg is.

Fuck. Fuck. Fuck.

I pull up my phone and open my period tracker. I've really slacked on using it lately, but four months ago, when I did track my cycle, it started on the fifth. And that was two weeks ago.

My skin starts to buzz and my blood pressure rises. As reality sets in, I toss my phone down on the mattress and throw my head back on my pillow.

With tears forming in my eyes, I scream the only thing I can think of at the moment.

"Fuck!"

SIX

Lucas

The house was quiet this morning when I left for campus. Isaac and I moved him into his new place last night. His room is empty of his things, all the personal touches that he embedded into that space—the mess of charging cables, discarded Gatorade bottles on the nightstand, a punk-rock Dolly Parton poster on the wall. All gone.

As I slipped on my shoes this morning, I berated myself for getting sentimental over the fact that his dirty boots were no longer by the door. Even if he was only there sporadically for days or weeks at a time.

Honestly, I need to get my shit together.

But today was the first day in nearly a decade when I had to accept that he's not coming back. There is no longer a physical space carved out for my brother in my home.

When I reach campus, I walk to my first class with a strange sense of anticipation. I wouldn't call it excitement or dread, but something in the middle. Because today is Friday, which means I will see Sadie Green again.

After the incident last week when she barreled into class

midlecture and got sick in a trash can in front of everyone, she's been a little off. Her sassy disposition is gone. Instead, she's been despondent and quiet.

Every day since, she's walked in on time, sat down in her normal seat, taken her notes, and walked out at the end. No eye contact. No sarcastic remarks. Nothing.

To make matters worse, her essay on *Paradise Lost* was phenomenal—probably the best in the class.

Why is this so terrible? Because I'm pretty sure it's something I said last week that sent her into this melancholy tailspin. I berated and insulted my best student.

What kind of teacher does that?

When I arrive at the lecture hall, Sadie isn't there. Even after the room fills up and I start class, her typical seat is empty. It grates on my nerves that she's missing, especially since today is the day I pass back the essays I've graded.

Her A+ paper is sitting on my podium, and I don't get to witness the look on her face when she sees it. It's like I want to rub it in that I was right.

Right about what, I don't know.

Less than halfway through the class, it's obvious I'm too distracted, so I call it and dismiss everyone early—again.

Before the room is even empty, I look up Sadie's phone number in the class directory. I'm calling as her professor, so I'm allowed to do this, although it does slightly feel like overstepping a professional boundary.

When she doesn't answer, I let out a huff.

Where is she?

Why must she always be so unreliable and disorganized? Why can't she just show up where she is supposed to show up, on time? I'm not being too harsh on her, but especially after reading this paper, I see the potential this woman has, and she's wasting it.

Growing more and more irritated by the second, I pull open her student record and find her address. I'm allowed to do this because she's a friend...sort of. We have mutual friends.

Before I know it, I'm in my car and driving down the interstate toward her side of town. It's an older, more established neighborhood, which seems a bit strange for a young woman in her twenties, but who am I to judge?

When I park in front of the address listed on her student profile, I feel a hint of apprehension. I should not be doing this—that much is clear. I would never do this for any other student, but after only five weeks in my class, it's clear that Sadie is not like any other student.

She's bold and not afraid to push my buttons or hurt my feelings. Maybe it's because she and I started out as mutual acquaintances that she felt that level of comfort, but whatever has happened between us by now has paved the way for my own personal entitlement to show up at her house unannounced.

I climb out of my car, her A+ essay in hand, and stroll up to the front door. I ring the doorbell with anxiety simmering under my skin. There are no cars in the driveway. The house is a brick ranch-style home with an expansive front yard and a large oak tree that provides shade.

When I hear footsteps inside, I straighten my spine. There's a large window to my right with a curtain that moves, revealing Sadie's astonished face through the pane.

She stares in shock at her grumpy English professor suddenly standing on her doormat. I don't wave or smile. I just stare right back at her and wait for her next move. Suddenly, her face disappears. Behind the door, I hear a muffled, "What the fuck?"

A moment later, the door opens.

"What...is happening?" she asks before I have a chance to speak.

She's dressed in an oversized sweatshirt and a worn-out pair of flannel pants. Her hair is piled on her head in a messy bun, wisps framing her face like a halo.

I hadn't quite prepared myself for what I'd say to her now that we're standing face to face, so I lift the paper in my outstretched hand.

"You weren't in class, and I wanted to give this to you."

Her expression twists with skepticism as she slowly reaches out to take the paper. As she looks down at the grade scribbled across the front, her face doesn't change.

Where is the surprise? The pride and excitement?

"You...brought me my essay?" she asks. "Why?"

"I thought you'd be excited to see I gave you an A," I argue back.

Her tense eyes lift up to my face. "Am I supposed to thank you for this?"

I scoff. "No. Why would you—"

She takes a step toward me, landing on the welcome mat and glaring up at me with lividity. "Because if you think you can just show up at my door to rub it in my face or act like I *owe* you something for taking pity on me, then you're even more of an asshole than I thought!"

Her furious tone has my molars clenching. Rather than surrender to her outrage, I step toward her.

"Watch your tone, Miss Green," I mutter under my breath. "I didn't take pity on you."

With a huff, she raises her arms. "That's right. You don't take pity on anyone."

"You don't need my pity," I snap back.

"Then why did you give me this grade?" she shouts.

"Because you deserved it!" I'm leaning over her, my face inches from hers, as she glares up at me with determination.

Amid the awkward and elongated stare-down, neither of us moves. But when her expression finally changes, it's not at all what I expect.

Her bottom lip quivers. Her nostrils flare. And tears fill her eyes.

Oh no.

"I'm really not in the mood for your jokes, Dr. Goode."

"I'm not—"

She steps away from me, covering her face with her hands. As she begins to weep, I curse myself again. Her shoulders tremble as she cries, and I awkwardly reach out a hand and rest it on her arm. Damn, I'm bad at this.

Not only have I humiliated, berated, and insulted my best student, but now I can add to that list—stalked, harassed, and made her cry.

If I don't get fired for this, I'll quit myself.

"I'm...sorry," I mumble awkwardly.

She pulls her hands away from her face and wipes the tears from her eyes. "It's not your fault," she says. Then, after a big sigh and a wincing expression, she mumbles to herself, "These goddamn hormones are out of control, and I cry at the drop of a hat."

"Are you okay?" I ask, unsure of what else to say.

"No," she mutters indignantly.

"What do you mean *no*?"

With a huff, she drops her hands and stares at me. "I don't know why I'm telling you this, but I'm...pregnant."

As she turns those tear-soaked eyes on me, I stand in silence. My eyes blink, and my throat turns dry. Her words are like bubbles, floating toward me only to pop the moment they reach my cold, lifeless exterior.

"Um..."

With a sad laugh, she turns away. "Please don't say anything. You'd probably say the wrong thing anyway."

"What is the right thing to say?" I ask.

"I don't know..." she says with exasperation. "Congratulations?"

"Is it...a cause for celebration?"

Turning toward me, she appears offended. "Of course. Right? Babies are little blessings we should be excited about?"

"Not always," I argue.

Her eyes are glued to my face as if she's confused by my reactions or trying to figure me out. Finally, she crosses her arms over her chest. "I shouldn't have even told you about it. I don't know why I keep talking to you. You clearly don't have a relatable, sympathetic bone in your body, so it's like I just gave you *more* ammunition to lecture me for being an irresponsible idiot and screwing a guy I didn't know without protection and *never* taking my birth control at the same time every day like I was supposed to.

"And it's not like you care that I now have to decide if I should keep the baby or not. Or that my parents would be furious with me because I can't seem to do anything right in my life. And how I probably won't graduate on time now and can't afford to move out, and everything is going to shit. But nope. You couldn't possibly relate, Mr. Perfect, because, as you said, some people just make smarter choices, right? Isn't that what you said?"

When she's done with her emotional speech, she places her hands on her hips, out of breath and clearly very emotional.

I don't have a response to anything she said because she's right. I did say that. And now, in this context, it sounds awful.

But at the same time, I hate that she's beating herself up for every little thing that's gone wrong. I don't want to just make her feel better—I want to make her *be* better. And by better, I mean... good enough for herself.

Reaching forward, I snatch the paper from her hand. "This paper is phenomenal, Sadie. Your writing is eloquent, captivating, and brilliant. You got an A on this paper because you earned it."

She scoffs. "Who cares about a fucking essay?"

"I do. You should. Because it's not about the essay, Sadie. It's about your potential. You are *not* an idiot. You are human and you made a few mistakes, but it doesn't mean you're not smart."

"Wow," she says, wiping her eyes again. "Saying I'm not an idiot is the nicest thing you've ever said about me."

I let out a heavy breath as I fight the urge to shake her. Sadie reminds me so much of Isaac. With so much potential but so little guidance or confidence.

Relating her to my brother probably motivates me to say the absolutely wildest and most unexpected thing.

"I have a spare room."

Her brows knit together as her head cocks to the side. "What?"

Forging ahead with this absolutely ridiculous idea, I continue. "What you need, Miss Green, is to find a sense of confidence for yourself with some guidance from me. I have a spare room in my house. Come and stay with me, and I will help you."

"Help me what?" she asks in astonishment.

"Help you with your studies, your time management, and your confidence."

She lets out a guffaw of a laugh. "You must be out of your mind."

I must be.

"I won't charge you rent, so you can save up for your own place. All I ask in return is that you listen to me. Do exactly as I tell you. Let me guide you the way you need, and if you choose to continue with this pregnancy, I'll make sure your schoolwork doesn't suffer for it."

Her jaw is hanging open, her eyes blinking slowly. "I manage a sex club, you know? I am perfectly capable of doing things on my own, and I don't need a *man* to tell me what to do."

Letting my eyes roll, I let out a sigh. "It has nothing to do with me being a man, Miss Green. It has everything to do with me being a..."

My voice trails off with a flat expression on my face. After a moment, she throws her hands up. "A what?"

I take a step toward her. It's not that I don't know the word she almost used to describe me—it's that I want to hear her say it. For reasons, even I don't understand. This is all new territory for me.

Leaning in, I ask, "You tell me. What exactly were you going to call me last week in class? Someone who gets off on telling others what to do..."

Her mouth closes. I watch the movement in her throat as she swallows. But she doesn't back away. Her voice is soft as she replies, "I don't need a Dom, Dr. Goode."

"Are you sure?" I ask.

"I'm sure," she replies, but her tone is weak. "And if I did, it sure as hell wouldn't be *you*."

There's something about the fire in her eyes that excites me. Her defiance tickles my brain in a way no one ever has before.

Stepping away with my brow in a stern line, I cross my arms. "Suit yourself, Miss Green. But think about it. No strings. No sex. Just an opportunity to scratch my back while I scratch yours."

"So you admit it then?" she asks, mirroring my stance and jutting her chin out toward me.

"Is that what you want to hear?" I ask.

"Yes. Admit I'm right."

"You were...close. No one has ever called me a Dom before and it's not something I do regularly. I don't *get off* on telling you what to do. There's nothing sexual about it. I just enjoy... teaching."

She makes a noise of interest, something between a humph and a laugh. "Well, I appreciate the offer, Dr. Goode, but being in your class is more than enough for me."

With a quiet nod, I hand the paper back to her. It takes her a moment before she reaches out to take it.

"I'll see you Monday, Miss Green."

Her eyes narrow as if she takes my words as a challenge—which they are. I have a feeling I'll be seeing Sadie before Monday.

In fact, I'm betting on it.

SEVEN

Sadie

M y stomach is churning as I park at the club, not only because of this not-so-morning sickness but also because I have to do the one thing I've been dreading since the double pink lines showed up on that pregnancy test.

And also maybe because I'm still thinking about Lucas's visit to my house this morning. I meant what I said—I don't need a Dom. I've never been interested in one, and I don't feel very submissive as it is.

But...

There's something about the way he talks to me. The firm, assertive tone of his voice. The unwavering confidence. The arrogance that is infuriatingly *sexy*.

I really can't stand him, which makes the way my belly tightened with arousal at his words this morning so irritating.

But I'm not thinking about that right now. Right now, I'm focused on the fact that I've managed to lure Jax Kingston back to the club, and while he thinks it's for another "room tour," he has no idea I'm about to knock him off his feet with a sucker punch of reality.

Tossing my purse over my shoulder, I walk inside. I've called in a lot this week. I can tell Sage is worried about me, and I feel bad that I haven't come clean with her either. I guess everyone is in for a surprise tonight.

The club isn't open yet, so I unlock the back door and enter the quiet space, immediately hearing my pink-haired boss talking in the back office.

"Oh, that feels so good," she moans, and I halt in my tracks. Halfway down the hall, I wonder if the door slamming behind me was loud enough to warn her and her husband that I'm now in the building.

"Hello..." I call.

"We're in here," she replies before moaning again.

"Umm..." Taking each step down the hall slowly, I wonder what exactly I'm about to walk into, especially after being invited in. But when I peek my head into the office, I relax my shoulders at the sight of Sage in one office chair and her feet in Adam's lap as he massages them with adoration on his face.

"Hey!" she calls with a tired but wide smile on her face.

"Hey," I reply, clearing my throat and averting my eyes from the scene of her partner so affectionately caring for her. No one will be rubbing mine anytime soon.

Sage picks up on my less-than-chipper greeting and pulls her feet from his hands. "What's up?" she asks.

"Nothing," I reply nonchalantly as I drop my bag on the counter and begin my club-opening routine.

"Bullshit," she snaps, rising from her chair.

When I tilt my head to the side and give her a flat look, she simply turns to her husband and touches his shoulder.

"Baby, will you give us a few minutes?" she asks softly.

"Of course, Peaches," he replies. As he stands from his chair, he plants his lips on her forehead and then on her protruding belly. On his way out, he gives me a simple smile and a wave.

I don't know why, but the gesture has tears forming in my eyes.

"Uh-oh," Sage starts when she sees them welling up. "If that Jax guy hurt you, I told you I'll kill him."

I laugh as a tear spills over. "No, it's not him. Well...not exactly."

Looking confused, she asks, "Did Luke do something?"

This has me cackle loudly, making me look and feel out of my mind. I can't even begin to get into the Dr. Goode situation right now. Instead, I just come out with it.

After a deep breath, I blurt out, "I'm pregnant."

Sage's jaw drops. Then, she waits for a moment as if she's trying to gauge my emotions before reacting. But since I really don't know how to react, I simply shrug and let another tear fall.

"Oh, honey," she says, pulling me into her arms. After patting my back for a few minutes, she just mumbles in my ear, "It's going to be okay. I promise...everything will be okay."

Pulling away from her embrace, I force a fake smile and wipe my eyes. "It was that night with Jax. I know it was stupid of me to have unprotected sex, and I know you're disappointed—"

"Sadie, stop! I am not disappointed. And you are not stupid."

Rather than argue with her and tell her exactly how stupid I feel, I give her a tight smile and try to force her words into my psyche. I'm *not* stupid.

"I don't know what I'm going to do," I say, letting out a sigh.

"Have you told him yet?" she asks.

"He's coming in tonight. I wanted to do it in person," I say before chewing the inside of my cheek.

"What are you going to say?" she asks, looking uneasy.

"I don't know," I reply with a shake of my head. "I don't even know what I want to do yet."

"Well, I am here for you, no matter what, and I'll be here tonight if you need me."

"Thanks," I mumble.

As I stare into Sage's eyes, I think about how we are in similar but *different* situations. Her pregnancy is a celebration. She is supposed to be happy for her baby.

And I find myself feeling incredibly...jealous.

I feel like a jerk even thinking that, so I shove the thought away.

Jax shows up two hours late. For a while I assumed he wouldn't show up at all. But when I see his Land Rover park out front again on the security screen, a sense of dread washes over me.

Here the fuck we go.

Leaving the back office, I head to the front to greet him. My stomach might as well be an Olympic gymnast for how much it's twisting in my gut. I can't believe I'm about to do this. I'm about to tell a hot, rich porn star that I'm pregnant with his baby. Is it too late to undo everything? I'd like a time machine to go back to that night six weeks ago and put that condom on him myself. Or rather, not have sex with him at all. I miss the days when I *pined* for Jax. Wanting is far better than disappointment.

"There's my sexy Sadie," he calls as he enters the club. He has the same wide, charming smile, and it makes my stomach turn even more. Why must he be so hot? It's distracting.

I force some enthusiasm on my face as I meet him in the middle of the lobby. I don't want to scare him away, so I have to make him think he's here for something fun. He's too close to the door for me to drop reality on him here.

"Thanks for coming in," I say in my high-pitched, flirty voice. He wraps his arms around me in a way that feels intimate.

"I'll always show up for you, sweetie," he murmurs against the top of my head.

My brows furrow against his chest. *Sweetie*? We barely know each other. Why is he talking to me like we have any relationship at all? We chatted through social media for a couple of weeks. I saw him in person for about five minutes. Then he stuck his dick in me and was gone before I could say *nice to meet you*.

When I try to pull away, he lowers his face to mine. Instead of letting him kiss me, I turn away and try to play it off.

"Care to join me?" I say, tugging him toward the entrance to the club. "I've got a little something to talk to you about."

A little something is right.

"Abso-fuckin'-lutely," he replies excitedly.

He links his fingers with mine as I pull him through the club toward the rooms in the back. I decide to take him back to the scene of the crime. The moment I drag him inside and let the door close, he's on me. His hands find my hips, and his mouth lands on my neck.

"This room again?" he mumbles against my flesh.

I back up, trying to put some distance between us. "Hey, can we talk first?"

"Mm-hmm," he replies without taking his lips from my skin. He's trying to maneuver us toward the bed, but I plant my feet and shove him away as nonaggressively as possible.

"Sorry," I mutter as he stares down at me in confusion.

God, did I really just apologize for that? I *hate* this.

"What's up?" he asks with a little bite in his tone.

"I really do need to talk to you."

His expression is guarded as he takes a step back. It's amazing how, when you remove the promise of sex, the mood can change.

"About what?" he asks solemnly.

"Well..." I wring my hands as I avert my gaze. "The last time you were here...we didn't use protection."

"Yeah."

I glance up at him to find his expression still guarded and confused.

"And unfortunately, I wasn't on the pill."

"Okay."

He's really going to make me spell this out for him, isn't he?

"So...I took a test last week, and I'm pregnant."

Every time I say those words out loud, they feel heavy on my tongue. They're awkward and hard to utter, and it doesn't get any easier once they're out.

To my surprise, Jax's expression doesn't change. He's still just staring at me as if he's waiting for me to get to the point of all this.

And here I thought I just did.

"It's yours."

"And?"

My jaw drops.

"And...I thought you'd want to know," I reply. My skin is unbearably hot under his scrutinizing gaze, and it's not that he's *trying* to be a dick right now, but he just is.

Finally, *finally*, he starts to show some sort of reaction. He takes a deep breath and runs his fingers through his hair. After doing a little panicked spin in a small circle, he turns toward me and paints a sympathetic expression on his face.

"Fuck, I'm sorry. I just...don't know what to say in these situations."

"It's okay," I reply with a tight smile. It's really *not* okay, but I'll cut him some slack.

"I hate that you're having to deal with this because of me. Just let me know how much it's gonna cost to take care of it, and I'll send it over."

Something sickening travels down my spine. I wish I could express how the words *take care of it* feel so wrong, but I can't. Nothing makes sense.

"I don't really know what I'm going to do," I reply, twisting my hands so tightly they ache.

He takes a step toward me and places his hands on my arms. "Hey, hey, hey," he says comfortingly. "Don't you worry about it. We'll fix this, and I'll pay for everything. It'll be okay."

He presses his lips to my forehead, and I find myself nodding.

"Yeah, okay," I reply.

Maybe he's right. We can just take care of it, and then everything will be back to normal.

Why, at this moment, with Jax's muscular arms wrapped around me, do I suddenly think about Lucas? The way he smelled and the sound of his voice. The safe and comforting way I felt with his nearness. He's never been half as nice to me as Jax, but in some very weird way...I crave him.

"Actually," I say, tearing myself away. "I don't know what I want to do yet. I might...keep it."

Wow. I've never said that out loud before. Those words don't feel nearly as awkward and heavy.

I glance up at Jax to find him gazing down at me with wide eyes. "Are you serious?"

I shrug. "I don't know. I just...haven't decided."

He lets out another heavy sigh, this one sounding a little disgruntled. He rubs at the back of his neck as he turns away. "Fuck."

When he turns back toward me, there's something like disappointment in his eyes, and I hate it.

"Look, I'm not asking you to do anything," I say. "I just wanted you to know."

"Yeah," he mutters to himself. "I appreciate you telling me."

Suddenly, I wish he'd touch me again. Hold me. Kiss me. Anything to be back in his good graces and turn around this dreary mood we're both in.

I find myself reaching for him. "We can still..."

My flirtatious smile barely changes his expression at all. He still leans in and kisses me on the cheek. But that's it.

"I don't know if that's a good idea," he replies.

My hands slide up his biceps. "Why not? It's not like you can get me *more* pregnant." I laugh, but he doesn't join in.

"I should probably go," he says.

Fuck. I messed this up. Me and my stupid ovaries fucked up everything.

"Okay," I say reluctantly.

"But let me know what you decide, and I'm serious; I'll pay for everything. You know, if you do decide to..."

"Yep. Got it," I reply.

As he opens the door, I feel such a sense of defeat. This was awful, but did I really expect anything different? Was there any chance of this conversation going well?

No. Because, deep down, I think I knew what I was going to say even before the words came out of my mouth.

I think I want to keep the baby.

EIGHT

Lucas

G rading papers can be a mind-numbing activity. Hence why I prenumb myself with two to three glasses of Macallan 18 before getting started.

It's a pathetic way to spend a Friday night, but until something more stimulating comes along, this is my life.

After the third glass, I consider calling someone to stave off the loneliness. There's a beautiful ethics professor that has flirted with me once or twice and probably isn't opposed to booty calls. Maybe I should text her.

There's some light jazz playing in the living room as I pick up my phone and scroll for Dr. Laura Hanson's phone number.

God, when was the last time I got laid? It's been too long. No wonder I've been so tense lately.

As I find Laura's number, I pause, hovering my thumb over the button to call her. Suddenly, I'm thinking about my visit to Sadie's house this morning, and the corner of my mouth lifts in a smirk.

I've never once considered myself a Dom or kinky at all. I

wouldn't dare ask a woman to do anything like that, but it does make me wonder...

With the right partner, it might be fun.

I wonder if Laura would submit to me. Would she crawl on the floor for me? Let me control her?

I doubt it. And she wouldn't argue back either. Not in a defiantly hot and bratty way.

And this is how I know I'm drunk. Because suddenly, I'm imagining one of my students and that smart mouth of hers. The way Sadie argues with me sets my body on fire. Almost like she *wants* to be punished.

I'd *love* to punish her. I'd put her over my knee. Spank the shit out of her ass until she promises to be good—even though we both know she'll mouth off again just to get me riled up. I'd love to fold her over this table and wrinkle up these essays as I fuck her.

Yep. I'm drunk.

It's so depraved, but I'm about to pull my cock out and run through the entire fantasy in my head when a banging at my door stops me. My first thought is that it must be Isaac, so I shove away my dirty thoughts, and my cock quickly deflates.

When I reach the front door, I pull it open to find the object of my fantasies standing on my doormat, and I blink in surprise.

"How does it feel to have people show up unannounced at your house?" she asks, hands on her hips.

I gaze down at her in confusion as I glance around the street behind her. "How did you find out where I lived?"

"Same way you found out where I live," she snaps back. Then, to my surprise, she shoves open the door to my house and lets herself in. I'm too dumbfounded to argue.

"Wait," I say as I slam the door and turn to find her standing in my living room. "I found your address on the student registry."

"Oh," she replies, turning toward me with a tilt to her head. "I just asked Sage for your address."

"And she gave it to you?" I say with an astonished laugh.

"Yeah, well...using the school registry to show up to a

student's house uninvited probably isn't allowed either, so we're even." She plants her hands back on her hips and gives me a quirky, crooked smirk.

It makes me smile, but I try to hide it. I'm supposed to be stern and commanding with her, but when she looks so goddamn cute, she makes it hard.

"What's wrong with you?" she asks with a notch in her brow. "Are you drunk?"

I nod toward the table where the bottle is sitting open amid a sea of ungraded papers and a stack of red pens.

"Oh," she replies with a nod. "Wish I could join you, but... you know..." She waves toward her stomach.

Passing her by, I head to my kitchen and retrieve a bottle of water for her instead. "So, what *are* you doing here?" I ask, trying not to think about the fantasy running through my head just a few minutes ago. "Let me guess," I say as I pass her the water. "You're here to accept my offer."

She rolls her eyes as she takes the bottle. "You wish."

I do.

"The truth is," she adds after taking a swig, "I need someone to talk to. Someone who won't be blindly supportive of everything I do. Someone who will tell me like it is and be brutally honest, maybe even to a fault."

"At your service," I say with a drunk smirk as I grab my glass and lead her to my living room. The vinyl has reached the end of the A-side, so I lift the case and turn it to the B-side. Resetting the needle, I wait until the soft music emanates from the speakers before closing the case and finding my seat in the soft brown leather chair.

She's folded up on my couch, one leg tucked beneath her as she hugs the other knee to her chest. My eyes land on the blue paint on her toenails, her sandals discarded across the floor of my house. She's wearing a pair of ripped denim shorts, and the way she's sitting exposes her entire thigh all the way up, and it's *incredibly* distracting.

"Go ahead," I say after taking a sip of my whiskey.

Sadie is chewing the inside of her lip as she stares at me, clearly feeling uneasy. I watch as she takes a long, deep breath, wincing before blurting out, "I'm going to keep this baby."

This statement doesn't really elicit anything from me emotionally. To be honest, I sort of assumed she'd keep it. I don't know why. And it doesn't matter either way.

"Say something," she snaps at me, and I blink a few times before reacting.

"What would you like me to say, Miss Green?"

She throws her hands up in exasperation. "Tell me I'm being irresponsible and that I have no place trying to raise a child when I'm such a mess myself. Tell me it's the wrong choice. Just tell me the responsible thing to do would be to get an abortion and get my own life together before bringing another life into the world."

My brows pinch inward as I stare at her and try to formulate my answer.

"You think that's what I should say?" I ask.

"Yes. I think that's what you *want* to say."

"That's not what I want to say," I argue.

"Why not? It's true, isn't it? And I asked you to be brutally honest."

I set my glass on the coffee table and lean forward. Taking off my glasses, I rub at the bridge of my nose, before putting them back on and looking at her. "Miss Green, do you *want* to keep the baby?"

I watch the subtle movement of her throat as she swallows. "Yes. But..."

"No buts. You'll figure the rest out. If that's what you want, then that's the right answer."

She stares at me for a moment, a wrinkle forming between her eyes. Then, she lets out a loud, guttural noise.

"Ugh!" she cries, slapping her hands over her face.

"What's wrong?"

"That is not helpful, and I thought you, of all people, would tell me that I need to be smart about this and do the responsible thing."

I pick up my glass and take another sip. "Sorry, Miss Green, but I'm not in the business of telling women what to do with their bodies."

"But I thought..." she argues.

As our gazes meet, I let my eyes roll as I stand up. "Not like *that*."

I can understand the irony of that statement since we literally had a conversation this morning about how I *may* or *may not be* the kind of guy who does, in fact, like to tell women what to do with their bodies. I am a bit of a control freak—I can admit it.

And while it's not inherently sexual, I can see how fun it *would* be.

But that is not what I'm talking about with Sadie, and she knows it.

Avoiding that topic of conversation again, I disappear into the hallway and flip the light on in the guest bedroom.

"Come here, Miss Green," I call in a low, commanding tone.

I hear her rise from the couch and make her way down the hall. As she appears in the doorway behind me, I turn around to find her arms crossed and her eyes scanning the cozy space.

"I never said I was moving in here," she states defiantly.

"I know you didn't, but I'm showing you anyway."

"And what about when the baby comes?" she asks, looking up at me with her brows raised.

"I'll be gone by then. I've applied to a program in England. I leave in the spring and I'll be gone for a year. You can rent this house and have it to yourself. Or move out by then. Doesn't matter to me, but what I'm offering you is more than a room, Miss Green. You understand? By the time the baby comes, you'll have your finances in order. You'll have graduated and you won't feel like you do now—like a mess."

Her curious gaze lingers on my face, and before long, it starts to burn.

"Who lived here before?" she asks softly, those warm, green eyes still focused on me.

I clear my throat. "No one."

When she doesn't look away, I get the feeling that she doesn't believe me. But Sadie is too closely tied to my family for me to be honest about this. I can't tell her that Isaac has been quasi living with me because she could pass that information on to Sage, who would then tell her husband, Adam.

And the last thing I need is a fired-up Adam on my case.

If she can see through my lie, she isn't arguing about it. Instead, she takes a deep breath and lets out a heavy sigh.

"Fine."

My head spins toward her in surprise. I have to quickly train my expression not to come off as too eager or excited.

"But—" she snaps, holding up a finger. "We need boundaries. I want your help, but you can't really control every aspect of my life. I'd smother you in your sleep if you tried that."

"That's fair," I reply, leaning against the opposite side of the doorframe with my arms crossed. "But you have to be open to this. I'm doing it for your own good."

"I'm open to it," she says with a shrug. "I am a strong, independent woman."

"I know you are."

"And even though I *don't* need a Dom or a man, I'm not going to lie...I need help."

"I want to help," I reply gently.

"I still don't understand why." The corner of her mouth lifts in a smirk, creating dimples in her cheeks and making the splatter of freckles across her nose shine in the room's overhead light.

Lifting my shoulders in a shrug, I say, "I don't either. Maybe it's just goodwill and benevolence."

A loud cackle flies from her mouth. "Ha! More like a God complex and arrogance."

I fight a smile as I nod. "Maybe."

As she steps into the room, surveying the queen-size bed and letting her hand glide over the bedspread, she looks back at me with a warning. "Please don't make me regret this, Dr. Goode."

My eyes float downward to the way her ass fills those ripped denim shorts. Those filthy fantasies of mine from earlier harken back to my mind.

Stop it. I can't be entertaining these thoughts if she's going to stay here.

As I back out the room, I coldly reply, "Then, don't disappoint me, Miss Green."

NINE

Sadie

"You're what?"

My mother is standing in the doorway of my bedroom, watching me as I toss my essential clothing into a box.

"I'm moving out," I answer. "I found a place to rent, and it's closer to work."

"And you'll have a roommate?" she asks, her voice rising in suspicion.

"Yeah. He's my friend's brother-in-law. He's trustworthy. Don't worry."

As I glance over my shoulder at her, I notice the scrutinizing way she has her lips pursed and her brow tightened. She's not so sure about this, but then again...I'm twenty-five. I'm far too old to be living at home as it is.

No, I don't tell her the part about how this man I'm living with is also my English professor.

And *no*, I don't tell her the part about how I'm also with child —and will remain with child. I figure one dose of big news a day is more than enough for my quaint suburban family's life.

"If you're sure..." she says uneasily.

When I hear footsteps down the hall, I tense, waiting for Jonah to appear next to my mother. Glancing over my shoulder, I watch as he stares with his mouth hanging open and his eyes wide.

"Where are you going?" he signs, the movement of his hands angry and urgent.

My shoulders sag as I turn toward him. With my mouth twisted in regret, I reply, both out loud and with sign language, "I'm renting a room in the city."

"Why?" he asks. The look of betrayal on his face hurts. Part of me knows that Jonah is just being a sarcastic, overdramatic teenager. He thinks it's fun to overreact to everything.

But part of me also knows that being so close as siblings has come from living together for so long, and moving out feels like leaving him behind.

"Because I'm too old to live at home," I reply. "And I found a great place to rent near work. The guy who owns it is going on some work trip to England, so I'll practically have the place to myself."

Jonah rolls his eyes and makes a waving motion as if to blow me off. I pick up a dirty sock and toss it at him as he tries to walk away. He flips me off before laughing and jogging down the hallway toward the kitchen.

"He'll be all right," my mom says once he's gone.

"I know he will," I say without looking her in the eyes.

"I was starting to think he was going to move out before you," she says with a laugh.

"Very funny," I reply, rolling my eyes. I slam the box down with a huff. "Well, you're in luck now because I'll be out of your hair, and you and Dad can focus on Jonah and all of his accomplishments."

"Now, don't be like that," my mom replies with a tsk.

"It's fine," I argue, starting another box, this time throwing things I need like my laptop and chargers in. "I've been a mooch for long enough. I should have moved out years ago, and you're right. I'm sure Jonah will be out the door the day after he graduates, probably with some sports scholarship at an Ivy League school, and I'll be working in some shitty nightclub."

I feel her approach, putting her arms around me from behind. "Stop pouting. We're proud of both of our kids."

"Sure," I groan.

My mom doesn't stick around to argue, and I know I am just being whiny and overdramatic, but it's hard not to feel the sting of her little comments.

I will show them how capable I am. I'm going to move out and get my life together and somehow figure out how to do all of that with a kid on the way.

My toiletry bag lands with a *thunk* at the bottom of the box, and I freeze as that thought washes over me—a *kid*.

God, what am I doing? Am I making a mistake?

I'm not a mother. I don't know the first thing about raising a child, and for some reason, just because some guy I barely know didn't wrap his dick, I think I'm ready to bring one into the world and raise it alone.

Before my thoughts can spiral, I close my eyes and hear Luke's calming tone in my head.

No buts. If that's what you want, then that's the right answer. You'll figure the rest out.

God, I hope he's right.

I manage to fit everything I need into three boxes. I cram them into the back of my Civic and hug my parents and brother goodbye. And that's it.

I drive away from the safety net of my childhood house and straight over to Luke's house. I mean, it's not like I'm going far. And I promised to come back once a week to check in, but as far as sprouting wings and leaving the nest goes, this is nothing more than a gentle shove without a big drop.

As I pull into the spot he told me to park in, I take a deep breath and ask myself if this is crazy. Am I moving too fast? Should I have given this some more thought? Weighed the pros and cons? Taken at least two or three days to decide?

Would it have made a difference?

Because I'm not only moving in with him. I'm basically handing my life over to him. I'm allowing him full control. He's going to tell me what to do, and I'm going to *hate* it. But it's what I need. Isn't it?

It's not like I'm naive to the benefits of a full-time Dom/sub dynamic, but it doesn't matter because we're not ready for that yet. There needs to be so much more trust between us before we go that far. And, as far as I know, Lucas doesn't know a thing about the full-time lifestyle. No matter how much I can see it intrigues him.

What if I get my life together, and it makes Jax look at me as more than just a quick fuck? What if he sees how good we'd be together and things actually work out between us?

One happy little family.

I just have to get through the rest of the semester with Dr. Control Issues, and everything will be fine.

Leaving the boxes in the trunk, I climb out of the car and head up to Luke's house. I knock on the door and a moment later, he answers. Like last night, he's in more casual attire—light jeans and a flannel button-down. It's annoying how handsome he is. Like, he's too much of a dickhead to be so hot. Too uptight. Too rude and selfish. Hotness should really be reserved for guys with fun personalities and laid-back attitudes.

"Come in, Miss Green," he says, opening the door for me.

"I left my boxes in the car," I reply.

"I'll get them," he says as he closes the door behind me. "But let's get situated first. Have a seat on the bench and take off your shoes. I don't like shoes in my home, so consider that the first rule."

It's a little early in the arrangement to be rolling my eyes, but here I am. Instead of sitting on the bench like he said, I just slip my Chucks off without even touching them. Then I kick them over to the corner near the bench.

Luke glares at me as his nostrils flare. "Line them up against the wall, Miss Green."

"Oh, we're starting already?" I quip back with a smirk. He doesn't find it funny. "Okay, okay, relax." With a huff, I line my sneakers up against the wall next to his brown leather shoes. They look so out of place together.

After putting my shoes where he wants them, I turn back and place my hands on my hips. "So, what other rules should I know about? I have a feeling there will be more."

"Yes," he replies dryly before moving into the house. I follow, noticing how he's not the same relaxed, drunk version of himself he was last night. I might need to get him to drink more. I liked him better with whiskey in his bloodstream.

"I don't like food in the living room," he says. "Clean up after yourself in the kitchen and throw away food when it's expired. You can help yourself to anything in the kitchen, even if it's mine. Don't leave anything in the sink and wash and put the dishes back after you use them."

"Sheesh," I groan as I stand behind him with wide eyes. "Will I get punished if I break the rules?" I ask playfully.

He turns, leaning against the fridge with his arms crossed. "Do you want to be punished, Miss Green?"

My brows shoot upward as I fight a smile. Just the image of Lucas Goode bending me over his knee and spanking me like a child makes me laugh...while also making my stomach flutter with something I don't want to think about right now.

"Okay, but seriously," I say as I hop up onto the counter. "I'm giving you control so you can help me figure my shit out, so how's this going to work? You want me to crawl around or fetch you coffee? You can pet my head and call me a good girl."

His expression turns to stone as he stares at me. After a moment, he has to clear his throat before speaking again. "Crawl around? That's not what we agreed to, and that's not exactly what I had in mind."

"Then, what did you have in mind?" I ask.

Ignoring my question, he narrows his eyes. "Is that what you thought this was? I mean...that's what you came for?"

I shrug. "I don't know what I came for, honestly. But when I'm around you..." My voice trails as our eyes meet, and I decide to choose my next words very carefully. I don't want to give him the wrong idea. "You have a way of making everything simple. You know what you want, and you know how to ask for it. I need that. I need crystal-clear expectations. Just...give me the chance to do something right."

Slowly, he nods. "I think I can do that."

"Thanks," I reply, a small smile creeping across my face.

"Start by getting off my counter," he says coldly.

My smile vanishes as I hop down and stand face to face with him.

"Good girl," he replies, the frigid, gravelly tone of his voice sending chills all the way down to my toes.

I can't hide my smirk now, but for the first time since I showed up, neither can he.

TEN

Lucas

Word travels fast. It takes my brother less than twenty-four hours to find out about my new roommate, and I'm willing to bet he didn't waste a minute before texting me about it. I can just picture Caleb sitting smugly behind his desk at work with his phone in his hand, laughing about the fact that I now have a woman living in my house.

No doubt he's making something out of nothing.

> You and Sadie, huh?

I grimace down at his text message.

> She's renting the spare bedroom at my place.

> Nothing more than that.

> Right.

> Dean rented a room at my place, too, remember?

I roll my eyes as I hustle across campus, staring down at my phone and trying to formulate a response. This is nothing like his situation with Dean.

First of all, I'm not going to be fucking my tenant.

Second of all, I won't be settling down or falling in love with anyone. That business is for my brothers, not me. Everyone knows that.

Adam tried to fake date his now pregnant wife and look how that turned out for him.

As for Caleb, he did his best to resist the much younger man living in his rental unit, but when his wife jumped on board, the three of them couldn't resist living in matrimonial bliss together.

And me? I'm married to my work, and I like it that way. I don't date to marry, and I never have. The idea of marriage and children is repulsive to me, so I'm content with my life the way it is.

> Unlike you, I know how to keep my dick in my pants.

> That's why you're the boring twin.

> No, just the smarter one.

> I had two sets of lips wrapped around my dick last night. So you tell me who's smarter.

> Please keep that to yourself.

> I have pictures if you want to see them.

> I'll block you.

He doesn't text back—*thank God*—so I pocket my phone and continue my walk across campus. Sadie is in my class today, but after that, I have a meeting with the Stratford Project. I haven't stopped thinking about it all week. It's the only thing distracting me from the fact that I have a gorgeous woman living under my roof, one who apparently has an affinity for punishment and praise.

This living situation might be harder than I thought.

When I reach the classroom, the students are filling in, and I realize I'm not as early as I normally am. In fact, class is due to start in two minutes, and I'm not nearly prepared enough.

On top of that, Sadie's usual seat is empty.

Frowning to myself, I put my laptop away and pull out my class notes along with the reading material for today.

When I start my lecture, she's still not here. At first, I begin to worry. Maybe she had an accident on the way in, or something happened at the house.

But roughly fifteen minutes into the class, the doors open, and she slinks in with a wince, avoiding eye contact as if that somehow saves her from my scrutiny. I pause my lecture to clear my throat.

"Thanks for joining us, Miss Green," I mutter under my breath.

"Sorry I'm late," she replies.

"Class starts promptly at ten. Is that a problem for you?"

As she takes a seat, she grimaces at me. "No. At least I didn't throw up this time."

"You have a response for everything, don't you?" I say.

"You have a complaint for everything, don't you?" she replies, echoing my words back to me.

The other students in the classroom become blurry in my periphery as I glare at her.

She is out of line. She is *always* out of line.

"Please stay after class, Miss Green," I mutter indignantly.

"Yes, sir," she replies with enthusiasm, and I find my molars grinding. I don't know what game she's playing, but if she's trying to push every button of mine, she's succeeding. It's like she sees insolence as a charming attribute rather than an infuriating flaw.

I'll break her of it. I swear I will.

Ignoring her remark, I turn toward the rest of the lecture hall and continue my discussion on the American literary movement.

"The most popular book during this movement that I'm sure most of you have heard of is *Moby Dick*." I hold up my copy of the book, and the students nod in recognition, typing their notes as they listen.

A small snicker from the left side of the room catches my attention. I turn my head to see Sadie smiling to herself as she jots down something in her notebook.

I should just leave it alone, but when it comes to her, it's obvious I can't seem to help myself.

"Is something funny, Miss Green?"

She looks up. "Oh, no," she replies, giggling again as she returns her eyes to her paper.

Is she really so immature that she finds the title *Moby Dick* to be funny? Against my better judgment, I persist.

"No, please share why you think it's appropriate to laugh during my presentation."

Her eyes lift again, this time piercing me with a stubborn expression. "Fine," she spits out with tenacity. "I was laughing because this guy and I used to use *Moby Dick* as a texting code with each other whenever we wanted to hook up. That's what made me giggle. Happy now?"

The class erupts in laughter, but Sadie's fearless gaze doesn't leave my face—not even as my cheeks start to heat up. I have to fight the urge to drag her out of her seat and show her what happens to impudent brats when they act like she is right now.

Rebellious, sassy, bold brats like Sadie Green.

"That's enough," I bark, tearing my eyes away from her and focusing on the class. "Thank you for enlightening us, Miss Green. For the purpose of today's lecture, we're going to focus on *Moby Dick*, the novel."

"Fine by me," she mutters under her breath.

But even as I move on and make it through the rest of the

class discussion, I can't shake the tension that has burrowed itself in my bones. How can I let her get under my skin like this? What is it about this woman that drives me so mad? It's not like she's the first student to talk back or the first woman to give me hell. But there's just something about Sadie that makes her different from the rest, and I wish I could put my finger on it.

After class ends and the students file out, Sadie doesn't leave her seat. She sits in her spot, crosses her arms, and glares at me as she waits for the room to empty.

The moment the last student leaves and the door closes, we unleash on each other.

"What is your problem?" she shouts.

"Is it too much to ask that you show up on time?" I yell.

"You do realize that I'm not the only person who shows up late to a college class, right?"

"Yeah, well, you're the only one who bothers me every single time you do it," I argue.

"Why?" Her hands fly into the air as she stands from her seat. "What is your *obsession* with me? You hate everything I do and you take it all so personally!"

"Because I see your potential, Miss Green. I see how brilliant you are, and you're wasting it!" My own statement takes me by surprise.

Her hands drop, and her face falls. "You think I'm brilliant?"

"It doesn't matter what I think," I reply, turning away to begin packing up my things.

"Clearly, it does, Dr. Goode. You act as if your opinion of me matters more than anyone else's."

Do I?

"My opinion of you does not matter, Miss Green. What matters is that you have real potential. However, rather than utilizing that potential, you show up to class late and unprepared, and what's worse, you disrupt the rest of the class with your giggles and comments."

She huffs with a sarcastic laugh, and I spin on her to see her face. "What's so funny?" I ask.

"You. You're hilarious if you think *I'm* the one disrupting class."

"What is that supposed to mean?" I take a step toward her. My palms start to itch, so I flex my hands in and out of fists to keep from doing something I shouldn't.

She takes another step closer, and my mind rings with alarm bells. This is dangerous.

"It means *you* are the one disrupting the class. Everyone can see how obsessed you are with me! Did you even notice the guy who came in a whole five minutes after me? Did you say a word to him? No. You just want to make my life hell because, for some reason, you want to be a massive *dick* to me!"

"Watch your tone, Miss Green," I say in warning.

Another step closer.

We're toe to toe now.

I should back up, but I can't.

"Or what?" she argues with her head tilted like she's presenting a challenge. "What are you going to do, Dr. Goode?"

"You know what," I grit through my teeth.

"Go ahead," she whispers. "You know you want to."

This is a mistake. A stupid, careless mistake, but she's pushing me to do it, and she's one-hundred-percent right. We both know I want to.

So I do something I never, ever do. I act without thinking. I don't process the consequences and I don't regard the warning signs.

I grab Sadie by the back of the neck, spinning her around to the nearest table. She doesn't stop me or fight back. She lets me bend her over, letting out a gasp as I do.

A gasp that goes straight to my dick.

Holding her chest to the surface, she waits, gripping the edges as I stare down at her ass in those tight black leggings. The round, luscious surface of it perched up in anticipation.

With all of the anger boiling under my skin, I rear back my hand and spank her on the left side of her ass. Not hard enough to hurt her or the baby, but enough to *show her*.

Show her what...I don't know.

She whimpers, gripping tighter to the table.

God, that felt good.

Too good.

So I lift my hand and do it again. And again. And again.

With each wallop on her ass, I grunt, leaning into the fervor and satisfaction of bringing her just a little bit of pain, making her *feel* how vehement I am. Like pouring my passion into her. It connects us. Makes us one.

It doesn't make sense. Nothing with her makes sense.

But in some weird way, it makes more sense than anything else I've tried to understand in the past six weeks.

I lose count of how many times I spank her, but when my hands start to sting, and her voice grows higher, I stop. My arm is raised in midair, and I'm gazing down at her like I'm recovering from some out-of-body experience.

Quickly, I back away.

As the adrenaline starts to fade, I realize there is a throbbing inside my pants. I turn away from her to hide my raging erection.

She rises from the table, breathing hard but not saying a word.

"I'm sorry, I just—"

I don't finish my sentence. I'm interrupted by the sound of her footsteps as she sprints out of the room, letting the door slam behind her and leaving me alone with my shame.

ELEVEN

Sadie

I'm sprinting across campus. My notebook and pen are still sitting on the table in the classroom, but there's no way I'm going back. Not today.

Tears sting behind my eyes, and I feel like I'm crawling out of my skin. I don't know if I want to cry or scream or hit something or *fuck* someone.

What just happened back there?

I wanted that—and I'm not just saying that. I really did want it. I craved it, needed it, and practically begged him to do it. I wanted Lucas Goode to release his aggression on me as much as he wanted to.

So why am I so upset?

It's like all my emotions bubbled to the top, and now they're begging to spring free.

I manage to make it to my car, locking myself inside before slamming my hands against the steering wheel and letting out a scream. It doesn't help. My body is still buzzing. My skin prickles, feeling every tiny sensation from the friction of my cotton panties against my sore ass to the heat of my car, causing sweat to build in my pores. I can feel every single one.

My breathing intensifies, and before I give myself time to think or stop, I shove my hand down the front of my leggings. My body is screaming with need as I smother my hand over my clit, trying to quiet this ache.

But I can't. Touching myself only makes it worse.

So I press my fingers over it in tight circles, rubbing myself as I replay the needy sounds he made as he spanked me. The way he unleashed something primal inside himself. The way the pain awakened my arousal and my emotions.

Throwing my head back, I whimper in the quiet, steamy confines of my car. My legs tense, and my back arches as my relentless fingers force my body into a hasty orgasm that feels like both a burden and a relief.

Crying out, I ride out the waves of pleasure, cursing Dr. Goode's name in my head. My free hand squeezes the steering wheel, and when the climax eventually crests the peak, my head starts to spin, and dots appear in my vision.

Quickly, I pull my hand out of my pants and start my car, cranking the AC to full power. It takes a moment for the air to turn cold, but when it does, I rest my forehead against the steering wheel and breathe it in. My head is soaked with sweat, and my legs are still trembling from the intensity of my quick orgasm.

It takes me a moment to realize I'm not upset anymore. It turns out masturbating really did relieve the intensity.

However, my ass still hurts, and I'm still mad.

Instead of going back to Luke's house—which, I guess, technically is my house now—I drive to the one person who will listen to me vent about this without judgment. When I pull up to Sage's apartment, I park in an empty spot across the street and dash into the laundromat.

She's not down here like I can sometimes find her, but the owner, Gladys, is. She's sweeping the floor and pauses to stare at me in shock.

"What the hell happened to you?" she asks.

Saying that I just got spanked by my professor and masturbated in my car probably isn't the right response, so I just shrug and reply jovially, "This heat!"

She chuckles to herself as I jog up the stairs to Sage's apartment. God, I sure hope Adam isn't home, and I don't walk in on something I don't want to see. When I tap on her door, her dog Roscoe starts yipping inside, and I hear her immediately try to shush him.

When she opens the door, she's obviously surprised to see me, judging by the expression on her face. "What's up? Are you okay?"

"Something weird just happened, and I need to talk about it."

"Come in." Quickly opening the door, she ushers me inside and meets me on the couch. "Want something to drink? I've got sweet tea."

"No thanks," I reply, tucking my sweaty red curls behind my ear.

Planting her hands in what's left of her lap, she waits for me to speak. "What happened?"

"First of all, you have to promise to keep this between you and me."

"Always," she replies without hesitation. "Adam is with his mom, so we're good. Tell me everything."

I drag in a breath before starting. "Luke...spanked me."

Sage's face is frozen in disbelief. "Spanked you?"

"Yes. After class."

Her expression tightens. "Did he hurt you?"

"No," I answer quickly. "I mean...not any more than I wanted him to."

"So...you wanted him to..." she says with the tone of a question.

"Yes..." I reply uneasily.

Sage shakes her head. "Okay, start over."

That's when I tell her everything, from the argument in class to the fight afterward, even last night's discussion about the terms of our new living arrangement and how things should be. She doesn't look less confused at any point in the story, which is a bad sign.

"Wow..."

"Yeah," I reply.

"You guys have some intense sexual chemistry."

My spine straightens. "What? No. That's not...no. We don't..."

With that, Sage begins to laugh. "Do you hear yourself?"

"Sage, Luke and I do not have sexual *anything*. He's a pompous control freak and not my type *at all*. We're just living together until he hopefully leaves for England. I can rent his place on my own. Maybe even date a *normal* guy and settle down."

She rubs her belly as her eyes narrow. "He just spanked you, and you rubbed one out minutes later. I'd call that pretty sexual."

"Ugh," I groan, putting my face in my hands.

"Maybe you two need to just do it and get it out of your systems," she says with a shrug.

"Absolutely not," I say, shaking my head.

"Okay, fine. But you have to admit that you're sort of falling into kinky roles with each other. It sounds to me like you want him to be your Dom, and he wants that, too."

Biting my bottom lip, I don't even bother trying to argue with that. She's right. I do want that in some weird way. I've even made it somewhat clear to him. But was I putting too much pressure on him today? Did I coerce him into something he didn't want?

Sage's soft hand touches my knee. "You need to talk to him. That's step one. Figure out exactly what you both want out of this situation. And hey, you can always have a Dom/sub dynamic without the sex. People do it all the time."

I roll my eyes. "No, they don't. Sex always becomes part of the equation. Trying to separate kink from sex is like trying to separate sex from feelings."

Sage shakes her head, clearly disagreeing with me but not bothering to argue.

"Listen," she says after a moment. "Take my advice. Talk to him because if you don't, and you just continue to get on his nerves to get a reaction out of him, I guarantee it will end with sex. So if that's not what you want...talk it out."

"Fine," I mumble under my breath.

After leaving Sage's, I head back to the house. Luke's not there, so I use that time to do homework and a bit of reading. I need to make a doctor's appointment to get this whole pregnancy situation checked out, but I'm dreading that, so it keeps getting shoved down the to-do list.

Halfway through my statistics homework, I stretch out on the couch and fall asleep with my book and calculator on my chest. But when I wake up, they're both stacked on the coffee table, along with the pen and notebook I left in class. I hear movement in the kitchen, but I pretend to be asleep for a while to avoid the awkward conversation I don't want to have.

I still don't know what I want to say. I'm a grown-ass woman who was spanked like a child—and I *liked* it. I can't ask for that. Not from someone I'm not even in a relationship with. If Luke and I were dating, it would be different.

When it becomes unavoidable, I eventually sit up from the couch and turn to face the man sitting at the dining room table.

"Hi," I stammer uncomfortably.

I can see his jaw clench from here before he awkwardly replies, "Hey."

"How did your interview go?" I ask to keep the conversation light.

"It was postponed." His mood is melancholy, and now I know why.

I climb onto my knees to face him. "Oh no. I'm sorry."

"It's okay," he says with a shrug. "They needed to reschedule for next month."

I don't know anything about this internship he's trying to get into, but I know enough from his mood and the way he talks about it that it's important to him.

When there's nothing to say for a moment, we sit in tense silence. He's the first one to broach the subject.

"Listen, Sadie..."

Just hearing him say my name, not Miss Green, sets my nerves on edge. It's too real and serious. I hate it.

So I quickly interrupt him before he can say anything else.

"Don't," I blurt out. "You don't need to apologize or say anything. I'm fine."

"Yes, I do," he argues. "I lost my temper."

"No, you didn't."

"It was wrong of me to put my hands on you," he continues, clearly not listening to me.

"Luke, I wanted you to."

"Still, I didn't know that at the time, and it was wrong of me."

God, this is so uncomfortable, but I can still feel his gaze on my face, so I decide to just come out with it.

"I liked it."

He pauses. "You did?"

Without looking into his eyes, I quickly nod.

Then, after clearing his throat, he mutters raspily, "Me too."

We're both quiet for a moment, soaking in this new tension between us. Finally, I'm the one to fill the silence. "I think we just found our form of punishment."

"Yeah..." he stammers. "I think we did."

More awkward silence.

"So..." he starts. "If you act up or don't listen to me, you want me to..."

"Yep," I reply.

"We should probably have a word or something, right?" He scratches the back of his neck and it's clear just how new all of this is to him.

"A safe word, yeah. I think *stop* or *no* will suffice for now," I say.

He shuffles his feet as he nods. "Perfect."

For the first time since the start of this awkward conversation, our eyes meet and something pure flashes between us. An almost friendly familiarity. And for the first time since we met, I feel a trust blooming between us. I can't remember the last man I really trusted, so this is nice.

"Now that we've established that," he says, "are you going to tell me why you were late this morning?" he asks.

There's something so satisfying about hearing that infuriatingly stern tone of his again. It feels so normal already.

"Well, if you must know. It's because I spent the morning throwing up."

He winces in disgust. "Is that normal? To be so sick all the time?"

"How the hell should I know? This is my first time doing this."

"Have you seen your doctor yet?"

I deflate into the couch. "No."

"Why not?" he asks in a scolding tone.

"Because I'm putting it off. If I make the appointment, then it becomes real, and I'm not ready for it to be real."

With a huff, he stares at the ceiling. "These things rarely wait until you're ready, Miss Green."

Oh, thank God. No more *Sadie*.

"I know that. I'm not an idiot," I argue.

"Then pick up the phone. And call them. Now."

Glaring at him obstinately, I grab my phone from the table. As I glance down at the device, scrolling for my doctor's number, I realize that I'm doing this because he's making me. Hypothetically. Not literally. But something about that makes it easier. Less overwhelming. More manageable.

When I find the number, I stare at it for a moment. Making this call is huge. I'll have to say those words out loud again. The words that my mouth seems to fumble. *I'm pregnant.*

"I think I need to...be alone for this." My voice sounds so small, but Luke doesn't argue or question it.

He just stands from the dining room table and says, "I'm going for a run." Then as he passes the couch, he lays a hand on my shoulder. It's so oddly comforting. The same hand that spanked me this morning. "You can do this," he says, and I swallow those words like medicine.

I can do this.

With that he leaves, and I hit the button.

TWELVE

Lucas

"Rise and shine, Miss Green."

Standing over Sadie's bed in the guest room, I cross my arms over my chest and wait for her to show signs of life. It's past nine and I know she worked late. She's lying on her side, curled up in the fetal position, hugging a pillow to her front with her long red hair braided over her shoulder.

Her lips are parted, and her cheeks are red. She looks so at peace, and part of me hates having to wake her up.

"Miss Green," I say again, nudging her on the leg. She stirs but doesn't wake up.

I let out a disgruntled sigh as I glance around the room. Her dirty clothes are piled in the corner, and there's a pile of empty water bottles on the nightstand. She really is like Isaac.

It's infuriating.

She's been here for two weeks now, and for the most part, it's been uneventful. She spends a lot of time at work or studying, but when she is here, I notice quirky little habits that drive me insane. Like how she is constantly singing something, even when there's no music playing. She dances in her seat when she eats, and she leaves her shoes all over the house instead of in their place by the door like I've told her.

But even with all of that, we haven't had another incident like we did in the classroom. I still don't understand what came over me that day. I've never done anything like that in my life, and I still worry that it was wrong. Even if she said she liked it.

It's one thing to assume Sadie wants that and another to think she's just saying that to please me. Communication isn't my strong suit, and having conversations like that isn't easy for me.

And it's pretty obvious how much communication is required for something like this.

"Sadie!" I bark, and finally, she jumps, her eyes popping open as she stares up at me in shock.

"What are you doing here?" she asks.

When she rolls onto her back, the thin tank top of her pajamas shifts, and her breast slips out of the top. Quickly, I turn away and rid the image of her pretty pink nipple from my memory.

"It's past nine, and your appointment is in an hour," I say, keeping my tone steady.

"Oh shit," she replies with a groan.

I leave the room as she crawls out of bed, but before I leave, I think about making a remark about the mess in her room or the fact that she should really set an alarm on her phone, but when I glance back, I notice just how defeated she appears, so I decide to save it for another time.

Going into the kitchen, I keep myself busy by fixing some breakfast. I ate mine two hours ago, but I don't have a class on my schedule today so I have nothing better to do.

When Sadie comes out a few moments later, her hair brushed in long waves and hints of makeup on her face, I place a bowl of granola with fruit and yogurt on the table next to a glass of juice.

"Eat," I say as I turn away and head back to the kitchen for another cup of coffee.

"I'm not hungry," she replies, sitting on the couch and slipping on her shoes.

I pause with my back to her and grind my molars together. "I fixed you breakfast, and you shouldn't be skipping meals. You have time before your appointment. So eat."

When she gets up from the couch, she doesn't head toward the dining room like I expect her to. Instead, she fumbles with her hair, clearly frustrated with it, as she stares in the mirror by the front door.

"Miss Green," I say in a warning. "Did you hear me?"

"Don't start with me today, Dr. Goode. I'm not in the mood."

My coffee cup lands loudly on the counter as I stare at her across the house. "I don't care if you're in the mood. You will eat breakfast," I say.

"Ugh!" She grunts in frustration as she starts fidgeting with her shirt, pulling it down to reach the waistband of her skirt, but it's clearly not to her satisfaction. "Only nine weeks and nothing fits me already! I hate this stupid shirt! And I hate my hair."

"Miss Green..." I call when I notice her starting to fly off the handle.

She finally rips off her shirt before tearing off her shoes, and I notice her lip starting to tremble.

"Come sit down," I say again as I make my way into the living room. But it does nothing to stave her breakdown.

"I can't do this!" she screams. Her face is red, and tears are brimming in her eyes. "I can't go to this stupid appointment, and I can't have this baby!"

"Sadie, sit down!" I shout, thinking it will snap her out of her fit.

It doesn't.

She gapes at me in shock before picking up one of her shoes and sending it hurling toward my head. I manage to dodge it just in time. "Stop yelling at me!" she shouts.

I turn to find the shoe lying on my kitchen counter, and I'm too stunned to move. Turning back toward her, my jaw still hangs open like a fish.

For what feels like minutes, I stand in the middle of the room at a loss for words. Finally, Sadie drops to the floor, her back to the wall as she sobs into her folded arms.

Clenching my jaw and forcing myself to swallow, I make my way slowly toward her. Standing over her, I watch her cry without knowing what I'm supposed to say in this moment. She wanted me to be firm with her and to tell her what to do, but that clearly didn't work today.

And finally I see what it is she's feeling. She's not angry or defiant—she's scared.

She once said my confidence brings her comfort.

Kneeling down next to her, I run a hand softly over her head. At first, she flinches, trying to push me away. But then, as I do it again, she leans into my touch.

Once her tears have subsided, I stand back up and rest my hands on my hips.

"Get up."

She sniffles before glancing up at me. "I can't do this," she cries.

"Yes, you can. Now, get...up."

When she doesn't move after a moment, a look of defeat washing over her, I reach down and pet my hand softly over her head again, this time touching her as if I'm admiring her.

"One thing at a time," I say as our eyes meet. "And first, I want you to show me you can get up."

Her hand reaches up and takes mine. Then, slowly and with a shaky breath, she rises from the floor. When she's on her feet, she stares at me as if waiting for the next step.

"Good girl," I say. "Now, go sit at the table."

"But—"

"No buts. Go sit at the table. Now."

She subtly nods before moving around me to the dining room table. I pick up her shirt from the floor and bring it to her as she sits down in front of her breakfast. Draping the shirt on the back of her chair, I stroke her head again.

As I stand next to her, I feel her lean toward me, and I let her. Her head rests against my side, and she breathes loudly as if trying to keep the tears from returning.

"I want you to eat," I say. "I know you can do that for me."

Again, she nods. With a sniffle, she takes the spoon and picks at the fruit first. She doesn't eat much, but it's something, and it's enough for me. I've never gained such satisfaction from watching someone eat before, but I swear I could sit here and feed Sadie all day. I want to watch her fill her belly. I want to see her full and sated.

This is inappropriate. I realize that now. This relationship between us is not the way a professor should be acting with his student, but as long as we're not having sex, then I'm innocent. I just have to resist any sort of sexual temptation, and I'm fine.

When Sadie sets down her spoon and takes a sip of juice, she places her hands in her lap and lets out a sigh.

"Good job," I say.

It's quiet for a moment, and I start to anticipate what she'll say even before the words leave her lips.

"Will you..." She swallows. "Will you come with me?"

Inappropriate.

That word rings so many times in my head that it starts to lose its meaning. I mean, we've already crossed into this forbidden territory with living together and the spanking, so what harm is me driving her to her doctor's appointment?

If anyone were to see me accompanying my student outside of campus—especially when she starts to look pregnant—I'd lose my job.

Oh well. I never liked this job much anyway.

"Of course."

"Thank you," she mumbles. "I'm sorry for freaking out. These mood swings are..."

"You don't need to apologize," I say, clearing my throat and picking up her dishes. "Just get your shoes on."

"Yes, sir," she replies with a hint of humor.

But I don't laugh because it doesn't feel like a joke, not anymore. I don't know what's happening between Sadie and me, but we are falling into roles I don't entirely understand. Roles that feel natural and wrong at the same time. And it's something I don't know if I'd stop, even if I could.

THIRTEEN

Sadie

The waiting room is stifling. Some relaxing piano music is playing overhead, and the women around me have various stages of round stomachs and excited smiles or expressions of discomfort.

When I start biting at the corner of my thumbnail, Luke reaches over and pulls my hand away from my mouth, so I hold it in my lap, picking at the nail where he can't see.

I hum along to the music, and he glances sideways at me.

"Relax," he says lowly. It's meant as a command, not a comfort.

"Easy for you to say," I reply in a whisper.

"One step at a time, Miss Green," he replies.

There's a couple sitting across from us. Their hands are linked between them, and they keep looking at me and Luke, the woman smiling tightly. I want to tell her to stop. We're not the same. But she has no clue. Luke isn't my boyfriend or husband, and this isn't even his baby.

I should tell him he can go. He doesn't need to be here.

But I can't bring myself to do it.

I don't even catch myself chewing on my thumbnail again until he stops me. This time, he holds my hand in place, squeezing my palm between his fingers. He's scolding me, and something about it grounds me.

"Sadie," the nurse calls with a clipboard and a grin.

My eyes widen, but instead of standing up, I freeze in place.

Luke squeezes my hand again. "Stand up."

I swallow and do as he says, but my hand doesn't release his. When I glance down at him, my eyes are pleading. I don't want to go in there by myself.

And he can tell.

Everyone in the waiting room is staring at us, even the nurse.

God, what am I doing? Am I seriously expecting him to go to my doctor's appointment? Why? We're not friends or lovers. He's my teacher. And something else I can't explain. This is ridiculous.

So I pry my fingers from his hold and walk away.

"That's me," I say to the nurse. She holds the door open for me and I walk through, but before it closes, Luke slips through.

I glance back at him in shock.

"Right this way," the nurse says as Luke and I have a silent conversation with only our eyes.

My body is tense as I follow her into the room and take a seat on the paper-lined table. Luke looks so uncomfortable as he sits in the chair. Regret washes over me that I'm forcing him in here with me. The minute this nurse leaves, I'm telling him to go.

What a disaster I am.

"Okay," the nurse says as she sits on the stool in front of the computer. "What was the first day of your last period?"

I cover half my face with my hand, blocking Luke from view. "August seventh," I reply.

She types that in. "And you've had a positive at-home pregnancy test?"

I wince. "Yep."

Her eyes track over to Luke in his chair. I can't even bear to look at him at the moment. "Well, we'll need a urine sample, and then the doctor will come in and do an exam."

"Okay," I groan.

After the nurse does all the vital stuff, blood pressure, temperature, etcetera, she leaves with an empty plastic cup and a paper gown I'm supposed to put on. I immediately look at Luke in the chair. "You can go."

"What?" he asks with mild surprise.

"You don't need to be here for this, and it was wrong of me to ask you."

He shifts in his seat. "I'm not leaving you here alone, Sadie."

"Why not? I'll have to do all of this alone, Luke. I can tell how uncomfortable you are, so just go. This isn't your problem."

His jaw sets in a firm line. Then he stands from his chair, and I breathe out a sigh of relief. But he doesn't move toward the door. Instead, he stops directly in front of me so my knees are pressed against his hips.

As he reaches out and takes my jaw in his hand, my eyes go wide and my breathing stops altogether.

"You don't tell me what to do, Miss Green," he says. "It's the other way around. Understand? Now stop being such a petulant brat and go pee into the cup. *Now.*"

Chills scatter down my body as I stare up at him. All of the anxious thoughts in my head quiet as I focus only on the touch of his fingers on my face and the commanding presence of his words.

"Okay," I whisper.

He lets me go and backs up to allow me to jump down from the table. I don't look at him as I slip out of the room toward the bathroom, and the entire time I'm peeing in that cup, I'm questioning how in the hell he does that.

How does he always know exactly what to say to silence my mind? Why does it have such an effect on me? I normally *hate* being told what to do. And in any other situation, I truly cannot stand Lucas at all. Which makes it that much more infuriating that he has a special talent of playing me like a puppet on a string.

It makes me want to scream. Everything he tells me to do, I want to do the opposite. I want to fight back against him just to see him get mad. As mad as he was in the classroom that day.

But in situations like this, when I *need* something to ground me, his commands give me exactly what I need.

I leave the pee cup on the table the nurse told me to before I wash my hands, change into the stupid backless gown, and head back to the exam room. Luke is still in the chair, staring down at his phone. I let out a huff as I sit back down on the exam table, wanting to tell him just how much of a prick he is.

He ignores me, and it makes me even angrier.

Just when I'm about to start a fight, the door opens, and the doctor walks in.

"Hello, Miss Green," she says in a warm, friendly tone. Then she turns to shake Luke's hand and I grimace to myself.

"He's not," I blurt out as Luke looks at me quizzically before shaking the doctor's hand anyway.

"So..." she starts, taking a seat on the rolling stool. "Your test came back positive. And according to your cycle, your due date should be around mid-May but we will get a better idea of dates after your scan."

Breathe. Breathe. Breathe.

"Okay," I mutter, not quite excited and not quite devastated. Somewhere in the middle.

The doctor looks at me with an uneasy smile as if my reaction is not what she expected, so I paste a big fake smile on my face. "I mean...yay."

Out of the corner of my eye, I see Luke smirk to himself.

"We're going to do a quick ultrasound to take a look at the baby," the doctor says.

My brows shoot upward. "Now? Really?"

"Yep," she replies, rolling toward me. And when she pulls out those humiliating stirrups on the table, I think I actually die of mortification. *Oh God.* "Go ahead and lie back. Dad, I'll have you come stand by her head."

Oh God, oh God, oh God.

"He's not!" I blurt out, and the doctor only replies with a smile.

I've never been in a more awkward room in all of my life. If there were a God, a meteor would collide with the planet right now and save us all from this humiliation. But no such luck.

"Lie down, Sadie." Luke's voice brings me back down to earth. Clinging to his calm demeanor, I recline on the exam table and stare up at the fluorescent lights and ceiling panels.

Even as he stands next to my head, he won't look down at me, not that I want to meet his gaze anyway. I work in a sex club. I literally watch people get naked and do shameless things every single day, but watching this doctor lube up a plastic-wrapped probe about to go inside me has me feeling more uncomfortable than I've ever been in my life.

"Ready?" she asks, and I quickly nod without looking at her.

Luke is just staring unfocused across the room away from my parted legs. After this, he's definitely going to kick me out of his house. And maybe even out of his class. We'll never survive this. It's too awkward.

I freeze as the doctor slips the probe inside me, and I pray she just gets through it all quickly. I keep glancing up at him to see how miserable he is. I wish he'd say something, like tell me to relax or tell me it's okay or—

A quick thumping sound fills the room.

My eyes shoot to the screen. So do Luke's.

"Is that..." he mumbles.

"That's the heartbeat," she says with a smile. "It sounds nice and strong."

"Holy shit," I breathe.

For a moment, I forget there's a medical-grade dildo stuck up my vagina, and my broody English professor is standing next to me. There's nothing else but that heartbeat.

Then, for the first time since I walked back into the room, he looks at me, and our eyes meet. We're sharing the same expression of astonishment. With that, he rests his hand on my shoulder, and I'm not sure why, but it's nice.

"There's just one, right?" I ask, looking at the screen, trying to make sense of the small pulsing black-and-white circle in the middle.

"Just one," she replies.

"Thank God."

"Hey, what's wrong with twins?" he asks, a sliver of a smile on his face. "I'm a twin."

"They usually run in the family," the doctor says before pulling the probe out.

"Yeah, but he's not—"

"He's not the father," the doctor says with a laugh as she touches my knee. "I understand, Miss Green."

I grimace with embarrassment as she removes her gloves and helps me up. After giving me the rundown on all the things I can't do and things I can't eat, she slides us a pamphlet and a long slip of paper with multiple photos of the white pulsing blob we just saw on the screen.

"Congratulations, Miss Green. We'll see you in four weeks."

And with that, she leaves.

The room is bathed in awkward silence, and I wish the heartbeat was still playing on the monitor. It gave me something to focus on. Instead, I'm starting to panic again. Sitting on the table in my paper gown, I close my eyes.

"Say something," I mumble.

"Get dressed," he replies, and I feel something soft touch my arm. When I open my eyes, he's holding my clothes out to me. "I'll be in the waiting room."

As he moves toward the door, I try to focus on his task and his command. But before he leaves, he turns back toward me with one hand on the knob.

"You can do this, Miss Green. The road ahead might be tough, but I believe you're tougher."

The door clicks as he opens it and disappears into the hallway before it closes again.

There's a gentle tug on the corner of my lips, and I swallow a smile of pride as I hop down from the table and start to get dressed.

FOURTEEN

Lucas

"We should get lunch," I say, as we head back out to the car from Sadie's doctor's appointment.

"Be careful, Dr. Goode," she says with a laugh. "You keep trying to feed me like this and I'm going to fall in love with you."

I let out a disgruntled sound as I open her car door.

Even joking about that shouldn't make me tense up as much as it does. I don't want to give Sadie the wrong idea. Because that is never happening.

Not with her. Not with anyone.

Sadie is a beautiful woman, and regardless of how infuriating she can be at times, I do like her. And the signals between us might get a little mixed at times.

But if she's holding on to any hope that this thing might turn romantic, she's going to be sorely disappointed.

It's nothing personal, of course. It's not just Sadie. I don't plan on being in a relationship with anyone. Even when it comes to casual sex, I like to keep it noncommittal. Not that that's what's happening between Sadie and me.

Climbing into the driver's seat, I start the car and glance over at her.

"What are you craving?" I ask.

She hums in contemplation. "I don't know. I don't really have any cravings yet, I guess. I mean, I'd love some sushi, but apparently, that's on the list of things I can no longer enjoy."

"No sushi," I reply flatly.

We settle on a taco joint. And after ordering, we have a seat at one of the small linoleum tables. Leaning back in my chair, I watch Sadie, replaying that moment in the doctor's office when the baby's heartbeat echoed through the room. Even for someone like me, who has no inkling of a desire to be a father, that moment felt significant.

I can't help but wonder how she's feeling about it now. Is this baby still what she wants? Parenthood seems incredibly daunting and exhausting and overwhelming and to think that she is embarking on this alone—it's both admirable and worrisome. I hope she knows what she's doing.

"Don't mind me asking..." I say after our tacos are delivered to the table and we start eating. "But what is the deal with the baby's father?"

The only thing she's really mentioned up until now is that it was a one-night stand. But I can't help but wonder about this man who got her pregnant while I was the one standing next to her during the doctor's visit.

Sadie shrugs casually as she wipes her mouth with a napkin. "It was just one night," she says.

"It generally doesn't require more than that," I reply mockingly.

She rolls her eyes at me, making me smirk before she continues. "He's a porn star of sorts who came into the club. And typical me, I basically threw myself at him, while *also* throwing caution to the wind. Like I said, I was stupid."

It irks me when she speaks so deprecatingly about herself.

Especially since I can't help but feel as if she's doing this on purpose because she thinks that's what I want to hear.

"You are not stupid," I reply flatly.

"Well, you know what I mean," she says before taking another bite.

"Does he know about the baby?"

"Yes," she replies. "I told him."

"So why wasn't he the one with you today?" I ask.

She hesitates, not meeting my gaze, as she picks up her drink and takes a sip. The look on her face is something like shame or regret. And it's not what I intended by asking that question.

"I didn't tell him about my appointment today," she says softly.

"Why not?"

"I don't know," she shrugs. "I like Jax. I like him a lot, actually," she adds. "And I kinda hope there's still a chance for us. But to be honest, I don't know if I want him to be involved in all of this."

"Well, you clearly didn't want to go alone," I snap back, not meaning for it to come out as harsh or as cruel as it does. But I can see her shrink down in her seat before glancing up at me.

"No, I didn't want to go alone."

As we stare at each other for a moment, it suddenly dawns on me that she didn't want to go alone, and she didn't want to go with him. But maybe she actually wanted *me* there—which doesn't make any sense. Why me?

Suddenly I'm reminded of the conversation we had this morning about the way Sadie feels when she's around me, about the way I calm her and give her guidance.

I don't respond to her comment, giving her only a simple nod. "Finish eating."

With a crooked smile, she does. I bite the inside of my cheek to stifle my smile every time she takes a bite and does a little side-to-side dance in her seat as she chews.

She's insufferable.

An enigma. Brilliant and bubbly and messy and so, *so* strange.

I can't stop thinking about the way Sadie reacts to my commands. All the way back to the house, I keep replaying every moment that I've ordered her what to do, and she either does it or rebels. But either way, she seems to like it.

And I seem to like it.

What is this? What are we doing?

I've never been in a relationship like this. I'm not like my brothers, and I never considered myself a very *kinky* person. I enjoy sex for what it is and nothing more. But this isn't sex. It's something entirely different. Something more fulfilling and rewarding. But where does it end? How much more can we do without crossing that line? My palms itch to test the limits, just to see exactly what she does. It feels too addicting to resist.

Once we're back in the private confines of my house, I feel restless. I have too much on my mind about Sadie to just let her out of my sight.

So, I decide to try something.

Sitting on the bench by the front door, I peel off each of my shoes and place them against the wall as I normally do.

Sadie stands next to me and does the same. But as she often does, she kicks hers off with the heel of one shoe under the toe of the other and flings them into the corner haphazardly. Then she makes brief eye contact with me—as if to challenge me. Like a child misbehaving on purpose.

I should be annoyed, but actually, I'm pleased.

Standing in the living room, I slowly roll up each of my sleeves.

"Miss Green," I say in a low voice. She turns around with anticipation on her face. Rather than just giving her a regular order, I change the inflection of my voice just a hair, testing to see if it changes the way she responds. "You have reading to do for my class," I say boldly. "Get your book and sit down and read." Then I add, "*Now.*"

The hairs on the back of my neck stand up, and my veins are thrumming with excitement. Maybe I'm misreading the situation.

There's a chance she could just pick up her book and sit down and read or ignore me and walk away, and this could all be in my head, but I have a feeling it's not. I have a feeling that little shoe kick a moment ago was her way of saying she's in the mood to be a brat.

Which is fine by me because I'm in the mood to punish her.

Sadie stares at me for a moment, eyes glancing back and forth between mine. "No," she says, shoving her shoulders back. It's one clipped and short syllable that carries so much weight.

"No?" I retort with a quizzical brow.

"I don't want to," she replies.

"You wanted my guidance and my direction, Miss Green, and now I'm giving it to you."

The corner of her mouth lifts in the smallest, subtlest of ways before she replies. "And I'm telling you to fuck off. I don't want to do what you say all the time."

Just like in the classroom, my blood begins to boil. And I find it fascinating that while *that* incident was in the heat of the moment, this one, which is a bit more orchestrated, feels just as powerful and intoxicating.

I take a menacing step toward her. "You will do as I say, Miss Green."

"Or what?" she replies defiantly, lifting her chin toward me. And those two words set me on fire. The *or what*. It's an invitation. Like a secret that only we know the meaning to.

"You know what," I reply.

Her eyes narrow as she tilts her head. "I don't think you have it in you, Dr. Goode. You certainly didn't do anything this morning when I threw a shoe at your head."

I let out a threatening-sounding laugh. "Oh, don't think I forgot about that, Miss Green."

She chuckles haughtily. "I am not afraid of you."

I take another step forward. "You should be."

FIFTEEN

Sadie

I don't know if I'm supposed to be turned on right now, but I am.

Maybe it's a pregnancy hormone thing. If you had told me a year ago that I would be getting hot and bothered by an arrogant man telling me what to do, I would have slapped you and called you wrong.

But here we are.

When Luke steps up to me, threatening me with this punishment that I so desperately crave, it feels like a game. I have to push his buttons. He wants me to. And I want to. The more I push, he pushes back, and we both play our roles to perfection. Which is why I raise my chin and utter a harsh "Fuck you" before turning on my heel and marching away.

Of course, I don't get far. But, to be fair, I don't want to.

He snatches me by the arm and hauls me toward him, dragging me across the living room toward the couch. Rather than bending me over it like he did in the classroom that day, he sits in the middle. My core tightens with arousal as he smacks his lap and mutters, "Lie down."

I freeze with my lips parted. "What?"

"Across my lap now, Miss Green," he says angrily.

It's somehow even hotter than being folded over a desk, except now I'm suddenly realizing that I'm wearing a skirt. Which sort of takes this to a whole new level. And I'm not sure we're ready for that. Because once I lie across his lap, my ass will be exposed and he'll be *touching* it.

Is that what he wants? Is that what *I* want?

Because to be honest, if he puts me over his knee and slaps my ass, I can't promise I won't come right here in his lap. And that might be a little embarrassing if that's not what we're going for.

When I don't move for a moment, he grabs me by the arm and tugs me down. As I drape my stomach over his legs, I realize it's only a matter of time before I won't be able to do this anymore. Eventually, my stomach will be too full.

God, what am I thinking? Are we even going to be doing this for that long?

I'm in my head too much right now.

But when Luke flips up my skirt, exposing the cotton underwear beneath, I feel him tense.

"You're a brat. You know that, don't you, Miss Green?" His voice is strained and a little hoarse.

"Yes," I whimper.

"And brats deserve this, don't they?"

"Yes," I repeat.

"Say it, Miss Green. Tell me you deserve this."

God, this is so hot I could die. "I deserve it," I say.

"Tell me to punish you, you little devil."

"Punish me," I squeak. "Please, Dr. Goode. Punish me."

When his hand grips the soft flesh of my ass, I squeeze my eyes closed because it's all too much. He seems so in control and out of control at the same time. It's erotic and exciting, but my mind is a mess—cleared only when his hand lifts from my backside and comes down with an echoing smack.

And then everything is quiet and *good*. A wave of tranquility drowns me immediately. It all feels so right.

Small yelps and moans escape my mouth with each slap of his hand. It doesn't hurt, not really. But even in the pain, there's something stronger than comfort. In some weird way, when he's doing this, I don't feel so alone. I don't feel like I'm being punished or hurt or degraded. For the first time in my life, it feels as if I'm getting exactly what I asked for from someone who might actually understand me.

I lose count of the smacks when Luke lets out a growly question. "Have you learned your lesson, Miss Green?"

I don't want it to end, so I shake my head.

"No? Very well then," he replies.

The spankings are rapid and loud but not too aggressive or hard. Of course, this time, they're on my ass rather than through my pants, so they sting a bit more. I love the idea of my backside turning red from his hand.

As I shift on his lap, I feel something hard against my side, and I know exactly what it is. And knowing this turns him on makes it even better for me. After a few more, his hand stills on my ass, squeezing again and rubbing the tender flesh.

"That's enough," he says, sounding breathless and spent.

But it's not enough. I crave more. Not more pain or even more punishment. Just more of this moment. It's exhilarating that we have somehow returned to this situation that at first was awkward and unexpected.

But knowing that we both wanted it so much that we found ourselves here again means something. It means that we can get back to this moment again. I know, and he knows exactly what we need to do—the roles we have to play.

As I climb off his lap, I feel a moment of satisfaction—mostly because I know, at some point, we'll get to do it again.

"Oh my god," Sage squeals, holding the flimsy page of black-and-white ultrasound photos between her fingers. "Look at how cute it is!"

"It is not cute," I reply, scanning the inventory on the computer. "It's a blob of cells with a heartbeat. Relax."

"Okay, but it will be cute," she says, which makes me chuckle.

"Well, I assume it will be, but right now, it feels more like a condition than a baby."

"Why didn't you tell me you had a doctor's appointment? I would have gone with you," she says as she sets the pictures down next to me.

I clear my throat and fidget in my seat. "Well, I didn't go alone."

"Don't tell me Jax went with you," she says with a huff.

I can't help but wince. "Actually," I say, "it was Luke."

After a long moment of confusion, her hand slams onto the desk next to me. "Shut up," she barks. "Luke as in Luke Goode?"

Recoiling, I nod. "That one."

She's gaping in astonishment. "Dr. Lucas Goode went to your ultrasound appointment today?"

Standing from the chair, I put my hands up in front of me in surrender. "Listen, before you make something out of nothing here, it wasn't like that."

"Okay, what was it like then?" she asks.

"Luke and I have a unique relationship," I explain uneasily.

"Unique *how*?" she asks.

My face screws up as I try to figure out a way to word this. "It's not romantic, and we're not even really friends," I say. "He's just taken an interest in helping me out."

"Oh, yeah, that sounds very normal." Her tone is laced with sarcasm. "Taking care of you, *how*?"

"Well, for one, he's letting me stay in his spare bedroom until I figure things out on my own.

"Okay..." she says. "And that's not against school policy?"

A laugh bursts through my lips. "Oh, I'm quite sure it's against school policy."

The other things we like to do are against policy, too, but I don't mention that part.

"Listen," I continue, "Luke is the kind of guy who just has his shit together, and I don't, so he's helping me get my shit together."

I knew Sage would be surprised by this development, hence why I waited so long to tell her. She's the least judgmental person I know, but even I can understand how shocking this is.

"So, is he like your daddy now?" she asks with a laugh, and I shove her softly on the shoulder.

I twist my face in disgust. "Shut up. He is not my daddy, and it's not like that. I told you."

She laughs again. "I can't picture anyone living with Luke."

"Actually," I say, dying to change the subject. "I get the feeling someone else lived in his guest room before me, but he doesn't seem to want to talk about that."

"Oh, really?" she asks. "I doubt he'd have a roommate without Adam knowing about it."

I shrug. "I don't know. Luke likes his privacy."

"True," she replies. "And for what it's worth, I don't think you're a mess."

"I appreciate that."

"So..." she says as she leans against the desk, placing her hands on either side of her hips, "tell me all about this doctor's appointment and what it was like to have Luke in the room with you while you got probed by your obstetrician."

My head hangs back as I laugh. I have to admit, it's kind of nice to have someone else to relate to with all of this. Sage is in the second half of her pregnancy, which means she's already gone through everything I'm about to go through, and it gives me a sense of comfort.

I tell her all about the doctor's visit and my neurotic behavior. After a good long laugh back in the office, we open the club and

Adam shows up to take Sage home. She's cut her hours back a lot in the past couple of months, and it fills me with a sense of pride that she trusts me enough to pick up the slack.

After she's gone, I take a little stroll around the club to make sure everything is going accordingly. I check in with the bartenders and then with the floor staff. Once done, I find myself meandering around less for work purposes and more for personal ones. I find myself watching the open playroom, and for the most part, it's pretty tame tonight.

It's funny how working in a sex club for the past couple of years has completely desensitized me to public sex and intimacy, which is what makes it so odd that today, on Lucas's lap, had such a visceral effect on me. I thought I knew everything about my tastes, kinks, and my desires. I don't get turned on by pain or bondage or even submission.

So it doesn't make sense why every time I'm around Lucas and he talks to me and treats me the way he does, I feel like I want to crawl out of my skin and not in a bad way. It makes me feel so alive. It consumes me with desire and passion.

As I watch a couple in the corner, the woman chained to the wall, and the man swatting at her ass with a flogger, I know it's not quite the same.

Is it him? Is it us? Today, he called me a brat, and not for the first time. Maybe that's what I am. Maybe that's what I want. Someone who doesn't just tolerate me in my stubborn, rebellious ways but celebrates it. Someone who enjoys it, gets off on it, participates in it, and plays the role that I so desperately crave.

Maybe this is something I should be seeking in the bedroom with an actual romantic partner and not my English professor. But Luke makes it so easy.

It's too good to quit.

I'm just worried about how long this can last and where it's going to go from here.

SIXTEEN

Lucas

"Thank you very much for your time today, Dr. Goode. We've enjoyed this discussion and we'll be sure to reach out to you after some deliberation," the woman says, her face smiling on the computer screen.

"The pleasure is all mine," I reply politely. "Thank you very much for your consideration, and I look forward to hearing from you."

We say our awkward goodbyes through the web meeting app before the screen goes dark and I close my laptop. I rub my sweaty palms against my pants as I deliberate on exactly how that interview went. I mean, I felt good about it. I did my best. I said everything I wanted to say. I think I sounded pretty intelligent.

There was only one unenthusiastic guy in the meeting, but the rest seemed to enjoy my speech and my answers.

"Knock, knock," a voice says as they open my office door. One of my colleagues, the professor of ethics and literature, Dr. Hanson, stands in the doorway with a polite smile. "How'd it go?"

"It just ended," I reply with a sigh.

This is only her second year on campus, but so far, I like her. She's not too talkative. She's very bright. She works long hours like I do. So essentially she's the female version of me. And we've become work friends.

"I think it went well," I say, "but there are so many fucking applicants I don't see how I could possibly have a chance."

"Oh, stop," she says. "You're educated and passionate about the topic. I don't see why they wouldn't take you."

"Thanks," I reply.

"That's not what I came in here for, though," she adds, crossing her arms in front of her chest. "Are you submitting any students for that grant?" she asks.

"Oh, shit, I forgot about that," I mutter to myself.

It's a grant that covers two years of tuition for a student in our class we find promising. The only requirement is that the student be a full-time English major with plans to either teach or write professionally after they graduate. Immediately, no one comes to mind.

At least no one that qualifies.

"I doubt it," I reply with a shrug.

"Yeah, me neither," she says. "But I didn't submit one last year either, and apparently the administration is cracking down. It starts to look bad on our entire program when we can all admit that we don't have any promising students."

I let out a disgruntled sigh. "Yeah, I get it, but..." My voice trails as one face comes to mind.

"Looks like you just remembered someone," she says, noting my expression.

"Yeah," I say in a mumble. "You remember me telling you about that paper one of my students turned in a few weeks ago?"

"Of course. Are they an English major?"

My mouth turns down into a frown. "No."

"That's the problem," she says. "No one wants to be an English major anymore."

Damn it, Sadie, I think. It really was the best paper I received in the whole quarter. Hell, it might be the best paper I've ever received, period, but that's how it is with Sadie. It's like she does it purposely just to piss me off. She has so much potential and chooses to waste it on a business degree, so she can run a sex club.

Not that there's anything wrong with a sex club or running a sex club, but with skills like that, she could be doing so much more.

"Yeah, I'll give it some thought," I say.

"Good luck," Dr. Hanson replies before disappearing through the door.

As she slips out into the hallway, she almost runs headfirst into the redhead walking straight to my office.

"Oh shit, sorry, excuse me," Sadie mumbles awkwardly.

"No worries," Dr. Hanson replies.

As Sadie slides into my office, I feel myself starting to tense. She's never been in my office before, and there are a lot of people currently in the building, so I hope she's not here to try anything or cause a scene.

"Hi, Dr. Goode," she announces casually. "I was hoping you had a moment to talk about this week's assignment."

I clear my throat. "Of course, Miss Green, come in."

She glances behind her before closing the door. I may not love this job, but I don't want to lose it. And it's not like having a private meeting with a student is inappropriate, but I feel guilty anyway. The people on the other side of this door might suspect something, and that haunts me as she takes a seat in the chair opposite me.

I stare at her expectantly.

"Relax," she says. "I really am here to talk about the assignment."

I breathe a sigh of relief. "What can I help you with?"

She digs into her backpack and pulls out the reading for this week—an excerpt from *The Scarlet Letter*. But before she asks about the reading, she pauses and smirks at me.

"Who was that?" she asks. "She was hot."

I clench my molars together as I glare at Sadie. "That is a colleague and a professor. If she's *hot*, I didn't notice, and it's honestly inappropriate to even make mention of it."

She scoffs and rolls her eyes. "Oh, come on, you're lying if you're telling me you didn't notice how hot that woman is."

Shaking my head, I turn away from her. It's clear she's not going to talk about the assignment. Of course, I noticed how hot Dr. Hanson is. I'm not blind. But that's where the attraction ends. Beautiful is just that—nothing exciting or worth pursuing. There's no real chemistry between us.

"Is she single? You should ask her out," Sadie presses, resting her forearms on my desk. Having her this close, I admire the freckles across her cheeks, which are more exposed when she doesn't wear so much makeup as she does at night.

"Again, inappropriate." My gaze drifts downward briefly to the cleavage pushing out of the top of her shirt. Quickly, I glance away before she can notice.

"I'll behave," she lies. She never behaves.

Regardless, I will be punishing Sadie tonight. The spankings have become an almost nightly ritual.

She mouths off to some degree, and I either put her over my knee or over the couch or table. And then I spank her until we're both satisfied. And that's it. It's an addiction, and I know it's not just me.

I love spanking Sadie far more than I would have ever expected to. And I may never understand why.

Sometimes, I do it fast and hard, and sometimes, I do it slowly. Each time is different, but they are all exhilarating.

It never goes beyond that. I mean, sure, I get hard every single time. And I imagine all the filthy things I could do to her if she let me. But it ends with the spankings, and we both walk away.

I don't know what Sadie does behind closed doors. But for me, I enjoy the resistance. I don't touch myself. I don't jack off thinking about her. I just let the erection fade away and count the minutes until the next time my hand meets her ass. At some point, something's got to give. I know that. But for now, I'm enjoying it for what it is, and I think she is too.

"What's wrong, Dr. Goode. You seem tense. Sounds to me like you need to get laid," Sadie says, and I immediately tense.

Letting out a discontented sigh, I glare at her. "I sure hope nobody from the administration can hear you on the other side of that door." She leans back, crossing her arms with petulance, and my palm begins to itch.

"And deny you the opportunity to punish me?" she says cheekily.

"Enough," I mutter.

As she snickers to herself, I force myself to look away.

"Besides," I say lowly. "I get laid plenty, thank you very much." I keep my voice quiet, although I'm quite certain there's no one on the other side of the door who could hear us.

Sadie scoffs. "You do not. I've been in that house for over a month now, and I haven't seen any sign of a woman."

It's true; I have been under a little bit of a dry spell lately, but I choose not to share that with her.

"That's out of respect for you," I say, which is a lie. I don't know why I haven't called anyone over in a while.

Even if what Sadie and I have isn't romantic, it would feel like a betrayal of sorts.

She puts her hands up. "Oh please, don't deny yourself on my account." Her tone is laced with sarcasm as if she knows that none of this is based on truth.

Sadie and I have never spoken about sex before, regardless of our new, strange arrangement. Never mind the fact that I have heard her moans and whimpers, and she's felt the rigid length of my arousal against her side as she lies across my lap nearly every night. Still, our relationship is not sexual, and it has to stay that way.

"No shame, Dr. Goode. It's been forever for me, too," she says, and suddenly my interest is piqued. Why does that make me feel a sense of relief?

She arches her back, stretching on the chair. The hem of her T-shirt lifts, exposing her soft, white belly. My eyes trail downward, focusing on her belly button peeking between the fabric.

And even though she's now approaching thirteen weeks along, I don't see much difference in her figure. I can't help but wonder what she's going to look like as her belly begins to round.

And the longer she lives under my roof, and the more we get to play this strange little game we're playing, the more intrigued I am by Sadie's body. I know it's wrong, and I have no intention of doing so, but I can't help but wonder what I would find if I were to peel back every layer of clothes.

Do the freckles on her face spread across her chest?

What do her breasts look like beneath that bra? If I were to cup them in my hand, just how much would they overflow?

How warm is the space between her thighs? And what would it feel like to bury my hand between them?

Suddenly I'm fidgeting in my seat, realizing that I really do need to fucking get laid.

"What about, uh, what's his name?" I ask with a hint of displeasure in my tone.

"Jax? He hasn't been in since I told him about the baby."

"You haven't spoken at all?" I ask.

"We've talked mostly through text or Messenger. And he has offered to pay for everything," she says as if that makes up for his lack of attention. Or the fact that he's not been around for anything, not for either of her two doctor appointments like I have. And he likely won't show up for anything now.

"I feel weird calling him now," she says, "especially for a hookup. Or even a date. But man, I'd like to…"

I feel my spine straighten and my muscles tense at the idea of him and her together. He doesn't deserve her. She should know that. Not even for just sex.

"What about you?" she says. "Why don't you call Miss Hot English Teacher out there and see if she wants to go on a date?"

I don't glance up at her as I reply, "I don't date, Miss Green."

"Then how do you get laid?"

"You are overstepping again," I grumble.

She rolls her eyes. "Whatever, punish me later. Answer the question. How come you don't date?"

I let out a sigh. "Because I'm not interested in a relationship, if you must know. I don't want a girlfriend or a wife or a family. I enjoy my life the way it is. I'm married to my work, and I'm not ashamed of it. As for sex, which, again, is an inappropriate conversation for us to be having, I have sex and plenty of it, thank you. But it's nothing more than a means to an end. It's about pleasure and intimacy but requires nothing long term or monogamy of any sort."

Staring at me perplexed, she lets her mouth fall open. "Oh my god!" she murmurs to herself with wide eyes.

"What?"

"You're a playboy!"

With a huff, I furrow my brow. "I am not a playboy."

"Yes, you are!" she replies with a laugh.

"Keep your voice down," I scold her, but she doesn't listen.

"That was probably the most eloquent way I've ever heard it expressed, but you're essentially just a manwhore, Dr. Goode."

"I am not a manwhore," I reply in an angry whisper. But even I can't keep the humor from my voice as I say that.

"You little heartbreaker!" she says with a smile. "You just love 'em and leave 'em."

I fight a smile and shake my head. "That's not what I meant." But she's enjoying this far too much. Leaning back in her chair, she smiles at me as if I've just let her in on the world's greatest secret.

"A regular literary lothario," she says with a grin.

"Knock it off," I mutter.

"A classical Casanova."

"Ha ha, joke all you want," I say. "But at least I'm not texting people *Moby Dick* like a teenager."

"I literally was a teenager!" she laughs. "It's not like I do it now."

I clear my throat, resting my elbows on my desk as I stare at her. "And what exactly do you do now?" I say. I do not entirely know why I'm approaching this subject this way.

"I don't know," she says with a shrug. "Usually just text somebody 'wanna come over?' and that does it. And what about you? What is the academic way to express 'wanna fuck?'"

I bite my bottom lip as I ponder the question, fighting a smile. "How about...I would emphatically appreciate the gratification of your company?"

She cracks up laughing. "A bit stiff, don't you think?" she asks.

And even I can't help myself now, laughing loudly and not caring who might hear us. "Very," I reply. "To answer your question, I text 'wanna come over?' just like everyone else."

Her laughter dies down, but her smirk remains. "Good to know," she says without tearing her gaze away from my face.

Suddenly, I find myself looking a little too deeply into her response.

After a few moments of silence, I stare at the paper in her lap, trying to shake myself out of the spell she put me under. "You said you were here to discuss the assignment."

"Oh shit, yeah," she replies. As she grabs her paper and launches into her questions about the piece, I can't take my eyes off her mouth, or wipe the smile from my face.

SEVENTEEN

Sadie

My phone is sitting in my hands, an unsent message haunting me on the screen. It's just past nine, and I'm so restless I could die. I wasn't kidding when I told Lucas today that it's been far too long for me.

It's not that I was used to getting sex every week, but I had a healthy sex life before this baby came along. Or maybe before I moved in with Luke. I don't know which one killed it more or if it was both.

So now I'm sitting here alone in the back office of the club, staring at my phone, contemplating this message. I've never been so desperate for sex in my life, but I figure if I'm going to scratch this itch, I might as well do it with him, right?

He is the father of my baby, after all.

> Busy tonight? Wanna hang out?

"Just hit send, you coward," I mutter to myself.

Something is holding me back, and I don't know what it is. Maybe I'm just determined to have a better night with Jax than we had the first time. Maybe Lucas has gotten into my head so much that I don't feel like myself anymore.

I have other past friends with benefits I could call. People in this club right now who would love some company, I'm sure. But I'm desperately clinging to something with Jax—this dream of something perfect. Which makes me feel out of my mind. I barely know the guy. Envisioning some picturesque life together with him and me and the baby is so out of touch with reality it's humiliating.

But I can't help it. That's what I want.

Suddenly, my thumb smashes the send button without hesitation.

It's a Thursday night. There's no way he's going to respond—

> Hey sexy. I'm not busy.

I bolt upright in my seat. My eyes scan the message three times to be sure I'm reading it right.

Then another text comes through and I instantly deflate.

> Having a few drinks at Club Max. You should come.

I hate Club Max. After a bad experience there a few years back, I haven't stepped foot in that club and going alone is the worst of bad ideas. But surely, I'll be fine tonight. I'll be with Jax.

Hesitantly, I type out my response.

> I'll be there in fifteen.

I hit send with a nervous smile on my face. Standing from the chair, I check myself in the mirror on the door. I'm wearing a sheer black crop top over a black bra and high-waist black pants. Turning to the side, I check my profile and notice that my stomach doesn't stick out any more than it used to. Although when I look at my body straight on, my waist doesn't have the curves it once had. I'm starting to fill out on all angles, but at least it's not obvious that I'm pregnant. No one wants to see a big pregnant belly at the club.

Grabbing my coat from the hook, I log out of the computer and dash out the door. There's another floor manager on duty tonight. I was supposed to get off at nine, but as I wave goodbye and rush out through the back door of the club, I briefly wonder if I should tell Luke that I'm not coming straight home.

Will he worry? I mean, I already know he'll be angry, but he's always angry.

Will he punish me for this? Is that weird, punishing me for hooking up when I was supposed to come home?

Oh well. That'll be tomorrow-Sadie's problem because tonight-Sadie needs to get off.

I climb in my car and make the short drive over to Club Max, trying to remember the *good* days before the very, very bad one.

Fresh out of high school, my friends and I would make our rounds every weekend night to each of the city's nightclubs. We were underage and high on our youth, but whenever my friends rejoiced at the clubs that didn't look closely at our IDs, if they even looked at them at all, I cringed.

My interest in nightlife always went a bit deeper than everyone else's. My friends were out to get drunk, get laid, and be reckless. But I was too busy looking deeper, seeing potential, seeing risks, and finding flaws.

Nightlife could be *so* much better than this. It didn't have to be seedy and dangerous. That's not what we wanted. We wanted liberation and expression in more forms than just shots and grinding on a dance floor with a stranger who smelled like cheap body spray and bad decisions.

In my early twenties, I discovered sex clubs, mostly by accident. I found a few online, and it opened my eyes to a whole new world. I toured for a year straight, absorbing everything I could learn, picking up small jobs here and there, apprenticing, and immersing myself headfirst in a world that was wildly flawed with so much potential.

Then I came home. Opened up my own consulting business. Worked at a few random clubs, and then picked up a job at Pink. And the rest was history.

Now, going back there with two years of meaningful work under my belt feels slightly good, like I've grown and changed since my time there. I'm not the same girl I was that night.

After parking, I pass the line waiting outside and breathe a sigh of relief when I see a doorman I recognize from the few times he's worked at Pink. His stern exterior breaks into a smile when he sees me.

"Sadie?" he says in a greeting before opening his arms for a hug. I let him embrace me and laugh a little at how soft and sweet most of these scary-looking bouncers really are. "What are you doing here?" he asks.

"Meeting up with a friend," I reply.

He lifts the red rope to allow me in before patting me warmly on the back. "Any creeps give you trouble, you just text me."

"I will. Thank you," I reply with a grin, feeling a bit better now that he's said that.

As I enter the club, I'm surprised to find it so crowded. Immediately, my skin starts to crawl and I feel a sense of unease wash over me. A sweaty arm brushes mine, and I resist the urge to scream and run.

Ignoring my rising panic, I wind through the masses toward the couches in the back. I have no doubt that's where Jax is. Someone like him doesn't sit at pub tables or around the bar.

"Sexy Sadie!"

His voice rings over the deafening beat of the music, and I look up to find him holding his arms up for me. Immediately I can tell by his smile that he's drunk, a slightly unsettling realization. I really don't want to hook up with someone who's intoxicated, but I'll give him a chance. Maybe I'm wrong.

When he pulls me into his arms, I breathe in the scent of his cologne and try to just savor the feel of his large frame engulfing me.

This is so nice.

"Come sit," he shouts over the music. "You want something to drink?" He tries to put his iridescent blue drink to my lips.

With a wince, I shake my head. "No thanks."

"Oh yeah," he replies before throwing his head back and laughing. "I keep forgetting." His gaze drops to my stomach and then back to my face. "How the hell are you? I got those pics you sent me, but I'll be honest, I couldn't see shit." He laughs again.

Forcing a smile, I shrug. "It's okay. I couldn't either."

I really don't want to talk about the baby.

As he tugs me toward the giant blue couch situated in a square around a round table littered with empty glasses, I notice the crowd as they all look up at me with scrutiny. It's mostly women, all thin and blonde and beautiful.

I feel like a monster invading the party.

Jax drops onto the sofa, pulling me down next to him. He nestles me under his arm, and I softly smile to myself. He really does like me, which gives me hope. All of the panic and paranoia from when I first walked in has started to subside.

As he and his friends laugh and drink, I stay quiet by his side, anxiously waiting for the opportunity to be alone with him.

My phone buzzes in my pocket, and I pull it out and glance at the screen.

Where are you?

Biting my bottom lip, I swallow down my guilt as I put it back in my pocket.

What the hell am I guilty of? I'm an adult. I can go where I want, when I want. I don't owe Luke an explanation. He's not my boyfriend or my father. He's just my professor and also maybe... my Dom?

Jax and his friends order another round of drinks, and I get cranberry and soda water to at least have something to sip on.

My phone buzzes again.

> You should have been home two hours ago. Where the fuck are you?

"What a control freak," I mumble to myself.

"Is that your boyfriend?" Jax's deep, slurring voice whispers in my ear.

I slam my phone face down and smile up at him. "Fuck no. Just my bossy roommate."

"Well, let's make him jealous then," he replies with a wink. He takes my phone and opens the camera app, pointing it at us. We fit perfectly in the frame as he snaps a few pictures.

Then, I watch with horror as he puts the photo in the message box and sends it to Luke. As he drops it in my lap, he grins.

"There. Now maybe he'll fuck off."

I laugh uncomfortably to myself, staring down when Jax's hand touches my chin and lifts my gaze up to his face. As he leans in to kiss me, I feel my phone buzz in my lap. Ignoring Luke, I let Jax's lips touch mine.

My lips part, and Jax's tongue invades my mouth as my phone buzzes again.

I'm fuming as Lucas continues to distract me during this kiss, but eventually, one of Jax's friends interrupts us. He slaps Jax on the leg as the waitress sets a tray of shots on the table. The ten of them all take the shots together, and when I expect Jax to direct his attention back to me, a woman approaches and asks him for a photo and his autograph.

When he stands from the couch, part of me knows he's not coming back.

And I was right.

He gets pulled away to the dance floor and to another crowd who fawn over his celebrity status. No one at the table starts a conversation with me, and after a while, I sink into my own pity party.

The lights are too bright and the music is too loud and harmful memories start to creep in again, as if there's not five years between then and now. It's all happening again.

To ground myself, I pick up my phone and glance at the texts from Luke.

> Where are you, Sadie?

> Just tell me you're okay.

My throat starts to sting as I stare at his messages, no longer abrasive and controlling but worried and attentive.

This thing with Luke has to end. It's gotten too involved and messy. We can't keep doing this. He can't keep worrying about me or trying to fix me because without fail, every time, I will fuck up. And I don't need another person to disappoint.

Blinking away the urge to cry, I glance up from my phone to find the rest of the sofa empty. Looking around the club, I don't see any sign of Jax or his friends—just their empty shot glasses and spilled drinks.

I'm alone.

My skin breaks out in painful goose bumps that prick the surface, tingling up my legs and arms and down my spine. My chest starts to heave and struggle to breathe like there's a weight on it. I squeeze my eyes shut and try to imagine I'm somewhere else.

I just need to get out of here. But I can't move.

I just need—

"Miss Green." That deep, calm voice tears my attention away from my frantic thoughts. My head snaps up as I stare at Lucas Goode standing over me with flaring nostrils and a clenched jaw.

The panic starts to dissipate immediately.

"What are you doing here? How did you find me?" I ask with a gasp.

He holds up his phone, a picture of Jax's Instagram on the screen. "I know how to stalk a local celebrity on social media."

I stand up and stare into his eyes, and something is so irritatingly comforting about it. Whatever I was just thinking about all just drifts away. Instead, I lunge, wrapping my arms around his neck and burying my face in his neck.

He winds his arms around my waist and squeezes me against him.

"Are you okay? Did he hurt you?" he asks.

"I'm sorry," I sob into his neck.

"What are you sorry for?"

"I should have just come home. I thought he would want me, but he doesn't." My chest aches with those words, but Lucas only squeezes tighter.

"Come on," he mumbles against my head. "Let's go home."

And I know it's not the same. I know that Lucas doesn't like me the way I want Jax to like me, but he's here, and he cares. It may not be the hookup I wanted, but right now, it means so much more.

Eighteen

Lucas

Sadie drives herself back home, but I follow her in my car. Tonight was a wake-up call for me. I worried about where she was, who she was with, why she hadn't told me. It was exhausting and I hated every second of it.

We've grown far too close and I think it's time to put an end to this little arrangement of ours. It was going to end eventually anyway, so tonight feels like the right time to do it. If only I could utter those words.

If she leaves, my house will be quiet again. I'll be alone again. No one to look after. No one to care about. No one to wait for. I should be happy about that. I'm one foot out the door anyway.

When we walk inside the house, Sadie seems despondent. She slips off her shoes like she always does, kicking them in the corner. I expect her to go into her room, but she lingers in the living room as if she's waiting for something.

Awkwardly, she stares at the floor as I approach.

I know what she's waiting for, but I can't bring myself to do it.

"Go to bed, Miss Green," I say coldly.

"Please," she whispers. "I need this."

Her plea wrenches my heart. Touching her arm, I draw her attention up to my face. Her expression is desperate and pitiful. The tracks of her tears cut through the makeup, revealing the soft spatter of freckles underneath.

"We can't keep doing this," I say weakly.

"Don't say that. There's nothing wrong with what we do. We both like it, and it's the only thing that makes me feel better." Her tone is earnest and needy, and it breaks me to deny her.

I want to bend her over this couch and give her exactly what she wants. But where does this end?

"That's the problem, Miss Green. You can't rely on me to make you feel better."

She throws her head back in defeat. "Please, Dr. Goode. Just this last time. I'm begging you. Punish me!"

"You didn't do anything wrong," I argue, moving to walk away.

"What are you talking about?" she cries. "I didn't come home. I threw myself at someone who doesn't even want me! I let him kiss me. And I ignored your texts. I fucked up and I won't be able to sleep tonight until you make me pay for what I've done."

Running my hands through my hair, I groan. *He kissed her.* "This is so fucked up."

She grabs my arm to pull me toward her. "I don't care that it's fucked up and neither do you. It'll be our little secret, Professor Goode. Please."

Our secret. That's the word that makes me snap. Spinning toward her, I find her throat with my hand and she stares up at me with desperation in her eyes. Our mouths are inches apart as I snarl at her.

"You've fucked me up, you little devil. This is all your fucking fault. I was fine until you came around, but now you have me acting like some kind of freak."

"Yes," she whimpers as I back her up toward the couch. Once her ass touches the back of it, I spin her around and force her into a bent position, careful not to hurt her as she perches her ass in the air.

Looking down at her ass in those black pants, I know I need to feel her bare ass. So I grab the waistband, and I tear them down, revealing her black lace panties, and it's still not enough. Hooking my fingers in the elastic, I rip those down, too.

She yelps in surprise because this is the first time I've ever had her fully naked from the waist down like this. Even I'm shocked by my actions. *What am I doing?*

My hand finds her soft ass cheek, massaging it like I normally do before rearing back my hand and spanking her without too much force. She moans in relief, gripping the back of the couch in her hands.

"Who gives you what you need?" I growl as I lay another gentle slap on her ass.

"You do," she replies with a gasp.

"And you went to *him*," I say contemptuously.

"I'm sorry."

I smack her ass again, this time massaging the flesh for a bit longer and noticing the way she presses backward against my touch, seeking more.

"I bet if I were to check, you'd be wet for this, wouldn't you, Miss Green?"

If there's a line we're not supposed to cross, it feels as if we just keep pushing it further and further away.

"Yes," she shrieks.

"Shall we check?"

She moans with her face in the cushion of the couch. "Yes, please."

I smack her ass again, making her jump, and then I slide my hand between her legs, along the seam of her cunt. And just as I suspected, she's soaked, warm, and wet for me.

My cock twitches, already hard and straining against my pants. My middle finger glides back and forth over her dripping core, and I can't believe how good she feels. So perfect.

Drawing my hand away, I rub the moisture from her arousal across her ass.

"Does he make you this wet, Miss Green?" I ask in a low growl.

She shakes her head.

"Does he make you come?"

I notice the way her knuckles tighten their grip on the couch.

She shakes her head again.

"Do you deserve to come?" I ask.

"Yes, please. I'll be good."

Fuck. My dick leaks at the tip. The desire and tension are so good. This wanting, *needing* feeling is so exhilarating, but it's so much stronger than normal.

"I know you'll be good, Miss Green. You're always *so* good." With that, I slip my middle finger inside her, and it seems like we both stop breathing. Sadie lets out a guttural groan as I focus on the tight, wet heat I'm plunging into.

Pulling out to the tip, I thrust my finger back inside her, savoring the way her body reacts. Muscles in her back strain as her pussy tightens around me.

It feels so incredibly invasive and filthy, but I can't stop. I fuck her with my middle finger before adding a second, moving faster now.

"Please don't stop," she groans.

My hand pulses quickly, slamming into her and waiting for the moment when her pleasure detonates.

"You belong to me. *My* little devil. Isn't that right?"

"Yes," she whines, her voice strained and breathless.

"You will not see him, talk to him, or let him touch you without my permission. Do you understand?" I thrust harder until she's on her tiptoes, her knees buckling as she struggles with the sensation.

"I understand," she murmurs.

"Now I want you to be a good girl and come for me, Miss Green."

Her groan is loud and throaty. When she tries to slip her own hand down to her clit, I bat it away.

"Mine," I growl as I find her clit with my free hand and rub it fiercely while still plunging into her cunt.

The combination makes her come undone. With a desperate scream, her body tenses and her legs tremble. I can feel the thrumming pulse of her cunt as she comes, and I keep up the motion of my hand so she can ride it out.

She quivers for so long that I start to wonder if her climax will ever end. My dick is the hardest it's ever been, throbbing painfully as I resist the urge to stroke it.

Before I pull out of her pussy, Sadie turns her head and stares up at me. Looking into each other's eyes, we face this new line we've crossed together.

I wonder if she feels the same remorse I do, and not because I regret touching her. I loved it more than she'll ever know. But because I was supposed to be pulling myself away, and I think I just dug myself in deeper. How am I going to push her away now?

My fingers are soaked when I pull them away, and I never want to wash them clean. I want to wear her scent like cologne so everyone knows she's mine.

Pulling up her pants, I help her to stand and look into her eyes for a sign of any distress. But there isn't any. In fact, she looks at peace.

Her angelic green eyes gaze up at me. I want to touch her face, tuck her hair behind her ear, and pull her into my arms. But I've crossed one line already today, so I don't need to cross another one.

"Go to bed, Miss Green."

With a defeated look in her eyes, she hesitates. For a moment, I expect her to argue or ask me to join her. But with a sigh, she finally relents. Pressing her lips together, she nods.

"Thank you for coming to get me tonight."

I touch her under her chin and lift her face toward mine. "I meant what I said. Don't call him again."

"I won't."

"Good girl."

With that, she smiles and turns toward her room. I don't move from my spot until her door closes. Then I stare at the couch before running my hand through my hair in exasperation.

This is getting out of hand. I just want to think clearly, but with Sadie, it's like I can't do that. Nothing makes sense, and I find myself acting more on impulse than critical thinking. If I'm not careful, she's going to fuck up so much more than my job.

When I eventually make it to my bedroom, my body is still strung tight. I tear off my clothes like they're suddenly strangling me. Instead of folding them neatly or putting them in the laundry basket, I'm tossing them on the floor, burning up.

My cock is still hard, but I hope falling asleep will finally make it relax. But sleep evades me. Lying in my dark room, I toss and turn with no consolation.

Eventually, I give in. Reaching into my boxers, I fist my cock and let out a moan of relief. Her name lingers on my lips as I stroke myself.

"Fuck, Sadie," I whisper to myself as I fuck my fist, imagining it's her tight cunt or warm mouth. I replay her moans and cries in my head, imagining she's in the room with me.

I lift my fingers to my nose, sniffing them for her scent. It makes me feel like an animal, but where she's concerned, I'm no longer a man with a complex mind. I'm a beast for her—feral and wild.

"Mine," I growl, licking her arousal from my fingers.

With my feet pressed down to my mattress and my legs open wide, I pump my hand over my dick, imagining the most depraved and dirty things I could do with her. My neck is strained as my head hangs back when my orgasm finally crests and my cock releases.

My own cum flies so far it lands against my cheek and neck, and I groan loudly. I hope she hears it. My ears are ringing, and my balls are tight as the onslaught of pleasure continues.

By the time my balls are spent, I collapse in exhaustion on my bed, covered in my own release without an ounce of remorse or shame about it.

The fantasy of Sadie in my head is the hottest vision I've jacked off to. And I know sex with her will stay a fantasy forever. It has to. Because eventually she'll have another man's baby and I'll be moving to England. So our relationship has to stop here, and any prospect of us has to remain in my head. Where she's safe. Because I can't break a fantasy's heart.

SECOND TRIMESTER

NINETEEN

Sadie

"What about this?" I ask, running my finger along the line on my laptop. "In *The Old Man and the Sea*, Ernest Hemingway masterfully employs his signature writing style to explore themes of perseverance and resilience, ultimately showcasing the power of the human spirit in the face of adversity."

When I look up at Luke across the table of the library, I bite my bottom lip and wait for his response. His eyes narrow as he contemplates my thesis statement.

"Make some mention of the iceberg theory, and it will be perfect."

I smile to myself as I nod. "Okay, I will."

Turning back to my laptop in the middle of a mess of open books and printed articles, I find a way to add the theory to my statement. Our last paper of the semester is due in two weeks, and I've been researching it since before Thanksgiving.

I got such a good grade on the last one I want to make sure I do this one justice. Luke has offered to help me. I don't know if that's allowed, but at this point, I don't really care. I'm going to pass either way. But if I can write something good to impress him, then that's just a bonus.

Glancing up over my laptop, I stare at him for a moment across the table. He's wearing that brown tweed jacket and blue button-down underneath. He's clean-shaven and staring down at a book through his round tortoise-shell glasses. His hair has grown out a bit since I met him too, and I like how long it's getting on the sides, although I know he'll be cutting it soon. He keeps everything neat and trim.

I wonder if Lucas even realizes how handsome he is. He certainly doesn't bother with caring what others think about him, and he's already said he gets laid plenty, but I doubt he's had sex even once since I moved in two months ago.

Ever since that night when he found me in the club and fingered me over the back of the couch, we haven't touched each other. Even the spankings stopped. I think we both knew it had to stop. We were getting in too deep.

But I won't lie—I miss it. I miss *him*.

Now, the only things we talk about are school and Ernest Hemingway. He doesn't put me over his knee and tell me what a bad girl I am anymore. Who knew I could miss something like that?

I glance back at the computer screen and read over my first draft again, finding little things to tighten up throughout. It makes me wonder if it'll ever be perfect.

As I stare at the Word document, I feel his gaze lift from his book to me. He stares at me for a moment in the same way I had stared at him.

Then, he puts his book down.

"Why don't you get an English degree?" he asks.

I pause midsentence and look up at him. "What?"

"I know you're getting a business degree so you can open your own club, but you're so smart, Miss Green. Why don't you consider changing? It suits you so much better."

"What the hell am I going to do with an English degree?" I reply with a laugh.

"You could write or teach."

"You just want me to get *your* degree, but that's not what I want," I argue.

"What if there was a grant that would pay two years of tuition for getting an English degree?" he says and my brow furrows.

"Oh great. That would cover half of what my tuition would be if I wanted to switch," I reply with sarcasm.

His mouth presses into a tight line. "You're not listening to me."

I cross my arms and place them on the table. "I am listening to you, but you're not listening to *me*. You think because I can write a good English paper I should quit the job I love as if I owe something to the literary world for having a brain. Dr. Goode, I don't want an English degree and I don't want to work in a university or a library or whatever. I want to own my own club someday and I want a business degree to do it. And there's no shame in that."

We have a momentary stare-down after I've finished my rant, and I swear I notice the corner of his mouth lift just an inch.

"You and your smart mouth," he mumbles under his breath.

For a moment, my heart beats faster. We haven't spoken this way with each other in over a month, and I swear if he threatened to put me over this desk right now, I'd let him.

"I do have a smart mouth," I quip back.

When he opens his book back up and reads, I stare at him for a moment longer. Were we just flirting? We haven't fought in so long. Is it weird that I miss that too?

As I focus on the essay again, I find myself touching my stomach more. It's nothing more than a little swollen and a little more poochy, but it's getting harder, and I definitely don't fit in pants the same way.

I haven't felt any kicks or flutters yet, which is disappointing. All the books we have say it should happen around sixteen to twenty-five weeks, and I'm approaching sixteen soon, so I'm getting excited.

The more this pregnancy progresses, the more real it feels. First, a heartbeat, and next, a kick.

And yet, the more this pregnancy progresses, the more anxiety I feel. I'm still living in Luke's house, wondering where the hell I'm going to raise this child. Who is going to help me when I have to work late? What if I can't afford it all? What if I can't give this child the life he or she deserves?

Those are the thoughts that keep me up at night.

What if this is all a mistake?

"It's getting late," he says as he sets his book down. "And you should eat."

"Yeah," I say, leaning back to get a full stretch. I feel my shirt slide up and notice the way Luke's eyes drift down to my belly. "Chinese? Or, ooh, pizza."

"Pizza it is," he says as he moves to stand.

My stomach starts growling at the prospect of melted cheese and garlic, so I hop up and start packing up my things. I see someone approaching to our right and turn to find that hot English teacher smiling at Luke.

"Dr. Goode," she says in a polite greeting.

He turns her way, with a moment of panic, as if tutoring me in the library is somehow inappropriate. "Dr. Hanson," he says excitedly. "I was just...tutoring my student for her final."

She looks at me with a tight smirk. "How's it going?"

"This is Sadie Green, the one I told you about. Her paper on *Paradise Lost* was phenomenal."

The woman reaches her hand toward me, but I'm too busy trying not to blush at his words. Is he lying to cover up our secret, or does he really feel that way?

"Nice to meet you," I say, shaking her hand. Her eyes dance down to my stomach, and I wonder if she notices the way it protrudes a little more than natural.

"He's told me so much about you," she says.

I clutch my book to my chest, soaking in the praise. But then she takes a side step closer to him, placing her hand on his shoulder. There's something intimate and infuriating about it.

As she turns to him, I feel as if I'm being excused from the conversation. I'm just a student, and they're the faculty, and I don't belong with them.

"A few of us from the department are going out for dinner if you'd like to join," she says softly to him.

I continue packing up my things, trying to pretend that I'm not here. But when I glance up, his eyes find me.

"Thanks," he says politely. "That would be nice. Can I meet you there?"

"Of course," she replies, touching his arm *again*. "I'll text you the location."

As I slam my laptop into my backpack, I toss it over my shoulder and mutter a quick goodbye. Then, I storm off toward the stairs that lead down to the exit. If he wants to stand around and let the hot teacher fawn all over him, he can. It means nothing to me.

Besides, it would look too suspicious if I stuck around and expected an invitation.

Maybe they've been screwing already, and that's why he's been in such a good mood lately. He's not so tense anymore.

Lucky me. I should thank her.

I let out a huff as I hurl my backpack onto the seat of my car and slam the door closed.

I am the one who told him to hook up with her in the first place, so I don't know why I'm so annoyed right now. Maybe I'm just hungry. He did say we'd get pizza and now he's ditching me to hang out with his lame academic friends.

That's fine. I don't care. I'll get pizza alone. I might as well get used to being alone anyway.

As I climb into the driver's seat without any sign of him following me, I start the car and peel out of the parking lot. The entire drive back to the house, I'm on edge, and I don't get why.

Because I feel betrayed? Or because I feel jealous? Maybe somewhere in the past two months, Luke and I have gotten closer than I expected. We fooled around with the whole spanking thing, and then that *one* night when he fingered me in the living room, but that was it. There are no feelings between us, so who cares if he screws some teacher?

Or maybe I'm more jealous of the fact that he so easily changed plans to hang out with someone else. I really need to make friends of my own. Sage is literally about to pop so she's focused on that, and my brother is doing his thing at school with his own friends. No wonder I've resorted to befriending my English teacher. Who else am I going to hang out with?

When I get to the house, I go straight to my room because I don't want to care whether or not Luke comes home anytime soon. Instead, I drop onto my bed and pull out my phone to order myself a pizza.

It doesn't work to keep me from obsessing over whether or not he's with her right now. Being alone only makes it worse.

When the front door opens, I glance up from my phone. No surprise, his footsteps lead directly to my room.

He doesn't bother knocking as the door opens, and he glares at me with narrowed eyes. "What got into you?"

It takes everything in me to keep my cool. With a shrug, I reply, "Nothing."

"You just stormed off. Are you mad about something?"

I look back down at my phone. "What would I be mad about?"

He breathes heavily out of his nostrils, and I recognize it as one of the signs that he's angry with me. My heart picks up speed again.

"Miss Green, stop being a brat."

Here we go.

"I'm not being a brat. I didn't want to stick around and make that teacher suspect anything," I argue.

He crosses his arms. "You were rude."

I sit up straighter. "No, *you* were rude!"

"Who was I rude to?" he barks.

"Me!" I shout.

"How was I rude to you?"

"You made plans to have dinner with me, and then right in front of me, you agreed to go with her!"

Letting out a laugh, he shakes his head at me. "Miss Green, are you jealous?"

"No, I'm not fucking jealous of you and your boring friends, but when you make plans with someone, it's rude to make plans with someone else."

His smile won't fade, and it's grating on my nerves. Letting out a huff of frustration, I climb off my bed and try to move past him in the doorway.

Of course, he doesn't let me. Blocking my path, he mocks me with his grin. "I had no intention of meeting them for dinner. That's why I said I'd meet them there."

"Bullshit," I snap.

"It's true."

"You're an idiot if you pass up the opportunity to hook up with her," I say, making my skin grow even hotter with anger and jealousy. Luke is standing just a few inches from me, and the intensity of his gaze is making me even hotter.

"I never had the opportunity to hook up with her," he says calmly.

Now, it's my turn to laugh. "Well, you're blind then because she couldn't stop touching you."

"Oh..." he says with a knowing smile. "That's what this is about."

I shove him to try and get past him without facing this conversation, but he doesn't budge. "You really are jealous."

"Fuck you," I mutter. Every time I try to move past him, he steps in my way, and the closer we get, the more I forget what this fight is about.

"Let me remind you that you were the one who told me to hook up with her in the first place."

"I don't care what you do," I lie.

His hand shoots out, holding the doorframe to keep me in the room. Suddenly, we're so close that I can feel his breath and smell his cologne. When our eyes meet, they burn with something I don't recognize. None of this is like it used to be. Usually, I'd argue, and he'd punish me, and that would be it. So why isn't he spanking me already?

"For what it's worth, Miss Green, if that woman did give me the opportunity, I wouldn't take it."

"Why not?" I breathe, staring into his eyes.

Seconds tick by as I wait for his answer, but it's as if he's struggling to voice what's on his mind. But his gaze never wavers from mine. And just when I see his lips part, and I'm ready for his answer, the doorbell rings.

TWENTY

Lucas

Pizza has diffused the situation, but for the first time, I don't know if I wanted it to be diffused at all. I liked seeing Sadie jealous. I had no idea she would feel that way. She was the one who pushed me to ask Dr. Hanson out in the first place.

Of course, I never did. I have no desire to screw another woman, but I certainly can't screw Sadie either. We don't need that complication right now. We already behave like a couple—we eat together, live together, study together, and hang out together. If we added sex to that dynamic, it would make it impossible to walk away when the time comes.

It was fun to watch her get all flustered over Dr. Hanson, though.

After our pizza, we both sit in the living room while the music plays on the record player, and Sadie finishes her paper. Neither of us broaches the subject again, although we both know we left it unfinished.

We veered a little too close to that line before the doorbell rang. I'm afraid of what I was about to say. But we can't go back there.

My gaze finds her over the book in my hands. She's curled up on the floor between the couch and the coffee table. She's resting her forearm on the table with her chin perched on her fist, her attention lost to the essay on her laptop. The essay, I have no doubt, will be stellar and brilliant.

Her long red hair is draped down her back in natural waves, and her black knit sweater is hanging off her shoulder to reveal the freckles that dance their way down her arm.

In my fantasies, I imagine losing myself in her body. Finding all the ways to show her pleasure. Kissing every inch of her flawless, soft skin. I've made no attempt to deny myself those fantasies since that night when I felt the heaven hiding between her legs.

Her gaze drifts toward mine, and I flinch as if she's caught me in the act.

Suddenly, she sits upright and closes her laptop. The hairs on the back of my neck stand as she stares at me.

"What is it, Miss Green?" I ask, keeping my cool.

"Don't you want to punish me for the way I acted today?"

I gaze back down at my book. "No. We're not doing that anymore."

"Why not?" she asks.

"You know why," I reply, glancing her way only briefly.

"What are you so afraid of, Dr. Goode?" She leans back and crosses her arms over her chest.

Getting attached. Falling in love. Breaking your heart.

But I can't say that.

"Losing my job," I reply.

"Who's going to find out?" she asks. "It'll be our little secret."

There's that word again—secret—the one that sets my body on fire with exhilaration. I want to keep secrets with her more than I'm proud to admit.

"Miss Green, stop it."

"Punish me, Dr. Goode."

"No. Besides, it doesn't feel right spanking a pregnant woman now that you're starting to show."

I glance up from my book, expecting her to relent. But she doesn't.

Instead, she moves onto all fours. "There are other ways to make me pay."

Fuck.

"Miss Green," I say in warning, but like the petulant brat she is, she doesn't listen.

"Come on, Professor," she purrs as she crawls closer. The sound of that word on her lips does things to me.

"What are you doing, Miss Green? Why are you trying to cross this line now?" I ask.

"Because another woman touched you today," she says with determination. "And I didn't like it. I'll do whatever I can to get your attention, Dr. Goode."

"Because you're a brat."

"Because I'm *your* brat."

I gaze down at her, my conscience lost between right and wrong. Want and need. Smart and reckless. Sadie exits somewhere in the blurry gray haze of virtue and sin. She muddles my cognition, obscures my principles, and obliterates my judgment.

As she reaches me, where I'm sitting in my brown leather chair, I've given up the fight. When she grabs the book from my hands and tosses it across the room, I don't even flinch. My eyes are focused on her and the temptation to discipline her for her tantrum.

"How exactly would you like to be punished then, little devil?" I ask, forcing myself to breathe.

"Let me make it up to you," she says. "Let me show you how good I can be."

From this angle, her eyes glisten, and her mouth looks delicious—those round, full lips. And I know what she's implying, but it's so wrong.

"Then go ahead," I mutter with a cold, hard expression. "Show me."

When her hands touch my knees, I breathe in her touch like

it's oxygen. This alone is enough for me, but as she slides them up my thighs, I feel like I'm dying a slow, beautiful death.

I shift in my seat as her fingers touch the button of my pants. With her eyes on my face, I watch her as she tears down another wall between us. Every line we aren't supposed to cross feels like a downhill slide. There is no stopping us now.

The sound of my zipper coming down echoes through the room as the next track on the record player starts up. Sadie lifts onto her knees, staring down at my groin as she slips her fingers under the elastic of my boxer briefs and tugs them down.

My cock is already hard, and I watch her expression as she feasts on the sight of it. Her tongue darts out to lick her lips as her hand reaches for me, petting her fingers softly along the velvety underside of my cock. My eyes fight the urge to roll back into my head.

"Oh, Dr. Goode," she murmurs softly, admiring the length of my cock.

As her fingers encircle the shaft, I reach out and bury my hand in her hair behind her ear.

"Is this how you want to be punished?" I mutter, bringing her mouth closer to the head of my dick. "Stick your tongue out."

She stares up at me through her lashes as her pink tongue lays across her bottom lip, parting her mouth as wide as she can.

With a grasp of her hair, I drag her face closer, running my cock along the soft, wet surface of her tongue.

"Will you let me fuck your mouth?" I ask, "Will you gag on my cock until I'm convinced that you're sorry?"

With drops of my precum smeared across her tongue, she nods.

"You won't let anyone else do this, will you?"

She shakes her head.

"Because you belong to me, don't you, my little devil?"

She nods.

"And you won't tell anyone your English professor fucks your pretty mouth, will you?"

Her grip on my legs tightens as she moans and shakes her head.

"Good girl. Now, show me just how sorry you are."

I release her hair and lean back in my chair. Instantly, her hand moves to the base of my cock, and her lips close around it. Her tongue lathers up the length as she moans around me, bobbing her head up and down enthusiastically.

Immediately, I ascend to heaven. Letting my head hang back, I grip the arms of the chair as she drags the pleasure from my body like it's the only thing that matters to her.

"Fuck, Miss Green," I rasp as I glance down at her, moving her hair out of the way to watch the way her mouth moves. "That's it. That's my girl."

Her mouth moves faster, and her hand squeezes tighter on the upstroke. I'm tempted to tell her to slow down, but it feels so fucking good I don't want her to stop.

"Don't stop," I growl. "You're doing so good."

My fingers dig into her hair on either side of her head as she slides me deeper and deeper with each thrust of my cock down her throat.

My body is on fire with pleasure. Her mouth is warm and wet and perfect, but it's her sweet little moans around my cock that push me to the edge. She hums with my cock in her mouth like she's starving for it.

"I'm gonna come, Miss Green. Are you ready for me?"

She moans louder as the orgasm crashes into me. Groaning loudly, I shoot my release into her mouth, and she sucks me down without hesitation. I continue to see stars in my vision long after the climax subsides.

When I open my eyes to stare at the ceiling, Sadie releases my cock and tucks it back into my boxer briefs. She rests on her knees in front of me as if she's waiting for a word of praise. Reaching out, I stroke her face, and she leans into my touch.

"That was very good," I say, and I watch her expression

soften. "You're forgiven now for your behavior earlier. Are you done with your paper?"

"Almost," she replies gently.

"Good. Go back to your computer and finish it for me."

"Okay," she says with a crooked smile.

And with that, she turns and crawls back to the seat on the floor. Picking up her water bottle she takes a drink and opens up her laptop. As she gets back to work, I stand from my chair and zip myself back up. Then I retrieve my book from the floor where she threw it.

On my way back, I stroke her head, amazed at how something so hot could feel so normal. The tension between us has melted away and left us both at ease.

As I sit back in my chair, this time with a glass of Macallan, I don't read my book, but I think about how this chemistry between us works so well. Why does Sadie like this so much? She wants to please me, and she acts out in order to get the punishment and praise she craves. Where did this behavior come from? Why does she lack so much confidence in herself that she fails to see her own potential?

The bigger question, the one that turns my stomach every time I think about it is, who will do this for her once I'm gone?

TWENTY-ONE

Sadie

E verything is fine, and I'm feeling good.

    Of course, it always starts out this way.

The music. The beat. The people.

It's fun, and I'm happy.

But then the space gets too hot, and everyone is standing too close.

Familiar faces blink into the mass of people before they're gone again.

"No."

Someone holds my hand and pulls me through the horde. It's Sage, and she's smiling, squeezing my fingers until they hurt.

But then her grip slips, and she's gone. They're all getting too close again.

"No, no, no."

I search the crowd for Luke, but he's not here. A distant voice reminds me he will never be here. He doesn't belong here. The comfort he brings, the security I feel with him, the warmth of his touch—none of that will find me here.

Someone touches my back, and I try to scream, but it comes out more like a wail.

Hands grip my arms, my legs, my hair.

They're tearing me apart.

"Stop!"

"This is all your fault," they say. Their voices echo in unison, over and over and over again.

I keep trying to scream, but nothing comes out.

Just wake up, Sadie. You just have to wake up, and they'll stop.

When a hand slips up my thigh, my stomach turns, and I feel tears stream down my face. As I surrender to the masses, letting their hands take their fill of me, I call out for him.

His name comes out in a slur and more of a cry than a call.

"Luke, please."

Rough hands shake me, and suddenly, through the darkness, he's there.

"Sadie, wake up."

He's kneeling on the side of my bed, his face illuminated by the glow of the night-light plugged into the wall.

I blink a few times, trying to reconcile if this is real or a dream. I can still feel hands on my body and the moisture on my face. I touch my face to find my lashes wet and a sheen of sweat on my forehead.

"Are you okay?" he whispers, brushing my hair from my face. "You had a bad dream."

Suddenly, I'm flooded with embarrassment. I haven't had a dream like that in a long time. I thought those days were behind me.

Oh God, what did I say?

"I'm fine," I say, shaking my head and trying to hide the tremble in my limbs.

He's staring at me gravely, without moving.

"I said I'm fine," I snap, turning away from him and resting my hand on the hard, round swell of my stomach.

"Okay. You scared me," he says, as if I should feel bad for my subconscious scaring him.

"Sorry," I huff, my voice shaking as I fight the urge to cry.

I keep waiting for him to leave so I can just let it all out, but the bed dips instead. Turning back, I find him crawling under the covers behind me. He's in nothing but plaid pajama pants and no shirt. And I'm in far less—a sports bra and a pair of cotton panties.

When the bare skin of his chest touches my back, I have to breathe through the tears. His arm wraps around my midsection, tugging me closer.

"Go to your own bed," I say, whimpering as I sob. I don't even bother trying to hide it now.

He squeezes me closer.

"No."

"Luke," I whine.

"Go back to sleep," he murmurs in the darkness.

"Now who's the brat?" I say, forcing a laugh that he doesn't return.

I don't fall back to sleep and not because I'm being obstinate, but because I can't. My mind is racing, replaying everything from the dream and then, of course, everything from that night the dream was an echo of. The tears eventually stop, but I lie in silence and stare through the night at the window and the gently moving curtain.

"Do you want to talk about it?" he whispers a while later.

I shake my head.

"Can I ask why you called my name?" His voice is gentle, with his hand resting on my stomach and my head just under his chin.

"I didn't," I argue, although I don't know what I yelled out loud. I just know what I felt.

"Yes, you did. You screamed it."

My eyes pinch closed tightly.

Then I feel his lips against my head as he gently mumbles, "You sounded terrified."

My fingers find his and I squeeze his hand in mine and tighten his grip around me, but I can't speak. Not yet.

"I don't want you to be afraid of me, Sadie. I don't want to hurt you."

"You don't hurt me," I reply in a breathless cry. I hate to imagine him thinking he's the reason I was so scared. It wasn't that way at all, but how can I tell him that?

He's not the nightmare; he's the dream.

"It was nothing, Luke. I promise. I was just scared, and I was looking for you."

Turning my head, I gaze into his eyes. His expression is dire, still a little frightened, but he never lets me go.

"Well, I'm here now," he replies, pulling me closer. "So you can sleep."

Nestling into the pillow and focusing on the cadence of his breath and the beat of his heart, I finally manage to drift off.

☦

Waking up in Lucas's arms is agonizingly wonderful. The lean muscles of his arm are still wrapped around me and our bodies fit together like they were made to.

How is this fair? Why does he have to be so perfect for me, except for that one minor flaw—he hates the idea of relationships or kids?

Count me out.

We've grown so close over the past couple of months. I wonder if he'll even look back when he leaves. Will it tear him up the same way it will me? I bet he'll board that plane and take off to live his dreams without an ounce of remorse or heartbreak.

How the fuck is this fair?

I blink my eyes open, slowly waking up as he shifts behind me.

As his grip on my waist tightens and he lets out a sleepy groan, my eyes pop open wide.

His impressive length is hard and poking my backside. Suddenly, my body is thrumming with excitement.

Is he awake?

He freezes for a moment, and I wait to see if he'll do it again.

"Sorry," he mumbles sleepily. "I'm not used to waking up with a beautiful woman next to me."

Shifting my hips back an inch, I reply, "It's okay."

He tightens his grip on my side. "Stop it."

"What if I don't?" I say. Biting my bottom lip, I rub my ass against him some more.

He buries his face in my neck, growling deeply right into my ear. I laugh, reaching back to bury my hand in his hair.

"Then I'll have to punish you again," he says, but there's not an ounce of severity in his tone. He's grinding himself against my backside now.

Briefly, in the back of my mind, I wonder when we got here. The spanking, the touching, the classroom, our relationship has evolved so strangely since we met, but no matter what our dynamic is, the comfort is there. Is he my friend? My Dom? My boyfriend?

All of the above, or maybe none of them at all. No words can quite describe what we have, and I love that.

As he groans in my ear, I close my eyes and smile. His right hand drifts down, slipping into my underwear and finding my clit as if he's already memorized the landscape of my body.

"Some punishment," I say with a hum.

"I changed my mind," he mutters darkly. "This is a reward."

"I like rewards too." My voice is high-pitched as he grinds against me faster, massaging my clit in fast, tight circles.

I wish he'd tear down my underwear and fuck me, but it's the wanting that makes this so good. We are so close to sex without quite having it yet, and it makes it that much more decadent.

His groans mingle with mine as we use each other to get off

like we're recording over the events of last night. He dismisses my nightmares with his touch. Luke is not taking something without permission. I'm giving him my body with a mind full of trust and a heart full of hope.

I already told him—I'm his.

"More," I whine as he cants his hips up and down against my panty-covered ass, seeking friction for his own pleasure.

"I'm gonna fucking come," he rasps.

Our bodies are tangled as we both find our climaxes, coming together for the first time.

He moans loudly in my ear as I whimper through my own orgasm, getting off on the reminder that I've made him come in his own pants. And something about that is so hot.

"Fuck," he murmurs into my hair.

"What a way to wake up," I reply with a smile.

Another day, another line crossed.

As he melts into the mattress to catch his breath, rolling onto his back, I stretch my body out next to him.

Softly, he mumbles, "I need to clean up—"

I gasp so loud he startles.

"What?!" he shrieks, looking at me with terror.

My hand flies to my stomach. "I felt something."

It was a tiny pulse, like a flinch but more than a flutter. Quickly, I grab Luke's hand and bring it to my belly, gently pushing his fingers where I felt the movement.

We stare at each other in anticipation. And after a moment, another tiny bump drums inside me.

"Did you feel that?" I ask excitedly.

Luke's eyes grow wide as his mouth hangs open.

"Oh my god," he says in awe.

After another moment, it kicks again. Luke lies back on the bed, apparently unbothered by the mess in his pants, as we lie together, our hands pressed against my stomach.

The moment is quiet and intimate, but I know in my heart that this moment is also cosmic and unforgettable.

Perhaps stuff like this is worse than sex when it comes to lines we shouldn't cross. Because sex is easier to walk away from. But *this* will be impossible.

If he keeps letting me get this close to him, he won't just break my heart—he'll obliterate it.

TWENTY-TWO

Lucas

"Dinner is at four," my mother says through the phone line. "Don't we normally eat earlier on Thanksgiving?" I ask as I walk out of the bathroom with a towel wrapped around my waist.

"Yes, but Adam and Sage are running the soup kitchen at the church in the morning, so I shifted ours to later in the day," she replies. I can hear the whirring of a stand mixer in the background.

"Makes sense," I say, running a comb through my hair.

"Are you bringing anyone?" she asks with a hint of mischief in her voice.

"Have I ever?" I reply flatly.

"No, but a mother can hope."

The line is quiet for a moment. There's so much tension in our family now and it makes the silent moments reek with it. As if the fact that our father is now in prison and our family has endured so much trauma in the last couple of years screams loudest when we're not saying anything at all.

I can tell my mom feels it too, especially when she brings up her next question. "Have you heard from your brother?"

My mother and I have grown accustomed to talking about Isaac privately over the last ten years, so I know that if she were talking about Adam or Caleb, she would have called them by name. She's asking about Isaac because while she has been in contact with him briefly, I am the one who talks to him the most.

"Last I heard, he was settling into his new apartment," I say.

"He's not alone today, is he?"

"I doubt it. He's got his band and the guys at the record label."

She doesn't mention how Isaac has spent every holiday over the past decade without his family, so I don't know how this one would be any different. Normally, he'd avoid Texas during the holidays altogether, I think, to avoid the temptation of joining his family when we're all together. And on the rare occasions when he stayed home during the holidays, I would find a reason to skip my parents' house and stay with him.

I would never deprive my mother of any part of her youngest son, but there is still a protective part of me that wants to put as much distance between all of them and him as I can.

"He's so busy now," she complains. "He used to call me more and send pictures, but now I get nothin'."

"He's not mad at you, Mom. He's just dealing with a lot."

"I know," she mutters to herself. "I'm proud of him. I just miss him."

Letting out a sigh, I realize just how much I miss him too. His dirty boots by the door. His Gatorade bottles on the floor. Hair products scattered in the bathroom.

"Oooh, sexy," a voice calls from behind me. "Drop the towel."

Spinning around, I stare wide-eyed at Sadie standing in my doorway.

"I'm on the phone with my mom," I mouth angrily. Sadie snickers as she covers her mouth.

"Who was that?" my mom asks with excitement.

"No one," I grit through my teeth, flaring my nostrils at Sadie.

"Sure," my mom replies. "I'll let you go then. See you at four."

"See you at four, Mom."

After hanging up the phone, I toss it on the bed, place my hands on my hips, and glare at Sadie.

"I'm in trouble, aren't I?" she asks, putting her hands behind her back innocently.

"You know it."

"Are you going to spank me?" she asks.

Sucking in through my teeth, my palms start to itch. I certainly didn't anticipate getting into this today.

"Yes, I think I will," I reply, taking a step toward her.

She's dressed nicely in a knee-length dress that hangs over her full breasts and hides her stomach.

Twisting her mouth to the corner, she wears the bratty expression so well, as if she was made for this role.

"You'll have to catch me first," she replies before turning and sprinting down the hall.

"Oh, you brat," I reply with humor in my tone. Taking off after her, I don't run but stalk her menacingly. There aren't a lot of places she can go, but when she reaches the living room, she's laughing, a bright smile stretched across her face. Using the couch as a barrier between us, she dodges my advances.

A throw pillow flies toward my head as she nods toward the towel still tied around my hips.

"Drop the towel, and I'll let you catch me."

With a lopsided smirk, I shake my head. "No, we don't have time for that."

She tries to maneuver around the couch to the kitchen, but I manage to catch her, hauling her toward me until her back is pressed to my chest. She doesn't put up a fight and lets me hold her by the throat with one hand and lift her dress with the other.

When I lay a smack on her ass, she smiles wickedly.

"Next time, you'll knock before entering my room, understand?" I mutter in her ear.

"I understand," she replies. As she turns her face up toward me, our eyes meet, and we both notice just how close our mouths are. It's an icy dose of reality.

I haven't laid my lips on hers even once. Regardless of all the other things we've done together, I won't let myself kiss her. It's too intimate. Something about that act would make everything between us too real.

And after that morning last week when we felt the baby kick, it's all been feeling far too real for my comfort.

I release her throat, and she moves away.

Just like that, we're back to being distant and detached.

"You look nice," I say after clearing my throat.

"Thanks," she replies, smoothing her dress. "I'm nervous."

"Why?"

"Because I haven't told them yet, and I think I'm going to do it today."

"How do you think they'll react?" I ask.

Inside, my stomach is turning with the thought of Sadie struggling through this alone or being berated by her family, but then I have to remind myself that not all fathers are like mine.

She shrugs. "They'll be disappointed. My mom might be excited, but I'm afraid my dad is going to look at me differently."

I swallow stiffly. "He won't be cruel, will he?"

Furrowing her brow, she shakes her head. "God, no. Why?"

"No reason. I just don't want you going alone if they're going to treat you poorly."

She chews the inside of her cheek and fights a smile. "That's sweet, Dr. Goode. But you have your own family to spend time with today."

I shrug. "Yeah, but they're all at the church, so we won't eat until later."

Her demeanor perks up. "Wait, really? You can seriously go with me?"

"If you want me to."

A smile curls around her mouth as she nods. "Yes, I would like that very much."

Shrugging, I add, "And you can come to my family's while you're at it."

This makes her flinch with disbelief. "You sure you want that? They're going to suspect..."

"Are you kidding? It would make my mother's day."

Sadie hops in place excitedly. "Okay, go get dressed then."

Soon, we're in the car, on our way to Sadie's parents' house. She laughs at the fact that I don't need directions because I remember how to get there. That felt so long ago, the day she didn't show up for class, and I was chasing her down like some lovesick stalker.

"You're not going to tell them it's mine..." I glance down at her stomach.

"Oh, God no," she replies. Resting her hand on her belly, she stares out through the window of the car. "I'll be honest with them. You and I are just friends, and the father of the baby doesn't want to be a father, so I'm raising the baby alone."

"Omitting the part about me being your professor," I add with a hand on the steering wheel as I glance her way.

"Of course."

I notice the way she's wringing her hands in her lap. It must be terrifying to have to face her family and tell them something that could change their perception of her.

I'm reminded of the night Isaac called me, erratic and hysterical. He had just come out to our family, and after our father had called him every vulgar name in the book, he packed his shit and disappeared in the middle of the night.

This is why I keep my distance from everyone. I'm just not a family man. I may never understand what makes it so worth the pain they cause. The moment I was old enough to move away, I did.

And I swore I would never give anyone that much power over me.

Reaching over, I clasp Sadie's hand in mine to try and calm her. Instantly, I feel her warm hands still.

When we reach her house, there are numerous cars parked out front, which I assume means it will not be a small, private event. After I climb out, I walk around to put a hand out for Sadie.

"I can get out of a car by myself." She laughs under her breath.

"I can still offer to help."

As she looks up at me, leveling a narrow-eyed expression in my direction, I know she's about to say something cheeky and sarcastic.

"You know, you can be a really nice guy sometimes when you try."

"I'm always nice," I argue.

"No, you're always controlling and bossy."

"I can be both," I say as I place a hand on her lower back. "Being so controlling and bossy is my way of being nice. It's because I care about you that I want you to do better."

She rolls her eyes with a huff. "Then you must care about me a *lot*."

With a laugh, she steps up to the front door of her house, but I swallow down the reminder that I do care about her a lot, and most people would find that exciting, but it feels like a noose around my neck instead.

Sadie pulls open the door to her house, and the deafening sound of family greets us. We're immediately ambushed by aunts, uncles and grandparents. Sadie has to tell them no less than ten times that I'm *just a friend*.

When we finally make it to the kitchen, Sadie introduces me to her mother. It's obvious where she inherited her copper-red locks from. Unlike Sadie, her mother is tall and slender, with straight hips and thin arms.

"Mom, this is my friend, Luke. The one I'm renting a room from."

The woman puts out her hand. "So nice to meet you," she says with a smile. "Thanks for joining us!"

"I hope I'm not imposing," I reply.

"Oh, not at all."

"Where's Jonah?" Sadie asks, turning her head to look around the house.

"Picking up his girlfriend," her mother replies, which makes Sadie's jaw drop.

"His *girlfriend*?"

"Yeah, she's a cute little thing too. A cheerleader," her mother replies while stirring gravy on the stove.

I notice Sadie's expression grow a little uncomfortable as she starts picking at her nails. I subtly grab her hand to stop her.

"Hey, Sadie's here," a deep-voiced man calls enthusiastically as he enters the kitchen through the back door. He's wearing oven mitts and carrying a serving tray with a beautiful, glistening turkey he must have been smoking in the backyard.

"Hey, Dad," she says, her mood instantly perking up as she places a kiss on his cheek. "This is my friend, Luke."

The man places the tray on the counter and pulls off an oven mitt to shake my hand. Although her mother gave her her red hair, Sadie resembles her father far more. Round face, big eyes, button nose, and a bit on the shorter and stouter side.

"Nice to meet you, Luke," he says with a smile under his thick, brown mustache.

Sadie's mother turns to appraise Sadie, who is standing with her back to the counter. From this angle, her dress lies against her frame, showcasing the round pooch of her stomach.

"Sadie, honey," her mother says with a tilt of her head. "You're putting on a little weight."

Instantly, Sadie straightens up and turns toward me. There is panic in her eyes, but I don't know what to do to defuse the tension in the room.

I consider blurting out something to save her from the embarrassment of having to do this right here, right now.

Before I can do anything, Sadie looks straight at her mother as she presses her shoulders back and proudly announces, "That's because I'm pregnant."

The kitchen falls dead silent.

TWENTY-THREE

Sadie

My mother is pacing back and forth in front of me as I sit cross-legged on my old bed. My dad is just standing in the corner, staring at the floor as he chews on the knuckle of one of his fingers.

Luke is somewhere in my house, surrounded by my relatives, who are no doubt berating him with questions.

"You should just move back home," my mother says after a long deliberation.

"No, Mom," I reply, hugging a pillow to my chest.

"How are you going to raise this baby alone, Sadie? Who's going to take care of it while you're at work?"

It. Ouch.

"Mom, you do realize I'm twenty-five, right? I'm not seventeen."

"Yes, but..."

"But what?" I reply, feeling irritated. "You had me when you were twenty-six."

"I was *married*," she says, and I tighten my lips to keep from arguing.

"Listen, this isn't up for debate and there's nothing you need to do. I can do this." I sort of wish Luke were in here to hear me say this to her because somehow, I do feel stronger and more confident than I was when I lived here.

I *can* do this.

"Where will you live, Sadie?" my dad asks. His expression is somber and contemplative, as if he's just been told his sweet little girl isn't so sweet and little anymore.

"For now, I'll live at Luke's. He's probably leaving soon for England, and he's going to let me stay there while he's gone."

My mom lets out a huff of frustration. "You need something more stable."

"There is literally no one more stable than Luke," I say, but she's not listening.

"And what about the father?" my dad asks.

"He's just a guy I hung out with once. He knows about the baby, but he's not really interested in raising him or her."

"He'll pay child support then," my mom states as if she's personally getting it from him like some ruthless debt collector.

I shrug in response and it's not enough for her, I can tell. But it's not really up to her, so I don't bother trying to explain.

My mom pinches her forehead in frustration. Meanwhile, I climb off the bed and walk toward the door. "Come on. Let's eat dinner. You don't need to stress about this for me. I can do this."

She looks up and stares into my eyes, not appearing to have any faith in me.

"Fine," she mutters under her breath.

Peeling open the door, I walk out into the hallway. The first person I look for when I reach the living room is Luke. But as I turn the corner and see him standing near the kitchen with my brother right in front of him, I freeze.

"I work at the university," Luke says as he signs every word. "I can put in a good word at admissions."

My lips part as blood rushes to my cheeks. I watch Luke from across the room and it feels as if I'm seeing him for the first time. It's like watching my heart split open.

He's signing with my brother. And the words he doesn't seem to know, he spells effortlessly. He's *signing*.

"Thank you," Jonah replies before clapping Luke on the shoulder.

Luke's eyes find mine and I'm suddenly barreled over with emotion. And I swear he can tell.

My brother turns toward me, an expression of excitement washing over his features.

"Sadie," he signs, putting his arms out for me. "There you are."

I swallow down the needles poking in my throat as I rush toward him, wrapping my arms around his waist and breathing in his familiarity.

When I pull away from his hug, he says, "I like your boyfriend."

"He's just my friend," I reply for the twelfth time tonight, but this time, the words hurt, so they come out weak and broken.

Jonah gestures to our parents, who are sneaking out of the hallway together, looking stressed and despondent. "What's wrong with them?"

"Umm..." I say, scratching the back of my neck. "I just told them my news."

The needles turn painful as I fight the urge to cry. Why is this so hard? Jonah won't be upset or mad to hear he'll be an uncle, but for some reason, breaking this news to him feels like I'm breaking some sort of bond.

"What news?" he asks.

Luke's eyes are on me, and I try to draw courage from them. I wish I could ask him to tell me I'm good. I'm doing the right thing. Tell me how strong and brave I am. Tell me anything.

I touch my stomach. "I'm pregnant."

Jonah's eyes widen, then shoot to Luke and back to me.

"It's not his," I sign.

Jonah's face splits into a smile as he stares at my stomach. He doesn't ask whose baby it is or what my plans are. He doesn't give me a disappointed glare.

"I'm going to be a cool uncle," he says in that overconfident teenage boy way, and it brings tears to my eyes.

"Yeah, you are."

I glance up at Luke again, and to my relief, he looks proud. It's enough to get me through the rest of dinner.

✝

"Thank you again for having me," Luke says to my parents as we walk together down the drive toward his car.

They wave from the door, caught somewhere between smiles and hesitation.

As soon as we get in the car, I look at him. "What the hell?" I bark.

His brow furrows as he turns his head. "What?"

"Where did you learn sign language?"

He seems offended. "My college roommate was hearing-impaired, so I learned. What's the big deal?"

The big deal is you're making me fall in love with you, and it's not fair.

I cross my arms over my chest in frustration. "It just took me by surprise. That's all."

"You seem angry about it."

"I'm not. I'm glad. Normally, anyone I bring home can't talk to or understand my brother."

"Then shouldn't you be happy?" he asks as he pulls out onto the street.

"Yeah, I guess," I mumble.

But I'm not. That image of Luke signing with Jonah is etched into my memory. I'm irritated by how much of an effect it had on me. I'm irritated that it's literally the *only* time this has ever happened. I'm irritated that it will probably never happen again.

"How are you feeling about your parents' reaction?" he asks.

I shrug as anxiety swarms in my stomach. "Fine, I guess."

Thinking about it some more, I realize it's not fine. Luke stays quiet as I deliberate.

"It's just..." I say as I stare out the window. "My parents have been telling Jonah his entire life that he can do whatever he puts his mind to. But it feels like they've been telling me the opposite. 'Sadie, you can't live on your own. Sadie, you can't raise a baby. Sadie, you can't just go back to college.'"

"Well..." he says, glancing my way. "Maybe telling you what you *can't* do is how they motivate you."

I screw up my face in confusion. "How the hell does that make sense?"

"I don't think they're doing it on purpose, but if I know you, and I think I do now, then I know that you like a challenge. You're motivated by rebellion. You want to prove them wrong. So by telling you that you *can't* do something, whether they know it or not, they're basically encouraging you to do it."

Mulling over his words for a moment, I smirk at him. "So I really am a brat."

He smiles from the driver's seat. "You really are a brat."

Pulling up to his mother's house a few minutes later, we park out front in the large, round driveway, which has enough space to accommodate at least thirty cars. Only two are parked out front.

Dean is sitting on the front porch steps, watching a little girl ride her bike around the massive circular drive.

It's comforting to know I have two friends here, so it won't be quite as uncomfortable. Luke's family intimidates me. They're Austin celebrities for both good and bad reasons.

Before a couple of years ago, they were a prominent family that nearly everyone in the city knew for their church. I was barely familiar with them, but then I got a job at the club and had a front-row seat to their downfall.

Luke's dad turned out to be a dirty hypocrite and liar, and now he's rotting in jail with a five to ten-year sentence for attempted murder.

Even if he's not here, the family still intimidates me.

A petite, beautiful, silver-haired woman walks out of the house and waves to us as we approach. Her jaw nearly drops to the ground when she notices me standing next to her son.

"Is that Sadie?" she asks with a smile. She's wearing baby-pink lipstick and has thin wrinkles around her mouth and eyes. She's one of those women who looks like she wakes up perfect.

I've met Luke's mother briefly at events, like Dean's dad's funeral. She's always sort of ignored me for the most part, and I don't think she was being rude, but until now, I was no one to her. Now, I'm showing up with her son.

"I'm so glad you could join us," Melanie says excitedly.

From the corner of my eye, I can see Luke's jaw click as he clenches his molars. I've picked up on all of Luke's tells since I moved in with him. I can tell when he's annoyed, uncomfortable or relaxed.

"Thank you so much for having me," I reply.

Melanie comes closer, putting her arm around my shoulders. With her head tilted toward me, she whispers, "I've heard the news. Congratulations."

"Oh," I stammer, glancing at Luke. He looks so uncomfortable I'm afraid he might jump back in the car and leave.

"Let's go inside," he mutters as he turns his back and marches toward the house. Melanie keeps her arm around my shoulders and ushers me behind her.

"Uncle Luke!" the little girl shouts as she comes riding toward us.

His demeanor softens immediately. "Hey, Abigail," he says. She ditches her bike and Dean scolds her for letting it drop to the ground instead of using the kickstand, but she's already bolting into Luke's arms.

I can't take my eyes off him as he kneels down to scoop up his niece with one arm. I've never seen him like this, but he is so effortless with her. Not stiff, uncomfortable or brash. Even the smiles he gives her are unique. I've certainly never seen them before.

It's another gut punch. Or rather, a heart punch.

Why does he have to be so perfect? What happened to the infuriating professor that was easy to hate?

To make things worse, he glances back at me as I walk behind him, as if he's looking to make sure I'm coming. He treats me like I'm with him, and all the *you're mine* talk is just a game. It's not real. But today, he's acting like I mean something to him.

What an asshole.

Meanwhile, Dean lets out a huff and an eye roll as he goes to pick up his daughter's bike from the drive. I smile to myself as I pass him by.

The only person less likely to become a parent than me was Dean. But he made the mistake of falling in love with a man and woman who already had a daughter.

I know the truth, though—he's in heaven. Even when he doesn't show it.

The inside of the Goode house is ginormous and smells *so* good. It's so clean and tidy, like it's been decorated by professionals, and has constant cleaners to maintain its pristine condition.

So this is where Luke gets it.

Sage waddles out of the kitchen with a beaming smile. Adam is close behind with a hand on her back as if she's going to tip over at any moment. Honestly, she's all stomach, so I wouldn't be shocked if she did.

I wrap my arms around her, although I see her nearly every night as it is. She's due next week, and she looks so tired but glowing at the same time. I can't believe they're going to be parents soon. It still feels so surreal.

My hand goes to my own stomach. What am I thinking? I only have a few months myself.

Sage drags me into the massive kitchen and offers me a sweet tea. Caleb and Dean's wife, Briar, are sitting at the kitchen island with a spread of books and papers between the peeled potatoes and casserole dishes.

"Don't mind me," she says, looking exasperated. "I just waited until the last minute, and I have a huge paper due Monday."

"You've got this, angel," Caleb says from the other side of the kitchen where he's basting the turkey.

Suddenly, I don't know what I've been so worried about. This family is so warm and casual, just like any other. Melanie hands me a glass of tea while Briar laughs with Sage while feeling the baby move in her belly. Dean kisses Caleb's cheek while he stirs something on the stove. Abby comes barreling into the room, trying to steal whipped cream off the pies before getting redirected by her mother.

It's all ridiculously perfect, and it makes my heart ache to know that this would be a wonderful family to raise a child in. Mine is great, too, but if I were in this family, I'd have sisters and a loving mother-in-law. My child would have cousins to play with.

A soft hand rests on my lower back, and I turn to find Luke standing next to me. My heart pitter-patters in my chest, and I force myself to move away.

Stop it, you jerk.

In fact, this whole family is acting like jerks. The audacity to make me fall in love with them in minutes.

TWENTY-FOUR

Lucas

Two Thanksgiving dinners are one too many. If I even see another potato, I might be sick.

Discomfort aside, I'm feeling oddly good today. I'm glad I chose to go with Sadie today to her family's dinner. They were very nice people, but I think having me there as she broke the news made things easier for her.

And to see her at this table, laughing and conversing with my family, is doing things to me. It makes me want to bring her around more. She fits in so well.

But she's being standoffish to me. So maybe I'm reading the signs wrong, and she's not as comfortable here as she seems. Maybe she doesn't like how intimate things are feeling with *me*. Sadie would rather keep things between us casual and noncommittal. I practically invented noncommittal. I should be fine with this.

But for some reason, I don't like it.

Reaching over to her under the table, I try to take her hand, but she subtly evades my touch. I swallow down my disappointment.

Get your head on straight, Luke. What is wrong with you?

"Let's all say something we're thankful for," my mother says from the head of the table. Most of us groan and Caleb shoots me an eye-rolling expression.

"I'll go first," Abby says brightly, kicking her feet in her chair next to Sage. The novelty of Dean has worn off, it seems, because she's back to being glued to Sage's side.

"Go ahead, peanut," Briar says.

"I'm thankful for pumpkin pie." She giggles before taking a bite of the pie in front of her. Dean wipes whipped cream on her nose, making her laugh hysterically.

"I'm thankful for pumpkin pie, too," Sadie says from beside me. She's grinning at Abby, and I feel something warm shoot down my spine. I wonder if she knows how good of a mother she'll be.

She puts a hand on her stomach before adding, "Among other things."

I glance at my sister-in-law, Briar, to gauge her reaction. After a long battle with infertility and deciding last year to stop trying, I'm sometimes worried that having two pregnant women at the table would be triggering for her. But she only smiles at Sadie and then reaches over to Sage and rubs her belly again.

Caleb wraps an arm around her back before kissing the side of her head. Something about the gesture makes me strangely jealous. For over a decade, I've watched my brother devote his life to this one woman, and never have I felt jealous or wanted that for myself.

In fact, there were times when I pitied him for the emotional roller coaster he seemed to be on in his marriage. From the outside, his love for her looked like a burden.

But now, seeing the way he connects with her, supports her, and touches her, I see it so differently. Maybe having Sadie live with me has gone to my head. These feelings are an illusion. I'm attached to Sadie because she has been in my space for so long now. Once I leave for England—hopefully—I'll be able to think clearly.

"What about you, Luke?" my mom asks.

"I'm thankful for..." I feel Sadie's eyes on me as she glances my way. "The opportunity to go to England in the fall. Even if I don't make it into the program, I'm thankful I got the chance."

No one reacts. In fact, everyone is just staring at me except for Sadie, who is now looking down at her empty plate.

Fuck, I'm an asshole.

I clear my throat to ease the tension. "Caleb, your turn."

He lets out an exasperated sigh but jumps in to take some focus off me. I'm staring at Sadie, noticing the way her pouty mouth is set in a thin line, and her eyes look more moist than usual.

I don't even hear what Caleb is saying when Sadie quietly excuses herself from the table.

Now everyone is *really* looking at me.

They just don't understand. Sadie isn't my girlfriend. We're not in love, and she's not having my baby. We're just friends, so what was I supposed to say?

Without a word, I rise from the table and leave the dining room to find her. She's not in the guest bathroom downstairs, so I creep up to the second floor in search of her, but she's not up there either. I start to panic a bit until I peek into my father's office and find her curled up in one of his large upholstered chairs, wiping tears from her eyes with a tissue.

I stop in the doorway, paralyzed with indecision.

"Go away, Luke," she says coldly. "I'm fine."

"I'm sorry," I say as I walk into the room and close the door behind me.

"What are you sorry for?" she asks with a humorless laugh.

"I don't know," I answer honestly.

She presses the tissue to her eyes and cries in silence. Something inside me shatters. Without knowing why she's upset or what I should do, I walk up to her and drop to my knees at her feet.

"I upset you, and I'm sorry," I say, staring pleadingly into her eyes.

"You don't get it." She laughs. "We're just friends, Luke. You're leaving soon. I know that, and I know I mean nothing to you, but to hear you say it out loud in front of your entire family..."

I lean forward and touch her leg. "You don't mean *nothing* to me."

"Sure," she says with makeup streaked under her eyes. "But you're all I have right now, and you're leaving me."

Whatever was left of my heart is gone now.

"I fucked up," I say, leaning toward her. "Sadie, you don't mean nothing to me. I promise. I'm sorry. I'm not good at this. You're all I have, too. I didn't even have friends before you came along, so I say selfish, inconsiderate things. How can I make this up to you?"

She shakes her head and tries to stand from the chair. I press my hands down on her thighs to keep her there.

"Punish me."

Her brows pinch inward as she stares at me in confusion. "What?"

"I'm serious," I say, kneeling in front of her. "Punish me."

She lets out a laugh. "What do you want me to do, Luke? Put you over your father's desk and spank you?"

My lips part, but nothing comes out. That's not exactly what I had in mind. That night in my house comes back to mind when Sadie crawled over to me and used her mouth to make it up to me.

My fingers slide to the hem of her dress as I slide it slowly upward. "Let me show you."

"Luke," she says but makes no move to stop me.

"Use me, Sadie," I whisper, pressing my lips to the top of her thighs. "Use my mouth until you're convinced I'm sorry."

"Your family is right downstairs."

The first thought that enters my mind is that my family is right *here*, in this room, but that's not the right thing to think. That's just an illusion, again.

"I don't care," I reply as I move my kisses up her thighs.

Her fingers run through my hair as she melts into my touch. Hooking my hands under her hips, I tug her to the edge of the chair and lower myself until I can reach the inner parts of her thighs.

Her legs dangle over my shoulders as I breathe in the scent of her cunt. My mouth waters, and I let out a subtle groan.

Slipping her panties to the side, I stare at her beautiful pink pussy, glistening for me already. Leaning forward, I lick her slit and nuzzle myself closer. Latching my lips around her clit, I flick the sensitive spot with my tongue, and she lets out a pleasure-filled hum.

I moan against her, creating vibration. She writhes on the chair, squeezing her thighs around my ears as I suck and nibble. When I find the movements that make her fidget more, I keep them up. It's like learning the secret code to her pleasure, and it's locked into my memory forever.

"Luke," she cries out in a low whisper. Her fingers grip my hair at the scalp as she pulls. The pain doesn't bother me. I'm too focused on her.

My face is soaked with her arousal, and I'm feral for how much I love this. This perfect little pussy is mine. This woman is *mine*.

Those are the lies echoing in my mind as I make her come on the brown upholstered chair. Because she's not mine. No part of this woman belongs to me. Not her body. Not her heart.

And that's my fault. No matter how much I want her to be mine, I can never give her what she wants.

My fingers grip her thighs as I press my face even closer to her cunt. I suck so hard on her clit, she has to bite her own fist to keep from screaming. Her back arches and her legs tremble as she climaxes on my tongue. I keep my mouth on her, feeling her pulse against my lips.

Eventually, I release her panties and ease her legs from my shoulders. When I look up at her, she looks completely spent and exhausted. Her hair is a mess, and her cheeks are red.

"Okay, I believe you're sorry," she says on an exhale.

Smiling, I wipe my face against her inner thigh.

I want to keep her taste on my lips, savoring the flavor of her because *I* am the only one who can.

Because she's mine. Or, I guess at this point, it would be more accurate to say I am hers. And I don't have any choice in the matter.

†

By the time Sadie and I get back to the house, it's late and we're both exhausted. We don't talk in the car except about safe, neutral topics like how cute Abigail was at dinner or how good the sweet potatoes were.

When we get to the house, Sadie kicks off her shoes in the corner and walks directly toward her room. But she hesitates in the hallway, and I wonder if she's feeling the same way I feel. After a long day of feeling like a couple, it's strange to be going to different beds.

For a moment, I consider crawling back under her covers, using her nightmares as an excuse. But after today, I've learned that I am too flippant with her emotions. I need to be more careful.

So, as she meanders slowly to her room, I let her. I don't even look up from where I'm unlacing my shoes. When the door closes behind her, it's chilling.

After I get to my own room, I drop onto the bed and stare at the floor. I can't make myself do anything I normally do—take off my clothes, brush my teeth, climb into my bed. It's like I'm frozen in this state of discomfort. Everything feels so wrong.

Pulling out my phone, I stare at the screen. I want something to quiet my thoughts, so I first go to my email, looking for a response from the Stratford Project. The feeling used to be hopeful and excited, but now it's laced with dread.

Dammit, why has she taken away the *one* thing I'm longing for? Before her, my desires were simple. Work, study, write, read. Alone.

Now, I can think only about her slipping off that dress, red marks on her inner thighs from the scratch of my five-o'clock shadow. Her full breasts under the cotton of an old T-shirt. The clean, floral scent of her hair and the round pucker of her lips.

This is what drives poets mad. Now, it all makes sense. This feeling is like hypnosis. Like I no longer have control over my own mind and body. It's driven only by her and this irrepressible need to be and give her everything she needs. She is the siren at the bottom of the sea, calling me to my own reckoning. And like the carnal creature I am, I would gladly drown.

Glancing numbly down at my phone, I pull up our text message thread. The world at my fingertips. With just a few words, I could express to her what I'm feeling.

Maybe it would ruin everything.

Maybe it would fix everything.

It doesn't have to be forever. Perhaps one night of lust would quench this thirst.

I type out and delete a hundred different phrases.

Wanna come over?

You up?

Moby Dick?

I delete them all. I'm being reckless. Even I know that taking this astronomical leap with Sadie wouldn't curb any of our desires but would only enhance them. I already feel so emotionally chained to her.

I need to be smart about this. Distance and discipline are the only things that could possibly cure this sickness I seem to be suffering from.

So, with that, I drop my phone on the nightstand. Then I tear off my clothes, leaving them in a pile on the floor, and crawl under the covers to fight off another sleepless night—alone.

TWENTY-FIVE

Sadie

"I've decided I don't want to know."

I'm standing in the kitchen, watching Luke wrap a Barbie doll for Abigail with green-and-red-plaid wrapping paper. He's taken twice as long to wrap his Christmas gifts as I have, and it's mostly because of his meticulous, crisp edges and my wrinkled, tape-covered messes.

"Don't want to know what?" he asks, not looking up from the gift.

"The sex of the baby."

With his finger pressing the fold, his head snaps up. "Really?"

"Yeah," I reply with a shrug. "I think it will be more fun to find out when the baby is born."

His shoulders sag as disappointment washes over his features. It almost looks like he's bummed we're *not* finding out tomorrow. "Well, it's your choice."

"It's not like I was ever going to cover the baby in pink or blue either way," I reply.

"Good point," he says, going back to his wrapping.

I watch him for a moment when that familiar tension rises in my gut. Ever since Thanksgiving last week, I've struggled to keep Luke at a distance. I never expected my heart to get so attached, but it has.

"Sage is throwing you a baby shower?" he asks.

"Yeah. Apparently, Briar and our mothers are in on it too," I add.

The room grows quiet again. Neither of us wants to discuss how *his* family throwing me a baby shower feels wrong—and somehow right.

Why did I say it like that?

I pick up my wrapped presents and take them into the living room. Luke didn't want to decorate for Christmas, but I smuggled in a small Christmas tree and placed it in the corner by his record player and *one* of his bookshelves. He didn't put up much of a fight when he discovered it. He just sort of rolled his eyes and ignored it.

"I assume tomorrow I'll come home to find stockings on the mantel," he muttered under his breath.

"Don't give me any ideas." I laughed.

I didn't, in fact, hang up any stockings. I considered it, but I realized that seeing his and mine together would make it look too much like we're a couple.

Just one more thing to drive the knife in a little deeper.

Returning to the kitchen island to get the rest of my wrapped presents, I notice Luke staring at his phone. His eyes are wide and he's as still as a statue.

"What's up?" I ask softly.

But I already know. This is the moment I've been waiting for and dreading. I cruelly wished that maybe he wouldn't get into the program in England. As wrong as that is for me to want his career to suffer so that I could have a few more moments with him, I wished for it with all of my heart.

And as I stare at his face now as he reads through something on his phone, I wonder what he's thinking. If he's going to erupt in elation at any moment, I don't want to be around to see it.

"You got in, didn't you?" I whisper.

His eyes lift to my face and he swallows, clearly uncomfortable and hesitant.

Then, slowly, he nods.

"Congratulations," I say, trying to force my voice to lie with enthusiasm, but I don't pull it off. "You can be happy, Luke. That's amazing. You wanted it so bad."

"I think I'm in shock," he says, his expression unreadable.

"We should celebrate!" I cheer.

"We don't have to do that."

"I'm seriously *so* happy for you," I say, plastering a wide grin on my face. Surely, a smile can hide everything, right? No one can see through a smile.

Finally, his expression comes to life, a slow, creeping grin appearing on his face. He bites his bottom lip to control it as he continues to read the email.

"Let's go out to eat!" I shout, clapping my hands together. "You can celebrate your new boring book thing, and I can celebrate soon having this place to myself."

His smile falters, but I'm moving too fast to let the feelings in. I hurry the rest of my presents to the living room and start searching for my phone.

"Go get dressed," I shout.

"Okay, I am," he replies, abandoning his gift wrapping and walking toward his bedroom.

I can't stop moving. If I stop, every emotion I've shoved inside the thick steel locker in my head will come spilling out. I don't have the time or energy to sift through all of that right now.

This is good, I tell myself as I amble from room to room, looking everywhere for my phone. He's leaving soon, probably before the baby is born, so it'll put some much-needed distance between us and we can finally get over whatever pseudo-relationship thing we're in right now. We both need to clear our heads. That much is obvious.

When my thorough search of the house is unsuccessful, I

head into Luke's room. His bathroom door is closed and I hear the shower running inside.

Cracking it open a few inches, I call, "Hey, I lost my phone. Can I call it with yours?"

The bathroom is steamy, but I can make out the foggy form of his naked body through the misty reflection. My gaze is stuck for a moment before I tear it away.

"Yeah," he replies with his hands in his hair as he lathers it up. "It's on my bed. The passcode is 0415."

I turn and grab his phone from the bed, punching in the numbers. I pause and think about them for a moment.

"That's not your birthday, is it?"

"No, it's my brother's," he replies from the shower.

"Caleb's?" I say, wincing as I hear him laugh.

"Caleb's birthday is my birthday," he says, teasing me.

"I know that," I mutter with an eye roll. "I was joking." Which is a lie. I had a total slip and I'll blame my pregnancy brain for that.

He's still laughing as I realize something.

"It's not Adam's. His was a few weeks ago."

I don't know if Luke didn't hear my response or if he's ignoring me, but he doesn't say anything for a moment.

Is there another brother no one has told me about? Is Luke keeping secrets from me? Is the whole family? What if this is a tragic story, and I just brought it back up? I'm sure there's a reason he's never told me but as he avoids the question, I don't press him for it.

Instead, I pull up my contact on his phone. For some reason, I hit the message icon first and it pulls up our text thread. I'm just about to hit the phone icon in the corner to call my phone when I notice there is an unsent text message in the bar at the bottom.

Moby Dick?

I stare at it for far too long before I realize what it means. My jaw drops.

When did he type this? Did it mean he wanted to...?

Why didn't he send it?

My ears are buzzing as I stare at his phone, connecting pieces to this puzzle. Luke typed this out because he wanted to have sex with me, but he changed his mind.

So he *doesn't* want to have sex with me?

Did he have second thoughts, or was he too embarrassed to send it? Did he realize that it would only make our relationship more complicated?

What would I have said if he had sent it?

The last text he sent was the day before Thanksgiving, which means this was after that. And that was a week ago.

"Did you find it?" he asks.

I was so enthralled by this unsent text, I didn't even hear the shower stop. Quickly, I hit the call button from his phone and drop it on the bed, rushing from the room to follow the sound of my own phone ringing.

I have to dig into the cushions of the couch to retrieve it, but after I do, I drop onto the sofa and mull over the text situation again.

It's a good thing he didn't send it with the news he got today. I can only imagine that if we had slept together, it would have made today's news hurt even more.

Numbly, I go into my bedroom and get ready. None of my pants fit me anymore, so I'm stuck wearing stretchy leggings and dresses. I settle for a long black-and-white dress that pairs well with black boots and a leather jacket.

When I walk out into the living room, Luke is standing there in dark, fitted jeans, a dark-red button-down shirt, and brown leather loafers. He's so good-looking it literally hurts my eyes.

I just have to get through the night. Put on a happy face. And then ignore him as much as possible over the next few weeks as he prepares to leave. I can do that.

"I got us a table at that steak house," he says, looking up from his phone.

"Perfect," I say, avoiding eye contact.

We're quiet on the way to the restaurant, and even when we sit down, the conversation feels stiff. He sips on a glass of whiskey while I run my finger along the rim of my water glass.

"You should come visit," he says and I glance up at him without reacting.

"In England?" I ask.

"Yeah, of course."

"With a baby?"

"They have babies in England." He forces a smirk on his face. "The program is only a year long."

I don't know what that's supposed to mean so I don't reply. Is he implying that I should wait for him for a whole year and *maybe* we can try to be an actual couple when he gets back? He must know how ridiculous he sounds.

"Listen, Luke. I really am happy for you. This is what you've always wanted and the literary world is going to be better off with you in that project."

He scoffs. "Don't be so dramatic."

"Well, I don't know." I laugh. "What you're doing is important."

"Is it?" he mutters, staring down at his glass.

"To you it is," I reply.

Then his gaze drifts upward to meet my eyes. "Sadie," he starts. His tone is soft and sweet, and it almost sounds like he's going to say something I want to hear.

But then, movement catches my eye across the restaurant, and I glance up to see a very tall, familiar man walking in with a small party of well-dressed people.

"Oh my god," I mumble, quickly averting my eyes. But I know it's too late. For a brief moment, our eyes met.

"What?" Luke asks as he turns around to see Jax staring at us. "Who is that?"

"That's the—"

My words are cut off as Jax comes toward us. "Is that sexy Sadie?" he asks too loudly.

Luke's mouth sets in a thin, straight line.

"Jax," I say with a smile as I stand up to greet him. Luke immediately stands up too.

Jax's eyes bolt down to my belly, hovering there the same way a deer stares into oncoming traffic.

I pull him into a hug to distract him from the sight of my swollen, fetus-filled belly.

"You look great," he says in a mindless sort of hypnotic way as his eyes bore into mine.

Is he high?

"Thank you," I say sweetly.

Luke's rueful glare from the table is focused on Jax, so I quickly ease the tension.

"Luke, this is Jax," I say, widening my eyes and touching my stomach as if I'm sending him secret messages. He gets it right away.

Straightening his spine, I swear he tries to make himself taller. They're both already tall guys, but Jax has Luke by a few inches, which Luke is desperately trying to make up for with his chest puffed out and his chin held high.

He puts out a hand. "Lucas Goode," he says proudly, and I'm mildly surprised he didn't toss the *doctor* portion in there to show off.

"Nice to meet you," Jax says with scrutiny. "Are you two on a date?"

"Yes," Luke replies quickly.

And I throw in a quick "No. Just celebrating."

The muscles in Luke's jaw click. I can see it. Jax can see it. The sommelier by the bar can see it.

There's a thick fog of tension among the three of us that's probably hazing up this whole restaurant.

"What are you celebrating?" Jax asks cautiously.

Luke doesn't pipe up to answer this one. Instead, I smile and answer for him. "Luke got into an overseas program in England. It was very competitive and prestigious."

"Wow, congrats," Jax replies with a smug nod. Then he glances at me.

"Does that mean you're moving to England too?" He seems so stiff and almost aggressive. This is not the same Jax I know from the club. He's no longer flirty and carefree.

I laugh and shake my head. "Oh, no. We're not a couple."

There goes Luke's clicky jaw again. He's going to wear down his molars if he keeps that up.

"Oh," Jax replies, his gaze dancing over my face and body again. "Well, it was nice running into you."

"Yeah, you too," I reply politely.

Luke is glaring at me. It's like I can already feel his punishment coming.

"Enjoy your dinner," Jax says. "I'll talk to you soon."

"You too," I say as I sit back down. Luke stays standing until Jax leaves.

A moment later, our food comes and we eat in tense, uncomfortable silence. All I can think is that Jax didn't mention anything about the baby. I'm nothing but a woman he slept with once, and that's it. I just happen to be pregnant with a child created from his sperm, and that's it.

Sperm doesn't make anyone a father. So I don't know why I'm holding on to hope that Jax will suddenly sprout feelings for me or this child.

Glancing up at Luke across from me, I can't fight the feeling that he's angry. I don't know what I did or what he has to be angry about, but all I know is that when we get home, he will want to punish me for it.

And I can't wait.

TWENTY-SIX

Lucas

When I park the car in the garage, Sadie and I sit in silence before either of us moves. I don't want to talk about it, and I don't want to try to understand what any of this means.

With Sadie, we don't ever need to talk about it. She feels it, too.

I wish I could understand why she is so nice to him. Why doesn't she tell him what a piece of shit he is for abandoning her through this pregnancy? Why doesn't she understand she deserves so much more?

I wish I could spank her tonight. I need to feel that connection to her that only comes from those intense, visceral moments. But I don't feel right doing that anymore—for multiple reasons.

I have another idea instead.

"My room," I say. My voice is deep, just above a whisper.

"Okay," she replies softly.

She opens the door and climbs out, but before she closes it, I say, "Miss Green."

Pausing, she stares at me and waits.

"Naked," I add. For a moment, I'm afraid she'll argue or hesitate. Maybe I'm going too far. Maybe this fire burning between us is just me.

We both know this is reckless, but after the news today, I don't want to push her away anymore. I want to pull her closer and savor every second I have left. And I'm not holding back anymore.

Her expression doesn't change as she nods. "Okay."

Then I watch as she slams the door and disappears into the house. As soon as she's gone, I let out a heavy sigh.

This is going to hurt like a bitch. That much is clear. Not tonight. Tonight will be heavenly.

But the day I have to walk away from her and the baby, that day will be torture.

Have I briefly considered backing out and staying behind? Yes. More than briefly, actually.

I pondered it a lot today. I tried to picture what my life would look like if I said fuck it and stayed with Sadie. Made her more than a friend. Raised a baby with her.

It looks beautiful—like a dream.

But it's not *my* dream. That's not my life. It's someone else's dream.

How long until I resent Sadie for ruining my future? How long until I regret it? Every moment with her and the baby won't be a dream. Some days will be awful and I'll grow bitter.

Then, before I know it, I'll turn into my father.

I'll begrudge them both for not filling the hole in my life with their presence and their love. I'll start to *hate* that love.

I won't do to Sadie and the baby what my father did to us. I'll love her until the very last moment, and then I'll let her go.

I've made my mind up. It's for the best.

As I climb out of the car, my blood is coursing through my veins so fast that I can practically hear the pulse in my ears. The house is quiet as I enter, and I make her wait as I remove my shoes by the front door, neatly setting them to the side.

When I reach my bedroom, there's only one small lamp lit, so the room is dim. Sadie is standing in the middle of the room, waiting for me.

Like I instructed her to, she's removed every stitch of clothing. I let my eyes take their fill of her perfect body. I've seen every part of her in small doses, but this view is enough to send me off to heaven. Her breasts are full and heavy with tight, pebbled nipples that match the freckles on her cheeks. The swell of her stomach is more evident than I've seen it before. Even her belly button has started to flatten, and even though it's not biologically my child in there, the sight of her like this has me feeling downright feral.

Her round, plush hips look so soft to the touch I'm practically drooling. All I want to do is grasp them, squeeze them, hold them while I fuck her. Her thick thighs beckon to me, and I can't wait to lose myself in them and feel them wrapped around me.

She's standing proudly in the middle of the room, so we're face to face. Slowly, I peel open each button of my shirt, and her eyes track the movement.

"You seem to have forgotten who you belong to," I say as I slide my shirt from around my shoulders.

She lifts her chin defiantly.

My little devil.

"I'm not yours anymore," she says.

"Think so?"

"You're leaving," she argues.

"I'm not gone yet."

I take a menacing step forward. Her eyes search my face, and I realize that this is the only person on earth with whom I can do this. This silly little performance of ours. It's how we communicate, and maybe it's not the right way, but it's ours. No woman will ever fill this role for me again. Once I leave Sadie, I leave this lifestyle behind, too, *for good.*

"Would you like me to prove it to you?" I ask, touching her chin. "Not that I need to. You're already standing here naked, like I told you to. So you must already know you're mine."

When she doesn't answer, I bring my mouth closer to hers. I

don't kiss her, and I never will. That's a line I refuse to cross. But I want her to know this is as far as I'll go in the distance between our lips.

"Don't you?" I say, pushing her for a response.

"Yes," she replies.

Moving my touch from her chin and down her neck, I let my fingers glide softly over every freckle until I reach her breasts. My finger swirls the tight bud of her nipple, and I feel her shudder.

"Take my pants off," I say.

The touch of her fingers against my lower abdomen makes me shiver, and the sound of my buckle coming undone has my cock twitching in my underwear. It's already throbbing and ready for her.

Once she has the zipper down, she slides my pants to my ankles, and I step out of them, kicking them to the corner. Her hand slides back up my legs until she reaches my boxers.

"Take them off, too," I say.

With her intense gaze on my face, she slips her soft fingers under the elastic and pulls them down. My cock pops out, falling forward and aiming directly toward her.

"Get on your knees and open your mouth, Miss Green."

She drops slowly to the floor, gazing up at me until her face is in line with my cock. Her bottom lip falls open, and her soft pink tongue peeks out. Holding my cock at the base, I rest it against her cheek, watching the way her eyes close and she revels in the weight of my shaft on her face.

Gently, I run the head of my dick across her lips and over her nose as if I'm marking her with my scent. *Mine,* it says to anyone who dares to touch her or come near her. *She's taken.*

As I slide my cock into her mouth, I let out a rasping moan as I'm engulfed in the wet heat. She closes her lips around me and slathers my cock up, sucking me slowly like a sensual worship.

Her hands stay on her lap as she lets me use her mouth, easing in and out. We're not rushing toward a climax. We're savoring every second.

But as the intensity of my pleasure escalates, I pull my cock out and take a breath.

Reaching down, I hold her chin and force her to look up at me. "I want to fuck you, Miss Green. It's not a punishment, though. Do you understand?"

"I understand," she whispers.

"I need to hear you say it. Yes or no?"

"Yes. You can fuck me."

Those words slide down my spine like honey. I practically melt to the floor myself from how good it feels to hear her say that.

"I want you to," she adds sweetly.

"Then get on the bed for me," I say. "Flat on your back. Spread your legs and let me look at you."

She crawls to the bed and climbs up, stretching out in the middle of my king-size bed. Her legs butterfly open, and I stand at the end, stroking myself as I stare at her.

I want to tell her that I won't fuck anyone else while I'm in England. It's a foolish thing to think, let alone say, so I keep my mouth shut. Will I feel the same way months in? Can I make that promise? How do I know I won't miss Sadie so much it will drive me into someone else's bed?

I don't. And I'm breaking her heart enough as it is.

But I do know with one-hundred-percent certainty that no one will ever be as perfect as her.

Walking over to the nightstand, I dig in the drawer for the box of rubbers and Sadie watches.

"I was tested at the doctor's office, and I haven't been with anyone else," she says, her eyes pleading.

"I haven't been with anyone either since I was last tested," I reply, dropping the foil packet back in the drawer. "Are you sure?"

"I'm sure," she replies. "I trust you."

Arousal sparks at the base of my spine from the idea of being inside her with nothing between us. Leaving my seed inside her.

It's strange how that means something to me now when, before, it was often more of a fear than a fantasy.

Going back to the foot of the bed, I take my time as I crawl over her, kissing my way up her soft, pale legs. When I reach the insides of her thighs, I suck harder, scratching her flesh with my coarse facial hair. I want to mark her.

Reaching her pretty pink pussy, I breathe in her scent and let out a satisfied groan. I kiss my way around every inch of her cunt, the top, the bottom, the inside, everywhere. She moans softly with every touch of my lips.

Then I work my way up, kissing her gently on the hips and the soft mound of her stomach.

I quickly shove away any thoughts about the baby inside—the baby that *feels* like mine. The baby, which is definitely *not* mine.

She reaches for me, and I continue my climb until I'm hovering above her. I think she's waiting for me to kiss her, but as I lower myself, I press my lips to her throat and then across her collarbones.

Reaching down, I hook an arm under her leg and grind my erection against her clit. She hums with pleasure as she touches my face and stares into my eyes. My heart beats faster, and I'm not even inside her yet.

Lining my cock up with her warm core, I stare into her eyes as I press myself inside her slowly. Her lips part as she gazes into my eyes. It feels like it's the first time I've ever felt the wet heat of an eager body before, but Sadie is unlike anyone.

As I reach the hilt, she lets out a mewling sound, and chills ripple down my spine. My face falls to her breasts as I hold myself there, savoring the way she feels around me. I pepper her with kisses, imagining it's her lips, wishing I could tell her what she means to me.

"We fit together so well," I murmur against her skin. "Like we were made for each other."

I release her thigh and she wraps them around my waist, using her legs to pull me even closer as if she can't get me in deep enough. I'd crawl inside her if I could.

I can't hold back anymore. Lifting up, I pull out to the tip and slam back inside her. She lets out a deep groan, letting her head hang back. When I do it again, I slam in a little harder. Biting her lip, she gazes into my eyes with a feral expression. Her fingers scratch at my chest like she's asking for a hint of pain.

So I slam into her again and again. On each thrust, I let out a grunt and feel a spark of pleasure at the base of my spine. She has me falling apart piece by piece.

Holding my hips, she pulls me inside her, tilting her hips to allow me deeper access. I can't stop, lost somewhere between pleasure and need.

"Right there," she whimpers, reaching up to her own chest and pinching the tight buds of her nipples.

Taking her right thigh, I pull her leg up to my shoulder and fuck her harder in the exact spot that makes her eyes roll. I reach down and press my thumb to her clit, massaging it in tight circles.

Soon, her body tenses as her moans escalate, high-pitched and breathless.

"That's my girl," I mutter as I feel her cunt tighten around me. "Come on my cock, baby."

She grabs on to my arms, digging her nails in as she shudders out the remainder of her orgasm. I pick up the pace of my thrusts, remembering that there's no condom between us. So when I do come, I'll be filling her up. Making her truly mine.

That's the thought that brings me to climax, fucking her through the wave of pleasure. I grab her hand on my arm and intertwine our fingers. I bring them to my lips as I ride out the rest, kissing her knuckles and wishing they were her lips.

Once we're both spent, I take my time before pulling out. Then I collapse on the bed next to her. My heart is beating so fast it feels like it's going to punch its way out of my body. I still have Sadie's hand in mine.

I turn my head to stare into her eyes, and she gazes back with a look that guts me. It's soft and hopeful.

Just as I'm about to get up and find a towel to clean her up, she pulls me back down and crawls into my arms. Our naked bodies are pressed together as she presses her lips to my neck and nuzzles herself there.

"Let's just stay like this for a while," she murmurs.

"Okay," I reply, wrapping her up in my arms.

"I want to pretend for a moment like this matters."

Her exhale is cool against the wet skin of my neck, and I stare at the ceiling as those words run me over like a train. I don't know if she's talking about the sex, my seed, which is still buried deep inside her or us.

It doesn't matter because she's right—none of those things matter.

No matter how much it feels like they do.

TWENTY-SEVEN

Sadie

I stay in Luke's bed all night. His body is wound around mine like a shield, and I sleep so soundly that I don't hear my phone buzzing on the nightstand. It's Luke who wakes me up and not on purpose.

But when the person lying next to me gasps, it's hard to stay asleep.

"What is it?" I say, turning toward him. He's staring at his phone through sleep-dazed eyes.

Without responding, he just rotates the phone toward me. And there on the screen is a bright photo of a newborn baby, wrapped tightly in a blue-and-pink hospital blanket with a tiny baby beanie on her head.

It's a text from Adam, and below the photo, it reads:

> Say hello to Faith Marie Goode. Born at 11:05 p.m. last night.

"Oh my god!" I squeal as I sit upright and steal the phone

from him to stare at the picture some more. "She's so cute and perfect!"

Next to me, Luke is grinning softly at the picture. "She is cute."

Realizing it's *his* phone, I pass it back to him and watch as he types out:

> Congratulations. She's beautiful.

My phone buzzes again, so I reach over to retrieve it. It's a text from Sage, and when I open it, it's the same photo and message that Adam sent Luke.

I quickly text back a reply.

> Hi, Faith.

> I hope everyone is doing well. Congrats to you both!

I'm sure Sage is sleeping, or at least I hope she is, so she doesn't respond. So, after staring at the perfect picture a few minutes longer, I set my phone back on the nightstand and lie back down on the pillow.

My hand goes to my stomach as the baby does a little karate kick to my rib cage. I don't know how or why, but I can't help but feel like he's a boy. And suddenly, I'm picturing myself sending texts out just like this one.

A cute, bundled photo with a perfect little name so I can show off my baby to the world. It feels so surreal and daunting.

Luke stretches out next to me. As our eyes meet, we don't say anything for a moment. The weight of what we did last night hangs over us.

Everything between us feels so confusing, but I do know a few things for certain.

First, I know that it won't be the last time we have sex. It's obvious to me now that Luke is done holding back and restraining himself from what he wants with me.

Second, I know he's still leaving. This fling has a shelf life, and it's in the vicinity of three to four months.

And because these two things are true—that he'll both have me and *not* have me, I know he won't kiss me. That seems to be some unspoken rule of his. Kissing is too intimate and real.

Can I live with this? Do I have a choice?

I want Luke. But the longer we continue with this, the more it will hurt when it's time to say goodbye.

When we finally get out of bed, Luke goes to the kitchen to make a pot of coffee, and I hop into the shower. The entire time I stand under the spray, I think about last night and relive every moment.

The way he looked at me as he filled me to the hilt. The sounds he made as he pounded into me. The feel of his fingers intertwined with mine.

That wasn't just fucking. Fucking would have involved far less eye contact and delicate touches. Luke made our first time special.

When I step out of the shower, I hear Sam Cooke playing in the living room, which means Luke is in a good mood. The semester is almost over. He just found out he's getting the job of his dreams. His brother just became a dad.

He's on cloud nine.

I wish I could feel happier for him.

I slip on a simple dress for class and throw some beach wave product in my hair because I don't have the energy to blow-dry and straighten it today. It's getting too long anyway.

As I'm throwing on some mascara, my phone buzzes again. Assuming it's Sage replying to my text, I pick up and freeze as I read Jax's name on the screen.

It was great seeing you last night. I realize I've been a total asshole to you. Do you have plans tonight? I'd love to see you.

I read the message over and over again. What is happening?
He wants to see me? For what?

Is this about the baby or about me?

Should I ask that?

Instead, I settle on something safe and noncommittal.

> It was great seeing you, too! I don't know my
> plans for tonight, but I'll text you later.

Then, because I start to feel bad, I add...

> And you totally have not been an asshole.

I mean, he sort of has. But at least he's acknowledging that,
right?

What if he wants to give us a try? What if there's still a chance
for a romance here? I owe it to the baby to at least try, right? Even
if Jax and I could just establish some sort of relationship, we could
co-parent, and I'd have some help. I need that.

As I walk into the living room, I decide not to tell Luke about
the text from Jax. I don't need him judging me for my response or
the fact that I'm considering this.

Besides, I don't want it to tarnish the good mood he's in.

We decide to ride together to class today. It's a risk, and normally,
we never do this, but I enjoy this reckless side of Luke. Showing
up to campus with his pregnant student in his car is definitely
enough to raise some eyebrows, but he parks in the back of the
student lot, and I get out first, walking to class before him because
I always have to stop at the bathroom first—even if I went right
before we left.

As I walk out of the bathroom stall, a beautiful, tall woman in black heels comes into the bathroom. I glance up from the sink and our eyes meet briefly.

"Good morning," she says in a greeting, and it seems like that's all she's about to say, but then she pauses and says, "Oh, we've met. You're Dr. Goode's student, aren't you?"

I swallow, drying my hands on a paper towel. "Yes."

"He talks about you a lot," she says, crossing her arms as she leans against the white tile wall.

All I can think about is that day at the library when she invited him to dinner and kept *fucking* touching him. And now, to hear that she talks to him a lot when I'm not around—even if it is about me—grates on my nerves.

"He does," I reply, not quite like a question but more of a statement.

"I think you make him like teaching," she adds. "Of course, don't tell anyone I said that. He *really* wants to submit your name for that grant, but as long as you're a business major..."

"I'm a business major for a reason," I reply a little too coldly.

"I understand," she says with a smug expression.

She's blocking the door, so I can't quite leave. I'm just standing here, awkwardly staring at her with my bag slung over my shoulder.

"He's just taken a real interest in you," she adds. Her gaze drifts downward to my stomach and then back up to my face. "I assumed it was just because he wanted you in our department. Because you're so bright, of course."

Is she...insinuating something?

"I should get to class," I mumble under my breath as I pass her by to get to the door. But as my shoulder breezes past hers, she touches my arm.

"A scandal would ruin his chances for that program," she says under her breath.

There's a lump caught in my throat as I side-eye her. "He's already in the program."

"He's been accepted, Miss Green. He's not in it yet. And losing it would devastate him, so please...be careful."

Her tone sounds sincere, but what she's implying is that I will be the reason Luke's dreams are crushed. She has no idea how much turmoil I'm already in. So I clench my jaw and turn to stare at her.

"I don't know what you're talking about," I mutter.

"Good. I think you should keep it that way."

She leaves my side and walks to the bathroom stall, her heels clicking against the floor as she walks. I storm out of the bathroom, fuming from the conversation. I'm tempted to just leave campus now and ditch the rest of the school day, but Luke drove, and if I don't show up, he'll worry.

So I walk into class and take my seat at the side of the room. He's already unpacking his things. His gaze finds me, and he gives a subtle wink that no one is paying enough attention yet to see.

I can't help the smirk on my face, but I can't get that conversation with the professor out of my head. If people suspect, does that mean the administration does too? Will I be the reason Luke's dreams fall apart?

Resting my elbow on my desk, I stare at him as he discusses something with another student.

If I were a good person, I'd step aside and ensure that Lucas doesn't lose his internship. If I were a good person, I'd spend more of my energy working things out with Jax rather than pursuing a passionate fling with my English professor.

But as he smiles at me again, I can't help but wonder...am I really a good person at all?

TWENTY-EIGHT

Lucas

I can't take my eyes off Sadie for the entire class. Finals are this week, and we should be focusing on that, but I can't stop thinking about how beautiful her moans were in my ear last night as I fucked her.

God, I can't wait to be inside her again.

How the fuck am I going to live without this for a whole year while I'm in England? No one will compare. Not only has this woman flipped my life on its head, but she's also ruined sex for me.

As the students file out at the end of class, a few stay behind to discuss their essay grades, but Sadie lingers around as if she's also waiting to talk to me. It takes forever, no matter how I try to rush through each discussion.

Finally, as the last one leaves, I turn my feral gaze on her as she stands with her ass pressed against her desk.

"Get down here," I say in a hungry command.

She glances at the door. "I don't know if that's a good idea."

"I don't care. I gave you an order," I say with a smug smirk on my face. I can't seem to keep my smile away these days.

She tilts her head to the side, narrowing her eyes as she deliberates her next move.

"Fine," I reply. "I'll come to you."

I take the steps up to where she's standing next to her desk, and once I'm stationed in front of her, she backs up and grips the surface as she gazes into my eyes. "You'll lose your job if anyone catches us, Dr. Goode," she says.

"Then you should keep quiet, Miss Green."

Taking her jaw in my hand, I tilt her head to the side and kiss my way down her neck from her jaw to her collarbone. She tastes so good, like perfume and *her*.

Grabbing on to her hips, I spin her around until she's facing the table. She plants her hands on the surface and pushes her hips back toward me.

"Remember when I spanked your ass on this table?" I say through gritted teeth.

"Yes," she murmurs.

I undo my belt buckle as I stare down at her back, arched in a soft black dress. Her red hair is draped down her spine. I want to bury my hand in it and pull, bringing her a hint of pain.

"I wanted to fuck you so badly that day, Miss Green," I mutter. "It drove me wild how much I wanted you."

The sound of my zipper coming down echoes through the room, and it sounds so wrong in here. But it's the wrongness of it that makes it that much hotter.

She whimpers as I flip up her dress and grind my stiffening length against her backside.

"We'll have to be quick," I say as I drag my cock out of my boxer briefs. It's already throbbing for her before I even drag her panties to the side and notch the head at her cunt. I thrust inside her without warning, and she lets out a loud gasp.

Reaching down, I cover her mouth as I begin to fuck her. With the other hand, I lightly spank her ass.

"I told you to keep it down, Miss Green."

She turns her head to stare at me, and I remove my hand to

find her biting her bottom lip hard between her teeth. She's struggling to keep quiet now, but so am I.

I'm fucking her fast, gripping tightly to her hips. I know we have to hurry, but I don't want this to end. She feels so good around me, warm and tight. I love her soft body in my hands.

"You like your professor fucking you over your desk, Miss Green?" I say breathlessly as I lose my composure.

"Yes," she whispers. "I love it."

"I thought about this during the entire class. I wanted to fuck you in front of them. I want to show everyone who you belong to."

"Yes," she says again, this time more like a whine than a word.

I imagine someone walking in right now. I picture them finding us like this, and it's enough to send me over the edge. Sadie is white-knuckling the desk as she trembles through a silent release. Meanwhile, I'm finishing inside her with a loud groan.

I don't care if they find us. Let them.

At the sound of voices in the hall, I pull out in a rush, turning to zip up my pants. Sadie bolts upright and fixes her dress. The door never opens. It was just a group of students walking past.

But as their voices retreat into the distance, Sadie and I glance at each other for a long, tense minute. Then we both break out in laughter.

She picks up her backpack and watches as I walk down the steps to get my bag.

"You ruined my underwear," she says with an uncomfortable grimace on her face. I imagine my cum leaking out of her, soaking her panties, and it sends a brand-new jolt of arousal to my cock.

I let out a chuckle, and she swats playfully at my arm.

"Don't laugh. I have two more classes after this."

"It's our dirty little secret," I say as I lean toward her. Suddenly, I want to kiss her. If I were her boyfriend, I'd take her mouth in a familiar and passionate kiss.

Instead, I back away and avert my gaze. Like the coward I am.

Within walking distance of the house, there's a DQ that has become a late-night staple over the last few weeks. The mint chocolate chip ice cream bars haunt her dreams, apparently. Never mind the fact that it's cold as hell outside. Sadie and I are strolling back together as she satisfies her pregnancy craving.

I'll admit, I derive an alarming amount of pleasure from watching her do that little side-to-side wiggle she does as she takes the first bite. As if it's so good, she can't help but dance.

I'll miss this.

"You know my schedule for next semester still has your name on it," she says, taking a bite of her ice cream bar as we walk.

"That's because I'm not leaving until the spring. As of right now, they want me there no later than June first, but I might go early to get settled."

"Oh, so I get grumpy Dr. Goode for one more semester," she says with a smile.

"Do people call me that?" I ask.

"I do. But it's catching on."

As she laughs, I grab her hand and bring her ice cream to my face, stealing a bite. "I'll show you grumpy."

When our laughter subsides, we walk in silence. It's hard to gauge Sadie's emotions about all of this. She was upset at Thanksgiving, and I know she'll miss me, but she'll be fine. She understands that I'm not a relationship man. This was never going to work, so we're having fun while we can.

"I can't help but feel like this baby is kicking you out of your own house. He comes, and you leave."

"He?" I say, turning toward her in surprise. Did she somehow find out the sex without me?

"It's just a hunch," she replies. "I tried saying *she* for a while, but it didn't feel right."

"Have you thought about names?" I ask.

She screws up her face in contemplation. "I like Henry."

"Henry..."

It doesn't matter what I think, but suddenly imagining this baby with a name makes it so much more real. It hurts to think about it. And picturing Sadie as a mother is like throwing accelerant on an already burning fire. It's too much.

"I like Henry," I reply under my breath as I stare down at the concrete. "Henrietta if it's a girl?

She throws her head back and laughs. "I like Isla if it's a girl."

"Isla or Henry. Both adorable," I say.

"Thanks," she replies with a cheesy grin.

"When is the shower?" I ask as we reach the house. Unlocking the door for her, I pull it open and watch as she peels off her shoes without unlacing them, kicking them into the corner next to a pair of brown cowboy boots lying on their side.

"Not until March," she replies. "My mother is hounding me to find out the sex."

I help her peel off her coat and hang it on the rack. "Do what you want," I say. "Don't let her pressure you."

"I won't," she replies. She's stretching her back as she walks down the hall toward her room.

I sit on the bench and start unlacing my own shoes when I hear Sadie's bloodcurdling scream. Bolting from my seat, I sprint down the hall toward her room.

"I'm sorry!" Isaac shouts with his hands up. He's standing in the middle of the hallway, and Sadie is holding a leather-bound book from my bookcase as if she's going to use it as a weapon.

I move between them, taking the book from her hand as I softly explain, "He's my brother."

"I knew it!" she replies, looking astonished. "You have *another* brother."

Turning around, I stare at Isaac with my lips pressed together. "What are you doing here?"

"I came to see you," he says with a shrug.

"You could have texted first," I mutter.

"Sorry. But in my defense, you've never had a life before."

With a sigh, I rub my forehead. "Sadie, this is my little brother Isaac. He's an idiot."

"Hi," he says with a wave.

"Isaac, this is my friend Sadie."

"Please explain what's going on," she argues.

"Let's sit on the couch," I say, turning her toward the living room. "I need a drink."

As I fill in Sadie on everything that's happened with my brother over the years, her wide eyes are in a constant state of shock.

I reach over and touch her knee. "Sadie, no one knows that Isaac has been living with me, and no one can know that he's back in Austin."

She puts up three fingers. "Scout's honor. I won't tell a soul."

As she stares at Isaac, who's sitting on *my* chair with his feet propped up on the coffee table and a beer in his hand, I notice the way her expression changes from guarded and stern to warm and welcoming.

"Wow," she mumbles. "Your dad is an even bigger piece of shit than I thought."

"Cheers to that," Isaac says with a smile.

"So, wait..." she says as she leans forward. "You signed with a record label. Don't you think people will start to recognize you?"

Isaac shrugs. "Eventually. I like being Theo Virgil, though. I'm not ready to be Isaac Goode again."

"Makes sense," she replies warmly. Then she turns to me. "Aren't you afraid Adam and Caleb will kill you when they find out you've been hiding him all this time?"

I roll my eyes as I lean back on the couch and take a sip of my whiskey. "It's okay. I'll be in England."

"Wait...you're really going to England?" Isaac says, bolting upright.

As I meet his gaze, I swallow down a dose of regret with my Macallan. Before I can speak, Sadie cuts in.

"He got accepted to some literature program in England that he's been wanting to do for years." She sounds excited for me. Either that, or she's a good actress.

"For how long?" Isaac asks.

"A year," I reply.

"And what about you?" he asks her.

She rubs her stomach and stares at him with a question on her face. "I'll be living here with the baby."

As Isaac's gaze travels back to me, I feel about two inches tall. I don't need to tell him the baby's not mine. Somehow, he knows. I don't need to tell him that Sadie is not my girlfriend either. He knows that, too.

How does he know? Because I never change. I don't defy expectations or surprise anyone. I am who I am. I don't evolve or shift. I put my work first ten years ago, and I'll continue to put my work first until the day I die.

It makes my life easy, predictable, and manageable.

It also makes it boring and lonely.

For the first time in my life, I feel the sting of disappointment —my brother's and my own.

TWENTY-NINE

Sadie

Jax has texted me every day this week. And he texted me every day last week too.

I'm doing my best to respond, but this is uncharted territory for me. He's not texting because he wants a hookup. He's texting because he wants a relationship.

I don't know where this came from, but all of a sudden, it's as if he actually cares about me and this baby. He wants to know how big the baby is, and he wants to see ultrasound pictures.

We had our anatomy scan last week, right before Christmas, and I purposefully didn't tell Jax about it. Somehow, I knew that if I told him, he'd want to go. But if he went, that would mean Luke couldn't. And Luke has been at every appointment. It didn't seem fair to suddenly push him out for someone else.

That someone else being the baby's father, but still.

I don't know where Luke and I are, and I don't know what this is between us. He cares about me, and he cares about the baby. And I can tell that he's torn. But at the same time, this is so confusing for me.

It's like he's acting like the father that's going to leave as soon as the baby is born. The father that doesn't love either of us enough to stay. At times, I'm so angry at him for this.

But do I really want him to stay?

Jax is the one that I should want. So why do I feel myself constantly reaching for Luke?

We are having a great little fling, and the sex is amazing, but... We can't seriously be together, can we?

I'm staring down at my phone as Luke and I meander through the grocery store together. The text from Jax is staring back up at me.

Let me take you out for New Year's.

My gut twists with guilt. I want to say yes. I should try to make this work. Instead, I pocket my phone without responding.

Luke picks up a box of the same granola he eats every morning and tosses it into the cart. I reach for a box of Captain Crunch and do the same.

"Well, hello there," a warm, feminine voice says from behind us. Luke and I spin around in surprise to find the hot English professor coming up to greet us.

Shit.

"You two grocery shopping together?" she asks as she glances back and forth between us.

"Uh..." Luke stammers. "Actually, I'm renting out a room to Sadie," he says quietly as he glances around to make sure no one else can hear.

"Yeah!" I chime in. "He had a room pop up and I was getting some very life-changing news," I say, as I rub my stomach. "And he sort of swooped in to save the day."

"Don't worry," the hot teacher says as she touches his arm. "Your secret is safe with me. There's nothing wrong with living in the same building with your professor."

When her eyes glance back over to me, I sense something devious in her expression. And it has me clamming up.

"It's actually kind of sweet," she says as she looks at him.

We make small talk for a moment about the holidays and the start of next semester in a week. She keeps touching his arm like she did in the library, and I busy myself by looking around at the cereal aisle like a child.

"Do you have plans for New Year's?" she says quietly as if to have a conversation without me in it. "A few of us will be going out and I was wondering if you would like to join us?"

The way she says that makes me feel as if it's not "us" that she would like him to join, but really him. I'm tensing some more.

"I really appreciate the invitation," he says in that formal way that Luke talks.

"You're more than welcome to join," she says to me. "Although it will be a group of professors so we might be a little more boring than you're used to."

"Oh, that's okay," I say casually. "I appreciate the invite, though. Luke, you should go. Sounds like fun."

I can see his throat move as he swallows. "Thanks, I'll think about it," he stammers.

"Of course, just text me."

"Will do," he says.

She moves to leave, giving us both a polite wave. "You two have a good day," she says before turning away. Her eyes cascade over my face for a moment too long.

She reminds me of a wolf or a fox using intimidation as a hunting tactic.

Luke and I don't say anything for a while as if it's not safe. It's not until we get in the car that I turn to him and say, "You should go."

He glances my way with his brow furrowed. "What are you talking about?"

"I'm saying that you should go out with her for New Year's."

"Why would I do that?" he asks.

"Because," I reply, "for one, it would ease some suspicion off you and me. I can't help but feel as if, if you don't go, she's going to assume that you and I have more than a roommate relationship. But if you do go and, I don't know, flirt with her a little, maybe even kiss her at midnight, then maybe she'll be convinced that there's nothing going on between us."

His hand squeezes the steering wheel as if he's uncomfortable. "I don't want to go," he says in that cool, demanding tone of his.

I cross my arms over my chest and turn away. He senses the change in my tone. When we get back home and unload the groceries, he keeps eyeing me as if to watch my behavior. It makes me feel like a petulant child, but right now I am being a petulant child because I'm frustrated and I'm angry and I'm not getting what I want.

Turning toward me, his demeanor changes as he takes on that dominant, disciplinarian tone. "Miss Green," he says in warning, "why are you pouting?"

"I don't want to do this right now," I mutter as I turn away from him. He grabs my arm to pull me toward him. "Luke," I say.

I purposefully address him as Luke instead of Dr. Goode to identify that I'm not in the mood to play.

"I'm serious," I say, my tone biting. "You should go out with her."

"What is this about?" he asks as his expression softens.

"What are we? What are we doing? You say that you want to spend New Year's with me, and we have sex and we grocery shop together. And it's like we have this relationship, but we're not in a relationship.

"And you're about to leave, and I'm about to have a baby, and everything we're doing has this expiration date. And I don't understand. I like it, but at the same time, I don't like it. And—"

"Okay, okay, okay, calm down," he says, putting his hands on my arms. Immediately, I push him away.

"Don't tell me to calm down."

He looks remorseful as he drops his hands by his sides and steps away. "Sadie, there's a reason that we are not in a relationship. And that's because I can't be in a relationship. I am not good at this. I don't know how to tell you what you want to hear. I don't know how to give you what you want. I cannot be the man that you want me to be. So, yes, we are just having fun.

"And I'll be honest, I don't know what we're doing either, but I know that I like it. But if you don't, then we can stop."

I don't want to stop.

But I don't say it out loud. What is the point? He's right. We have no future. Even if he wasn't leaving, Luke doesn't want a wife or a child. He can never give me what I want.

"I think you should go out with her," I say, my tone defeated and exhausted.

"What about you?" he asks.

"I'll be fine," I reply.

None of this feels right. I hate the look on his face. The sadness in his mannerisms. I miss the *us* we were before this fight. This...indescribable, uncategorizable version of a relationship that isn't labeled or serious, but just *us*.

With that, I walk away, and I feel his eyes on me as I go.

When the night of New Year's Eve rolls around, I watch Luke get dressed. I smell his cologne wafting from his bedroom. And as much as it hurts, I know this is the right thing.

As he walks out into the living room in a pair of tight black pants and a gray button-down shirt, looking so good, I consider changing my mind on this entire thing. Maybe I should tell him to stay.

I bet if I asked him, he would. If I told him to curl up on the couch with me so we could watch a movie and eventually get each other off with our mouths, he would definitely take the bait.

But that's not what either of us needs. What we need is some distance and some time to reflect on what it is we're doing.

"Be safe," I say as he grabs his keys from the dish by the door.

"Are you sure you're okay just staying home?" he asks.

I give him a thumbs-up because I don't trust my voice not to crack if I speak. He lets out a deep sigh as he turns and moves toward the door. I'm buried under blankets on the couch, deep into my one-thousandth watch of *10 Things I Hate About You*, when I get a text message on my phone. It vibrates in my lap and I pick it up to see it's from Jax.

I get that tiny little spark of excitement before I hit the button to open the text.

> Come out with me tonight.

It's not a request. It's not an invitation. It's a command. And as it turns out, I kind of like commands. Which makes me wonder that if I say no, will Jax put me over his knee and spank me?

The image is immediately repulsive, as if completely unnatural, and I don't like it. So, I file that thought away before replying.

> Well, where are you?

He types back immediately as the bubbles pop up on the screen, and a moment later, the message comes through.

> Out with a couple of friends. It's a pretty chill bar. Nothing like the club that night.

I don't know if Jax could sense how much I disliked that club that night, but I appreciate the fact that he knows I didn't like it.

> I don't want to impose if you're out with your friends.

Which is true. I don't want to go out with Jax if he's going to give his attention to someone else. I want to go out with him to be with him, and I want his attention on me, and I don't think that's asking for too much.

He replies immediately again.

> I lied. I'm here alone, and I just want to
> see you.

As I stare at those words, my stomach twisting with something I don't recognize, I quickly type back.

> I'm on my way. Send me your location.

In a rush, I get dressed and bolt out the door.

As I walk into the bar, which is obviously packed because it's New Year's Eve, I find Jax waving at me from a bar table at the back. I weave through the crowd to take the seat next to him, but before I can sit down, he hoists me into his arms. He squeezes me in a tight bear hug as he mumbles in my ear, "I'm so glad you came."

After releasing me from the embrace, he looks down at my stomach and puts his hands over the small mound of my belly.

"Oh my god, look at how big you're getting," he says. I wince before he quickly corrects himself. "I'm sorry. That's not what I meant. You look beautiful."

"It's okay. I know what you meant. And yeah, it's getting kind of big."

"Shit, how much longer do we have?" he asks.

The word "we" in that sentence sends a chill down my spine. "Well, about halfway, actually," I say. "About four and a half months to go."

"God, it feels like forever," he says as he takes a seat at the table. He lifts a brown bottle of beer to his lips as he waits for my response.

"Yeah," I reply on a sigh. "Actually, it feels like it's flying by. Four and a half months doesn't feel long enough."

"Are you nervous?" he asks.

"Um," I reply, "not really. I'm actually kind of excited."

"Yeah, me too," he says. "Fuck, I've never been around kids. I haven't seen a baby in I don't even know how long." He laughs.

I chuckle awkwardly. "I'm sure a lot of it will come naturally."

"For you, maybe," he says. A few minutes later, a waitress comes by to bring me some water. I order a Shirley Temple and Jax and I struggle our way through some pretty awkward small talk.

During the entire encounter, I can't stop thinking about Luke. I'm wondering where he is. Is he with her? Will he kiss her at midnight? Will he come home to me? He wouldn't bring her home, but would he go to her house?

This is just how badly he's gotten into my head. I'm here with Jax, the man of my dreams, the guy I crushed so hard over for months, and whose baby I'm about to have by some miracle. And I can't stop thinking about my grumpy, possessive English teacher.

What on earth have I gotten myself into?

Jax tells me all about how he's trying to expand his business from *Fan Vids* to "real porn," as he calls it. But he doesn't want to be written off as some porn star. He wants to be *next level*.

Although I don't really understand anything that he's saying, I do my best. I try to write off the fact that some of his comments are a little problematic by telling myself that he just doesn't know any better and he means well. But the way he talks about sex work is sort of demeaning and disappointing.

He continues to get drunk while I am painfully sober. And it's only ten thirty. I start to make a plan for how I'm going to sneak my way out of this date before twelve because there's no chance I'll be here at the stroke of midnight.

When I get up from our table to go use the bathroom, it's on my way back that I hear a very familiar voice from near the bar. I stop in my tracks as I stare at the tall, blonde, beautiful woman with her hand resting on Luke's arm. He says something that makes her laugh, so she throws her head back and cackles loudly.

I watch her nails dig into the gray fabric of his shirt as she squeezes his arm. Everything in me tenses when he smiles at her. The way they're standing so close, the way they're looking at each other, the way she leans in to hear what he's saying—it all stabs relentlessly at my heart.

I need to get out of here.

It's the first thought in my head. I can't be here to witness this. I'd rather be home.

The old me would have used this as fuel to throw myself at Jax. I'd make sure Luke was around to watch me kissing Jax at midnight. I'd make sure that he saw me just to make him feel the way he's making me feel right now.

But I'm not out for revenge. Right now, I'm just trying to breathe through how painful this feels.

Then the tall blonde looks right at me. Quickly, I avert my gaze and make my way over to Jax.

Except there are two girls sitting in my seat. They are sharing my one barstool with their two tiny asses. They're young and beautiful, and they're flirting with him. Oohing and aahing over his muscles and his dimples and his bright smile and how tall he is.

"Sadie," a voice from behind me gets my attention as I turn to find Luke staring at me.

Immediately, I try to discern which version of Luke I'm getting right now. Is it my friend who often shows concern and can laugh with me? Or is it the stern, broody professor who likes to find reasons to discipline me?

"What are you doing here?" he asks. And the inflection in his tone tells me that it's the former, but I'm not exactly sure which one I was hoping for.

Maybe I wanted the Dominant to bend me over this barstool and spank me to make me feel better.

I point behind me, where Jax is still talking to the two young women. "He invited me out for a drink," I say. "I had no idea you were here."

He glances behind me to see Jax, and I watch his expression change. His brow furrows, his mouth tenses, his jaw clicks.

The tall blonde comes up behind Luke, resting her hand on

his shoulder almost possessively, and I resist the urge to lash out and bite her.

"Oh, hey," Jax says as if he just noticed I'm giving my attention to someone else. His hand rests on my hip, and he tugs me toward him so the four of us are all just staring at each other. The two girls are gone, so Jax casually invites Luke and the hot English teacher, whose name I still don't know, to join us.

I grimace internally.

This is going to be a disaster.

THIRTY

Lucas

I'm fuming, and I have absolutely no right to be.

She's out with him *again*. But what did I expect? For her to sit at home alone while I was on a date with another woman? Although I don't know if I would call what Laura and I were doing tonight a date.

The more I get to know Dr. Hanson, the more I realize she's competitive, arrogant, and a bit self-absorbed. She constantly tried to one-up me on everything I said. She used every opportunity she had to talk about Sadie, and not in a nice way. She clearly doesn't approve of our relationship. And I know deep down she senses it's more than just Sadie living with me.

But I think because of her competitive nature, she's trying to steal me from her. It's not flattering, and I don't like it.

Now, the four of us are sitting at a bar-top table on New Year's Eve, and I can't take my eyes off Sadie.

"So, Jax, what do you do?" Laura asks from beside me. Sadie stiffens as Jax smiles widely.

"I'm actually an adult film star," he says.

I can see Laura's jaw drop in my periphery as Sadie takes a sip of her little red drink, her eyes averted to the side.

"Interesting," Laura replies.

"Yeah," Jax says smugly. "I'm actually on FanVids at the moment, but I was just telling Sadie that I'm hoping to move to directed productions soon."

The table grows silent as we all avoid eye contact.

"It's okay," Jax says, trying to break the tension. "I know it's kind of a unique job, but I like it."

"That's great. Congratulations," Laura says. "And what about you, Miss Green?" she says, turning toward Sadie.

"Oh, she owns a sex club," Jax says, and I wince inwardly as Sadie slaps his arm.

"I don't own a club. I manage a club."

"But you want to open one someday," I say, my eyes focused on her. "Isn't that right?"

As our gazes meet, the connection fiery and intense, she nods. "Yes, that is why I'm getting a business degree. Because someday I'd like to start my own."

"That is incredible," Laura says.

"And you're both professors," Jax replies.

"Yes," I mutter in response.

"And Sadie here is one of Dr. Goode's star pupils," Laura says, and I breathe out a breath of frustration.

I need another drink.

By some miracle, the waitress happens to walk by, and I tap her on the arm to order two shots of Jameson and two beers.

"Oh, I don't like beer," Laura says, but I quickly shake my head.

"Oh, those are both for me."

This gets a laugh from the table. Jax puts in his order, as does Laura, while Sadie continues to sip on her nonalcoholic drink.

"Is that true?" Jax asks. "Is Sadie one of your students?"

"Actually, yes," I reply confidently. "She is. She's probably the brightest student I've ever had." I make sure to look her in the eye as I say this.

"Stop it," she replies, rolling her eyes.

"I'm being serious," I say. "Her writing is intelligent and thought-provoking. It's as if she takes the topic that I assign and completely flips it inside out. She thinks like no one else I know. She's changed my mind on literary topics so many times now I've lost count. And it's not just how well she writes, but it's also how interesting and creative her writing is. Everything she does is so... refreshing."

Laura is smirking beside me as Jax's jaw hangs open. But it's Sadie's expression that I'm focused on. The softness in her eyes, the warmth in her expression. She loves being praised, and I'm not just doing it to make her feel better. Every word I just said is true. She's brilliant and fearless, and I don't think she knows that. But God, I wish she did. And if I have to, I'll spend the rest of my life telling her until she finally gets it.

"Damn," Jax says. "I'm having a baby with a genius."

"I am not a genius," Sadie snaps back.

"Yes, you are," I mumble.

"You know," Laura says on my side, "I believe that the grant we were talking about would apply to minor degrees. You know, it's not too late to make business a major and English a minor. It would qualify you for that grant."

"I'm not applying for that grant," Sadie says, averting her gaze. I drop the subject, not wanting to pressure her too much, especially in front of everybody else, but Laura has a great point.

As the table falls into casual conversation and we've all guzzled down our drinks far too quickly, we order another. Suddenly, everyone seems to be feeling lighter and more comfortable.

Jax and Laura are having a side conversation next to us as Sadie and I sit together, staring at each other in silence. I wonder if she can feel how much more chemistry she and I have than her and Jax or me and Laura. I wonder if everyone can tell. Is it just the unspoken thing that nobody is acknowledging?

"So wait, you two live together, and he's your professor? Is that allowed?" Jax asks.

"Technically, I don't even know," Sadie says. "But honestly, he's a terrible roommate anyway."

"Excuse me?" I reply, gawking at her in surprise. "*I'm* the terrible roommate?"

"Yes," she boasts. "He is so picky about where you put your shoes after you take them off. So I purposely just kick them in the corner just to piss him off."

"I knew it!" The table breaks out in laughter as Sadie rolls her eyes.

"You can't have dirty dishes in the sink overnight," she continues. "You have to wash them immediately after you use them or load them in the dishwasher. And as soon as the dishwasher is done cleaning, you have to empty it immediately."

"You're joking," Laura says as we all laugh again.

"What? I like to keep a clean house," I argue.

"It's ridiculous," Sadie laughs.

"Me? What about the fact that you are constantly singing, even if there's no music playing, just constantly humming a tune or singing a song for no reason in every room of my house at all hours?" I reply with a smile.

Suddenly Sadie is grinning from ear to ear as she tries to hide her smile. But I continue on.

"Whatever, you listen to boring music," she argues playfully.

"Jazz is not boring," I say.

"Well, you have a drawer in your kitchen just for takeout menus. Like seriously, they're all on the internet now. Why do you need those?"

"Well, you dance while you eat," I say, with a grin on my face. She throws her head back and laughs.

"How does that make me a bad roommate? That's not annoying. It's adorable," she says.

It is adorable.

But I don't say it out loud.

"Okay, so she's not the worst roommate," I say, glancing up at the two other people at our table. Laura and Jax have both lost their wide smiles, and they're sort of staring at us as if they can tell something that we can't.

I realize all of a sudden that I'm a little drunk, and the music feels louder. The bar is ridiculously crowded, and while Jax and Laura break off in their own conversation again, I find myself reaching for Sadie to pull her toward the dance floor. She grinds her feet into the floor to stop me.

"We can't," she says under her breath.

"Why not?" I ask.

"Because you're here with someone else, and so am I," she says.

"Then let's leave them," I mutter under my breath.

She rolls her eyes. "Luke, stop it."

"You don't want to dance with me?" I reply.

"No," she replies, pressing a finger against my chest. "I *do* want to dance with you. That's the problem. I want to dance with you, and I want to kiss you at midnight, and I want you to take me home, and I want to have loud, wild sex, and then I want to sleep in your bed, and I want you to hold me all night."

"I will do all of those things," I reply.

"Even kiss me at midnight?" she whispers.

"Yeah," I reply, even though I'm drunk, and we both know it, and promises made when intoxicated aren't really promises at all. She seems to stare at my face for a moment, her eyes drifting down to my lips before back up to my eyes. And I think she's going to kiss me, but she shakes her head instead.

"No, Lucas, we can't keep doing this."

With that, she lets go of my fingers and moves toward Jax, who is still talking to Laura. If I wasn't so numb from the alcohol, I'm quite certain this would hurt a lot.

Then, a few moments later, when the countdown begins, she's staring at me. The crowd around us is raucous and loud, moving like they're stuck in slow motion.

I hear every number of the countdown like a shot. And when the clock strikes midnight, everyone shouts, "Happy New Year."

I watch with an ache in my heart as she turns her head from me and looks up at Jax. He leans down and presses his lips to hers.

I can't tear my eyes away.

"Happy New Year," a soft voice whispers in my ear. I turn my head to find Laura standing next to me. She slings her arms around my neck and kisses me hard on the lips.

I am a coward. I'm nothing more than an asshole with commitment issues. I have been dragging Sadie around for months. Then I dragged this woman out tonight and convinced her, for a moment, that there could be a future between us.

But the truth is, I have a future with no one.

This is just what I do. I break hearts. I have no consideration for other people's feelings or emotions. I bring people close to me long enough to let them believe a lie, and then I tear it all away. I've never realized it until now when I'm about to break the most important heart of all.

"Happy New Year," I mutter sadly.

"You want to get out of here?" Laura whispers in my ear.

I couldn't leave with her if I tried. Even if I had my brain convinced that sleeping with someone else would be a good idea, there's no chance I could get my body on board with that.

Sadie has ruined me. There's no one else I want to touch, no one else I want to see naked and waiting for me, no one else I want to make moan and whimper and cry sounds of pleasure.

"I'm sorry, but I'm a little too drunk," I say, which is a cop-out excuse. "I think I'm going to grab a cab home."

"I understand." Laura nods. "Well, I had fun tonight."

"Yeah, me too," I say.

"Congratulations again on getting into the Stratford Project. Maybe if we convince Sadie to change her major, she'll be my student in the future."

"Yeah, maybe," I say with a fake chuckle.

As I turn toward Sadie, my heart nearly stops in my chest. I grow cold as I watch Jax continue to kiss her. It's not a New Year's kiss. His tongue is in her mouth. His lips are on hers. His hands are roaming her side and her back. His body is pressed against hers, and their heads are tilted, their mouths never breaking apart as they devour each other.

Suddenly, I feel as if I'm going to be sick. I mutter a clumsy goodbye to Laura as I bolt for the door, sucking in cold, fresh air once I'm outside.

This is what she wanted all along. She wants him because he is right for her. He's the father of her child. He's not leaving or putting his job before her.

I should be happy for her. And yet, I'm stumbling into a cab by myself instead. Not even the alcohol is strong enough to dull the shattering pain of my heart.

I stare out the window of the cab on my way home, trying to convince myself that this shouldn't hurt. I shouldn't be in any pain. That kiss means nothing. *She* means nothing. She's a student, a roommate, a friend, a fling even. I don't have feelings for her, and I'm certainly not falling in love with her.

I keep trying to convince myself, but of course, none of it rings true.

THIRTY-ONE

Sadie

"**P**lease come inside," Jax begs in my car while we're parked in front of his house. I offered to drive him home since he was clearly drunk. And I'm...very sober.

"I really don't think it's a good idea tonight, Jax," I say, squeezing the steering wheel tight in my grip.

The old me would have climbed out of this car so fast there would have been smoke left in my wake.

The old me might have looked past the fact that he was drunk.

The old me might have looked past the fact that he was a selfish lover in bed. Or that he has a track record of being flaky and dismissive.

But the old me had a weakness for hot men.

Which is exactly how I got myself into this situation in the first place.

At some point, a girl's gotta learn. Don't get me wrong, I still want a relationship of some sort with Jax. But after tonight, I'm starting to doubt more and more that that relationship will be romantic. And maybe that's okay.

"Why not?" he whines. Leaning over to take my hand in his,

he interlaces our fingers, squeezing them tight as if that somehow binds me to him like handcuffs. Like if he holds my hand then I'll have no choice but to follow him to bed.

I rest my head against the headrest and stare at him through the late-night darkness.

"For one, you're drunk," I say.

"I am not!" he argues with a condescending tone. As if I didn't just watch him throw back half a dozen Fireball shots and almost a case of beer.

"Second of all," I add, "it's late. I'm tired, but I had fun, and I really appreciate you inviting me out."

He lets out a despondent sigh as he stares at me from the passenger seat. "I already blew it, didn't I?" he asks. He looks like a sad puppy who just pissed on the carpet and knows he fucked up.

So I go easy on him. "You didn't blow it," I say softly.

I don't have anything to add to that, so I stay quiet. Internally, I note the fact that Jax considers blowing it or screwing up our chances for a relationship as equal to not getting sex tonight. And that should be a giant red flag right there.

"I'll call you tomorrow, okay?" I offer, trying to end this conversation so he'll get out of my car.

"I really do think I want to be, you know..." His voice trails as he releases my hand from his grip.

I wait for him to finish his sentence before finally saying, "A what?"

"You know," he stammers, "a dad, to the, you know, to the baby."

It takes everything in me not to start laughing. The fact that Jax still seems to be hesitant about whether or not he wants to be the father of this child without fully acknowledging the fact that he is one hundred percent the father of this child is downright hilarious.

Suddenly, I see Jax for exactly what he is: a boy in the body of a man. I don't know much about his personal life or how he was raised, but I get the sense that Jax was never quite forced to grow up. He's been coasting by on his good looks, maybe his parents' money. The adrenaline high of a little bit of fame. And he's never had to face what true adulthood is like. He lives without consequence, and there's a good chance he always will.

I tap the top of his hand softly as I say, "I think that's great, Jax. I really do." Then I rest both hands back on the steering wheel, and I stare at him as I wait for him to get out of the car.

Eventually, he picks up the signal and opens the door. Before leaving, he leans over, presses his lips to my cheek, and softly whispers, "Night, sexy Sadie."

"Good night, Jax," I reply.

On the way home, I replay the entire night in my head. All in all, it was actually a pretty fun evening, but most of my recollection of it featured *him*. The way he kept talking about how smart I was. The way he constantly watched me. The palpable chemistry between us, even when we were there with other people.

There's a comfort I can't explain with Luke. A yearning just to be near him. I know he feels it, too. When I return to the house, I open the front door quietly, unsure of what environment I'm about to walk into. For all I know, he could be asleep, passed out in his room, or he could be up waiting for me. Perhaps in the mood to punish me for staying out too late, kissing someone else, or behaving as if I don't belong to him.

When I walk into the living room, I find Luke sitting on the couch. He's still fully dressed with his jacket and shoes on, reclining against the back with his legs splayed. He's staring at me as if he's lost, despondent, ruined, and I feel the pangs of pity in my chest.

I did this to him. *We* did this to him. This affair we've been having for the past three months is like a disease, and the symptoms are agonizing. Because I feel it, too.

I drop my purse on the bench by the door. Then I shuck off each of my shoes, tossing my coat on the rack before turning to stare at him.

Neither of us says a word until he softly mutters, "Come here."

I don't hesitate. I move like water sliding through rock. I'm hiking up my dress before straddling his lap on the couch. He doesn't move except for his hands, which glide softly up my thighs.

His eyes devour me like he's savoring every inch. As if he's glad I'm here.

"You came back," he whispers. His gaze doesn't leave my face.

"Of course I did," I reply.

"Why? Why would you come home to me, Sadie? I can't give you what you want."

My heart lurches as those words slice it in half. His hand reaches up to cup my cheek. The way he looks at me now, like he's *admiring* me, is like nothing I've ever felt before. I've never felt so seen.

I don't have an answer to his question. Because wanting a man I can't have bears no explanation, at least not a good one. So I shrug.

"I don't deserve you," he mumbles.

"Don't say that," I argue. It feels like we're crossing lines we haven't crossed yet. Are we finally at the precipice, ready to speak the unspoken truth? Our genuine feelings. Instead of brushing them under kinky behavior and sex.

"It's true, Sadie," he says, sitting more upright and pulling me closer. "I will never be a good husband or a good father. It's why I will never marry or have children. I refuse to disappoint someone the way my father disappointed me."

Tears sting my eyes as I stare at him. "That's why you don't want to settle down? Lucas, *fuck him.* Don't let his curse write your story. You're not him."

I watch him swallow as he stares at me with something that looks like hope on his face. "What if I let you down? What if I let you *both* down?"

"You could never let me down," I reply, leaning forward to press my forehead against his.

He tightens his grip on me.

"Tell me we can make this work, Sadie. And I'm yours."

There isn't an ounce of hesitation in my mind. "We can make this work."

"You and the baby could come to London," he says with a sense of renewed excitement.

"Or you could come visit here," I say. There's a tingle of hope crawling up my spine, like standing on the edge of something amazing.

As his gaze drops to my lips, I freeze. I'm ready to seal the deal. I want the intimate touch of his mouth on me more than I've wanted anything.

"I should have kissed you at midnight," he says as his hands glide slowly up my spine.

"We can make our own midnight," I reply in a gentle whisper.

He replies with a soft smile. "I like that idea."

"Then count down," I reply.

"Ten," he mutters as his touch drifts back down to my legs. "Nine, eight."

His fingers reach the hem of my dress.

"Seven, six."

He pulls it up, slowly revealing my body until he's tugging it over my head. I'm straddling his hips in nothing but a bra and black lace panties.

"Five, four."

I lean closer to him, my mouth just inches from his, as we whisper the last three together.

"Three, two, one."

"Happy New Year," I say as our eyes meet.

I barely get the words out before his hand is on the back of my neck, and he's crashing his lips against mine. His kiss is ravenous as we both moan into each other's mouths like wild animals that have been caged for too long.

He licks and sucks on every part of my mouth he can: my tongue, my lips, my face. I let myself drown in his kiss, closing my eyes as I throw caution to the wind, kissing him like this means forever.

Our lips are tangled for a long time. I don't think I've made out like this since high school. The entire time, I grind on top of him, and I feel his cock beneath me, quickly hardening as he grips my hips.

"Take your bra off," he commands, nodding toward my bra. His mouth is red and swollen, and I can't stop myself from crashing right back down for another kiss first. Then I reach behind and unclasp my bra, letting it fall off before flinging it to the floor.

Being this exposed with Luke doesn't make me feel insecure like it sometimes does with other men. He's fully clothed, and I'm almost naked on top of him.

When his eyes drift down to my breasts and then below to my belly, I know he's not scrutinizing the soft rolls at my hips or the stretch marks on my breasts. He licks his lips at the sight of me, and I know it's because he celebrates every perfect inch.

He doesn't even flinch at the sight of my swollen stomach as I grind myself on him. He urges me on, guiding me as I tilt my hips and seek friction on his now rock-hard cock.

I let out a whimper, and he squeezes me tighter.

"There you go," he mumbles softly. "Keep going."

I pick up speed as my head falls back, and I pinch my own nipples. Pleasure radiates from the pain, and with my eyes closed, I imagine him at the table tonight—watching me. I imagine he claims me. Calls me his. Tells everyone how smart I am. How beautiful I am. He tells everyone I'm his.

I grow breathless as I rock myself against him, shameless in pursuit of my orgasm.

"That's my girl," he whispers. "Show me how you get yourself off, Miss Green. Use my cock. It's all yours."

My response is a deafening, husky groan. Bringing my gaze

down to him, I stare into his eyes as I pinch my nipples, rubbing myself all over him like an animal in heat.

Even when I lean in to press my lips to his, he talks me through it, mumbling against my mouth.

"Don't stop," he whispers, dragging my body down harder on his stiff length. "Let me see you get yourself off."

I'm whimpering and moaning wildly, and when I finally reach the crest, my body explodes with sensation. It travels up my spine like fire, dousing me in ecstasy. I clutch tight to Luke's arm as my body seizes. I stop breathing as I ride out the waves while he watches.

I've barely come down before Luke reaches down and unbuckles his belt. I shift out of his way as he unbuttons his pants and tears down his zipper. His movements are rushed and desperate as he pulls out his cock and yanks me back up on his lap.

Tugging my panties to the side, he guides himself in and pushes my hips down until he's fully seated inside me.

The look on his face is both relieved and euphoric, as if not being inside me was torture for him. For a moment, he doesn't move, and neither do I. I feel his cock pulsing like he's struggling to keep himself from coming already.

Once he has himself composed, he grabs my hips again and guides my movement. I grind on him again, slowly at first, kissing him as I move. His hands meander their way around my body. Over my waist and around my belly, then up to my breasts and down the fleshy valleys of my sides.

Suddenly, his composure slips, and he loses control. Gripping my ass, he grinds me harder and harder on top of him.

"Tell me who the fuck you belong to," he mutters against my mouth.

His cock reaches so deep inside me that I feel myself coursing straight toward another climax. My body is buzzing for him, needing more, wanting more.

"You," I cry out.

"That's right," he says through the sounds of our bodies slapping together. Then he reaches out and grabs my face, forcing me to look at him. "And that's my fucking baby too, isn't it?"

Heat swells inside me. And there isn't a moment of hesitation as I cry out, "Yes."

"I'm the one who fills you up, Miss Green," he says as I move faster. "I am the one who makes you come."

My second climax hits me like a train—this one overwhelming and intense. It's like pleasure from the inside out.

As I'm screaming through the orgasm, Luke thrusts upward once, then twice, and stills as he empties himself inside me. His groans mingle with mine until we look and sound and feel like one.

When all is said and done, I collapse on his chest, pressing my face in his neck and breathing him in. My heart swells and beats against his.

There isn't a doubt in my mind now.

I love this man. Against all odds, I fell in love with the one person I wasn't supposed to.

And I think he did, too.

But loving him doesn't mean getting to keep him. In this case, loving him means eventually letting him go.

THIRTY-TWO

Lucas

Sadie rests in my arms for so long that I think she's fallen asleep. Her warm breath tickles my neck, and I don't have it in me to move her, no matter how much I want to kiss her again.

It's almost ironic how much more intimate a kiss is than what we've already done together. But it was so much more than a kiss. It was a vow. A declaration. It spoke volumes more than words ever could. More poetic than the most eloquent sonnet ever written.

Kissing her erased every shred of doubt in my mind. I love her.

I love her in a way that makes me think I've never loved anyone or anything before.

I love her in a way that makes me think I can have both. I can keep my job. I can go to England. I can do something important. I can make something of myself and still have her.

Eventually, she lifts her head from my chest and stares down at me sleepily with a happy smile on her face. Then she leans in and presses her soft pink lips to mine.

"Let's go to bed," I whisper when our kiss ends. She climbs from my lap and grabs a tissue from the table to clean up. Then I stand from the couch, taking her hand as I guide her back to my room. I quickly pull off my clothes and throw them into the laundry basket before climbing into bed next to her.

As soon as my head hits the pillow, she rolls closer, resting her head on my arm and draping her leg over me. When we lie together like this, I wonder how I went so long without her or how I thought I was going to live without her after this.

We kiss for a while longer, like a couple of teenagers, and it's not rushed or heated. It's kissing for the sake of kissing. When she finally pulls away, she rests her head on the pillow next to mine, staring into my eyes.

Softly, she asks, "Did you really mean what you said? Do you really think we can make this work?"

I run my fingers through the soft red strands of her hair. "I'm not sure there's any other choice," I reply.

Her brow furrows. "What do you mean?"

"I mean..." My voice trails as I let out a sigh. I'm not good at this. I don't know how to express what I'm feeling, which is ironic for someone who expresses a lot in writing, literature and poetry. I should be good at this. "I mean, I tried desperately to *not* want this. But I do. I want you. I want us, and I think we can make it work. I think if we try...I think if we really work at it."

"So you're still going?" she asks.

"Of course," I reply instantly. "I have to go, Sadie."

The expression on her face isn't entirely disappointed, but not hopeful either. It's somewhere far too neutral for my comfort. I can tell there are thoughts worrying in her head that are too complicated to express. But I'm giving as much as I can.

"Okay." She nods gently. "We'll make it work."

I lean forward and capture her lips again because speaking doesn't seem to work as well for me.

After a moment, she rests her head again on my arm, softly tracing her fingers around my chest.

"Can I ask you a question?" she says.

"Of course."

"Why are you so adamant about not wanting to get married or have children? What was it that stopped you?"

I've never given thought to this question at all. It's just always been something in the back of my head for as long as I can remember. But as I ponder it over in my head, I realize there is a moment that this question leads to in my memory.

But am I ready to be this vulnerable with her? Emphatically, the answer is yes.

"My father hated me," I say.

Immediately, Sadie tenses and glances those big green eyes up at me. "You don't mean that," she says.

"Yes," I reply, "I do. He hated me."

"Why would he hate you?"

"I don't know. To be honest," I start. "Probably because I wouldn't fall in line. I never believed anything he preached. I was argumentative. I never had faith. Not once in my life. I don't even know what it feels like. My brother Adam was the embodiment of faith. Caleb could fake it enough to get by, even if he didn't believe it. I was the difficult one when it came to religion. While my father spouted scripture, I retorted with logic, and he hated that."

"But he didn't hate you," she says.

"He did. On my thirteenth birthday, he beat me over the head with a Bible."

Her head snaps up again, her averted gaze on my face. "No."

I let out a heavy breath. "I argued with him, as I often did. And he usually responded with some authoritative discipline, often in the form of a backhand. But that day, he looked at me like he couldn't stand me. I could see it in his eyes. He wanted me gone."

Moisture brims in Sadie's eyes as she touches my face. "You didn't deserve that," she murmurs.

"It's okay," I reply softly.

"No, it's not. It's not okay, Lucas," she argues vehemently. She rests her elbow on the bed, propping up her head as she stares at me. "The way our parents treat us defines what we think we deserve. Your father mistreated you, and he made you believe that is what you deserve. And so you carried that with you your entire life, thinking you don't deserve love. You don't deserve a wife. You don't deserve a child because your own father never demonstrated that for you."

I've never felt such discomfort from words before in my life. How can something ring so true and be so painful at the same time? It makes me want to argue with her and tell her she's wrong; this isn't possible because I don't like it. I don't like the way the truth feels when it hits so hard.

I'm stroking her face softly as I gaze into her eyes. "How did you get so wise?" I ask.

"I'm not," she replies sadly. "I just..." She forces herself to swallow. "I think my parents were always disappointed in me, and it's taken me a long time to unlearn that."

My brow furrows as my spine tenses, goose bumps erupting across my skin. "How could anyone be disappointed in you?" I ask.

"They just never gave me very much attention, so once I found out I could get attention from boys... Let's just say there were some dark moments."

I stop breathing altogether. "What kind of dark moments?" My voice has gotten lower. My muscles are taut and uncomfortable. I don't like to think about anyone hurting her.

Her gaze bounces back and forth between my eyes for a moment as if she's working up the courage to speak. I run my hands up and down her arms softly, squeezing her closer, making her feel as safe as possible.

"You don't want to hear about this," she replies before looking down. I touch her chin and lift her face until our eyes meet.

"You don't have to tell me if you don't want to, but I will listen to you. No matter what," I say.

Her eyes don't leave my face as she breathes slowly. I think she wants to tell me whatever it is, so I wait as she works up the courage.

"I developed really early in my life," she says. "So, I noticed when I was really young that I liked the attention. As I got older, I liked to flaunt it."

Immediately, I don't like where this is headed, but I try my best to train my features not to show my discomfort.

"In high school, my friends and I would get into clubs because someone always knew one of the bouncers, so we would go all the time. That's where I would get the most attention. And I would make out with a couple of guys or dance with guys and get free drinks and it was always fun.

"But it progressively got worse. Until one weekend, I was out with some friends, and we caught the attention of a group of college guys."

My molars clench, and my blood feels like it's boiling in my veins. I don't know if I can listen to this. I want to go back in time and murder somebody already and I haven't even heard the whole story yet. I don't know if I need to. I think I know where this is going.

"Anyway, my friends sort of took off without me. And the guys just kept giving me drinks. And I liked it...at first."

Her voice cracks as she begins to cry.

"I think for a long time, I blamed myself for what happened. I shouldn't have been with them. I shouldn't have flirted so much. But I was young, and I didn't know any better. I had no idea what I was getting myself into. I mean, I don't even really remember much after we left the club. I just..."

I reach for her, holding her face as if I can protect her from something that has already happened to her.

"I just remember asking them to stop. I remember fighting against them, but I was too drunk. And the next thing I knew, I woke up alone in a hotel room. And..."

I can't bear to hear the rest. I feel like a coward. I pull her into my chest, her face in my neck as I squeeze her tight.

"I don't want to ever hear you say that that was your fault again. Do you understand me?" I say in a deep, scolding tone.

She nods against my chest and I feel her tears dripping against my bare skin.

"You didn't deserve that. That should have never happened to you."

She nods again, this time with a whimper as she sobs. My throat burns like needles. I've never felt so sick with rage in all my life. I don't know what else to say aside from *I'm sorry* so I mutter it quietly over and over again as I stroke her hair and her back. It's not fair that something so awful could happen to someone so perfect and innocent.

As her tears subside, she relaxes against my chest.

"I think that's why I always dated guys like Jax. Guys who were interested in my body first. I always thought that's what I deserved. I thought I could make them love me. So when we were at the bar last night, and you talked about how smart I was..." Her voice quivers with her tears.

"I said that because it's true," I say.

"I know. I've just never had anybody talk about me like that."

"Sadie, you deserve better," I say.

"I think I get that now," she whispers softly. After a few moments, she adds, "So that's why I always wanted to manage clubs and why I wanted to own one of my own. Because I wanted to give women like me someplace safe. Something we deserve. I wanted to change the world so that nobody ever had to go through what I went through."

"And you will," I say with encouragement. "Because that's the most noble fucking cause I've ever heard."

She laughs against my chest. "I don't know about that."

"It is. And I'm sorry for ever making you feel like you needed to do something different to be more important. Because that is important and you are so important."

She lifts up and presses her lips against mine again. "Thank you," she whispers.

"You don't need my approval," I add. "And you never did."

A soft smile stretches across her face. "No one has ever made me feel the way you do."

Suddenly, I remember all the times I berated her. Patronized her. Made her feel as if she needed me to somehow make her life better. And I realize now all of that was such bullshit.

I was the one who was a mess. And what I realize now is just how much I need her.

THIRTY-THREE

Sadie

The last week has felt like a dream—a dream I do not want to wake up from.

Jax has been ghosting me again, but honestly, I couldn't care if I tried. Most of the last six days have been spent in bed with Lucas. There have been more orgasms than I can count.

And if we're not screwing, we're kissing and talking. And it feels like the first real relationship I've ever been in.

We don't talk about the future, not yet, but it looms over us like a storm cloud on the horizon. I hate that he's still going to England, but I understand. This program is important to him, and I can support that—even if it means spending an entire year apart while I'm raising a baby and he's making his mark on the literary world.

Lucas believes he is meant for great things, and I believe that, too. I have faith that once his time with the program is done, he will come home and put me and the baby first. I believe that. I have to believe it because if I don't, it will ruin the greatest relationship I've ever been in.

Today is the first day of the spring semester. We each have a very busy day, so we drive separately to campus. The car ride alone is the most time we've been apart since New Year's Day. But I have a little something for him planned during our first class to make up for the time we're going to be apart today.

It might be a little diabolical of me, but it's just the first day. All he's really doing is passing out the syllabus and talking about all the essays and books we have to write this semester. He can handle a little distraction.

After parking in the student lot, I reach into my bag with shaky hands and pull out the toy Sage suggested. It's a U-shaped pink silicone vibrator and I did lengthy internet research to ensure it was safe for pregnant women. It takes a moment to figure out which way to put it in, and once I slide it into place, I pick up the small black remote and gently click it on.

I nearly fly out of my seat. The vibration is gentle but surprising since I feel it both inside and out. It feels so good it makes me want to skip class and enjoy it right here. But then I'd miss out on the best first day of school ever.

Our class is in the same lecture hall as last semester, so as I walk in, I veer subtly toward the front of the room first. Lucas is talking to another faculty member near his podium, but I shoot him a casual greeting before discreetly dropping the black remote next to his laptop. Thankfully, no one seems to notice.

Then, I find a seat in the fourth row, right in the middle.

And I take this specific seat for a reason.

Lucas looks up from the clipboard in his hands and notices me, his brow furrowing as he tries to figure out why I'm wearing such a mischievous grin and a new outfit. Crossing my legs under my desk, I bite my lip as I glance down at my class schedule for the semester, waiting for our class to start. The toy currently inserted inside me feels like such a dirty secret, and I'm so turned on by it.

I'm in a classic schoolgirl skirt and white button-down top. Something I definitely didn't have on this morning. I watch with a smirk on my face as he clears his throat to speak to the other professor.

If this is going to be my last semester with Dr. Goode, then I'm going to make it memorable.

A few moments later, the other students usher in, and our class is due to start. The other teacher he was talking to leaves, and Dr. Goode turns toward us, ready to start his lecture. Then his eyes trail down toward me, landing under my desk, where my legs are spread wide, and he gets a perfect view right up my skirt.

He freezes, and his eyes widen. I can see his jaw clench from here as he glances up at my eyes angrily. I'm going to be punished for this, and I cannot wait.

My eyes flash downward to the table, and his gaze follows. When he notices the black remote sitting there, he quickly snatches it and shoves it into his pocket. Then he glares at me and I can't keep the smirk off my face.

Luke struggles through his introduction, tripping over his words, trying his hardest to keep his eyes from between my legs. Every few minutes, I take pity on him and press my knees together so he can focus. But when I get bored with that, I simply let them drift open again, gently pulling up my skirt and scooting down in my seat to make his view even more tempting.

When the first few minutes go by and he doesn't turn the vibrator on, I start to feel a hint of disappointment.

I'm hardly paying attention to what he's saying, but as he starts a discussion with one of the students, I don't even notice him put his hand in his pocket.

As a burst of vibration hits my core, I let out a shriek and hop in my seat. It goes away quickly, but everyone in the room turns to gawk at me. I cover it up with a cough and notice Luke laughing to himself.

After a moment, he pushes it again. The setting is low and virtually silent, but it feels so good I struggle to sit still.

I watch his eyes trail toward me, gazing at me intently as I grip the edge of my desk and squirm in my seat. The vibration is a tease, and he knows it.

He moves to stand behind the podium instead of walking

around the front of the room like he normally does, and I know exactly why. I'm willing to bet he's pitching quite a tent down there.

I let my eyes close with my legs spread, enjoying the rapture of this feeling. It's a slow, subtle ride down a river of pleasure and I'm loving every second.

"Miss Green," he calls, and I pop my eyes open to stare at him. He reaches into his pocket and hits the button again to increase the intensity. I bite down a yelp.

"Yes?" I squeak.

"You read *Paradise Lost* last semester, didn't you?" he asks.

With a painful swallow and a quick fidget in my seat, I reply, "Yes."

"Would you like to share your thoughts on the religious allegory of Milton's poem?"

I clear my throat. "Um..."

He clicks it again. My legs slam closed, and I straighten my spine, trying to reconcile the room full of eyes on me and the unimaginable pleasure coursing through my pussy.

He lifts his brows, waiting for me to continue.

"I, uh..."

"Maybe another time?" he asks with a coy smile.

"Sure," I squeak. "Thanks."

He can't keep the grin off his face. Especially as the class continues their discussion but his eyes rarely leave me.

I can feel an orgasm building, tightening between my legs as I struggle to keep still and quiet. Eventually, I have to hang my head and pretend I'm reading the paper in front of me as pleasure assaults me in a tense, never-ending orgasm.

I'm breathing heavily through my nose as I hide what's happening to me on the inside. When I finally glance up, I notice him watching me intently before readjusting himself in his pants.

I can't help thinking about how hard his cock must be behind his zipper.

Then he reaches into his pocket and clicks the button again, shutting off the vibration, and I fall backward in my seat, satisfied and spent. The corner of his mouth lifts, but he manages to play it off with the rest of the class.

My legs fall open again and I catch him staring, probably enjoying how wet I am down there now. All I know is that I can't wait for my punishment.

When our class comes to an end, he is inundated with students asking him questions, a line trailing up the steps of the lecture hall. I choose not to wait in it, instead texting him that I'll be in the library studying as I slip out the door.

We have a regular table in the back corner of the library, and since it's only the first week of the semester, there are practically no students in here. Before taking a seat, I make a pit stop in the bathroom, pull out the vibrator, and quickly wash it in the sink before anyone can come in and find me. How embarrassing would that be?

Making my way back to the table, my hands are shaking from exhilaration. I can't believe I just did that. It takes about twenty minutes until I hear the sound of his shoes on the thin carpet in the library. I smile to myself as he approaches, more eager to see him than I've ever been.

"Get up," he mutters.

Glancing up through my lashes, I smile at him. "Hello, Dr. Goode," I say innocently.

He grabs my arm and makes more of a show of hauling me out of my seat than actually doing it, taking gentle care as he pulls me toward a dusty shelf in the back corner where there's no one around.

Grabbing my hand in his, he slams my palm against his cock so I can feel how hard it still is.

"Did you think that was cute?" he mutters under his breath playfully, even as he plays the part of a grumpy Dom. It's clear to me just how happy he is in this moment, and I eat it all up. "I had to walk across campus like this."

I giggle to myself just thinking about it and it only makes him more irate.

"There are consequences to your actions, Miss Green," he whispers.

"I know there are," I snap back in my bratty tone. Our voices are so quiet it's not even a whisper, but this library is quiet too. One little sound and I'm afraid we'd be heard clear across it. But we're hidden so far in the back among old sports magazines and encyclopedias nobody uses anymore that I'm quite certain we won't be caught.

"You did it just to be punished, didn't you?" he whispers against my lips.

"Yes," I breathe. "But, Dr. Goode, you can't punish me here. We're in a library."

"Watch me," he replies, playing along.

Silently, he slips the button of his pants open and quietly tugs down the zipper before pulling his cock out in his fist. I stare down at it as my mouth waters, the tip of his head leaking already.

I'd like to wrap my lips around it. I'd like to slip my tongue in the slit at the end.

"Look at you," he mutters as he strokes himself. "Look at how bad you want it."

"I do want it," I reply silently.

"This is a punishment, not a reward, Miss Green."

I let out a squeak of disappointment as I realize he won't even let me touch it, let alone take it in my mouth the way I want.

Instead, he strokes himself hard and makes me watch.

The whirring sound of the air conditioner overhead barely covers the slick cadence of his fist over his cock. I quickly peek around each corner to ensure no one is coming near us and we're alone.

I press my back against the wall of the endcap and I stare down, watching his fist move in rapid motion.

I once told Jax in our very first meeting how much I enjoyed watching videos of him masturbating, which was true at the time, but nothing compares to this. Making the man I love so turned on he can't help himself as he fucks his own fist in front of me.

His expression is almost tortured and pained, and it's so hot to me that I did this to him. I have to hold my breath to keep from moaning along as I watch him, waiting for him to make a mess all over my shirt.

"You are such a *bad* girl, Miss Green. You know that, don't you?" His features are tight and his teeth are clenched as he whispers those filthy words in the small space between us.

"Yes, I am," I reply. "So punish me, Dr. Goode."

When his lips part and his breathing slows, I know this means he's almost there. So I drop to my knees, open my mouth, and stick my tongue out for him. He glances around quickly to make sure nobody is watching before he unloads all over the surface of my tongue.

I'm rewarded with warm, salty jets of his release and a look of euphoric torture on his face; so much for this being a punishment. I'm loving every second. I gaze up at him with love in my eyes as I close my lips and swallow.

Standing with a wicked smile on my face, I help him tuck his cock back into his underwear and zip up his pants for him.

"You're gonna be the fucking death of me," he whispers before pressing his lips to mine. I couldn't stop smiling if I tried. Winding my arms around his neck, I pull him in, and we kiss for a long moment.

We can make this work, I tell myself again. We have to. There is no one else for me. I don't want another man. No one could ever measure up to what Luke and I have right now.

When he's fully composed, we go back to our table, and I pick up my books and things, shoving them into my backpack before we make our way toward the exit of the library together.

"When is your next class today?" he asks.

"In about forty-five minutes," I reply. "When's yours?"

"I have a faculty meeting around then," he says with a sigh.

"Soon, you'll be out of here," I say.

I wish I could link my arm through his. I wish we could intertwine our fingers, and I could kiss him goodbye as we separate.

Instead, I have to train my emotions not to reveal us. I can't be too smiley, too flirty, too affectionate. As we walk across campus together, I have to pretend that Dr. Lucas Goode means nothing to me.

My next class is in the math building, which is just past the English one. So we stop in front of his building before it's time to say goodbye.

But as we approach, I notice there is a horde of very official-looking faculty standing near the door. Chills run down my spine, especially when all four of them turn their gaze and stare at us.

Suddenly, I know something is very, very wrong. Luke can feel it, too. He tenses by my side, slowing his steps as if he can prolong the inevitable.

As we approach the bottom of the steps, a woman in a pantsuit steps forward, staring at Luke by my side.

"Dr. Goode," she says with a very stern tone. "Ms. Green," she adds, looking at me, and my blood runs cold.

"We will need to speak with you both immediately."

THIRTY-FOUR

Lucas

It wasn't fucking in our classroom.
And it wasn't me jacking off in the library.
It wasn't me spanking her over the desk.
It was fucking carpooling.

That's what tipped off the dean's office to our inappropriate relationship. *Carpooling.*

Sadie sits beside me in the chair of the office as we stare at a photo of us getting out of a car together in the student parking lot.

At the moment, my mind is frazzled, and I'm thinking of all of the things this fucking ruins. My job, my eligibility into the program, and Sadie's education. I can practically feel her fear radiating from her skin. I want to reach over and hold her hand, touch her back, hug her against me, and tell her everything is going to be okay.

"Dr. Goode, do you understand that this footage of you and one of your students was found on our security cameras? You understand that any physical and intimate relationship with your student is strictly forbidden at this university, don't you?"

"I understand," I reply flatly.

"I'm asking you now," he says, placing his hands on his desk. "Has there been an intimate and physical relationship between you and Miss Green?"

"No, sir," I answer emphatically, staring him in the eye. To my left, I feel Sadie's gaze shoot my way. He turns toward her.

"Ms. Green, has there been an intimate and physical relationship between you and Dr. Goode?"

She swallows and hesitates, her lips parting, and I watch.

"You understand you'll be questioned separately, but considering the nature of these accusations, I thought it best to bring you both in. I'm asking you both to be honest, but as you know, this could jeopardize your position here at the university."

"I understand," I mutter.

"Ms. Green, have you had an intimate relationship with Dr. Goode?" I watch the light die from her eyes as she stares at the floor.

"No, sir," she says.

"And I understand that you are currently pregnant?" he asks, his eyes glancing uncomfortably down to her stomach.

Softly, she nods as if she's ashamed, and it makes my blood boil.

"Then I assume this child is not Dr. Goode's?"

How could he accuse her of secretly carrying her professor's baby? The audacity.

"Correct," I say before she has a chance to respond. "It's not mine."

Sadie's shoulders slump away from her ears as she stares at the floor.

"Is that true, Ms. Green?"

"Will you please leave her alone?" I argue. "She's done nothing wrong."

She nods despondently anyway.

I can't help but feel as if I'm doing something wrong, but I'm trying to save her education and my career. Why do I feel like shit doing it?

That's not a lie; the baby isn't mine, and all we have to do is deny that we've had sex, and we'll be fine.

"I simply give Sadie a ride sometimes to campus. She's a family friend of ours, so we know each other from outside the classroom," I explain.

"I understand," the dean replies with a nod. "Ms. Green, do you have anything to add to this?"

She glances up from the floor and stares at his face a moment before turning toward me. Her gaze is piercing, and I feel it deep in my core.

"No," she replies without tearing her eyes away, making me feel about three inches tall.

And suddenly, I realize it. I'm a coward.

"Well, I'm relieved," the dean says as he sits back in his chair. "Dr. Goode, the university is very proud to have you on staff and thrilled about the work you'll be doing with the Stratford Project later this year. We would hate to lose you, so we appreciate your honesty in this matter.

"And, Ms. Green, I apologize for having to bring you in and putting you in this situation. Please accept my sincerest apologies."

Sadie nods softly before standing from her chair and bolting toward the door. It takes everything in me not to rush after her. Instead, I stand up and shake the dean's hand before saying my goodbyes and leaving his office.

Sadie is practically running. I have another class to attend today, but I need to see her first. I need to speak to her.

"Sadie, wait," I call when we reach the parking lot. She doesn't turn back. She doesn't respond. She's just marching angrily toward her car.

"Miss Green, stop!" I shout, but she doesn't listen. She gets to her car and tears open the door, and when she turns back to get in, I notice the tears streaking across her face.

"Sadie," I call with alarm.

Before she can slam the door on me, I grab it to keep it open.

"Leave me alone, Luke," she cries.

"What's wrong? Everything worked out fine. We got out of it."

"Oh, yes. Thank God for you, right? Thank God you still have your job." Her tone is laced with bitterness and rage.

"What?" I reply in shock.

"Since I know that is the most important thing to you, right, Luke?"

"Sadie," I say, "I need my job."

She bursts out of the car and stands chest to chest with me as she shouts.

"This isn't about needing your job, and you know it. This is about you thinking that you need your job. Because it is the most important thing in the world to you, right? It is the number one priority. Your job, your work, this program, how special it'll be, how you were made for this, and so much more, right? I was a fool for ever thinking that I could be one of your priorities ranked anywhere near the top. You're right, Luke. You lied to the dean, and you told him I meant nothing to you, and that was exactly what you had to do to keep your job.

"But you know, it made me realize something. It made me realize that I will never be everything to you. I will always come in second. I will always be the runner-up, and I deserve so much more. You can't even deny it because you know that it's true."

I'm staring at her dumbly, my mouth hanging open with no response. Probably because she's right.

"You think this is what I wanted? I told you I didn't want to be in a relationship, Sadie. I told you I couldn't be the man you needed," I argue, which was the wrong thing to say. She throws up her arms and rolls her eyes.

"No, Luke, I get it. You've told me before. You never wanted me. You never meant to fall in love with me. Being so in love with me is just a huge problem for you, right? Well, how about this?

How about I just make this so much easier for you? I won't be a problem anymore. How about that?"

"Sadie, please," I beg. The panic building inside me has me suddenly not caring that we're in a public place and people are watching. Suddenly, I don't give a shit about that. "That's not what I meant," I say.

"I don't care what you meant, Luke. You didn't mean any of it, right? You didn't mean to fall in love. You didn't mean for this to happen. You just wanted to work and fuck and go to England and be in your stupid project, right? You were never gonna put me first. You were never gonna sacrifice your work or this program for me. Meanwhile, here I am, in love with you, ready to give you everything. But all you were going to give me was a sliver."

"Sadie, stop," I say, feeling frantic and desperate. The words coming from her mouth terrify me.

"You tell me that I deserve so much more, but you were never going to give me everything, were you?" Her voice cracks and I have no response as the words trail, unfinished. "But this is what you do, Luke. You don't realize this power you have. You let women fall in love with you just so you can run away and break our hearts. You did try to warn me."

"Sadie," I whisper pleadingly, "I'll give you everything. I'm sorry."

"Yeah?" she asks, more tears streaming down her face. "Okay, prove it. Prove you'll give me everything."

But I don't move. I can't. I'm a coward.

"It's fine, Luke. It's okay to be married to your job. It's okay to want more from your life than raising someone else's baby. But next time you take in someone, offering to help make their life better, do not let that person fall in love with you. Do not do to somebody else what you've done to me."

"Can we please just talk about this when I get home?" I ask, reaching for her as she pulls away.

"I won't be there, Luke."

"What?" I ask.

"I'm moving out. This is over."

"Stop being so rash. This is ridiculous," I say.

"Is it? You're leaving anyway, right? What difference does it make? Why not just tear this Band-Aid off now before you're not just breaking my heart?" As she touches her stomach, she adds, "And his too."

I stand numbly as she climbs into her car and slams the door. Even as she pulls away and speeds out of the parking lot, I can't move. I feel paralyzed. I feel numb.

And I realize...this is what heartbreak feels like.

THIRTY-FIVE

Sadie

It doesn't take me long to pack up my things. I didn't bring much, but as I glance around the house with my bags at my feet, I realize how much I accumulated. Memories. Lessons. Love.

These are the things I wish I could leave behind, but they're coming with me whether I like it or not.

While I'm packing, my anger subsides and is replaced with grief. I'm not angry at Lucas for lying to the dean and protecting his career. It was never about that. It was about always putting his career first, and that isn't his fault—it's mine.

Because I knew. He did try to warn me. He made it clear from the start that he would never have a wife or family because he would always put his work first. I was just the fool who thought I could change him. I thought I could be the exception.

As it turns out, neither of us have changed at all—he's still Dr. Goode and I'm still the fool who finds love in all the wrong places. Idiotic Miss Green.

When the door flies open, I scream and turn to find Lucas frantically rushing in. He's disheveled and worked up, his eyes wide with shock as he marches toward me with his hands up in surrender.

"Sadie, please," he begs, his gaze flashing downward toward the bags at my feet. "Don't be so impulsive. We can work this out."

"How, Luke? You're moving to England and I'm having a baby. We both have bigger priorities than each other."

"That's not true," he argues.

"Yes, it is," I reply. "It was a fling, Luke."

"No, it wasn't," he barks as if I've just offended him. Stepping toward me, he takes my hands and stares into my eyes. I've never seen him look so scared and broken. He's always Mr. Composed and Confident.

And for a moment, I consider listening. I could just nod my head and agree that we could work it out even though I know that we won't. I could let him put his arms around me and kiss me and it would feel so, *so* good, but for how long? Until May, when I'm laboring alone, and he's off in another country living his dreams?

I pull my hands away and take a step back. My eyes are raw with tears as I stare at him.

"I asked you to help me get my life together. To help me make better decisions, and you did exactly what you were supposed to."

His shoulders melt downward, the look on his face despondent and grief-stricken. Because he knows I'm right.

This is the right decision, and for once, I'm the one making it.

"I have to go," I whisper.

"Where?" he asks. "Let me at least get you a place. I'll find you somewhere to rent, and I'll pay."

I shake my head. "I need to do this on my own."

Picking up my bag, I sling it over my shoulder and walk toward the door. I feel Lucas's eyes on me the entire way, but I fight the urge to turn around. I'm afraid if I look back, I'll never leave.

My mother is taking my return with more sympathy and compassion than I expected. I really thought I was going to return to a whole lot more *I told you so* than I did.

Instead, she wrapped her arms around me and just let me cry into her shoulder. Then she brought me into the kitchen and sat me at the table to make my favorite comfort food—grilled cheese and tomato soup straight from the can.

"You ready to talk about it?" she asks as she takes a seat at the table across from me.

"I told you," I reply. "Luke and I just didn't get along. We're too different to live together."

"I wasn't born yesterday, Sadie. It was more than living together."

I glance up from my soup as I stare at her in surprise. Before I can respond, she continues.

"I saw the way he looked at you at Thanksgiving. If you really were just friends, he wanted to be far more."

Looking back down, I swallow the emotion building in my throat. "Well, unfortunately, he doesn't have room in his life for anything more than friends. He wasn't willing to put me above his work."

"So you left him?" She sounds surprised, and I'm ready to defend my actions and explain *why* I wouldn't settle for less when a smile splits across her face.

Hesitantly, I nod. "Yeah. I didn't want to be second best."

My mom reaches over and places her hand on mine. "That's my girl."

I stare at her, stunned for a moment. "You're not disappointed?"

"Disappointed? Honey, I'm *proud*. You should be the top priority."

At that, I can't help but scoff and pull my hand away.

"What?" she asks.

I can't bear to look her in the eye as I mindlessly stir my soup. "It's just..." The words get caught in my throat, unable to come out. So I have to force myself to say what I've always wanted to say. "You and Dad always put Jonah first. I always felt like second best."

My mother gasps. "Sadie June Green, is that really what you think?"

"It's how I felt," I reply, looking into her eyes.

"Honey, I'm so sorry we made you feel that way." Tears well in her eyes as she reaches a hand toward me again. "You were *never* second best to anyone. You were our first baby. Our beautiful, headstrong, funny little girl. And when your brother came along, we loved you both equally. I'm sorry if sometimes it felt like we celebrated Jonah's accomplishments more. That was wrong of us. The worst thing about parents is that we're people too.

"You'll learn this soon, but we mess up sometimes. We do the wrong thing, and most of the time we don't know it was the wrong thing until it's too late. We try not to mess our kids up, and in some way, we always fail. But no matter what, we always love. That's the easy part."

A tear slips over my lips as my hand goes to my stomach. She seems to notice because she grabs a tissue from the table and brings it to me, crouching down in front of me. As she wipes my tears, she places a kiss on my forehead.

"I'm so sorry, Sadie. I couldn't be more proud of who you've become. And I know you're going to be such a fantastic mother."

I wrap my arms around my mom's neck and hug her tight. She squeezes me back and it feels like the first real hug we've had since I was a kid.

After lunch, I go into my room and lie on my bed. But it doesn't feel like mine anymore.

As I lie here, I think about what my mom said. There are probably a lot of ways I'm going to mess this up, but one thing is for sure. This baby will never doubt my love a day in his life.

Thirty-Six

Lucas

"I'm sorry," I mutter into the phone. "I'm still under the weather. Can you have someone continue to cover my classes?"

"Of course, Dr. Goode," the woman on the line replies. "We'll go ahead and get you covered for the rest of the week. If you could please keep up correspondence with your students via the classroom portal, that would be great."

I rub my forehead, stifling a groan. "Of course."

"Feel better soon, Dr. Goode," she says in a chipper tone.

I hit the end call button without a response. Setting my phone down on the coffee table, I recline on my couch with a glass of whiskey resting in my lap. Half-eaten cartons of Thai food are scattered across the coffee table, right next to a group of empty beer bottles, stationed like sentinels at my feet.

They keep me from feeling too much. Not everything, though. I wish they could protect me from feeling everything, but the regret and loneliness still seem to slip through from time to time.

Sadie left two weeks ago. For the first few days, I was able to pretend I was okay. I even managed to teach for a couple of days. But every chance I could, I reached for the bottle and by the weekend, I dove headfirst into the swamp.

Then, I started wallowing, and now I'm on day nine of this spell, and at this point, I wallow on a professional level. I've made a living in this swamp.

I've even taken to writing humiliating and depressing poetry. Burned that as soon as I woke up the next day. Turns out there was nothing romantic about the old drunk poets of the past—just pathetic misery.

I miss her so much it hurts. I miss the way she hummed songs, even in the silence. I miss the way she danced when she ate. I miss her fucking shoes kicked all over the house.

"Lucas."

I must have fallen asleep because I peel my eyes open to find my shirt cold and wet from the whiskey I spilled and someone standing over me, silhouetted by the TV playing behind them.

He slaps his hand over his chest, gasping for air as if I've somehow scared him.

"Jesus, I thought you were dead. You scared the shit out of me."

Wincing, I force myself to sit up and face my younger brother, who is somehow standing in my living room.

"What are you doing here?" I ask. "You don't live here anymore."

"Maybe I should..." he mumbles as he scans the current state of my house. "Look at this place."

"I'm not feeling well this week so housework has fallen a little behind."

"A little?" he snaps. Then, he glances around the house. "Where's Sadie?"

"She left," I groan.

"Left..."

"She left me," I say as I lean forward, squeezing my eyes shut and wishing my headache away. I'm still too drunk to be hungover, but lucky me, I seem to be caught between both states at the moment.

"Oh no," Isaac murmurs. He sits on the couch next to me as he places a hand on my back. "Luke, I'm sorry."

I swipe his hand away. "I'm fine. It was nothing. Just a fucking fling. I'm not really a relationship guy anyway."

"So you're not drunk and living in squalor because of a bad breakup?"

"What?" I grunt. "No. That's ridiculous."

"Sure, it is," he replies like he doesn't quite believe me. "I'm going to make coffee and open some fucking windows. It smells in here."

I lie back down on the couch and cover my eyes as Isaac tears open the curtains and throws open the windows to let some light and fresh air in. Immediately, I hate it. I want to vomit or cry or yell or something.

It's the middle of the fucking day and I'm drunk, trying to hide in the dark. How goddamn depressing.

But then I smell coffee and it gives me a small thread of hope. My stomach growls like it's hungry and I welcome the warm mug my brother hands me.

"Tell me everything."

So I do. I try to play it off as something casual that doesn't matter, but quickly, it turns into something more serious. And by the end, when I'm telling him how she left, my voice is cracking from emotion.

"Damn, Luke."

That's all he says, and I don't know if he means it as *you really fucked up* or a show of sympathy, but it hurts either way. Because *damn*.

"So, what's your plan?" he asks.

"Wallow my way through the hard part, I guess," I reply. "It'll go away eventually, right?"

He shrugs. "I don't know. I've never been in love. Do you want it to go away?"

Fuck no.

"What choice do I have?" I ask as I take a sip of the coffee.

"I think that's pretty obvious."

Is it?

"Sadie left because I'll never measure up to the man she deserves. She's literally better off without me," I say.

"No, she left because you care about your work more than her."

"That's not true," I argue.

"Isn't it? You're still going to England. You denied a relationship with her to save your job. Luke, you're a genius, but not when it comes to relationships. If you want Sadie back, then you need to show her that she means more than your job."

Setting the cup down on the table, I bury my hands in my hair. "You don't get it. My work is my whole life. My work is who I am."

Isaac doesn't speak for a moment and when I look up at him, I notice the tight-lipped way he's holding back.

"What? Say it," I mutter.

"Don't get mad at me," he replies.

My brows pinch inward as I glare at him. "No promises."

With a sigh, he shrugs. "Fine. I was just going to say...this whole workaholic thing you have reminds me of someone."

"Who—"

I don't even get the question out before I realize, and it steals the air from my lungs. Not because he's being cruel or mean but because he's right.

Our father.

He always put his work before us. It was what defined him. His legacy was his everything. He was Icarus who flew too close to the sun, and while we all reveled in watching him burn, it was too late. The damage was done.

Our entire childhood was tainted by the way he treated us. All of us. And while I've hated him more than anyone on this earth, it didn't stop me from following in his footsteps.

"I'm sorry. You okay?" my brother asks with a wince.

"No," I groan as my head falls forward. "I just realized I'm no better than Truett Goode, and I need a minute."

Isaac slaps a hand on my back. "Well, that's not entirely true," he says with a laugh. "You're not a hypocritical, self-indulgent homophobe."

"No, but I don't want to end up like him."

"What, in prison?"

"No," I reply. "Alone."

"Well then, I think you have some groveling to do."

✝

After Isaac leaves, I pick myself up off the couch. Still more than a little drunk, I stumble my way around the house, picking up garbage and dirty clothes as I go.

My life fell apart when I was sober, so it's ironic that drunk me is able to start piecing it back together.

As I'm cleaning, I can't stop thinking about what Isaac said. Am I really turning into my father? Deep down, did I always know how much like him I am? That's why I tried to spare anyone else from spending their life with me. I refused to treat the people I love the way he did.

Dismissive. Abusive. Manipulative.

I didn't run away the same way Isaac did, but I did run away. And I've been running ever since. Even when I returned to Austin, I was never fully present, at least not with my family.

Which means all the things I wanted to say to him have been left unsaid. Years and years of resentment and anger and hurt have just been lying dormant inside me since I was a kid. And rather than face it, find closure, and heal, I've been silent.

But I'm done being silent now.

✝

I've never been to a prison in my life. Growing up in a quote-unquote *good Christian family*, there was never an opportunity.

So, as I sit at the round metal table in the visitors' center of the Hill Country Penitentiary, I feel more out of place than I've ever felt in my life.

After Isaac's visit yesterday, I took a day to sober up and get my shit together. Then I drove up here with a headful of rehearsed lines I wanted to say to him. Right now, those lines are getting jumbled in my head. They sounded so eloquent when I practiced them in the car.

When the door opens, and they usher my father through the opening, I feel my stomach turn. He's not in cuffs or chains, but there is a guard at his side. I hardly recognize Truett as he walks toward me. He's a shell of the man he once was.

I used to think of my father as a mountain, strong and immovable. But now, with the dark circles under his eyes and barely any meat left on his frame, he looks like a weak, dying tree that could break with the smallest gust of wind.

His expression is guarded, staring at me with his brow furrowed as he takes a seat across from me at the table.

"What happened?" he asks, his voice a raspy crackling sound. For a man who once delivered sermons and shook walls with his verses, it's just another example of how far he's fallen.

"What do you mean?" I ask.

"Is it your mother? Is she okay?" He leans forward, his arms on the table as his gaze bores into me.

"Mom's fine. Why?" I'm genuinely perplexed, and I hate that he spoke first. I wanted the upper hand in this conversation.

He leans back and narrows his eyes. "Why are you here?"

"I want to talk to you," I say.

My father and I are strangers. I never realized it until now, but he and I have probably never been in a room alone together since I was a small child, and even then, I'm not entirely sure. We've never had a private conversation, and I can't remember the last time he looked me in the eye as long as he is now.

It's unnerving.

"I'm the only son who will still talk to you," I say as the realization dawns. That's why he thought I was here to deliver bad news. Adam and Caleb would both wring his neck before saying a word to him, so when he heard it was me, he assumed I was here to say something neither of them could.

He doesn't reply to that. Just sits back and crosses his arms.

"What do you want, Lucas?" he mutters indignantly.

What do I want?

All the lines I rehearsed vanish as I stare at him across the table while two guards watch us in silence.

"Four sons and the only one who will talk to you is the one you hate the most," I say with a hint of humor in my tone.

His brow furrows deeper. "I don't hate you. How could you say that?"

This time, I laugh, and one of the guards tenses.

"You've hated me my whole life. That's if you bothered to even consider me that much. Every time I opened my mouth around you, you looked ready to knock my lights out. Sometimes you almost did. Remember those times, Dad? When spankings turned into punches? All because I had the audacity to speak my mind around you."

His expression doesn't change, even as a fire begins to brew inside me.

"Is this why you're here? To remind me of what a terrible father I am? Adam and Caleb have already delivered that message, Lucas. I don't need to hear it again."

"You really were a terrible father," I say. "So, why did you have us? Why have *four* kids if you didn't want us? You could have been a great man. Maybe nobody would have faulted you for your vices if you had an ounce of humility, but you hurt the five people who loved you most. The people you were supposed to protect. So I guess I'm just here to understand...why?"

For the first time since I sat down, he seems to let his guard down. It's as if he realizes I'm not here to attack him but to just understand him. He lets out a deep breath I'm sure he's been holding for a long time.

"I wanted to be a good father, Lucas. When Adam was born, I really did think I was going to be the best father. Then, you two were born, and then..." His voice trails as he thinks of Isaac, and something inside me stiffens. I breathe a sigh of relief when he doesn't utter his name. I hate that my brother even exists in my father's head, so I don't know if I could bear to hear him speak about him.

Truett lets out another sigh as he leans forward and rubs a hand over his face. "I loved my boys." When his voice cracks, I fight the urge to flee. The last thing I want to do is hear my father cry like a victim in any of this.

"But I wasn't the father I wanted to be. And there were days I regretted having you. I considered leaving. But then I would show up at the church, and everyone loved me. Do you understand what that's like, Luke? To find more joy in your work than your own family? It was more powerful than I could have imagined."

"It's all you cared about," I mutter under my breath.

To my surprise, he nods. "It is all I cared about."

The rage inside me boils hotter but as I glance up and look into his eyes, seeing him for what he really is—a man who never should have been a father, the fire starts to die off.

As a son, to hear this hurts. To know my own father didn't want me. He loved *something* more.

The fact that he's finally owning up to his own behavior shakes me to my core.

I bury my fingers in my hair and let my head hang forward. Right now, the world feels so heavy, it's practically pulling me under. How could I have almost promised myself to Sadie with even a sliver of a chance that I could end up like this?

"I don't want to be like you," I growl into my hands.

To my surprise, my father lets out a chuckle. Which turns into a laugh, and when I peek through my fingers with confusion, I find him smiling and it's the most perplexed I've ever been in my life.

"You? Like me?" he says with a laugh.

"What's so funny?" I say with annoyance.

"Lucas, of all my kids, *you* were the least like me. Adam, sure. I could see Adam following in my footsteps, and even Caleb had a mean streak I recognized, but you? If your twin brother didn't look so much like me, I'd have thought you were another man's child."

"Well, bad news. I'm a workaholic, and guess who I got that from," I snap.

"I wasn't a workaholic," he says, which only grates on my nerves. Just as I'm about to argue with him for trying to escape the blame once again, he holds up his hands in surrender. "It wasn't my work I loved. It was the fame. The attention. The *power*. I didn't give a shit about the work."

"Wow..." I say as I shake my head. "Prison has really beat the humility out of you, hasn't it?"

He shrugs with defeat. "What the fuck do I have to lose now? You think I care anymore? I have nothing left, Lucas. So yeah...I can admit now what I've done wrong."

Neither of us speak for a moment. All of this is so hard to take in. It's so incredibly foreign to hear my father talk about himself in a way that isn't dripping with self-righteousness.

"Why are you all of a sudden so worried about being like me?" he asks, but before he can answer, his mouth forms an *O* shape as if he suddenly realizes. "You're about to be a father, aren't you?"

"Maybe," I reply. "I want to be."

It's the first time I've really admitted that out loud, and it feels good. I want to be with Sadie, and I want to raise this child with her. He might not biologically belong to me, but it feels like we've made him together. So much so that there's an ache in my chest for him. Something I've never felt before in my life.

"What the hell are you so worried about, then?" he asks with a shake of his head. "You've clearly expressed everything I did wrong. So, do the opposite."

"It's not that easy," I argue.

"Sure it is," he replies, and I immediately hold up my hand.

"I'm not taking parenting advice from you."

He puts his hands up in surrender before continuing. "All I was going to say is..." But then he pauses, and a tense silence fills the space as we stare at each other. "Being a father is easy, if you try. Just look him in the eye. Don't make him afraid of you. Listen to him when he talks. And tell him you love him. That's it."

I'm not taking parenting advice from my father. Ever.

But...him just advising me to do everything he *didn't* do as a father does ring with truth.

Neither of us say anything for a while. We sit in tense silence.

"Time's up," the guard says as he steps behind me, putting a hand under my father's arm.

We don't bother with goodbyes or other sentiments. He puts the familiar scowl back on his face as he's carted away from me.

For the first time in my life, I feel like I can finally put something behind me. Hearing Truett admit to what he did wrong as my father is just the first small step in healing, but it's enough to take the step forward I need.

THIRD
TRIMESTER

THIRTY-SEVEN

Sadie

My mother sets a gift bag on my lap. With over thirty people watching excitedly, I reach my hand in to retrieve a tiny white onesie covered in orange ducks. There's a collective *aww* through the crowd as I hold it up to show everyone.

The onesie is so small it practically fits in my hand. It's hard to believe somebody will be wearing this. I drape the onesie over my round stomach as I reach in to pull out the rest of the gifts in the bag. It's a tiny bathrobe, a yellow baby towel and a pack of itty-bitty washcloths.

Smiling at the front of the room, I thank my aunt for the gifts —while silently wondering to myself why on earth a baby needs his own towels and washcloths in the first place.

I'm surrounded by gifts and diapers. There's a cake by the window covered in yellow flowers. I tried to tell my mom I hate the color yellow. But she insisted that since I wasn't going to find out if the baby was a boy or a girl, it was either yellow or gray.

Honestly, I would have preferred gray. I could have tried to explain to her that a boy can wear a pink onesie and a girl can wear blue pants. But it would have been futile.

Speaking of futile, my gaze scans the crowd once again. But of course, he's not here. When Sage and Adam offered to host the baby shower in the rec room of his church for free, I agreed, knowing there'd be a small chance he could turn up.

You can take the girl out of hopeless, but you can't take the hopeless out of the girl—or however that saying goes.

It's been a little over a month since I left Luke's house. Another professor has been covering his courses. I transferred out of his class, and I deleted his number from my phone to resist the temptation to call him back. In fact, the shower today is probably the first time I've even bothered putting on makeup since we ended things.

I did the right thing. I know I did.

But it still hurts.

I guess that's the thing about being an adult that nobody really warns you about. Mature decisions suck. Indulgent immaturity is way more fun.

I'm just a little bitter that while I'm sitting here wallowing in self-pity, he's probably packing up and getting ready for the adventure of his life.

I thought being excited about the baby would distract me from missing Luke, but during the first half of my pregnancy, Luke was part of this. It felt like we were on this journey *together*. So now every doctor's appointment and kick from the baby just reminds me that he's not here.

Once I've gotten through all the presents, I stand from my chair and stretch my arms up to the ceiling. This baby is taking up so much room already, I have no idea how I still have two months to go.

According to the baby books, he is roughly the size of a zucchini. Which is impossible because it looks like I'm carrying about a hundred zucchinis right now.

"You hungry?" Sage asks as she rests a hand on my back.

"No thanks, I'm good," I reply. Faith is sleeping in a bundle against her chest, wrapped in a swathe of cotton. I'm a little jealous at how naturally Sage seems to be transitioning to motherhood. It helps that she has a supportive, loving husband and partner to carry the load.

Meanwhile, I'll be doing this alone and struggling while still living at my parents' house. My situation feels less like stepping into motherhood and more like being thrown off the side of a cruise ship with my ankles tied while taking care of a baby.

My excitement has turned into apprehension. Every day, my mother keeps asking if I want to go stroller shopping or to pick out a crib, and I have zero motivation to do any of that. I don't want to set up a crib at my parents' house.

Sage's sister-in-law, Briar, approaches with her daughter Abby by her side. Something tightens in my chest being around these two. Sage is my best friend, and I really like Briar, but they're each married to one of Luke's brothers. And that reminder feels like an alarm going off inside me.

It's like feeling as if I belong and don't belong at the same time. For a moment, I thought I could be Lucas's wife. I thought we had a future together. It was brief, but it was there, and it was more exciting than anything.

And I walked away from that—for my own good.

A pair of tiny hands press against my stomach, and I look down at Abby as she smiles up at me, waiting for the baby to kick.

"Abigail," her mother scolds, "you have to ask permission before you touch somebody, honey."

"Sorry," she says. "Can I touch your belly?" she asks without ever taking her hands off in the first place.

I chuckle. "Yes, of course."

I give the baby a gentle poke from underneath, which usually gets him or her to do a little kick. When Abby feels it, her eyes widen with excitement.

Briar smiles softly at me. "Thanks for inviting us. You look beautiful."

"Thanks," I reply. "I'm glad you could make it."

In the corner, the men are standing together, Caleb, Dean, and Adam, each with a beer in their hands.

I was adamant to Sage and my mother that I didn't want a traditional baby shower. No silly games. Even the men could come if they want. And yes, maybe underneath all of that was some ulterior motive in hopes that Lucas might show up.

But apparently, that was being too hopeful.

For all I know, he could have left already. Even though the semester isn't over, and as far as I know, he's still teaching, although I haven't seen him.

But he could also be out with a hot English teacher, or he could be on a plane to England, or he could be sitting in his house alone with jazz playing on the record player and a book in his hand with a glass of whiskey by his side. What hurts is that I have no idea which one it is.

Briar, Sage, and Abby disperse, leaving me to peruse the food table alone. When I glance up through the window of the rec room and see a familiar man standing in the parking lot with his back to me, I freeze. As I watch him, my heart begins to hammer in my chest and I'm flooded with sickening hope.

"Stop it," I scold myself quietly. "He's not here for you. Nothing has changed."

And yet, I can't stop myself as I turn from the food table and walk toward the door. He turns to face me right as I step outside, and our eyes meet.

All of the days since we have seen each other suddenly feel insurmountable. His eyes trail down to my stomach and back up to my face.

"Hey," he says casually.

"Hey," I reply.

"You look great," he stammers.

"Thanks."

I don't quite know what this is, so I don't know how to behave. Is he here as a friend? Did he stop by just to say hello? Do

I mean nothing to him? I don't have it in me to hope for anything more, so I force myself to stay neutral.

"I didn't know if I should come," he stutters, "but I just thought..." His voice trails as if he doesn't know what else to say.

I stare at his face and remember what it felt like to kiss those lips. I wish I could feel his arms wrapped around me one more time.

I wrap my arms around myself, like a reflex, even though it's not cold. A bit chilly for March in Texas, but nothing near as cold as this interaction between us.

Part of me wants to ask about the program and if he's excited about it, but I stop myself. I don't think I can bear to hear about it.

Instead, I blurt out something I know he will want to hear.

"I changed my major."

He freezes and stares at me with his mouth hanging open. "You did?"

"Well, sort of. I added English as a minor. Apparently, it was enough for me to apply for that grant. Not sure it makes up for how many more classes I have to pay for," I add with a laugh. "But I like my literature classes. And my new professor thinks I'm pretty good too."

I notice the way his jaw clenches, and I smile to myself.

Making him jealous was always my favorite.

"I'm proud of you," he says, looking at the ground and scratching the back of his neck.

"Thanks," I reply softly.

"And you and Jax...you've worked things out?"

I let out a scoff. "God, no. He's ghosting me again, so I think he might have changed his mind about wanting to be a dad."

Lucas does his best to tone down his reaction, but I can see the way his eyes roll. He shoves his hands in his pockets to hide the way they're clenched.

"You're better off without him," he says.

"Yeah, I know."

We stare at each other for a moment, and I can't help but feel like he wants to say something else, but he hesitates.

"Sadie..." he starts.

"Sadie, honey!" my mom calls from the door, and I turn to find her waving at me. "People are leaving. You should come say goodbye."

"I'll be right there," I reply. Turning back to Luke, I force myself to back away when what I really want is to run into his arms. "I should go."

He clears his throat. "Yeah." Then, with a quick shake of his head, he adds, "Wait. I brought you something." He holds up the package in his hand. It's shaped like a book, no surprise.

"Thanks."

After another moment of hesitation, he takes a step back.

So I do, too.

It feels like a mile.

Then he steps closer to me again, and my heart picks up speed. "Can I call you later?"

I open my mouth to reply. *Yes. Please.* But then I remember why I left in the first place.

"You're still leaving, though..." I reply sadly.

"It's complicated," he replies, and I just nod in understanding.

"I'm sure it is." Nodding, I take a step back. "It was good to see you."

He surrenders, letting his hands fall to his sides. "You too, Miss Green."

A buzz of warmth shoots down to my stomach at the sound of him calling me that. No matter how much I want to stay here with him, I pull myself away.

It feels like the hardest step I've ever taken, but at the end of the day, I'm proud of myself. I'm finally advocating for the love I think I deserve. He should be proud of me, too.

Even if it costs us everything.

THIRTY-EIGHT

Lucas

"You just gave her a book and left?" Isaac asks from across the living room.

My elbows are on my knees, with my hands buried in my hair. "I'm not good at this, Isaac," I groan.

"Clearly," he replies sarcastically. "Did you tell her you were quitting your job?"

"No. She just changed her major to my program. I don't want this to distract her."

"Fair, but you have to do something to show her you've changed," he says.

"She'll have to talk to me first," I reply.

"Well, you're not going to accomplish that by sitting here with me," he argues.

"Apparently, I'm not going to accomplish it standing in front of her either," I say with a moan.

"Come on, Luke. If you quit your job and turned down the chance of a lifetime for her, I think she'd like to know!"

"Stop yelling at me," I snap.

"Nice try, brother, but you can't just boss me around. And

right now, you need to hear this." Isaac breaks out in laughter. "It's kinda funny when you think about it. She came to you so you could help her get her life together, and now you're the one whose life is a mess. That's a coincidence."

"It's called irony," I reply with a grimace.

"Whatever."

"And I'm fully aware of how ironic this is," I mutter into my hands. Picking up my phone, I pull up our text thread and stare at it aimlessly. "Should I text her?"

"Fuck texts. You should go see her."

"I can't just show up at her house," I say. "I don't even know what the fuck to say."

"Start on your knees," Isaac says distractedly. My head snaps up to glare at him as he rolls his eyes.

"I didn't mean it like that. I meant that you have some begging to do, brother."

It feels wrong when I think about it, picturing myself on my knees for her. Kneeling is submitting. It's relinquishing control to someone you trust, and I trust Sadie more than I've ever trusted anyone in my life, but handing over control? That isn't something I can do so naturally.

And yet she's done it for me countless times. She trusted me to never hurt her too much. To never make her feel inferior or unappreciated. She trusted me with so much. And not just in a physical way, but she trusted me with her life. To help her. Guide her. Care about her.

And what did I do in return?

I put myself before her. I prioritized my *fucking job* when a perfect living, breathing, beautiful human wanted my devotion.

Fuck, I need to do more than kneel for her. I'd set myself on fire just to keep her warm.

But she never asked for anything so dramatic. No, what she asked for was so much more simple than that.

What is wrong with me?

I shove my phone into my pocket.

"You're right," I say as I bolt to a standing position. "I need to see her. Now."

Isaac looks up in shock from the baby name book she left behind. "That's more like it. What are you going to say?"

"I'll start with I'm sorry and see where it goes from there."

"Good start," he replies. "I'll get out of here in case you two come back here to *rekindle* things." He makes a squeamish face as he drops the book on the table and stands. As he grabs his keys from the table, I pause and give him a concerned look.

"Are you sure you're okay being alone?" I ask.

Shooting me a perplexed look, he replies, "I'm always alone, Luke."

For some reason, that comment slices me open like a knife. I'm always alone, too. But I don't want to be alone anymore, and it's the first time I've actually accepted that.

I don't want to be alone anymore.

In fact, the idea sends chills down my spine because what if she doesn't accept my apology? What if it's not enough for her, and she doesn't take me back? Then, I will be stuck alone forever. Something I once dreamed of now feels like my worst nightmare —all because of her.

Isaac seems to notice my heavy expression. "You okay?"

Solemnly, I nod. "Yeah. Or...no, I guess."

"Crystal clear," he retorts sarcastically.

As he tries to walk past me, I grab his arm to stop him. "You don't have to be alone, you know? Just because you don't want the family we were given doesn't mean you can't find a new one."

Isaac's expression turns serious, which isn't all that common for him. So, I appreciate the lightness in his eyes.

He turns them down to the floor as he uncomfortably mutters, "I know that. It's just not easy dating as a closeted country musician with trauma and emotional baggage."

"I don't believe that at all," I reply.

As he turns his gaze back up to my face, he forces a tight smile. "Thanks, and for what it's worth...it's not that I don't want the family I was given. In fact, I was thinking...maybe soon, I could... you know..."

My molars clench and something inside me tightens. I've come to recognize this as my protective, territorial side. Because I know what Isaac is implying—he's thinking about coming back into the fold of our family. Reuniting himself with Caleb and Adam and even our mother in more familial, less-guarded circumstances.

I don't know how I feel about this. I've had Isaac to myself for so long; I don't want to lose this. He's mine. My little brother. And it's been my job to keep him safe for the past ten years, but can I really keep him safe? And for how long?

But my insecurities shouldn't be the reason he's deprived of a family who loves him. If he is ready to come home, then I should support him. Besides, the monster who drove him away is gone now, and our brothers would only show him love. So what am I so afraid of?

I clap a hand on his shoulder as I force my own body to relax. "Whenever *you're* ready, I'll be here to support you."

His eyes glisten as he nods and looks away. "You always have."

Now it's my turn to look down and blink away tears. This feels like the end of something significant. Something I'm not ready to let go of. But life rarely happens when you're ready.

"Okay, seriously, go. Get that phenomenal girl back." He pushes me toward the door as he follows behind. I watch as he shoves his feet into his boots, getting hit with a wave of nostalgia. It's as if it's the last time I'll watch him do that.

I don't spend the drive rehearsing lines I won't say. There's no point. My mind is blank as I drive until the next thing I know, I'm standing on her front porch steps, ringing the doorbell at almost nine o'clock at night.

Her father comes to the door with a disgruntled expression.

"Hi, sorry," I stammer. "I know it's late, but is Sadie here? Could I please speak to her...sir?"

I've never felt like a bigger fool in my life, and I've never not cared so much, either.

"She's at work, Luke," he says impatiently. I'm sure he doesn't think highly of me at the moment, and I don't blame him. I don't think too highly of myself either, but I'm working on it.

"Work. Of course," I say with a shake of my head as I step away from the door and move to my car. "Thanks again," I call back as I retreat into the darkness.

But before I can get away, another figure steps out onto the porch steps. Sadie's brother, Jonah, stands about three inches taller than me and crosses his arms over his chest like a pissed-off guard dog.

Their father has already disappeared into the house, and I'm left to face Sadie's fiercest protector.

"Hi, Jonah," I say with an awkward wave.

He launches into a tirade, his hands moving angrily as he signs, almost too fast for me to follow.

"My sister is the best person I know," he says. "And she always dates the worst guys, but then when she brought you home, I thought you would be good for her."

"I know," I reply, softly tapping my forehead in defeat. "I'm sorry."

"Don't say sorry to me," he argues.

"I'm trying to find her to say sorry," I reply. My sign language is slow and awkward, but Jonah is quick to understand but not so quick to forgive. And somehow, this makes me like him even more.

"I thought you were smart," he says, which makes me laugh.

"I thought so, too."

"But you're not. You're stupid," he argues, and I laugh a little more. Suddenly, I'm reminded that Jonah is still a kid, fueled by base emotions like anger and fear. It makes things simple. I fucked up, and he's mad at me for it. He doesn't care that these things are complicated, and there are so many layers of my own personal trauma that made me the way I am, Sadie too.

According to Jonah, I made his sister cry. Which makes me stupid. And it's as simple as that.

I couldn't agree more.

I tap on the side of my head again. "I know."

He breathes angrily through his nose as he glares at me. Finally, he adds, "Don't hurt her."

"I don't want to," I reply. "I...I love her."

"She loves you too," he says, and I don't know if he knows that because she told him or because he could tell. Neither one makes me feel better. I know that she loves me, but I still didn't do right by her, so what should feel good to know only feels like shit.

"I want to take care of her," I say. "I want to make her happy. I'm going to put her first."

He stares at me for a while as if he's judging me. I've never wanted someone's approval more than I want his—an angry kid who loves his sister more than anyone.

"Good," he snaps. "Prove it."

"I will."

With that, he backs up toward the door until he reaches the handle, keeping an eye on me as he goes. I awkwardly wave goodbye to him before climbing back into my car.

THIRTY-NINE

Sadie

I'm spinning in the office chair, staring at the ceiling with boredom. I don't spend as much time on the floor as I used to. If I can manage to hide my stomach with oversized clothes, I do, but these days, that's more and more impossible. And no one wants to see a pregnant woman at a sex club.

I'm like a walking consequence.

So, I spend most of my shifts balancing books, checking numbers, and reviewing incident reports, which is less and less frequent now.

Most of the floor staff can handle the club. So I let my eyes drift closed and relive the baby shower today. Not the presents or the cake or seeing my family again.

But the awkward encounter in the parking lot.

Did he really come just to give me a book? It wasn't even a gift for the baby. It was a collection of poems from Henry Wadsworth Longfellow, which I assume was meant as an homage to the baby's (possible) name.

I glanced through it, but once I realized they were mostly

romantic poems between him and someone else, I just got sad and threw it on the shelf.

Why would he give that to me? And why today?

If I know Luke, and I think I do, I'd say he's still very torn about what he wants with me. He gave me that book because he couldn't do *nothing*, but he is still married to his job, so he couldn't give me anything more. This means nothing has changed and he still won't commit.

Deep down, I'm proud of myself for not giving in and rushing into his arms the way I wanted to. Indulging in unhealthy behavior will not solve any of my problems.

Look at me...such an adult now.

Turns out being an adult fucking sucks.

The office door opens and I peel open my eyes to see Dean standing in the doorway. "Feeling okay?" he asks.

"Just peachy," I reply.

"Right..."

"How are things on the floor? Need me?" I ask, desperately wanting something to distract me until closing time.

"Umm..." he says, and I bolt upright, staring at him expectantly.

"What is it?"

"Someone is here, and I would be very comfortable telling him to fuck off if that's what you want," he says with an astute tone.

My shoulders drop in disappointment. "Is it Jax?" I really don't have the energy to deal with him right now.

"Actually, no," Dean replies, scratching the back of his head.

"Then who is it?"

"Luke."

A sound escapes my lips that sounds too aggressive to be a laugh. "Very funny."

"I'm serious," Dean replies with a wince.

My face drops. "What? Luke? As in Lucas Goode...is *here*. In this sex club. Right now?"

"Yes, but—"

I burst out of my chair and look toward the security cameras to verify what Dean is saying right now. And there on the screen is a familiar body, sitting at the bar with what I assume is an expensive glass of whiskey in front of him.

"I can tell him to leave, Sadie. I'm serious."

"Did he...ask for me?" It feels like wishful thinking, and I'm terrified that maybe Luke came here for someone else, which would be so wild and out of character, but crazier things have happened.

"Yeah, he did," Dean replies.

"What did he say?"

"He asked to see you. When I pressed him for more information, he seemed pretty desperate and slightly embarrassed. But he wouldn't tell me why."

It's sweet that Dean is so protective of me when it's his own brother-in-law who broke my heart. It's touching, really.

I stare at Luke on the screen for a while, trying to decide what I want to do. Would it be reckless to see him? What if he's just here for sex, and nothing has really changed? Will I be able to turn him down if that's the case? Crawling back into bed with Lucas would only set me back, and I can't bear to feel that pain again. Losing him gutted me, and I can't relive those days.

But do I really have the heart to turn him away without a word? It feels impossible.

I run a hand over my stomach when I feel the baby kick. He or she is my first priority now. I have to protect them, and I have to protect myself. If I let them grow attached to Lucas only for him to leave or brush them aside, I would never forgive myself.

"Tell him to meet me in the Ethereal Room, please." My voice is flat, and Dean agrees softly. When the door closes behind him, and I'm left alone to stare at Lucas on the screen, I decide that I will hear what he has to say, but I've come too far to let him pull me back into a relationship where I don't feel valued.

I can do this because I'm not just doing it for me anymore.

On the screen, I watch Dean guide Luke toward the room where it all started. I make him wait for a few more minutes. Then I slip out of the office and make my way toward the room where he's waiting for me.

I am not fully prepared for what it will feel like to be alone with him again when I enter the room and see him standing there. The door clicks behind me as it closes and I have to repeat the mantra in my head over and over.

Do this for the baby.

"Can I help you?" I ask, and the coldness in my voice shocks even me.

His mouth opens as if he's about to speak, but nothing comes out. I stand here, staring at him, wishing he'd just find the words he needs to say. But he struggles for so long I nearly turn and leave.

Then, before he can move, I watch as he drops to his knees.

"What are you doing?" I ask.

"I don't know what to say, Sadie. I don't have the words, and maybe there are none. But this..." He gestures with his arms open at the way he's on the floor for me. "This is what I'm here to say."

"I don't know what that means, Luke," I say with a shrug. "Kneeling isn't enough. Saying sorry isn't enough."

"I know it isn't," he says with a wince.

"Then, figure it out—"

"I quit my job," he blurts out, and I freeze as I stare at him. "I'm not going to England, and I don't even fucking care about it anymore."

"Why?" I whisper as I move to take a step toward him. It makes me both sad and hopeful to hear that. I don't want Luke to give up his dreams for me. I don't want to steal away the things he loves. I just want to be one of them.

I also don't want to hear him say that he's given up everything for me because he thinks that's what I want. I need to hear why, and I'm terrified he won't express it right.

"Because...that's what you wanted, Sadie. That program was

my dream, but I gave it up for you... I mean, fuck. That's not what I mean."

"So I ruined your dreams?" I ask.

"No, Sadie. You became my dream. Getting to be with you, getting to raise a baby with you...that's my dream. That's all that fucking matters to me. I would still love to do my job, and I would love to get to study in England someday, but not at your expense. Never at your expense."

Tears prick my eyes as I let those words wash over me. Is this enough? Is this what I wanted?

It feels like everything I need to hear, but something is missing.

I chew on my bottom lip as I stare at him, blinking one tear down my cheek. He flinches at the sight of it as if he wants to lunge from the floor and wipe it away.

"Please, Sadie. I'm not good at this, but I'm trying."

"I don't know, Lucas," I mumble under my breath.

God, why does this hurt so much? I just want to run into his arms and let him hold me, but is that the right choice? How do I know he's changed and he won't resent me for taking away what he's worked so hard for?

I don't. And I may never know for sure.

"I'm begging you, Sadie."

"Begging me for what?" I ask as another tear falls.

"Another chance," he replies sadly. "What do you need to know I've changed? What can I do to prove it to you?"

"I don't know," I mutter under my breath. I'm torn apart by the fear that I'll never be able to fully trust him. That there's nothing he could do to prove his devotion.

He puts a hand out, reaching for me. "Punish me."

"Lucas, I can't..." I say with a shake of my head. Sex is not the answer right now. I know that, and the last time he asked me to punish him, he ended up with his face up my dress. The memory alone sparks arousal between my legs, which makes it nearly impossible to say no.

"Sadie," he begs. "I trust you. I want you to see that I'm truly regretful for the way I've behaved. So let me prove it to you. Punish me."

The way he says those two words, imploring and desperate, makes me lose my breath. He's serious.

"Hurting you won't make me feel better, Luke."

"Yes, but it will make me feel better. And it will prove to you just how much I trust you."

I take another step toward him. When he can finally reach me, he puts out a hand and touches my leg, nudging me closer until he can rest his face against my stomach. His cheek is pressed to my belly, and his arms wrap around my thighs.

Is this the same man who was once so controlled and dominant? Right now, he is on his knees for me, begging me to do the things to him that he once did to me. And I realize at this moment how much I want to.

This is so different from what we did before. When I would act out on purpose to receive my punishment. What Lucas is asking for now is a chance to pay his penance, to rid himself of his guilt by enduring something painful, to sacrifice his comfort for mine.

His head turns until he's staring up at me.

I stroke my fingers through his hair. It hits me just how much I've missed him.

"I want to hear you say this is what *you* want," I say. "Not just what you think *I* want."

He squeezes me tighter. "I want this. Sadie, I *need* this."

Feeling renewed with purpose, I take a step away from him. He releases me reluctantly and gazes up at me as he waits.

"Stand up," I say, leaving my hands by my sides. My tone is flat, and my face is expressionless. He eagerly moves to his feet. "Take your clothes off."

With an unsteady breath, he unbuttons his shirt and pulls it from his shoulders. I don't take my eyes away from him for a second, watching him without a hint of emotion on my face. But as he unbuckles his pants and slides them down with his underwear, exposing him from top to bottom, I falter. I feel myself warming at the sight of his body. His cock is still soft, and I take that as a sign of how serious he is about this. Not to say he won't be turned on by the intensity of what's about to happen to him. It just means he's not in this for the sex.

After he's slipped off his shoes and pulled his pants from around his ankles, he stands in front of me, completely naked and waiting for my instructions. I let my eyes rake over him, appreciating just how perfect Lucas is. On top of being brilliant and confident, he's also stunning—the most handsome man I've ever met. And on top of that, now he's showing vulnerability for me, and it makes my heart swell.

Already, I forgive him. At this moment, I know I'm taking him back and letting him have whatever he wants. Because this small gesture alone is enough to prove to me that he's not the same man he was six months ago. He cares about something more than himself.

He cares about me.

"Turn around and bend over the bed. If you want me to stop, say the word *stop*, and I will."

"Okay," he says without hesitation. Then he gives me one last glance before turning around and folding himself over the bed. It's too low to lay his body against, so he holds tight to the footboard. From this angle, he's even more exposed and vulnerable, and I take a moment to appreciate that.

There is nothing sexier than vulnerability. Lucas is a strong, powerful man, but I've brought him to his knees. I have him at my mercy. He's granting me the most delicate part of himself and laying everything aside for me. I have to swallow down the emotion this brings to the surface.

Walking over to him, I lay my hand against the bottom of his spine and slide it over his back, feeling the goose bumps rising across his skin. Then I slide my hand down, floating over the crack of his ass and feeling him stiffen. I massage each side slowly, and a thrum of pleasure builds in my core at the sight of his body like this.

Leaving him briefly, I move to the cabinet of toys against the wall. Opening it, I find a light-blue paddle that matches the aesthetic of the room. With a hint of a smile on my face, I lift it from the hook and carry it back over to where Lucas is bent over for me.

"Let's start with twelve swats from the paddle, and I want you to count, Dr. Goode. Don't forget to call me by name after each one. And if you are good and take your punishment, I might let you feel the flogger next. Understood?"

He lets out a shaky breath. "Yes, Miss Green."

"Very good."

Rearing back my hand, I rest a hand on his back as I let the paddle fly. I put everything into that first swing. Everything he wants. Like bleeding out the pain I've felt. The hope, the love, the fear, the anger. I give it all to him.

And judging by the howl he lets out, he feels it all.

FORTY

Lucas

The paddle hurts a lot fucking more than I expected. But I love it. I want it. I *crave* it.

I need to feel every ounce of pain that Sadie wants to give me. After only a few smacks of the hardwood against my ass, I'm starting to sweat. With each one, I let out a stifled grunt of pain, but I endure it. There's pride in endurance.

I'm doing this for me, and for her, and for us.

Getting to feel things from her perspective gives me so much more respect for her. Feeling submissive takes more trust than I had realized, which is why I want her to see just how devoted I am. She can have all of me. Nothing comes before her. Not to me. Not ever.

"Ten, Miss Green," I mutter with a groan.

Her hand strokes my ass, and I wince from how tender it is already. "How are you feeling?" she asks. "Do we need to pause?"

"No," I grunt. "More, please."

She squeezes my ass, and the mixture of pleasure and pain makes my dick jump. It's hanging stiffly between my legs, and that's unexpected. I'm almost ashamed of how turned on I am from this. This is supposed to be punishment. I'm not supposed to be enjoying it, but my dick has other plans.

Another smack from the paddle makes me groan from the pain. "Eleven, Miss Green."

The sting reverberates through my body, never fully dulling before the next hit, so it's like I'm consumed by the pain. It's a part of me now.

"Twelve, Miss Green," I say loudly after the hardest hit of all.

I want to look back at her. I'm desperate to see the look on her face. Is she enjoying this? Is she happy with me? Am I doing enough?

The paddle lands on the bed, and I feel her standing flush behind me. Her hands slide up my thighs and then across my abdomen. She gently nudges me to a standing position, and I feel her protruding stomach against my back, putting space between us.

When her hand finds my cock, I let out a groan.

"You did enjoy that," she purrs against my back.

"My cock did. Is that bad?" I ask.

"Not at all," she replies. "What about you? Did you enjoy that?"

"No," I mumble quietly, hoping it doesn't disappoint her.

"Good," she breathes against my back. "And how are you feeling now? Would you like to stop?"

"No," I say again. "I can take more."

She squeezes my cock in her hand, and I let out another groan. It's a tease of pleasure, which just feels like more punishment.

"Good," she repeats. "I'd like to show you more."

I want to ask if I take more, will that be enough for her? Will she forgive me and take me back?

The idea of getting my hopes up practically guts me.

Sliding her hands away from my cock, she presses them under my arms and guides them up over my head. The bed has a four-poster canopy, and the bars across the top seem sturdy, which makes sense for the activities that take place here.

"Hold on to the bar," she commands, and I do. Suddenly, I feel exposed all over again. My back is stretched out, and I know she's about to hurt me again.

Her body disappears from behind me, and I hear her open the cabinet again. A moment later, I hear a *thwack* as she slaps the flogger against her hand.

"We'll do less of these, but if it's too much, just say stop, and I will. Understand?"

I hesitate. Part of me is excited to feel the pain from this toy. I'm eager to show her how much I can take. For her, she can have it all.

"I understand," I say on an exhale.

"Good. Are you ready?"

"Yes, Miss Green."

"We'll start with six. Don't forget to count."

I drag a heavy breath in through my nose, but before my lungs are even full, pain explodes in dull, agonizing fireworks across my back. The sting doesn't fade at all; it intensifies.

Letting out a loud wince of pain, every muscle in my body tenses, and I squeeze the bar above my head.

"Let me hear you count, Dr. Goode."

"One, Miss Green," I groan.

She strokes my back. "That's it. You're taking it so well." When her touch reaches my head, she scrapes her nails against my scalp and I lean into the touch. After she pulls her hand away from my body, I take another breath because I know there will be another strike of the flogger.

The second one is worse than the first. I wince again as the sting scatters across my back in tiny bursts of pain.

"Two, Miss Green," I say through clenched teeth.

Sweat drips down my spine, and my blood feels like lava in my veins. It's strange how the pain tingles through every inch of me, throbbing like pleasure but stinging like torture.

Sadie lets out a grunt of exertion as she hits me again. My head falls backward as I breathe through the pain, this time letting it flow through me instead of fighting against it.

"Three, Miss Green," I say breathlessly.

"How are you doing?" she asks with concern. Her fingers trail over the raw, battered skin of my back, but I groan in appreciation of her touch.

"Good," I sigh.

"We can take a break."

I shake my head. "No. Keep going."

The last thing I want right now is a break. I want to ride this wave and see where it goes.

"Okay," she replies. With another grunt, she hits me again. I can't tell if she put more into it or if I'm just that sore, but it stings the worst.

Then my mind goes to a really strange place. Images of our church flash through my mind. A man on the cross. My father's words about sacrifice and sin. He spoke about a pain I couldn't understand. Love I couldn't fathom.

And it's ridiculous, but as the pain Sadie serves me flows through me, I feel this overwhelming presence that brings tears to my eyes. Fuck, it's not God, but it's *something*. Maybe it's me. Maybe it's her. But it's like my eyes have been opened, and I see colors that didn't exist a moment ago. Enlightenment by way of flogger. I didn't know that was a thing, but right now, I'm drowning in it.

"Lucas," she whispers. Her fingers touch my face, wiping moisture from my cheeks.

When I peel my eyes open, I stare at her in this room that looks like heaven.

"Four, Miss Green," I whisper.

"That's enough. We're stopping," she says as she tries to pull my hands from the bars.

"No," I blurt out angrily. "More. Please."

"I don't want to hurt you anymore," she says, and her voice shakes with pain.

"You're not hurting me," I reply. I hardly recognize my own voice from the rasp and gravelly tone in it. "You're healing me."

Her brow furrows as she stares at me. It sounds absurd and a little cheesy, but it's true. I need my penance. I want to feel it again.

"Are you sure?" she whispers.

"Yes. I'm begging you."

Before she picks up the flogger, she stands on her tiptoes and kisses my lips. I want to hold her, but I refuse to let go of this bar until my punishment is over.

After the kiss, she moves behind me.

"Don't hold back," I mutter under my breath.

And she doesn't. The next hit hurts the worst out of all of them. I don't scream or wail. I breathe through the pain, letting it burn through my mind and body. I see red behind my eyelids and it's beautiful. Warm copper strands of auburn dancing in my vision like hair strewn over my eyes.

"Five, Miss Green," I rasp.

It's excruciating, but I almost don't want it to stop. I feel changed. Renewed. A new, more whole version of myself born from the broken pieces of who I used to be.

"Last one," she whispers. And like the good girl she is, she gives it her all. With a roaring sound, she hits me so hard that I nearly tumble forward. My grip on the bar burns as fire spreads like tendrils over my flesh.

This time, I can't hold it in. I let out a wail as the adrenaline courses through me. All of my senses are heightened as the pain dulls into a throbbing sensation across my back.

I hear the flogger hit the floor as Sadie climbs onto the bed in front of me. Her warm arms wrap around my middle, her hard stomach pressed against mine, and her soft lips peppering the surface of my neck.

I'm breathing heavily, still hanging from the bar, as she kisses me. When her mouth finds mine, she tries to kiss her way into my mouth, and I finally let go of the bar to hold her. But my body is heavier and more spent than I realized. So I practically fall into her, but she holds me up.

"Six, Miss Green," I mumble against her shoulder, and she laughs with her lips against my cheek.

"You did so good," she says with a smile. "Come lie down now."

I blink open my eyes as she pulls me toward the head of the bed. "On your stomach," she says comfortingly.

With a sigh, I collapse onto the bed. It's softer than I expected so I sink into the mattress with my face in the pillow. My cock is still hard, pressed between my body and the bed, but I'm not doing anything about that right now. With everything my body just experienced, my cock hardly matters.

I had no idea pain could feel so good. Don't get me wrong; it still hurt. It was still awful, but it was also incredibly powerful. Like a few lashes of pain unleashed all of the adrenaline and endorphins in my body, more potent than the heaviest drug.

I feel the bed dip a moment before Sadie's warm hands stroke the tender skin of my back. It takes me a moment to realize she's wiping something on me. I lift my head to see what she's doing.

"It's a salve," she explains. "It will help with bruising."

Bruising? Why the fuck would I care about bruising? It felt like my body was being cracked open and torn apart. A few bruises are nothing. But the nurturing movement of her hands on my flesh is nice, and I feel like I might fall asleep.

Once she's done, she comes back a moment later with a thick, warm blanket, and she drapes it over my naked body. Then, her face comes into view, and she wipes mine with a soft cloth.

"How are you feeling?" she whispers.

I reply with a grunt and a nod, hoping it conveys what I'm feeling, which doesn't have any discernible words to describe it. Good. Bad. Tired. Refreshed. I guess those would do, although they don't make much sense.

"Would you like me to leave you alone?" she asks, and I lift my head from the pillow.

"What? No." I lift a hand to reach for her.

"Okay, I'm just making sure. Some people like alone time during aftercare," she says.

"Sadie, just please get the fuck over here."

With a smirk on her face, she crawls onto the bed and lies next to me on her side, facing me. I hook an arm around her leg and tug her closer. She scoots onto my pillow until our faces are inches apart. My hand rests on her hip as I stare into her eyes.

We don't speak for a moment. It feels like the punishment scrambled up everything. Like it picked us up in one place and dropped us in another. I forgot what I wanted to say an hour ago.

But as she strokes my face and stares lovingly into my eyes, it doesn't feel like we need to say anything at all.

Eventually, two words find their way to my lips, and they're simple and poignant enough to cover the rest.

"I'm sorry," I murmur.

"It's okay," she replies. "I know you are."

"I was stupid."

"No, you weren't," she says, stroking my cheek.

"Yes, I was," I reply. "Your brother told me so."

She freezes. "What? Jonah called you stupid?"

I smile as I nod. "Yes, but rightfully so."

"You're not stupid, Lucas."

Tugging her closer, I press my lips to hers. "Not anymore."

She deepens the kiss, hugging her body close to mine. I am more at peace than I've ever been in my life. This doesn't resolve everything between us—not even close. But it feels like we've expressed so much with our actions tonight.

I am forgiven.

I am hers.

FORTY-ONE

Sadie

L ucas comes out of the shower, standing in nothing but a towel around his waist as he uses another to dry his hair. I'm sitting cross-legged on his bed, staring at him with adoration in my eyes.

Watching him take his punishment tonight felt like an out-of-body experience. He didn't just apologize or make excuses for his actions. He *showed* me.

After about an hour on the bed in the Ethereal Room, we drove back to his house, and he went straight into the shower. Dean covered closing the club tonight so I could go, and I'm grateful for that. I think Lucas and I need to be together.

Neither of us says a word as we stare at each other. I notice the way he keeps looking down at my stomach. It has grown a lot in the last couple of months. It's no longer a cute belly but a full, round mass that makes everything difficult.

I want to ask him about the baby. Does he really mean what he meant about raising this child with me? Is he saying he wants to give *us* a try? Is he actually committing? Does he fully understand what he's getting into?

Tossing the towel in his hand onto the counter, he switches off the bathroom light and comes toward me. Sitting on the bed in front of me, he stares into my eyes before dropping down until his face is close to my stomach. His lips press against my belly before he rests his head completely in my lap.

"Maybe we should talk about this before we go any further," I say softly as I stroke his hair.

He lets out a heavy breath as he nods. Part of me worries that he's just preparing himself for the hard part. That he's about to say something difficult like how he wants me but isn't prepared to be a father. Anything less than unwavering confidence might break my heart right now.

"You don't owe us anything, Lucas. Just because you want to be with me doesn't mean you have to be ready to raise a child. But we can't do this if you're not—"

"I'm ready," he says. His tone sounds assured, but I'm still skeptical.

"If you want me, then he or she comes with me. You're not just getting a girlfriend; you're getting a child, too."

"I know."

"Are you ready to raise someone else's child?"

He stares up into my eyes with his hand resting on my stomach. "Sadie, this is *my* child."

Tears prick intensely behind my eyes. I blink to keep them from brewing more.

Lucas sits up and brings his face level with mine. Then he stares into my eyes. "You are mine, so he is mine. Understand?"

I try to nod, but it only makes my tears spill over, so Lucas pulls me into his arms. Softly, he murmurs against my head. "I never understood family until now, Sadie. I share blood with my own father, and he never showed me a day of love in my life, so I'll be damned if I let genetics determine how much I love this child. I'll love him or her with my whole fucking heart. And I'll tell them every day."

A sob racks through my chest as I squeeze myself closer to

him. This feels like a dream. It's everything I ever wanted. I just started imagining the wrong person at first, but now I know that this is how it was meant to be all along.

When I've dried my tears, I sit up, and Lucas presses his lips to my forehead. "Come here. I want to show you something." He climbs from the bed and reaches a hand toward me.

I stare at him with confusion before letting him help me up. Then I follow him out of his bedroom and down the hall to the room I once occupied.

As he opens the door, I look at him, wondering what this is all about. Does he want me to move back into this room? I was sort of hoping that he and I could take our relationship to a new level and I'd actually sleep with him.

But then he turns on the light and I let out a gasp.

"It's not finished, but I sort of had to make sure you'd talk to me again before I got it all done."

I press my fingers over my lips as I step into the room and take in the new furniture. There's a dark-brown crib against the wall and a changing table on the right. In the corner, a rocking chair with a stuffed elephant sits on the seat.

Suddenly, I'm crying again because I'm standing in my child's future bedroom, and it all feels so surreal. When I finally turn back toward him, he has tears in his eyes, too.

"Lucas..." I whisper through my tears.

"I wanted you to know that I was serious. I wanted you to see that if I was making room for you, I was making room for him or her too."

He nods toward my stomach, and I squeeze my eyes closed, feeling another round of sobs rack through me.

Then I'm crossing the room and burying myself in his arms. He squeezes his tightly around me and I've never felt more safe and at home in my life. Lucas is my home. He sees me the way no one else ever has. He has carved out a space for me in his heart and I know if I spend the rest of my life with him, I'll never doubt his love for a single moment.

He and I fit together like poetry. We are different, messy, and melodic, but we fit. It's not seamless, but it is beautiful.

"I love you so much," he mutters into my neck. "I promise nothing will come before you."

"Thank you," I cry in return. "I love you too."

When I pull away from our embrace, I stand on my tiptoes, and our mouths come together with passion. His kiss is needy and gentle at the same time, but the more he kisses me, the more I need from him.

Desperate hands roam my body, caressing every inch. I pull him out of the nursery and down the hall to his bedroom. We eventually reach his bed without ever having to separate our lips from each other.

I tear his towel from his hips and he lifts my shirt. I shrug it off in a rush and we both move for my leggings next. I'm eager to be naked for him but nervous at the same time. Will he still find me attractive? Will he be too scared to fuck me in this state?

Lucas doesn't falter for one second. He releases my bra with one quick swipe at the back and then moves to his knees to help me out of my pants.

And then he rises in front of me and lets his eyes cascade over the length of my naked body.

"God, you're so fucking beautiful," he mumbles under his breath.

He grips my breast in one hand, squeezing as his lips find the other. I let my head fall back as I succumb to the pleasure of his mouth on my body. My long hair drifts down my back as he fondles me appreciatively.

With every swipe of his teeth around my nipples, arousal detonates in my core. I'm so turned on for him, I feel like I could die from it. I need him so desperately.

"Please, Lucas," I groan as he moves to suck on the opposite breast.

"Please, what?" he asks with my nipple in his mouth.

"Please fuck me," I beg.

Letting out a husky sound, he grabs my ass and grinds his hard length against my leg. "Such a dirty mouth on you, Miss Green."

"Please," I cry.

As he straightens up, his hands continue their way downward, stroking slightly around my belly before stopping between my legs. As he slides his middle finger through my folds, I let out a gasp.

The other hand holds me by the back of the neck as we stare at each other. When he finds me wet and ready for him, I watch the way his lips part and his eyes dilate with arousal.

Then, he sinks his middle finger inside me and doesn't let me avert my eyes from his for a second. I'm so needy for him, it feels like I could come already. The intensity of his gaze and the comfort of his touch is almost too much for me.

I let out a mewling sound as he fucks me slowly with his middle finger. Then he adds another one and I have to cling to his arm to keep me upright.

"Does that feel good, Miss Green?"

"Yes," I cry out. "Please, more."

He picks up the pace, thrusting harder until it feels as if my body is wound so tight I'm about to explode. I need more. Rougher, harder, faster.

I moan with pleasure, but then a gasp leaves my lips as he grinds the heel of his palm against my clit. I'm writhing, chasing my orgasm as Lucas backs me up to the bed.

I nearly fall back onto it, holding myself up and staring into his eyes as he continues to fuck me with his fingers.

"Come on my hand, Miss Green."

I let out a raspy cry. With my legs spread wide for him, I let his talented fingers carry me straight down a landslide of pleasure. As my orgasm slams into me, the feeling is so divine, I nearly cry. Back arched and pulse thrumming, I scream through the sensation as it swims through every extremity of my body.

I collapse onto the bed, trying to catch my breath. My gaze

catches on the hard length of his cock, jutting out toward me with a droplet of cum leaking from the tip. Without touching himself, he lifts his arousal-soaked fingers to his lips and licks them with one long stroke of his tongue.

"I love the way you come for me," he murmurs around his digits. "Now get on the bed."

He nods toward the pillows, so I shimmy my way up. I'm lying naked on my side as I stare at him with love in my eyes. As he slowly crawls up toward me, he peppers my body with kisses. Starting from the tops of my feet, to my calves and my knees, up over my thick thighs, and then across the soft flesh of my belly.

As he situates himself behind me, he gathers me in his arms. The warm comfort of his long, strong body engulfs me in bliss. I turn my head and stare into his eyes. He's perched on his elbow, staring down at me as his lips softly find mine. It's a slow, sensual kiss that feels like a vow. When Lucas kisses me, I know it means that he takes us seriously. This is more than our bodies seeking pleasure—it's our hearts seeking a bond stronger than sex.

It's love.

When I feel him guide his cock toward my core, I hum with anticipation. As he presses himself inside me, his lips find mine. He moans into our kiss as he slides all the way to the hilt.

Our legs are tangled, and our hands intertwined as our bodies move together rhythmically. Having Luke inside me feels so natural to me already. He belongs here. We belong together.

I open my eyes to watch his face as he finds pleasure in my body. His moans in my ear. His breath on my face. It's enough to warm my body all over again so I feel as if I'm about to come again.

His thrusts grow faster and rougher, and I cling tighter to him as we chase our orgasms together.

"Harder," I plead. He pounds into me from behind, but the angle is awkward so he moves to his knees, lifting me to all fours.

Gripping my hips in his hands, he fucks me harder, grunting with every thrust.

"No one else will touch you for as long as we live, understand? You're mine, Sadie. All fucking mine."

Squeezing the blankets in my fists, I push back against him. "Yes," I scream. "I'm all yours."

"I'm about to come. Are you going to take every drop?"

"Yes," I moan into the mattress. "Give it to me."

With another three forceful thrusts, I begin to shudder and shake from the intensity. Then he stills, and I feel his cock flex inside me. He groans out his release as his grip on my hips tighten.

We're moaning and trembling together, and the sensation is so good I don't want it to end.

It feels as if Lucas comes, and comes, and comes. Honestly, it makes me wonder if he's even touched himself since we've been together last. But the idea of his full load filling me up makes me shiver with contentment. I want to take every part of him.

When he finally does finish, he pulls out and drops onto the mattress next to me. I curl onto my side, feeling him drip between my thighs. But I love the stickiness of him there, so I don't move to clean it up.

I rest my head on his arm and drape my top leg over his. Breathlessly, he turns and places a kiss on my forehead.

"I love you," he mumbles against my skin.

"I love you, too," I reply, squeezing him tighter.

And there's not a doubt in my heart that he means it.

FORTY-TWO

Lucas

Two months later

My mother sets a cake covered in candles in the center of the table between Caleb and me as the family starts singing. Abigail is bouncing on her feet next to me as I stare at my twin brother without blinking.

It's a stupid tradition we started when we were about eight years old. An annual stare-off over the birthday cake while everyone sings to us. Honestly, it's better than awkwardly staring at everyone while they sing an off-key version of the worst song in existence.

Sadie sticks out her tongue at me from behind my brother, and I crack a smile that makes me blink.

"You lose!" Abigail cheers as everyone laughs through the last line of the song.

Caleb beams triumphantly across from me. Thirty-five years old and we still act like children.

"You lose, Uncle Luke," Abigail repeats, which makes me laugh.

"I know, Abby. It's okay, though. Your dad always beats me."

She giggles as my mother cuts the cake. Technically, our birthday was on Thursday, but Sadie and I had tickets to a play downtown, and Caleb wanted to spend it at home with his own family, so we're celebrating with the big family at Sunday dinner.

My mother just had a new table delivered a few days ago, so it's our first one at the much larger version that seats all of us, with room for more. I glance at the empty one in the corner, still reserved for Isaac. And I remember what he said that night.

He's almost ready to come back. I can't even begin to imagine what that must be like. To be estranged from most of your family for so long that you feel like a stranger in your own home. I've hardly seen him since that night. He's been in the studio a lot working on the album. It's all recorded and set to come out in August.

We should be sharing a cake at the table for that accomplishment alone.

Maybe someday he will.

He has been texting nearly every day to check on Sadie. She's officially full term, which means the baby could come any day now. But technically, her due date isn't for another three weeks. She's miserable ninety percent of the time, and it's killing me. I want to ease all of her pain. Her backaches, her heartburn, her rib pain. I hate to see her suffer.

I take a bite of my cake, chocolate with vanilla sprinkle frosting because that's all Caleb and I could agree on as kids. Mom has taken it to heart ever since.

But as soon as I set my fork down and push the sugary sweet plate away, I have a baby thrust into my arms.

"Hold her for me, will you?" I glance up at my brother, Adam, who drops Faith into my arms. The bald-headed baby stares up at me with round blue eyes as she blows bubbles through her tiny lips.

"Uh...sure," I say, sending him a grimace as he laughs.

Then he picks up his plate and walks over to where Sage is

sitting and talking to Briar. He feeds her a bite of cake and takes a seat next to her. They're lucky they have so many open arms to help them with their baby.

I guess in less than a month's time, we will too.

Faith smiles up at me, and it takes up her entire face. A big toothless grin and dimples in her adorable chubby cheeks. There's a rubber giraffe in her hand that she slams into her mouth with little to no coordination. As she chews on the leg of the toy, she just stares at me.

I have two nieces, and it never fails to knock me off my feet how someone can be so incredibly loved from the moment they're born. I love Faith and Abby with so much of my heart, it's unbelievable.

There's a small hint of worry that creeps in every time I look at them, though. Will that same natural love bloom in my heart when our baby is born?

My gut tells me yes—emphatically yes.

But my cynical mind dwells on it.

Regardless, I will give him or her everything. I will love them no matter what. But I can't wait until that day. I can't wait to hold them and stare at the child that I already love as my own.

Sadie has had a couple of conversations with Jax about the baby and his role in his or her life. She's worried he'll only show up enough for the child to get attached but not enough to be a devoted parent. She wants to protect her baby, and I love her so fiercely for that. And we have a lot to figure out when it comes to how exactly we're going to raise this baby with him, but I have no doubt we'll know what to do when the time is right.

As for me, I'll be here no matter what. To support her. To love them both.

Looking up from the baby in my arms, I find Sadie watching me from across the room. She's hiding a gentle smile behind her hand as her eyes grow moist. I shoot her a crooked smirk just as Faith smacks me in the face with a drool-covered giraffe.

Sadie laughs loudly as I look down at Faith. For a moment I'm

afraid she might cry, but then she breaks out in a smile again, which warms my heart. Leaning in, I press my lips to her soft head as she coos in my arms.

After dessert, Sage takes Faith from me so she can feed her. Sadie and I help my mom take dishes into the kitchen. When I notice Sadie wincing from the pain in her back, I dry my wet hands on the kitchen towel and wave her toward me.

"Come here."

She waddles closer and assumes the position. Pressing her back to my chest, she leans against me as I hook my arms under her round belly. Then she subtly drops her weight against my chest as I rock her gently from side to side.

It's the only relief she gets on her back these days. Letting me hold her and take some of the pressure from the weight of her stomach.

"Want me to get you a heating pad?" I mumble softly against her ear.

Her eyes are closed as she holds on to my arms. "No. I'll be okay until we get home."

Kissing the side of her face, I look up right as my mother walks into the kitchen.

"Oh, poor Sadie. You okay, honey?" she asks.

"Yeah, I'm okay. Just ready to get this baby out of me."

My mother softly pats Sadie's stomach. "Pretty soon. It'll be here before you know it."

"How did you do this with twins?" Sadie asks.

Laughing, my mom shakes her head. "Don't ask me." After dropping some silverware into the sink, she turns toward us. "You know, Lucas and Caleb were born right on their due date. Right on time."

Sadie looks back at me with a smile. "Why am I not surprised?"

"Twins hardly ever make it to term, but Lucas was on a schedule, and he refused to be any earlier or later than he was supposed to be."

Sadie laughs as I smile, kissing her head again. "Well, I hope this baby comes early. Three weeks sounds like ten years right now."

"I know it does," my mother drawls as she touches Sadie's face affectionately. "Honey, why don't you go lie down in the living room? The birthday boy can help me clean up."

Sadie lets out a sigh and stands, moving away from me. "Don't tempt me with a good time."

As she leaves the kitchen, I turn toward my mother because I know she's manipulated her way into alone time with me for a reason. She nods toward the sink, gesturing for me to dry the dishes after she washes them.

This is where deep, significant conversations would happen growing up. Mom would draft each of us individually to drying dishes in order to get us alone and conjure up some personal topic. This is where Caleb admitted to her that he was in love with Briar—and again when he was in love with Dean. This is where I was standing when I first talked to her about how I was moving to New York for college and she promised that she would always love me, no matter how far away I was.

As she hands me a sopping wet plate, I glance over at her in expectation.

"How are you feeling with all of this?" she asks in her sweet Texas drawl.

"You mean the baby?" I ask.

"You're essentially about to be a father," she says, glancing sideways at me as she scrubs a pan. "And you just quit your job. You're going through a lot, sweetie."

I fall silent as I put the dry plate away in the cabinet. My mind is searching my emotions for how I truly feel about all of this.

"Believe it or not," I say with a sigh. "I feel good. Everything with Sadie might have happened quickly, and I wasn't planning on being a father, but I *chose* this. I chose to walk away from my job and move Sadie in. I chose to step up for the baby. Not because I feel like I have to, but because I want to."

She smiles to herself as she nods. "I always knew you'd be a good father."

I laugh as she hands me another plate. "That makes one of us."

"I mean, look at the way you've taken care of Isaac all these years." She glances behind herself to be sure we're alone and no one else hears. "You're a caretaker, Lucas. You love fiercely and loyally. And you don't hesitate to protect your family at all costs."

As I think about it, I realize she's right. I did always feel a sense of protectiveness over Isaac, and when he left, I felt that for Sadie.

"I didn't have much for a role model, though," I say under my breath. We don't like to talk to Mom about our father because she has her own baggage where that monster is concerned. But she has to know that he had an effect on me and how much I never wanted to end up like him.

"You didn't need one, Lucas. You would have paved your own path anyway. You make your own rules, and you're not afraid to do it alone."

I chuckle lightly to myself. "If you say so."

She glances sideways at me, grinning, and for the first time in a long time, I feel a sense of gratitude that I came back to Austin. I never wanted to return home. For a while, I saw returning here as a sense of failure. No one is ever supposed to come back home.

But now that I'm here, and I get to watch my nieces be born and grow up, and I get to dry dishes next to my mother, and celebrate birthdays with my brother, and bring my own child home for Sunday dinner... I'm so incredibly happy to be here.

FORTY-THREE

Sadie

"**W**ell, it's official," I groan from the middle of the bed. "He's late."

"He is your child, after all," Lucas replies with a smile as he leans over and kisses my temple.

"Very funny," I mutter. I'm lying in misery on top of the covers because I'm always so *fucking* hot. My back hurts. My feet hurt. My breasts hurt. Every single part of me is in pain all the time, and at this rate, I'm pretty sure I'm going to be pregnant forever.

"You should be glad he didn't come early," Lucas says as he tightens his tie. "You were able to finish the semester and pass every class."

He's picked up a teaching job at the community college and his last week of classes is this week. Technically, it's a big step down for him, but he doesn't care. He makes enough money to keep us comfortable in the house. The people at that England project were disappointed he passed on the position, but they offered it to him later down the road if he wanted. He passed on that too.

But he's happy. I can see it in his eyes every day now. He doesn't seem too restless, like he has one foot out the door. Both are firmly planted here in this house with me.

"Don't leave," I groan into the pillow.

"I'll only be gone for a couple of hours," he says, kneeling on the bed and brushing the hair from my face. "And Isaac will be here in about thirty minutes."

"I don't need a babysitter," I reply.

"No, but you do need someone to help you tie your shoes or to pick up things you drop on the floor."

I pick up a pillow and swing it at him, but he dodges it with a laugh. "Watch it, Miss Green," he says with a tsk. "One more outburst like that, and you'll be punished."

"Promises, promises," I reply with a shake of my head.

He gently swats my ass and I give him a coy smile as he kisses me again. "I love you," he mumbles against my lips.

"Love you too," I reply.

After he's gone, I manage to roll out of bed and start up the shower. Staring at my naked body in the bathroom mirror, I marvel at how much it has changed in this pregnancy. I feel huge, but I also feel sexy too. Every part of me is so full and round, and even with how uncomfortable I am, I am going to miss this.

Lucas certainly can't get enough either.

After my shower, I walk out into the living room to find Isaac cracking open an energy drink in the kitchen.

"Hey, mama," he says, looking at my stomach. "How you feeling?"

I try to stretch, but it feels like I might have slept on my back wrong because it's more tight than usual today. "Am I glowing?" I ask sarcastically.

"Radiant," he says with enthusiasm.

Isaac and I share the same sense of dry humor. Half the time, Luke feels left out when the three of us are together. Isaac has been around a lot lately. I'm getting the sense that he wants to be a part of this family, which is making things complicated.

At some point, he's going to have to take that step if that's what he really wants.

Since most of the work for his new album has been done and it's in the hands of the producers, he's mostly free to hang out here. He's been here nearly every day.

He kept me busy while Lucas was gone. We went for a walk around the neighborhood, watched *Coyote Ugly* on cable television, ordered a pizza, and ate it in the living room, of course. We mostly talk about stuff like the music we like, what makes Taylor Swift so amazing, and how stupid Texas can be sometimes. We agree on literally everything, except for the fact that he thinks the new country version of "Fast Car" is better than the original, which is a shame because he's just dead wrong.

All in all, I love Luke's secret brother, and he's exactly the friend I need right now.

"Have you talked to Jax lately?" he asks as he cleans up the evidence of us eating on the couch before his brother comes home.

"No," I reply. "Honestly, I wonder if I ever will."

"You really think he doesn't want the baby?" he asks.

"My fear is that he doesn't want it now, but someday he'll come back and want a part in the baby's life. It would be so confusing for them."

"So put Lucas on the birth certificate and tell Jax to fuck off," Isaac says as he drops back down on the couch.

My back stiffens again so I shift my position to find some relief. It doesn't work.

"It's not that easy," I laugh.

"Either way, the baby will be loved," he says, and I answer with a nod.

He fires up a video game on the TV, and I try to join him, but I'm so uncomfortable that I can hardly focus. I consider lying down for a nap, but standing up and walking around is the only thing that seems to relieve the pain.

Isaac is playing *Gran Turismo* as he glances sideways at me.

I'm leaning against the couch with my forearms as I let my belly hang and sway side to side, moaning from the discomfort in my hips.

"Uhh..." he says as he sets his controller down. "You okay?"

"Yeah," I reply. "My back just hurts today."

"Like a deep throbbing pain that comes and goes, radiating from your lower back to your hips?"

I pick my head up and stare at him, bewildered. "That was oddly specific."

"I read some baby books. It said early signs of labor include lower back pain that radiates to your hips. Is that what you're feeling?"

"Okay...first of all, it's adorable that you're reading baby books, and second...yeah, sort of."

Isaac leaps up from the couch. "I'm going to call Lucas."

I put up a hand to stop him. "Isaac, calm down. It's not even that bad yet."

"Still!" he shouts.

"It could be nothing. False labor happens all the time."

"So does *real* labor!"

The look of terror on this face is sort of adorable, and it makes me laugh. But my laughter is quickly cut off by another spasm in my back that does, in fact, radiate up to my hips.

Fuck.

✝

Labor is awful. I've been stuck at five centimeters for hours. I'm starving. Everything hurts. And the fucking anesthesiologist isn't here yet.

"Want me to go check again?" Isaac asks from the chair in the corner. I'm hanging on Lucas, but it's not helping as much as it normally does. Everything just hurts worse and worse and worse.

Luke growls angrily as he holds me. "I'm going to go raise hell in a minute," he argues.

"Just knock me out," I whine. "Someone please just put me out of my misery."

"That's it," Lucas growls. "Isaac, come hold her."

I'm in so much pain, I don't even care who's holding me. So when Lucas's familiar frame is replaced by Isaac's more gentle, narrow build, I don't even blink. I just hang on him and let him sway me gently to ease some tension in my back.

Then we both pause as we hear Lucas shouting through the door of my labor room. He sounds erratic and desperate, hollering at some nurse about how I've been in pain for hours without any relief.

"Don't worry," Isaac says. "If he gets kicked out, I'll be here with you."

"Thank you," I mumble.

A few minutes later, a nurse comes shuffling into the room, followed by an irate-looking Lucas.

She's grumpy about it, but suddenly stuff starts happening. She checks me, and I'm finally at six, but it's still not enough to start pushing.

And by some miracle from God himself, the anesthesiologist comes in and gives me the sweet, sweet relief of the epidural. Within minutes, I'm drifting off to sleep, and Lucas stays stationed at my side, holding my hand and rubbing my forehead softly with a wet cloth.

He seems at ease now that my pain is gone.

"What if I can't do it?" I whisper as I wake up with a bout of nausea.

"Of course you can do it," he replies. "You can do anything."

"No, I can't," I reply, fighting the urge to throw up all over this hospital blanket. I don't know if it's from fear or the medication or both.

"Sadie, you're the strongest, smartest person I know," he mumbles against my fingers.

"You used to think I was a mess," I reply.

"You did show up to the first day of class without any paper to write on." He laughs.

"And I threw up in the middle of your lecture."

"And you still made me fall in love with you," he says softly.

"Okay, maybe I can do anything."

I smile at him with sleepy eyes as he grins back. There's worry in his eyes, though. He thinks he's hiding it, but he can't hide anything from me. And I know that his worry is mostly from labor in general and the fear that something could go wrong, but I find it sweet that he's trying to encourage me when he's so obviously anxious.

The next hour passes so slowly it feels like a dream. I fall asleep and wake up to see the clock has barely moved. The nurse comes in to check me again, and when I'm still at six, I can tell there's a new level of concern.

Now, I can't fall back to sleep. And Lucas's anxiety is more apparent.

Isaac does as much as he can to support us, keeping the conversation light and staying by our side even when I notice how uncomfortable he is.

I don't even know what time it is when the doctor comes in and checks me, but when the labor hasn't progressed, he says a lot of things that make me start to cry.

Things like how the baby's heart rate drops with each contraction. And how his position isn't ideal for delivery. And how we should consider a C-section.

Lucas's grip on my hand becomes an anchor. Suddenly, I'm shaking violently, and I don't understand why. I've never felt fear like this before. No matter how much the doctor assures me, I can't shake this feeling that things are out of control.

And when I look over at the man I love and find his head bent and his eyes closed, that's when I really start to worry.

FORTY-FOUR

Lucas

I haven't prayed since I was a child. I can't remember the age I was when I believed there was a powerful man in the sky who would grant wishes if you hoped for them enough. Even when I was older and my mother made me bow my head in church, I recited words I never meant.

Those prayers never came from the heart.

But this one does.

The first time I heard the thump-thump of the heart rate playing in the room slowly during Sadie's contractions, I nearly shouted in my head for God's help. I begged him. Apologized. Promised I'd do better. He could have my soul if that's what He wanted. My undying devotion.

Just don't take either of these two people from me.

The doctor is nice enough to warn Sadie and me that he's about to hit an alert button that will make everything feel very frantic and scary. He tried to warn us. But when nurses and doctors start rushing in and things start moving around, there is no warning that could stop us from feeling this terror.

Sadie is sobbing, reaching for me as if I can stop any of this. If I could, I would.

All I can do is pray.

A sweet nurse tries to console her. She tells her these things happen all the time, but it's like she doesn't understand. This is *our* baby. It might happen to other people's babies, but never to ours.

As they whisk Sadie out of the room, they explain to her that I'll be prepped as well and will meet her in the room, but nothing could prepare me for what it's like to feel her hand let go as she's rolled away.

The tremble in her bones transfers to mine.

One of the nurses guides me to where I'll need to be prepped, and I feel Isaac behind me. He follows me for as long as he can, but then we reach a door he isn't allowed to cross into. I turn to him with panic and fear in my eyes, and see that the expression is mirrored in his.

"I'm not going anywhere," he says astutely. "I'll be here for you. No matter what."

I could cry with how good that feels. "The family," I mutter through chattering teeth.

"I'll call Mom," he says.

"The rest," I stutter.

He pauses. And my brain is so drunk on adrenaline I don't realize what I'm asking. After a deep, sober breath, he nods. "I'll call them too."

"Isaac," I mutter but the nurse behind me touches my arm.

"We have to be going," she says briskly.

"It's fine," Isaac says, waving me away. "Everything will be fine."

I want to hug him. I want to cry into his shoulder and let him convince me that everything will be fine, but I have to be with Sadie. So I follow the nurse.

It's a whirlwind from there. I'm rushing through the whole

process with shaking hands, but she assures me that they won't start without me. I'm scrubbed up, covered from head to toe, and guided down another hallway until we're in a sterile, cold operating room.

I see Sadie strapped to a table, tears streaming down her red face, and I practically sprint across the space to get to her.

The doctors and nurses are all talking, prepping things, but I can only focus on her. As our eyes meet, it feels like something cosmic and powerful. It's a new version of us, a new couple that experiences terror and trauma together. But I don't want her to know either of those things so I quickly pull it together and softly stroke her face.

"Everything is going to be fine," I whisper. "You're doing so good. Look at how amazing you are."

"Just keep talking to me," she cries.

So, I do. I just keep her eyes on me as I tell her every good and amazing thing about her that I love. Like how she sings to herself and dances when she eats and leaves her shoes all over my house. She manages a smile just before the doctor announces that she's going to feel some pressure.

Sadie seems drugged and dazed but she holds my eyes as we wait, the curtain draped over her abdomen to block our view from the rest of her body. I assume this is going to take a long time. It's quiet for a moment.

And then...

A cry.

A loud, wailing screech, vigorous and mighty.

Just like that, there's a new person in the room.

Everything that was sped up a moment ago now moves in slow motion.

Sadie's eyes widen as my heart bursts straight out of my chest. I bolt upright to look and there he is. Small, white limbs stretch furiously as the nurses work to clean his nose and check his heart and lungs. They place him on Sadie's chest, and he screams in anger.

"Lucas," Sadie gasps in a small voice from my side.

When I turn my head to look down at her, I feel tears streak down my face, and I hadn't even realized I was crying.

"It's a boy," I say, emotion strangling me as I try to speak. "And he's perfect."

Frantically, I look at the doctors and ask, "Is Sadie okay?"

The doctor gives me a quick nod. "Everything went perfectly."

The feeling of relief after so much terror is almost too good to absorb. There's still a shudder in my bones like I couldn't relax if I tried to.

The baby is still vehement as they clean him off and transfer him to a table nearby. I watch as they tightly swaddle him in a blanket and wipe something clear across his eyes. Then, they pop a tiny cap on his head before turning to look at me.

"Congratulations, Dad," one of the sweet nurses says. "Would you like to take him over to Mom?"

The world stops turning entirely. I'm frozen in place as the nurse picks up the baby and hands him to me. It's like nothing I've ever felt before, to be handed a newborn and feel so incredibly inadequate and unprepared.

But then he's in my arms and suddenly it's like the first day of my life.

Holding him tightly to my chest, I carry him over to where Sadie is still lying, strapped to the operating table. She searches for him with her eyes as I lower him toward her.

She turns her head his way, and I swear he does the same, as if they're looking for each other. They're pressed together, cheek to cheek, and I've never felt anything so raw and powerful in my chest before. She cries and just rejoices in feeling her baby against her skin. Meanwhile, he roots for her like he's still a part of her.

"Look at him, Sadie. I'm so fucking proud of you," I cry as I crouch near them both.

There was once two of us, but now there are three.

"Is he okay?" she squeaks. "Everything is okay?"

"Everything is okay," I say with a weepy smile.

She squeezes her eyes shut with a tight expression of gratitude on her face. Then she opens them and kisses the side of his head.

"Hello, Henry," she whispers. "We love you so much."

She looks up at me as if she's trying to gauge my emotions like it's not evident by the trails of tears streaking across my face.

"Yes, we do," I add, leaning down to kiss him right where she did.

Our time is cut short and the nurses put Henry in this tiny rolling bassinet. They invite me to walk with them to the nursery, and Sadie urges me to go. As if she doesn't want me to let him out of my sight. I'm way ahead of her. I walk protectively behind them as they push him down the long hall to the nursery. Then, they let me watch through the window as they give him a quick bath and do a few more tests.

He gets so angry at them when they unswaddle him, and it makes me smile. I love to see him scream in fury.

As I'm standing outside the nursery, I briefly realize that I left Isaac somewhere in the hospital. And the rest of my family is likely here, too. It's too late for visitors right now, but if I know my family, they're here whether or not they're allowed to be. They'd sleep in the waiting room if they had to.

I feel bad for leaving Isaac to deal with them alone. I don't know how they'll react when they see him, but right now, it's not my priority. My focus is this baby and the woman I love. Everything else is just noise.

Once they're done with Henry in the nursery, they wheel him to our recovery room. Sadie is already there, sleeping now.

His nurse smiles down at the baby. "Let her sleep for now, but if he wakes up and wants to nurse, we'll be around to help her."

"Okay, thank you," I mutter nervously.

Then, the nurses just leave me alone with them, and it all feels too surreal. How can I suddenly be responsible for a baby?

"Hey," a soft voice calls from the doorway. I spin around to see Isaac standing in the room.

The relief and emotion that washes over me in that moment

practically brings me to my knees. I cross the room in a rush and pull him into my arms.

"I had to bribe a nurse to let me back here this late," he mumbles against my shoulder.

"I'm so glad you're here," I reply, my voice tight.

As we part, his eyes find my face and there's something somber in them. "I couldn't do it," he confesses.

"Do what?" I ask.

"I couldn't call them. I'm so sorry, Luke."

The remorse on his face guts me. Grabbing him by the back of the neck, I haul him toward me and stare into his eyes. "I don't care," I say with a shake of my head. "I'm sorry I asked you to."

"I'm not ready to be around them all yet. I don't feel like part of the family anymore," he stammers, tears in his eyes. "I wanted to do it for you, but I just...couldn't."

"Isaac, I don't care."

"I'm sorry," he mumbles.

"I'm thankful you're here."

"I never left," he says. "I was afraid if I called one of them, then I'd freak out and leave, but I promised you I'd stay."

"I'm glad you did. And you might be ready one day, and you might not. But that is up to you, and there's no right answer, Isaac."

He hugs me again, and we don't say anything else. There's nothing left to be said.

As we pull apart, he glances over at the bassinet, so I guide him toward it quietly and watch his expression change as he sees Henry lying there.

"Holy shit," he whispers.

"I know, right?"

"That's a baby," Isaac mumbles.

"Pretty wild."

"You guys have a kid." He stares in awe for a while, but when I let out a yawn, he stands up and pats me on the shoulder. "You're exhausted. Get some rest. And text me tomorrow, okay?"

"Okay," I reply.

Silently, Isaac slips out of the room, and I collapse onto the stiff couch near the window. Rolling Henry toward me, I watch him for as long as I can. No matter how tired I am, my eyes don't drift closed for even a second.

Five minutes later, he lets out a hungry-sounding cry. His eyes are still closed, but his mouth opens and closes as if he's looking for something. I burst up from the couch and carefully lift him from the bassinet.

He stops crying for a moment as if my presence alone is enough to soothe him. Then I just hold him, staring down at his perfect little face. The first thing I notice is Sadie's button nose. Everything else is too hard to determine yet, but that one small feature alone makes me smile.

I remember how I worried that my love for him would not come as naturally as I wanted, which now I realize was incredibly futile. Because I've never known love like this. I don't need to give Henry my heart because he already has it. His presence alone is a miracle.

Did God have a hand in this moment? It feels like some higher power did. Not that I'm suddenly devout and ready to go back, but I feel closer to a small part of myself that I shut off decades ago. This faith I once had has been renewed.

Even if God doesn't exist, Henry does. And that is just as powerful to me.

I always thought I was meant for something more in this life. I wanted to do something people would remember: a legacy to outlive me. I thought I was so smart and had it all figured out. But now I realize I was meant for this. I was meant to be his father and her husband. Because this feeling is the greatest thing that has ever existed.

And I almost missed this. By some miracle from God, I didn't.

FORTY-FIVE

Sadie

I peel my eyes open to a dark room and slivers of light peering through the edges of the curtains. My body feels like I've been run over by a truck, and I'm too afraid to move.

I turn my head to see someone standing near the window, staring down and swaying softly from side to side.

"Luke," I whisper, and he turns toward me. Henry is bundled up and sleeping in his arms.

I lift my arms toward him, desperate to finally hold my baby. Luke walks toward me and gently places Henry in my arms.

I've never seen anything so perfect in my entire life. Perfect. From *me*.

My heart expands so quickly in my chest—it's incredible. It swells and pulses and grows so large that it's almost hard to breathe.

There is no question of *how* I can love someone so immensely so quickly—I just do. I place a kiss on his forehead and breathe in the strange but familiar scent of him. It's like a drug. So I do it again.

Lucas perches himself on the side of my bed and puts an arm

around my back. "You did it, Sadie," he whispers. "Isn't he amazing?"

"He's so amazing," I say, tears brimming in my eyes. "But is it bad if I say yesterday was terrible?"

Luke smiles. "Not even a little bit."

The trauma of that day feels like it's rewritten the chemistry in my brain. It was painful and long and terrifying and I never, ever want to relive anything like it. Even if this wonderful person is worth every single second.

Through all of it, Lucas was by my side. It was a true testament to his loyalty. If I ever doubted that I was a priority to him, yesterday proved it. Lucas would walk through the fires of hell for us, and he wouldn't regret it for a second.

Resting my head against Lucas, I smile. "Thanks for being there. I don't know what I would have done if you weren't there."

"Of course, I was going to be there, Sadie. I promised you that I'd never leave your side. And I meant it."

I look up at him, somehow loving him even more now. "And you love him...right?"

His brows pinch together as he lowers himself until he's lying next to me, gently touching Henry's head.

"I love him so much it feels impossible." Then he gently touches his forehead to mine. "You're mine, so he's mine, remember?"

I blink a tear out of my eye and it streams down my cheek. "I remember."

We lie there for a moment before one of the nurses comes in to check my stitches and take my vitals. She encourages me to try and feed Henry and like a little champ, he figures it out immediately. It feels like needles being sucked through my nipples, but watching him eat is worth it. So glad no one warned me about that.

"What about my mom and Jax and everyone? Have you called them?" I ask.

"I did. Your mom and dad are on their way. My family will

probably be here later. And...no answer from Jax yet," he says as he gently strokes Henry's head.

Looking down at the baby in my arms, I try to imagine what it will be like when or if Jax shows up. Will Lucas be angry? Will there be tension?

I glance up at him to see how he's feeling about that, but I laugh to myself instead. He looks like a mess. His hair is disheveled, and there are deep bags under his eyes like he hasn't slept in days.

"Do you want to go get some sleep? I'll be fine here."

"Nah," he says, sinking deeper into the bed at my side. "I'm going to stay right here."

My parents show up about an hour later. They coo and fawn over Henry. When my brother walks in and sees the name scrawled across the top of the bassinet, he starts to cry.

Henry Jonah Green

And then the Goodes show up one at a time. Sage and Adam first. Then Melanie. And then Caleb and Dean. Briar and Abby are out of town together on a mommy-daughter retreat, apparently. Part of me wonders if all of these babies being born in her family is affecting her, and I'm sure it is. But she's taking it in stride. I'm glad she's getting some quality time with her daughter. When she's ready to see Henry, we'll be here.

After everyone has come and gone, and our first day of parenthood is coming to a close, I've never felt more tired and in love in my life. I still can't stop staring at Henry, and clearly, Lucas feels the same.

Our hospital stay lasts roughly two hundred and fifty days. Or at least it feels that way. Apparently, getting a C-section qualifies you for an extended stay, all-inclusive, of course. Bad hospital food and monster-sized pads are complimentary.

By the time we come home with Henry, I almost forget what a real bed feels like. Or what normal feels like. I can get around, but not comfortably and not fast.

Lucas is amazing. He does all the burping, bathing, changing, rocking, cleaning.

Not one single second does he appear to be a man who never wanted kids. He slipped into this fatherhood role like he was born for it.

As for Jax, still nothing. I think he's scared. And I don't blame him. I just hope he decides on something soon so we can stop waiting, but realistically, he may never fully decide.

For now, Henry is taken care of and that's all that matters.

While I'm enjoying the best shower of my life, Luke gets Henry changed and cleaned up. We settle him into his bassinet next to our bed and Lucas pulls back the covers to make room for me to lie down. Once I do, he crawls in next to me. I rest my head on his chest, and he strokes my back.

It feels like the first day of the rest of our lives.

For some reason, I think about the day I moved in and how different it is from today. Lucas was cold, abrasive, and controlling. Since then, I've watched him thaw like ice.

I still love that dominant side of him, but I think he was so scorned by his own family that he never allowed anyone to see this side of him. He built a barrier around himself as a form of protection, and it makes me love him so much more to know that I get access to a part of him no one else does.

Henry and I both do.

"I'm going to ask Jax to sign over his rights," I mumble against Luke's chest.

I feel him tense beneath me. So I lift my head and look into his eyes. "I want you to be Henry's legal father."

His gaze softens as he brushes the hair from my face. "That's a big decision, Sadie. I don't need to be his legal father to call him my son. You know that."

Nodding, I smile. "I know that."

"I'm committed to you and Henry, no matter what," he adds with a furrow in his brow.

"I know you are," I reply as I sweep a long brown lock of hair from his forehead. "But...Henry deserves to have your name."

His chest inflates as his eyes grow wider. Then he takes me by the chin and lifts it closer until our lips are just inches apart. Gazing into my eyes, he whispers, "And so do you. If that's...what you want."

A smile spreads across my face. "Of course, that's what I want."

"Then it's yours. Take my name, little devil. Take it all."

Our lips meet in a warm, passionate kiss. I cling to him as he deepens the kiss, and although we both know this is going nowhere sexy, he cradles my sore and tired body in his hands and delicately kisses me like he means it.

FORTY-SIX

Lucas

One month later

My phone buzzes in my pocket as I'm perusing the aisle-long array of diapers on the shelves. How can there be so many options? I pull my phone out to see Sadie's name on the screen, so I quickly swipe the answer button and hold it up to my ear.

"Does Henry need diapers for crawling yet?" I ask.

She laughs into the phone. "He can't even hold his head up yet. He needs diapers that don't blow out the back. Is that an option?"

I scan the aisle again. There is a brand that specifically advertises *blowout protection.* "Got 'em," I say as I grab a package in his size.

"I'm hungry. Will you get me some sushi while you're there?" she pleads.

"Grocery store sushi?" I ask with a grin as I make my way up toward the deli area.

"Listen, it's been ten months, and I'm desperate."

"You got it. Anything else?" I ask.

"Nope. Just you," she adds sweetly.

"I'll be home soon."

"Love you," she says through the line.

"Love you too," I reply before hanging up.

I catch sight of myself in the glass doors of the deli section and realize what a mess I am. I desperately need a haircut, to shave my beard, and apparently check the state of my shirts before leaving the house. This one has a spit-up stain right on the shoulder.

After picking up a variety of sushi rolls for Sadie, I make my way to the register. A text from Adam on my phone pings as I drop everything on the conveyor belt.

> Need to talk when you have a chance.

It's about time. I can't say I'm surprised to get this message. Apparently, when we were at the hospital, Mom let it slip that my *brother* was with me, but he did some digging and found out that the *brother* wasn't Caleb.

I knew this day would come, and I'm not nearly as worried about it as I once was. So Adam found out I've been in contact with Isaac. He'll deal with it.

There's a man in a suit standing in front of me, checking out with the cashier as I stare at the text from my brother. The reason I notice the man is because he keeps glancing back at me suspiciously.

Is the spit-up stain that bad?

Once he pays, he politely smiles at the cashier and tells her, "God bless."

Then as she starts to ring up my items, the man takes his time putting his wallet away, glancing at me more than twice. I'm officially weirded out now.

After I pay, I grab the bag and take a step toward the door, but the guy is still there.

"Caleb Goode?" he asks as he steps in line next to me on the way to the parking lot.

I pause. "No..." I reply skeptically. "You must be looking for my brother." Which is weird because Caleb and I don't even really look alike. I look more like Adam if I'm being honest.

Finally getting a good look at the guy, I notice that he's well-dressed, handsome, tall, and probably about my age. Nothing about him gives me reason for concern, except for the fact that he knows my twin brother's name.

Laughing, he shakes his head. "It was a fifty-fifty chance. You must be Lucas."

"I am, and you are..."

"Sorry," he says, putting out his hand. "Jenson Miles. You don't know me, but there were still pictures of you and your family when I moved in. And we've never been properly introduced."

"Moved in?" I ask without shaking his hand.

"To the church."

For some reason, my mind immediately goes to Adam's church, the one we went to as kids before our father opened a megachurch and sullied his reputation and lost it.

"Redemption Point. I'm..." he stammers for a second as if he's surprised I don't know who he is. "I'm the new pastor."

If he's waiting for a reaction from me, he's going to be sorely disappointed. Instead of congratulating him on his new gig, I continue the walk to my car. "You'll have to understand, Mr. Miles, that it's a bit of a sore subject for me and my family."

He walks briskly beside me. "I understand, and I didn't mean to ambush you."

"Well, if you're here to talk about what a great man my father is, you're barking up the wrong tree." I unlock my car, in a bit of a pissed-off mood now.

"I don't think your father is a great man," he says as he stops behind me. The words make me pause. I turn to glance at him skeptically. "And if I can be frank, I think your dad is pretty deplorable, not only for tarnishing your family's good reputation but the congregation's as well."

"Well, then you and I do agree on something, after all," I say as I toss the bags in the trunk. "It was nice meeting you," I add, trying to end the conversation.

He steps up to stop me, a look of hopeful determination on his face. "I think seeing your family back at the church would be amazing. Find common ground with our followers. They were hurt, too."

"I bet," I reply before moving to get in the car again, only to be stopped by him again.

"Just take my card. And think about it."

He fishes in his pocket for a business card as I let out a sigh, hoping to get out of this conversation. The guy seems nice and genuine, nothing like my father or the other smarmy pastors with fake smiles and bullshit personas. This guy seems down to earth, but it changes nothing for me.

"Listen, it's not you," I say with a sigh. "You just ran into the wrong brother. You'd have better luck with—"

Music starts playing on his phone and the words are cut from my mouth. Because it's not just any music—it's my little brother's most popular country song. It's his raspy singing voice with backup guitar strums and a low drumbeat.

"Sorry," Jenson says as he silences the call and shoves his phone back into his pocket. "My ringtone is too loud. I know, I know, no one uses songs for ringtones anymore, but I just love that one so much." He's bumbling nervously with a sheepish look.

"You a big fan?" I ask, narrowing my eyes at the man.

"Of Theo Virgil? Huge fan. You know of him?"

"Yeah..." I say as I shuffle my feet and scrutinize him even more. "I've heard of him."

He smiles at me for a moment before handing me his card. "Your family is always welcome at Redemption Point."

"Thanks," I mutter as I take the card.

I don't bother telling him that I'll never step foot in that church, or any other for that matter, ever again. But he seems nice enough, like he might actually have good intentions. So I wave goodbye to him as I climb into my car to leave.

"Take care, Luke," he calls as he walks away.

As I sit in my car, I stare at the card in my hand. I haven't given my father's church a single thought since everything went down. And it doesn't mean anything to me to be invited back, but I wonder if it will mean anything to Caleb or Adam.

And, of course, I can't help but wonder—when he said our family was welcome there, did he mean Isaac, too?

✝

When I get home, Sadie is sleeping on the couch while Henry naps in the bassinet next to her. One of her hands rests on the edge of the crib, and I smile to myself as I lean down and press my lips to the side of her head.

After putting away the diapers in the nursery and storing Sadie's sushi in the fridge, I hear a soft coo from the living room. Going over to his bassinet, I find him staring up at me with wide, alert eyes.

I wonder how long the sight of him will steal my heart from right out of my chest the way it does now.

Leaning down, I scoop him up from his bassinet. When he starts to fuss, I pick up his pacifier and put it in his mouth. He sucks on it contentedly as he stares up at me in wonder.

As I gently trace the soft curve of his nose and the shape of his brows with my finger, he flutters his eyes closed for a second before opening them back up and gazing at me some more.

I carry him over to my leather chair on the other side of the room, and I quietly sit, propping my feet up and nuzzling Henry close. His eyes don't leave my face, and I smile down at him.

"'When I compare what I have lost with what I have gained,'"

I whisper softly, remembering the old Longfellow poem by memory. "'What I have missed with what attained, little room do I find for pride.'"

Henry stops suckling on his pacifier, letting his mouth hang open, enthralled by the sound of my voice as I continue.

"'I am aware how many days have been idly spent. How like an arrow the good intent, has fallen short or been turned aside.'"

I whisper the rest of the poem to him, kissing him gently on the forehead as I finish.

"'But who shall dare to measure loss and gain in this wise? Defeat may be victory in disguise. The lowest ebb is the turn of the tide.'"

Then, out of nowhere, Henry's lips tug upward at the corners, and I stare in shock as he smiles gently up at me. His first smile.

Tears prick my eyes as I gape at him with so much love in my heart I swear it's about to burst.

"He likes poetry," Sadie mumbles softly from across the room.

"He just smiled at me," I reply with tears in my eyes.

"Read us some more," she says sleepily as she closes her eyes again.

Reaching over to the table next to my chair, I pick up the book of poems I bought for Sadie just a few months ago. I read each one out loud to Henry until he falls asleep in my arms.

The moment screams with significance. I could have missed this, and for what? Like the poem said, the loss of my previous life was no loss at all when I look at what I've gained.

I pushed away love for so long out of fear, and that fear almost cost me *this*. All because my own father shattered my heart into pieces.

But these two people, my new *family*, have somehow found a way to put it back together again.

SADIE'S EPILOGUE

About a year later

"I've been naughty," I whisper to Lucas as I step behind him. His face stretches with a grin, but he won't turn around to look at me.

"You're always naughty, Miss Green," he mutters as he looks upward.

"Not Miss Green for long," I whisper as I trail my fingers up the back of his neck.

"And it's bad luck for me to see you before the wedding."

"Since when are you a superstitious man?" I ask, winding my arms around his body to stroke my hands over his chest.

"Since I have so much on the line," he replies, gripping my hand in his and kissing my knuckles.

"Come on. We have thirty minutes to kill. My mom has Henry," I plead.

"What do you want, little devil?" he asks, and I feel his resolve fading.

Lifting up to my tiptoes, I whisper into his ear, "I want you to fuck me one more time before I'm your wife."

He lets out a growl before finally giving in. "You tempting little brat."

I giggle quietly as he turns toward me and pauses for a moment, taking in the sight of me with my hair and makeup done in a long white gown with lace over my freckled chest and shoulders.

"Jesus fucking Christ, Sadie," he mumbles with his mouth hanging open.

"You like it?" I ask with feigned innocence.

"Like it?" He scrubs a hand over his jaw before backing me up to a bookshelf and looking at the door to make sure it's locked. "It's a good thing you showed me now, or I would have tried to fuck you in front of our friends and family."

His mouth attacks my neck, sucking and kissing me ravenously. Pulling up my dress, he runs his hands along my thighs and lets out another growl.

Having my body back to just being *mine* again has been so nice. I can finally seduce my soon-to-be husband without a giant belly in the way. He adores every single inch, no matter the stretch marks or scars. He loves me in every shape and size.

But more importantly, I love myself. This body gave me Henry. For nearly a year, it continued to feed Henry. I have never been more in love with my own flesh and bones just the way they are.

And right now, it's a vessel for pleasure. Luke reaches the apex of my thighs to find that I'm not wearing any underwear and he moans loudly against my neck.

"Get up here," he mutters as he lifts me onto the low table. "You locked the door?" he asks as he unbuckles his own belt.

"No," I say, shaking my head and biting my bottom lip. "Someone could walk in at any moment."

"You are so bad, Miss Green," he mutters before kissing my lips.

"Punish me already," I reply.

"Oh, I plan to."

Heat swells in my belly as Luke drags me to the edge of the table. His eyes bore into mine before he looks down and guides his cock to my core. As he presses himself inside, I let my head hang back with delight.

He hooks an arm under my leg and fucks me hard with violent thrusts. His free hand clamps over my mouth to stop me from crying out. As the sleeve of his jacket slips down, I catch a glimpse of the red devil tattoo adorning the back of his arm.

"Don't you dare come, Miss Green. I'll be forced to punish you again tonight."

I couldn't stop it if I tried. At this angle and this roughness, it only takes a few moments of circling my clit with my middle finger and I'm stifling a scream in the palm of his hand.

He feels my cunt pulse around his cock. "You are in so much trouble," he grunts before losing his own composure and unloading inside me with a groan.

A few moments later, there's a knock on the door. "We're about to start," Caleb calls, sounding slightly uncomfortable.

Luke and I laugh quietly together before he eventually pulls out. When he reaches into his pocket for something to wipe me up with, I stop him.

"Don't. I want to feel you dripping out of me when I say my vows."

He lets out another growl as he leans down and kisses me again. "God, I love you so much."

"I love you too," I reply with a smile.

He helps me down from the table and zips himself back up in his pants. "I came in here to admire the collections." As he gazes around the room, I stare only at him.

"I'm happy we chose this location then," I say, taking his hand.

"Who wouldn't want to get married in a library?" he asks with a shrug.

We walk hand in hand toward the door. "Right?"

When he places his hand on the knob, ready to open it, he pauses and stares down at me. "Are you ready?"

"Ready to be Sadie Goode? I don't think I've ever been more ready for anything in my life."

He smiles before leaning down and kissing me again. "Then let's get married."

LUCAS'S EPILOGUE

Eight years later

Sadie sets the cake down on the table as my family around us starts to sing. The twins stare at the single flame over the number-one-shaped candle with wide, wondrous eyes. It only takes a moment before Ezra starts to cry and Dylan looks at him in confusion.

Sadie softly strokes Ezra's head as everyone sings to them. And when the song ends, we try to entice them to blow the candles out but neither of them move. Ezra just starts crying more under the pressure.

Henry bounces excitedly next to his brothers. "Can I blow them out, Dad?" he begs.

"Yeah, go ahead, bud. They can't do it yet," I say, ruffling his warm, copper locks.

Reaching over the table, he blows the candles out, and Dylan lunges for the melted wax, but my mother snatches the cake away before he can get it.

Then she cuts the cake and nudges two tiny slices toward the two boys. Dylan doesn't waste a second, burying his tiny hands in the frosting and bringing them to his mouth.

Ezra is still crying and doesn't stop until Sadie picks him up and nuzzles him against her chest, whispering sweet words in his ear. Dipping my finger in the frosting, I give him a tiny taste. That makes him perk up a little, but he still doesn't want to return to his high chair. Nothing beats Mommy's arms.

"I think Dylan won," Caleb mutters to my right.

"It wasn't a competition," I reply with a shake of my head.

"Well, if it was, my money is on Dyl."

He playfully knocks my shoulder with a laugh.

"I think that's enough," Sadie says, nodding toward the other twin. We all look down at where Dylan has nearly demolished his entire slice, which means he'll be up and wired for the rest of the day. I have to be the bad guy and take the plate away, incurring his adorable baby wrath.

My mom scoops him up as he screams and takes him to the kitchen to clean him.

I catch Sadie's eye as she sits with Ezra on her lap, gently feeding him tiny bites of birthday cake. She grins up at me for a moment, and I swallow down my overwhelming gratitude.

"I love you," I mouth to her.

"I love you too," she mouths back.

It's just another moment of my life that screams significance.

Not all of them are this magical. When we're trying to balance having *two* babies at home, her erratic work schedule, and my demanding job, there are moments that don't feel like a dream. They feel like work—exhausting, unforgiving, thankless work.

And then there are moments like this. When Henry is playing with his baby brothers, and Sadie is smiling at her three perfect boys, my heart explodes with love—this is when I remember what I almost gave up.

I look back on my childhood, and I try to understand how my dad could have so easily brushed us aside. He must have closed off a piece of his heart because there's no way I couldn't love this family as much as I do. And now that I sit in a seat that looks quite a lot like his, I remember those wise words he told me one day in a state penitentiary—look your son in the eye, listen to him when he talks, and tell him you love him. All the things he never did.

Fatherhood is easy if you just try.

Maybe he should have spent more Sundays preaching that. Then I might have listened.

The moment Henry was born, my life changed and I knew I'd never end up like my father. There wasn't a day of Henry's life when he wasn't my son—bloodline or not.

Jax signed over his parental rights before Henry turned one. He could acknowledge that being a father wasn't the right choice for him, and Sadie and I both appreciate him for that. He still sees him from time to time and Henry knows the situation, but I don't let a day go by without telling my son just how much he means to me. I don't want him to doubt it—*ever*.

Henry loves to hear the story about how I fell in love with his mother while he was in her belly. So, in a way, I was falling in love with him too. Of course, his favorite part of the story is when his mom threw up in front of the classroom while I was teaching. He cracks up every time we tell him that part.

"All clean." My mother passes me Dylan in nothing but his diaper. His wispy dark hair is wet, and there are still streaks of green icing under his tiny fingernails. Of course, he wants nothing to do with being held with all that sugar coursing through his system, so I set him on the floor.

Immediately, he crawls to the other side of the house. The first person he meets is Dean, who looks down at him curiously as if he doesn't know whether to pick him up or pass him a beer.

Then Dylan crawls to Isaac, who doesn't hesitate to lift him from the floor. He manages to hold the squirmy one-year-old long enough to plant a kiss on his cheek before putting him back on the floor.

Dylan makes his way across the living room to a pile of toys in the corner. He occupies himself for a while there, banging blocks against my once pristine coffee table, and I don't even flinch anymore.

I watch him as my family around me converses together. Sadie is talking to Sage and Briar with Ezra now nursing under her shirt. Henry and Faith are playing a board game in the kitchen. Abigail stares down at the phone in her hand as if no one here could possibly interest her more than the device. And Adam is talking to Caleb near the record player.

I feel a soft hand on my shoulder as I turn to see my mother standing by my side. It's a soft moment. I can feel it.

"I don't think I tell you this enough, but I'm proud of you," she whispers.

I let out a huff as I think of my accomplishments over the years: work promotions, new literary articles and accolades, and supporting my brilliant wife as she finished her book.

But I have a feeling my mother isn't talking about that.

She's talking about the fact that I once feared turning into my father. And now that I am a father, I'm ten times the one he was.

"Thanks, Mom," I reply.

With lots of therapy over the years, I've learned to forgive my mother for never standing up to my dad when we were growing up. There was a hierarchy in our household that didn't put her in a powerful position, and I recognize that now.

Those hard years are built into the DNA of our relationship, but we're still healing. Always healing.

Dylan accidentally knocks his head on the side of the table and starts wailing in the living room. When he sees me approaching, he raises his arms for me.

"Dada!" he cries, seeking me out for comfort. I quickly pick him up, kiss his head and sit on the couch with him.

Lifting him up, I blow raspberries on his belly to make him squeal with laughter and distract him from the pain. This draws Henry's attention, so he joins us, tickling Dylan to make him laugh more. After a moment, Sadie and Ezra are with us, too.

"Picture!" my mother announces as she sees my family together on the couch. So the five of us squeeze in together: me, my beautiful wife, and our three amazing sons.

This picture will go in a frame, and it doesn't matter that Ezra is crying again, that Dylan is still in just a diaper, or that our life looks like a bit of a mess.

Because it's a beautiful fucking mess. And it's all ours.

✝

ACKNOWLEDGMENTS

Thank you for reading *The Heartbreaker*.

Lucas and Sadie stole my heart, and I hope they stole yours too. Look at me writing something heartwarming (and still very kinky).

When I set out to write this series, I had no clue that this family would have such an effect on me, but they have. I've loved every second of breaking them down just to build them back up again.

I have an excellent team of people to thank for everything it took to make this book happen.

My beta readers—Jill, Becca, Adrian, and Lori. Thanks for sticking with me through the tight deadlines and self-doubt. I couldn't do this without you.

My assistant—Lori Alexander for lifting me up and encouraging me when I get hard on myself.

My incredible agent—Savannah Greenwell.

My amazing editor—Rebecca.

My brilliant proofreaders—Rumi and Rose.

My stunning cover designers—Lori Jackson and Emily Wittig.

My PR company—The Author Agency

My friend and assistant—Misty Frey. I love having you on my team.

My forever hype girl and friend—Amanda Anderson.

The moderators and members of Sara's Salacious Readers.

All of my readers for letting me work out some religious trauma and following me through it all.

Thank you all!

ALSO BY SARA CATE

Salacious Players' Club

Praise

Eyes on Me

Give Me More

Mercy

Highest Bidder

Madame

The Goode Brothers series

The Anti-hero

The Home Wrecker

The Heart Breaker

The Prodigal Son - coming in 2025

Age-gap romance

Beautiful Monster

Beautiful Sinner

Wilde Boys duet

Gravity

Freefall

Black Heart Duet

Four

Five

Cocky Hero Club

Handsome Devil

Bully romance

Burn for Me

Fire and Ash

Wicked Hearts Series

Delicate

Dangerous

Defiant

ABOUT SARA CATE

Sara Cate is a USA Today bestselling romance author who weaves complex characters, heart-wrenching stories, and forbidden romance into every page of her spicy novels. Sara's writing is as hot as a desert summer, with twists and turns that will leave you breathless. Best known for the Salacious Players' Club series, Sara strives to take risks and provide her readers with an experience that is as arousing as it is empowering. When she's not penning steamy tales, she can be found soaking up the Arizona sun, jamming to Taylor Swift, and watching Marvel movies with her family.

You can find more information about her at
www.saracatebooks.com

Printed in the USA
CPSIA information can be obtained
at www.ICGtesting.com
JSHW031904240724
66787JS00003B/3

9 781956 830309